✦ MAGIC ✦
TREE HOUSE®

NIGHT OF THE NINJAS

MARY POPE OSBORNE'S

✦ MAGIC ✦
TREE HOUSE®

NIGHT OF THE NINJAS

THE GRAPHIC NOVEL

ADAPTED BY
JENNY LAIRD

WITH ART BY
KELLY & NICHOLE MATTHEWS

A STEPPING STONE BOOK™
RANDOM HOUSE 🏠 NEW YORK

This is a work of fiction. Names, characters, places, and incidents either are
the product of the author's imagination or are used fictitiously. Any resemblance
to actual persons, living or dead, events, or locales is entirely coincidental.

Text copyright © 2023 by Mary Pope Osborne
Art copyright © 2023 by Kelly Matthews & Nichole Matthews
Text adapted by Jenny Laird

All rights reserved. Published in the United States by Random House Children's Books, a division
of Penguin Random House LLC, New York. Adapted from *Night of the Ninjas,* published by
Random House Children's Books, a division of Penguin Random House LLC, New York, in 1995.

Random House and the colophon are registered trademarks and A Stepping Stone Book
and the colophon are trademarks of Penguin Random House LLC. RH Graphic with
the book design is a trademark of Penguin Random House LLC. Magic Tree House
is a registered trademark of Mary Pope Osborne; used under license.

Visit us on the Web!
rhcbooks.com
MagicTreeHouse.com

Educators and librarians, for a variety of teaching tools, visit us at RHTeachersLibrarians.com

Library of Congress Cataloging-in-Publication Data is available upon request.
ISBN 978-0-593-48878-2 (pbk.) — ISBN 978-0-593-48879-9 (hardcover) —
ISBN 978-0-593-48880-5 (lib. bdg.) — ISBN 978-0-593-48881-2 (ebook)

The artists used Clip Studio Paint to create the illustrations for this book.
The text of this book is set in 13-point Cartoonist Hand Regular.

MANUFACTURED IN CHINA
10 9 8 7 6 5 4 3 2 1
First Graphic Novel Edition

This book has been officially leveled by using the F&P Text Level Gradient™ Leveling System.

Random House Children's Books supports the First Amendment and celebrates the right to read.
Penguin Random House LLC supports copyright. Copyright fuels creativity, encourages diverse voices, promotes
free speech, and creates a vibrant culture. Thank you for buying an authorized edition of this book and for
complying with copyright laws by not reproducing, scanning, or distributing any part in any form without
permission. You are supporting writers and allowing Penguin Random House to publish books for every reader.

For
Ada and Georgia McCulloch
—M.P.O.

For Mary Pope Osborne
A true storytelling master

An empty page waits
She sits, imagines what if—
Whoosh! The mind takes flight.
—J.L.

To everyone who loves
to read and learn
—K.M. & N.M.

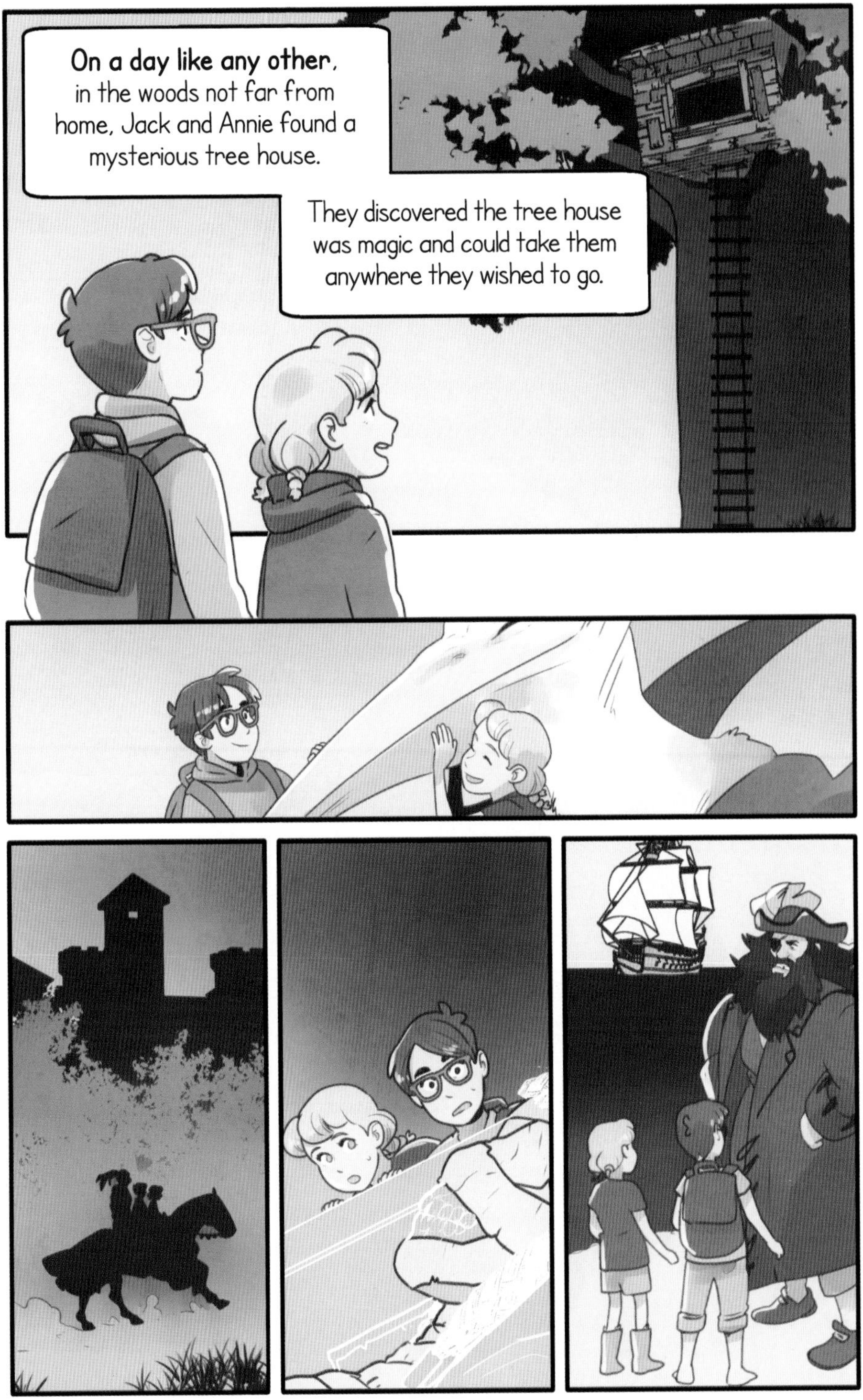
On a day like any other, in the woods not far from home, Jack and Annie found a mysterious tree house.
They discovered the tree house was magic and could take them anywhere they wished to go.

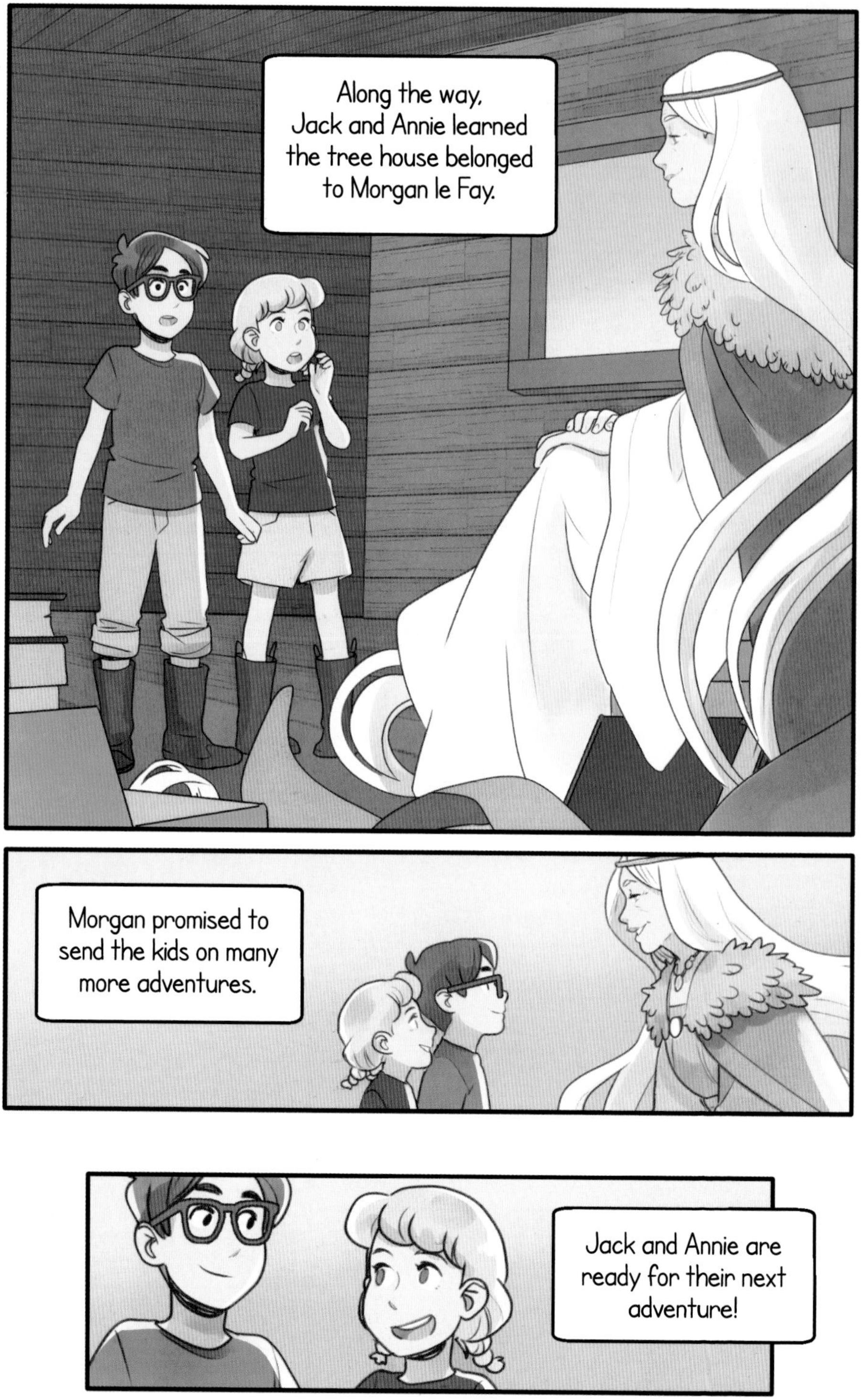
Along the way, Jack and Annie learned the tree house belonged to Morgan le Fay.
Morgan promised to send the kids on many more adventures.
Jack and Annie are ready for their next adventure!

CHAPTER ONE
Back into the Woods

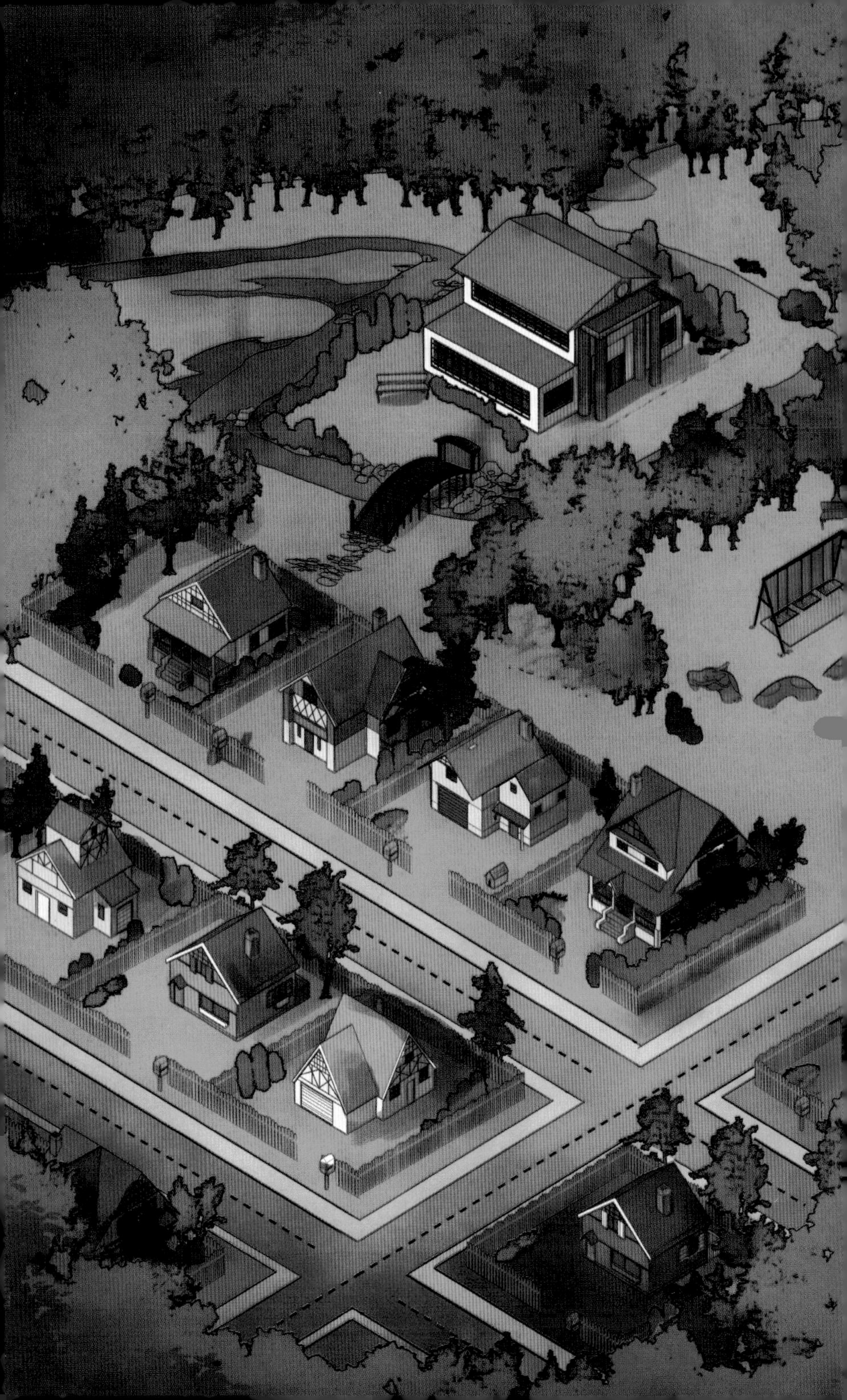

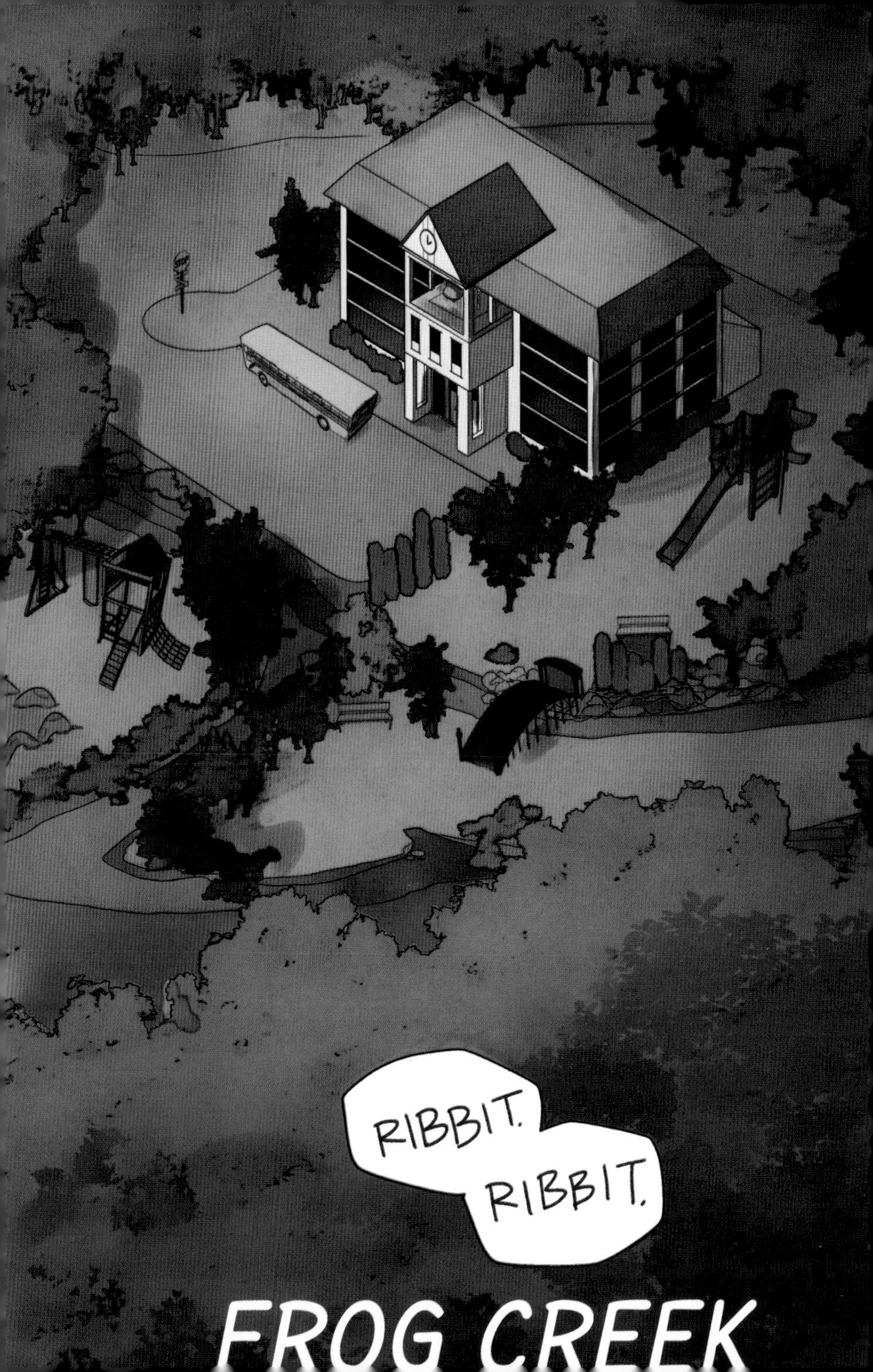
RIBBIT.
RIBBIT.
FROG CREEK

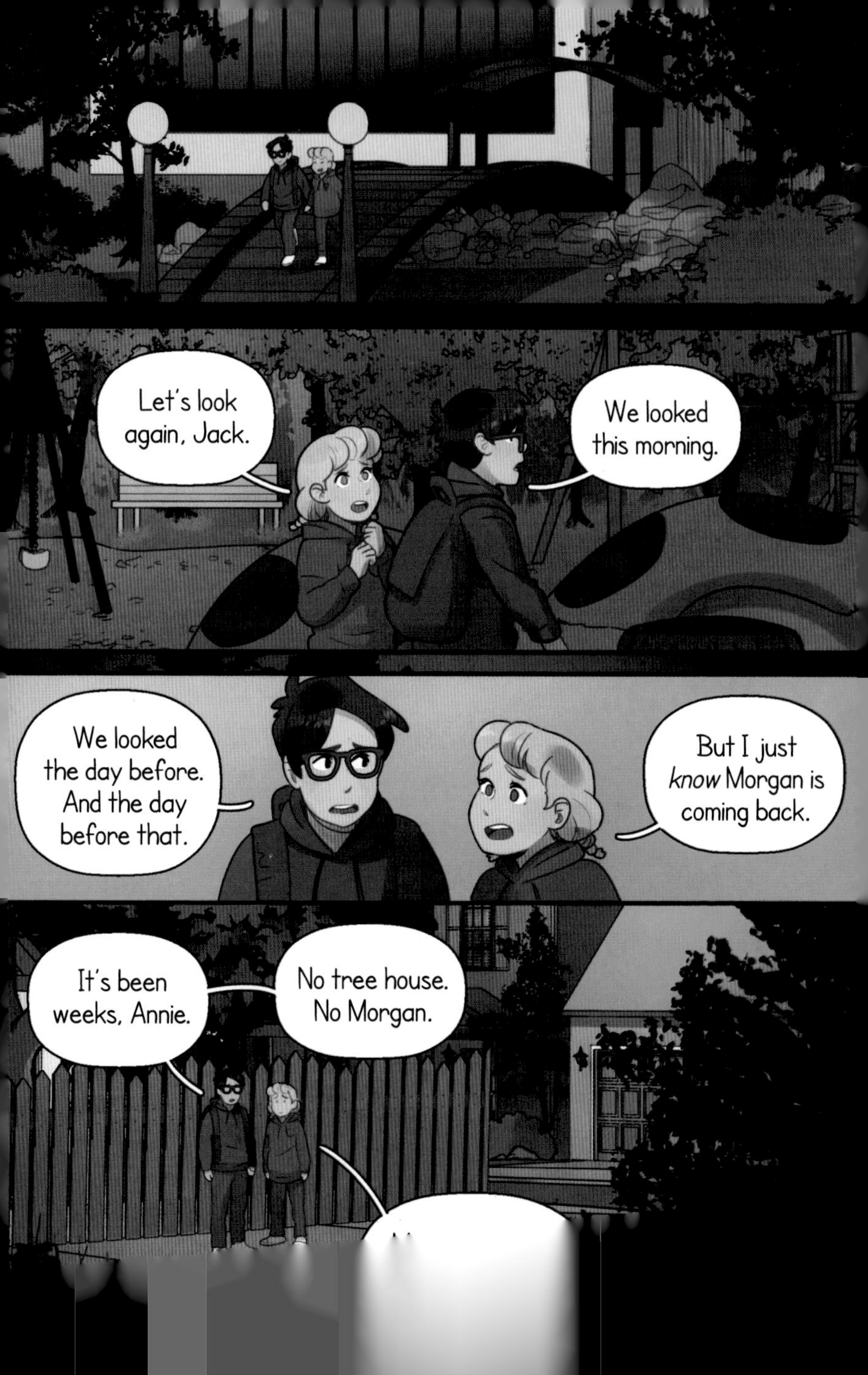
Let's look again, Jack.
We looked this morning.
We looked the day before. And the day before that.
But I just *know* Morgan is coming back.
It's been weeks, Annie.
No tree house. No Morgan.

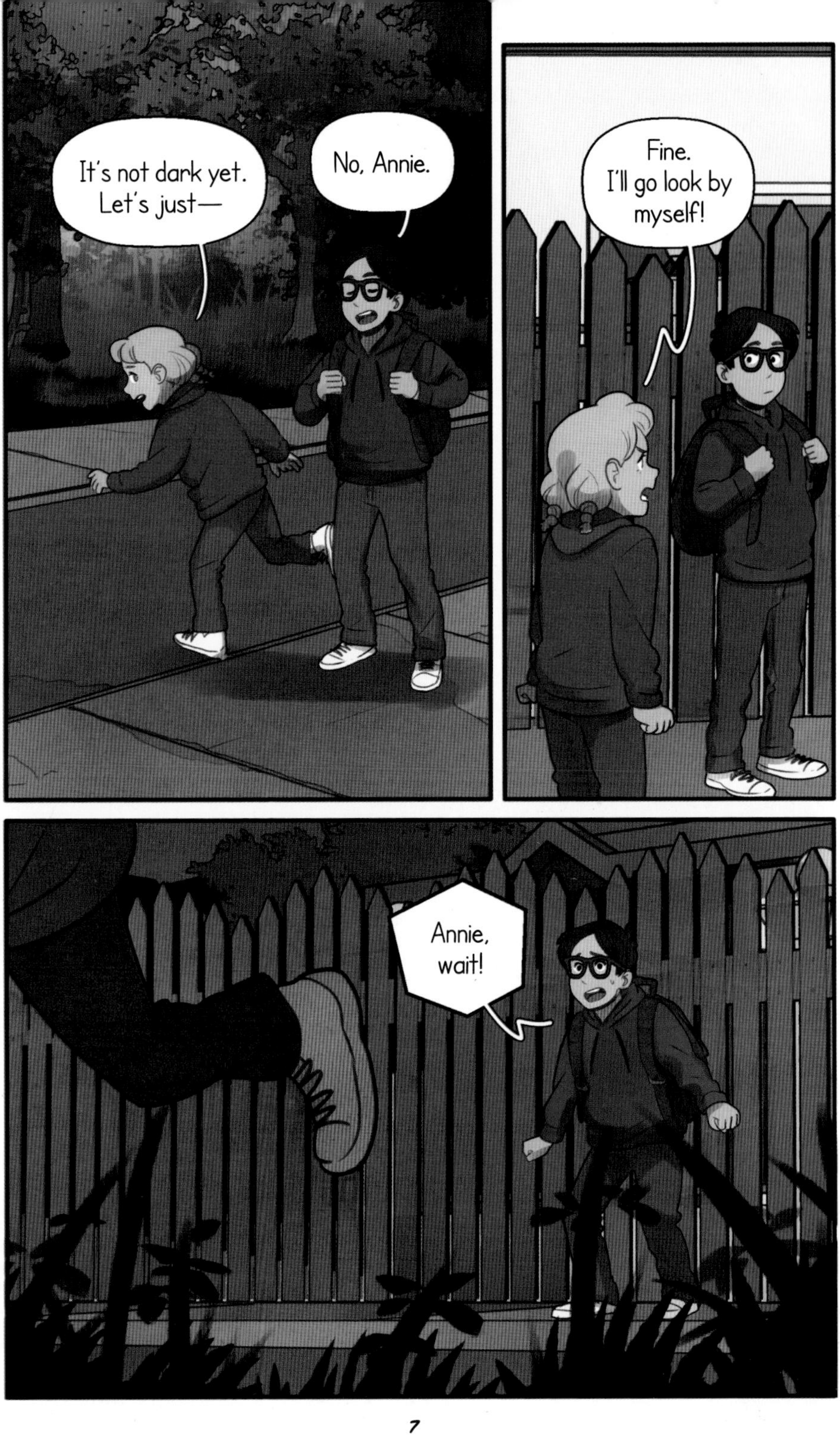

It's not dark yet. Let's just—
No, Annie.
Fine. I'll go look by myself!
Annie, wait!

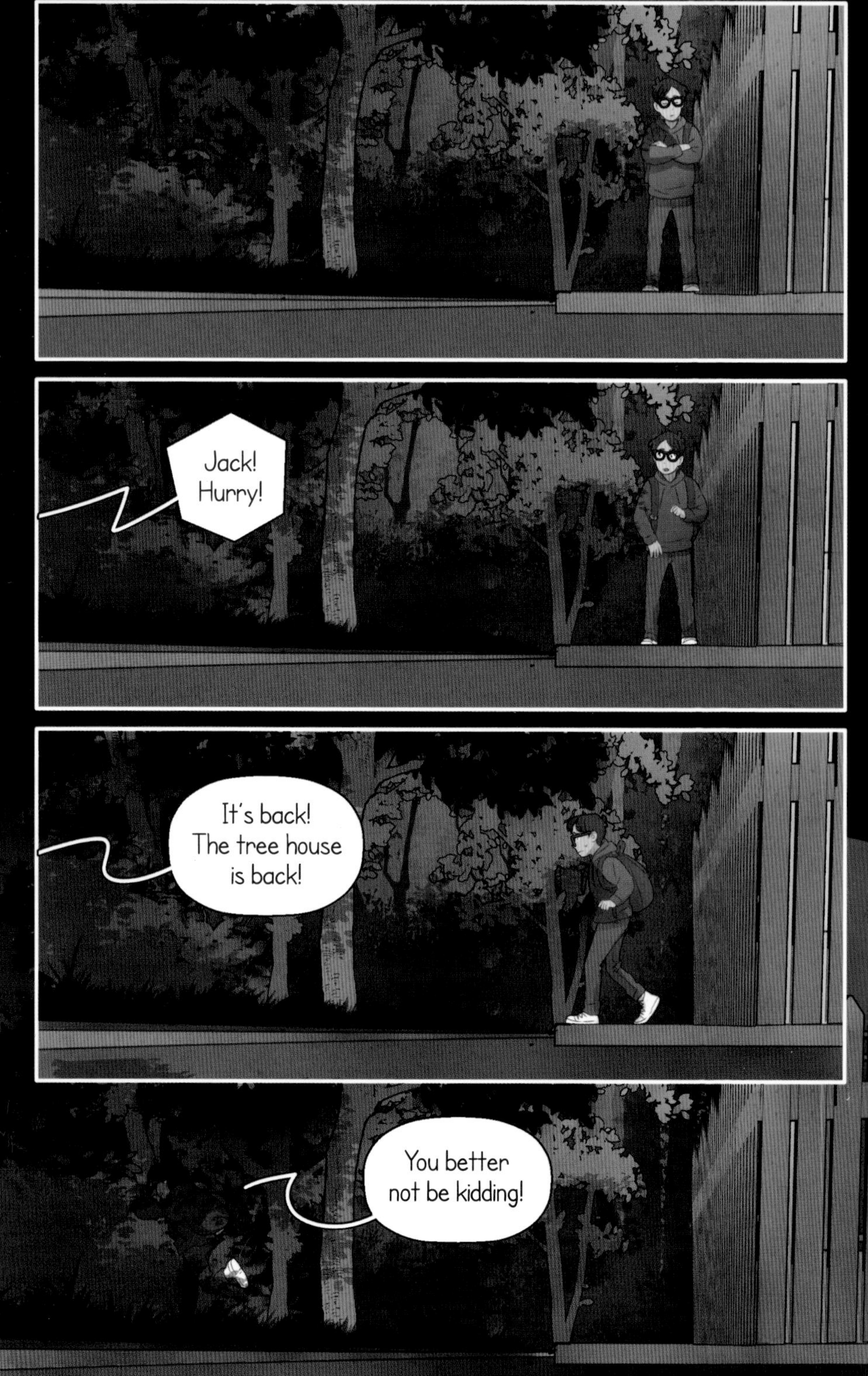
Jack! Hurry!
It's back! The tree house is back!
You better not be kidding!

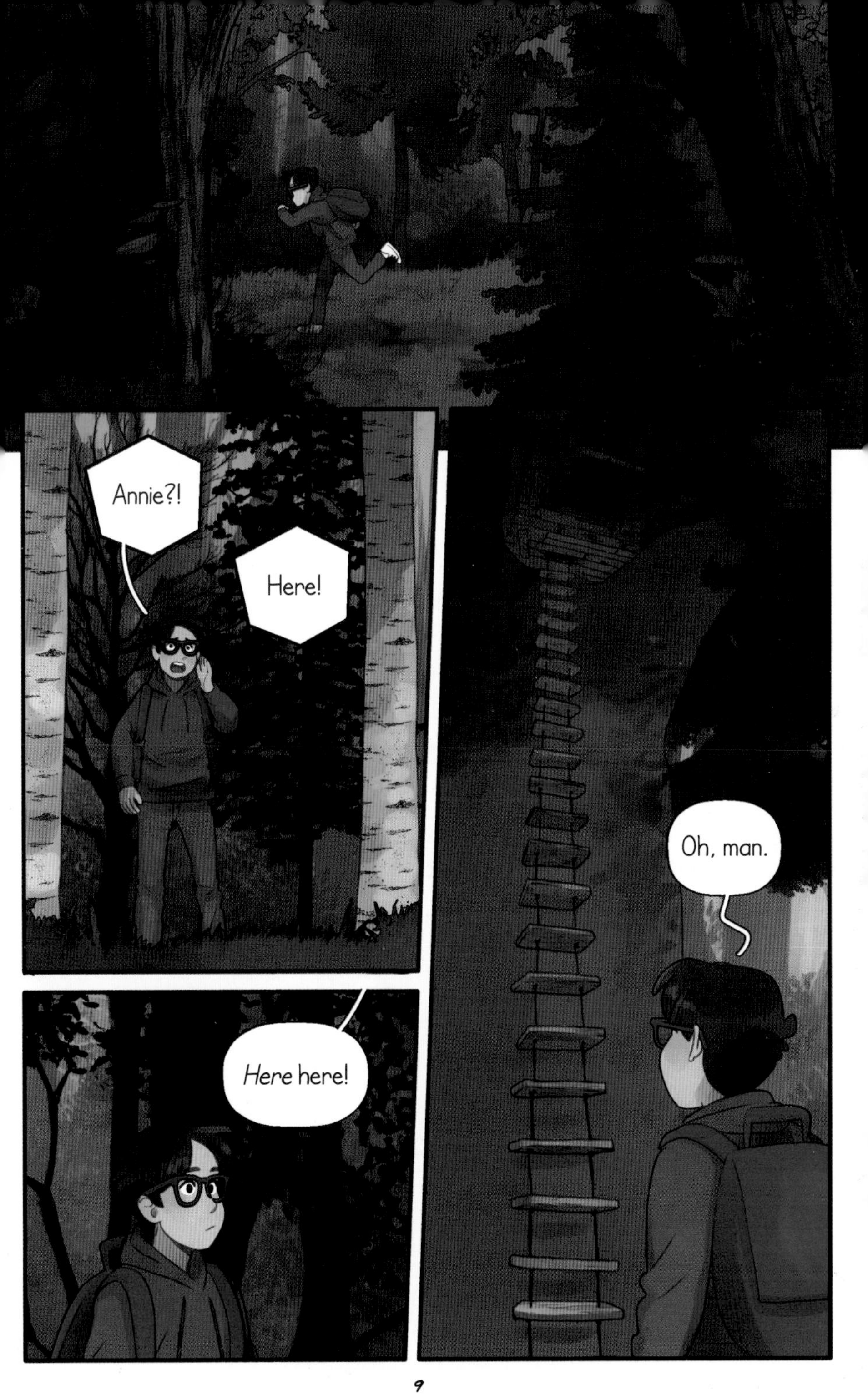
Annie?!
Here!
Here here!
Oh, man.

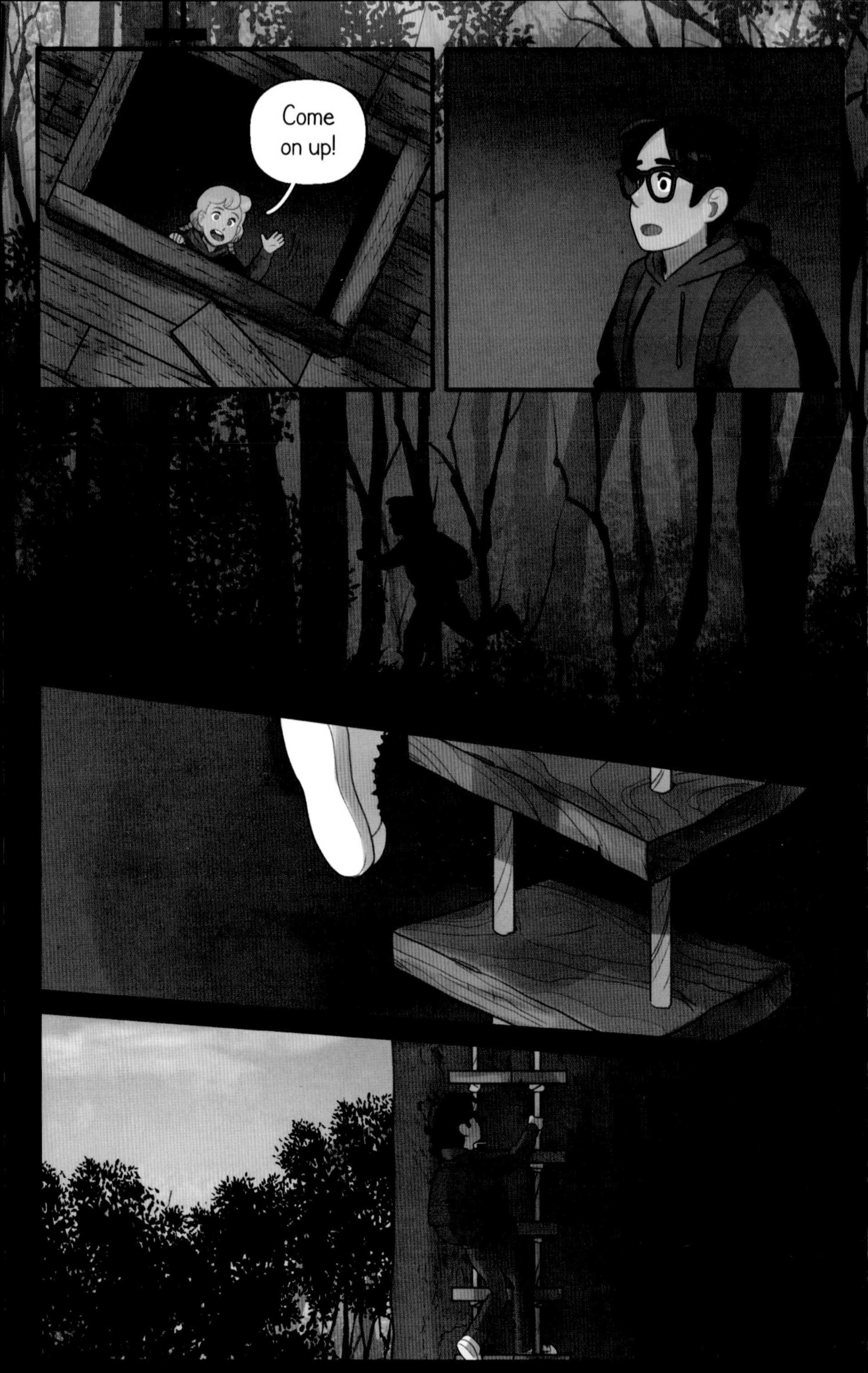
Come on up!

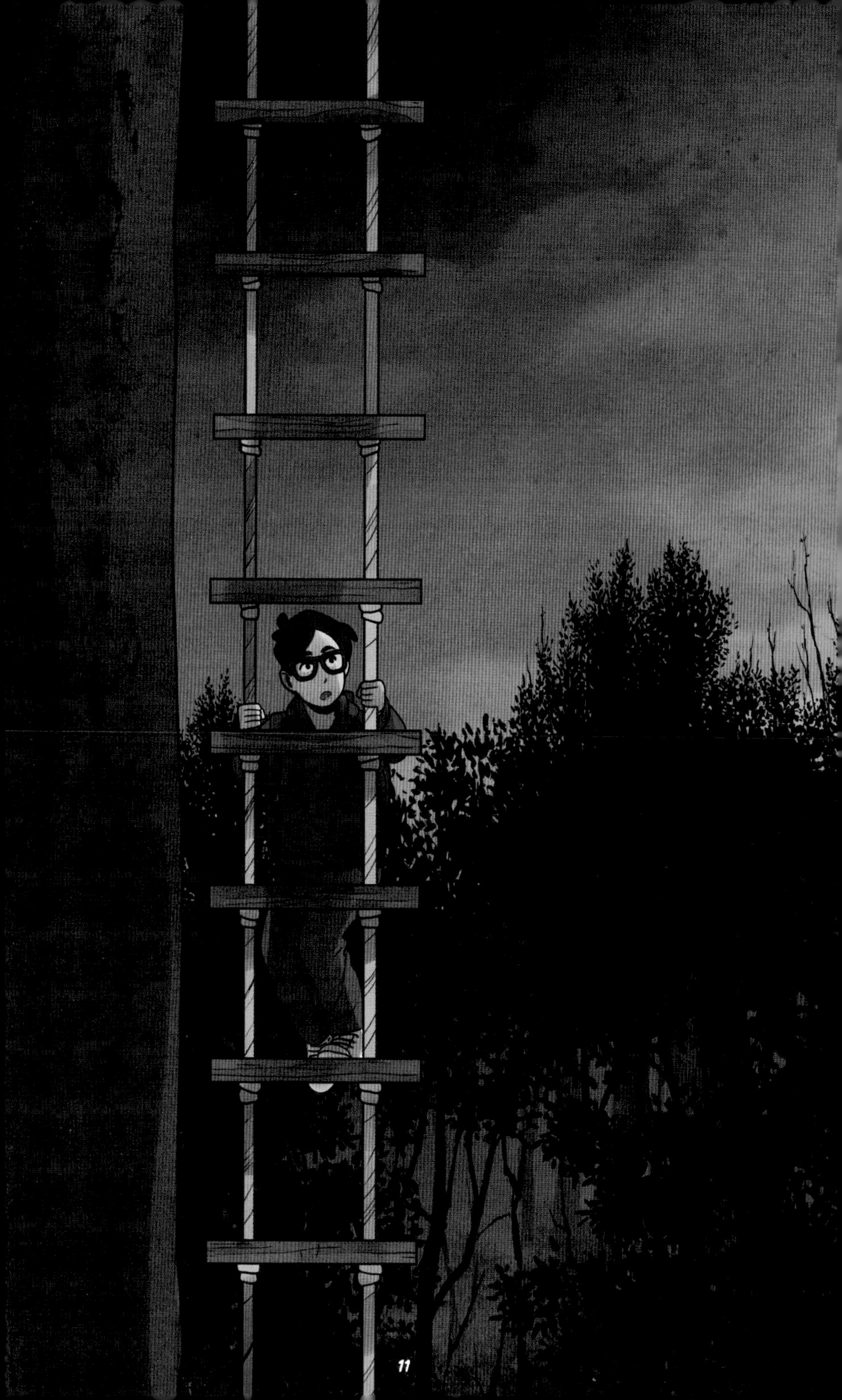

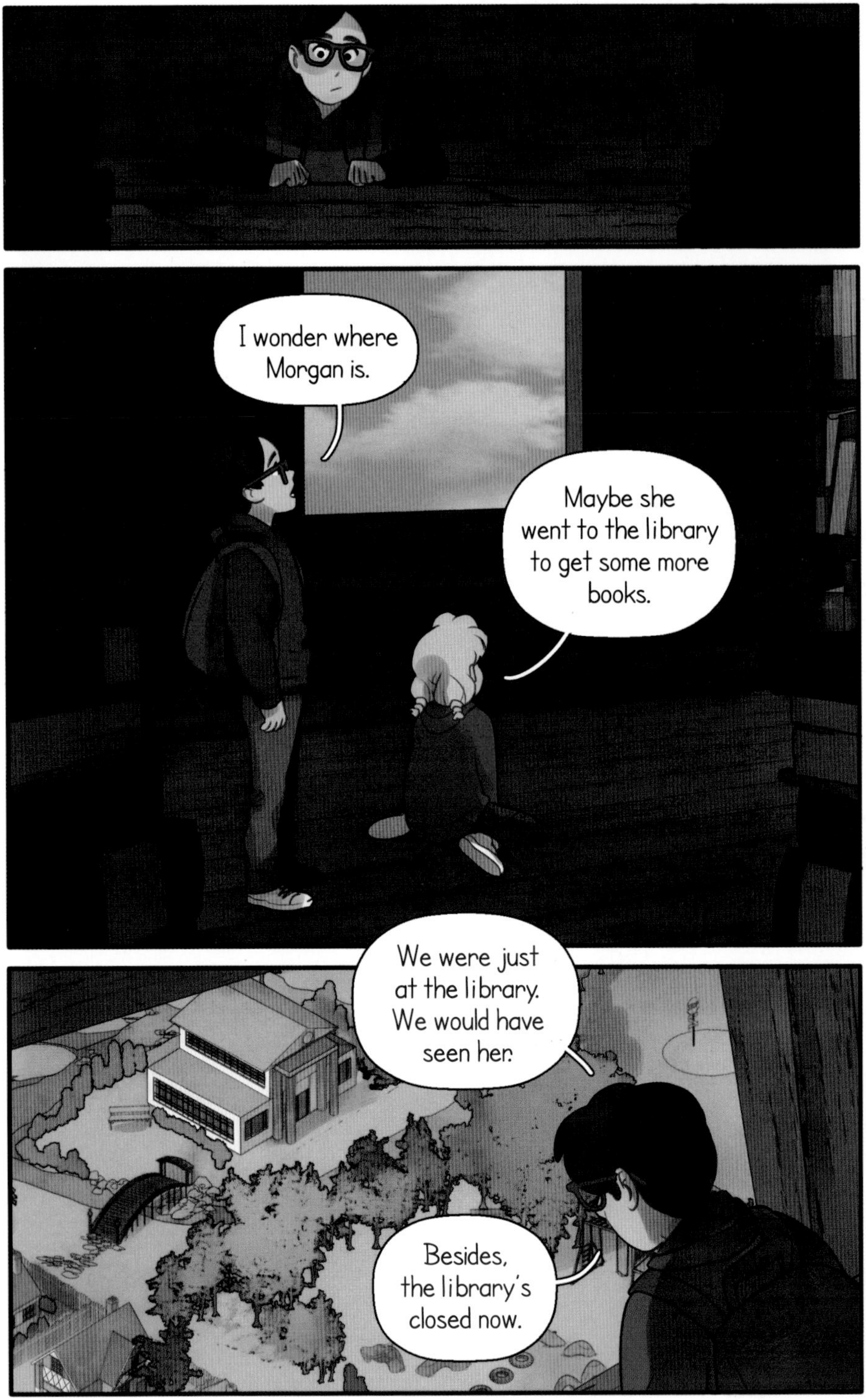
I wonder where Morgan is.
Maybe she went to the library to get some more books.
We were just at the library. We would have seen her.
Besides, the library's closed now.

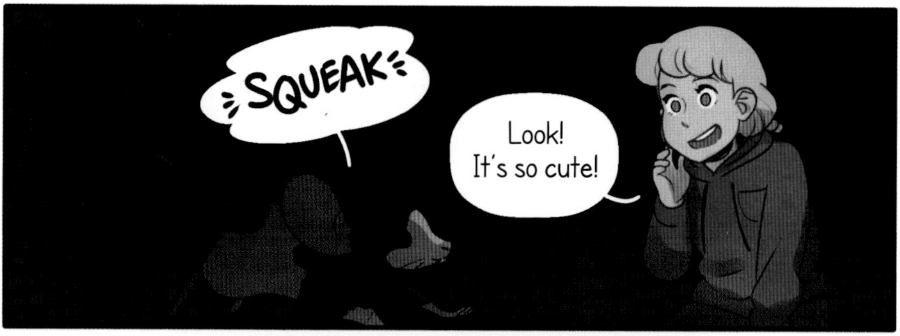
SQUEAK
Look! It's so cute!

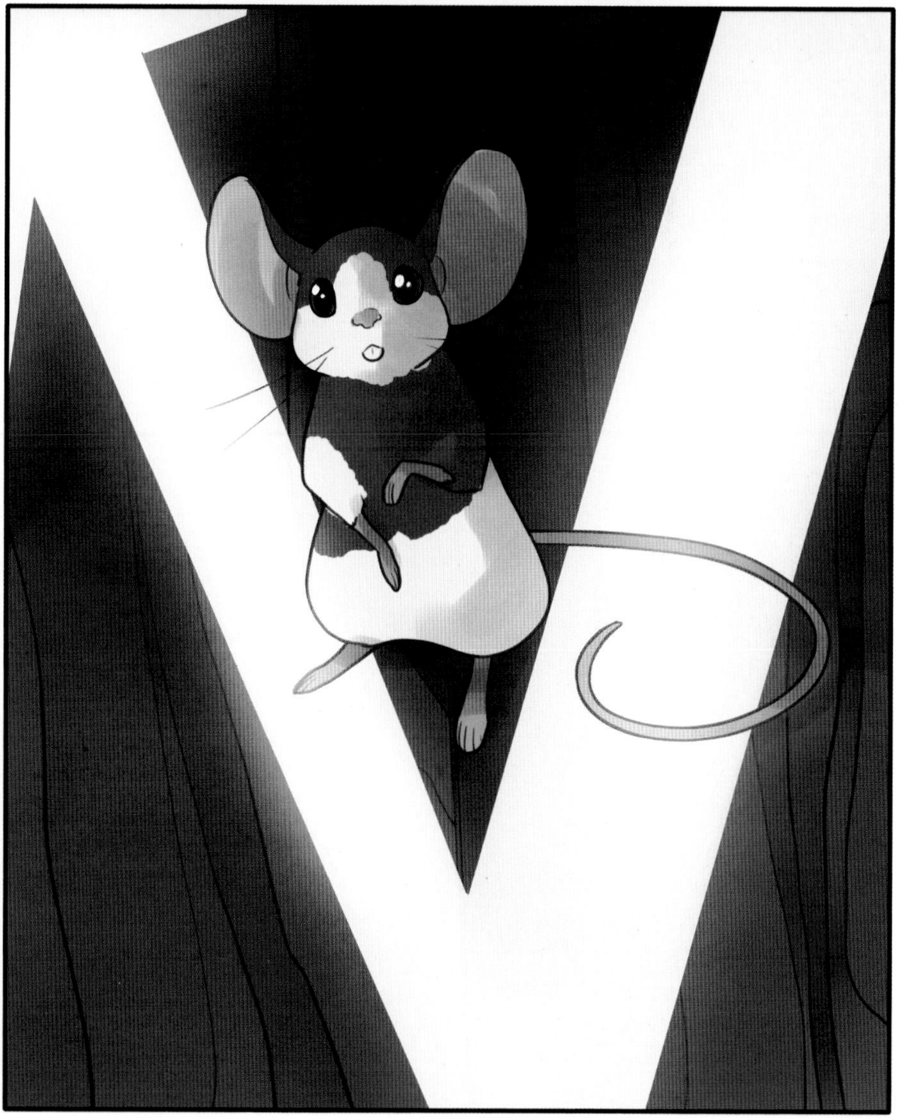

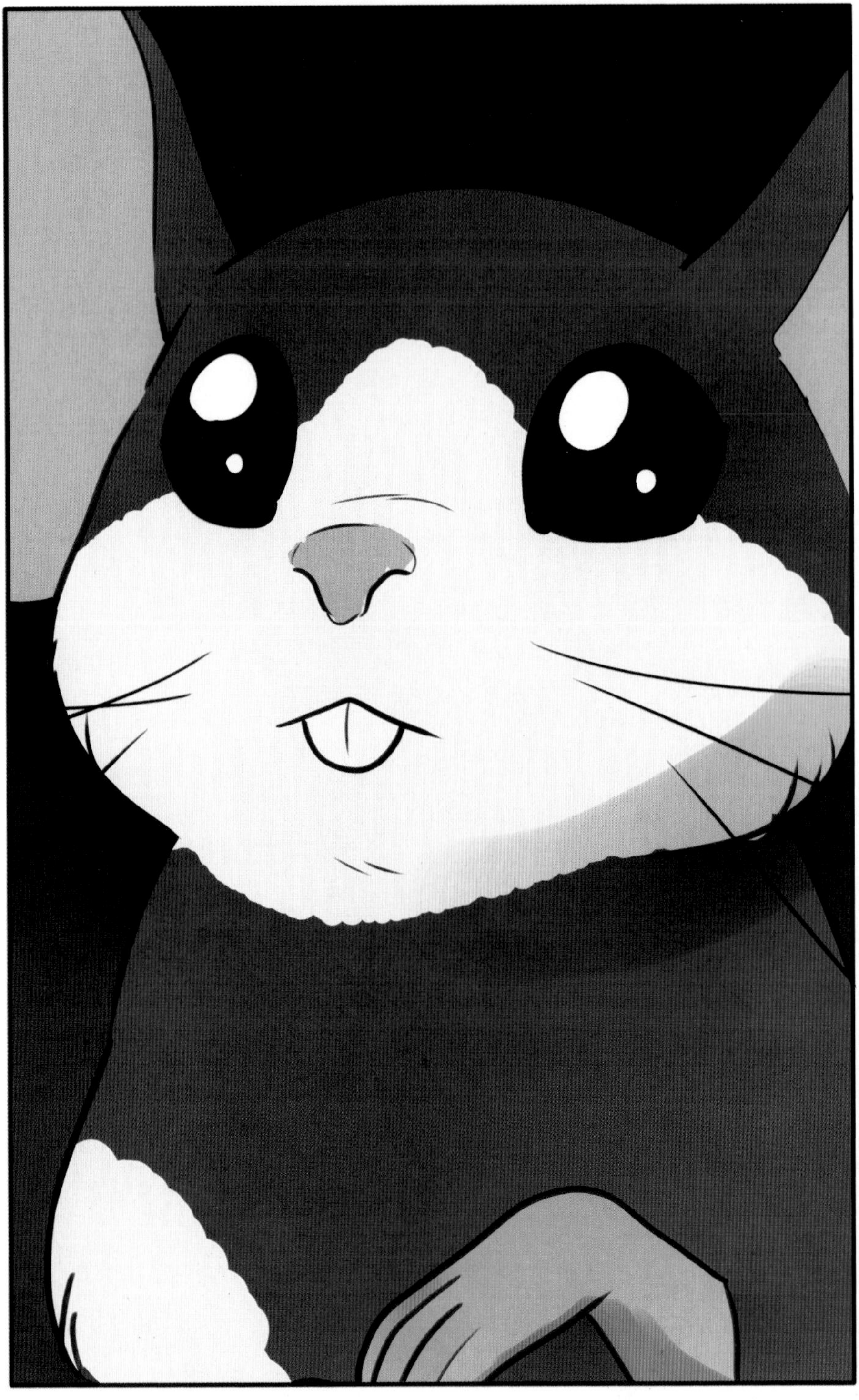

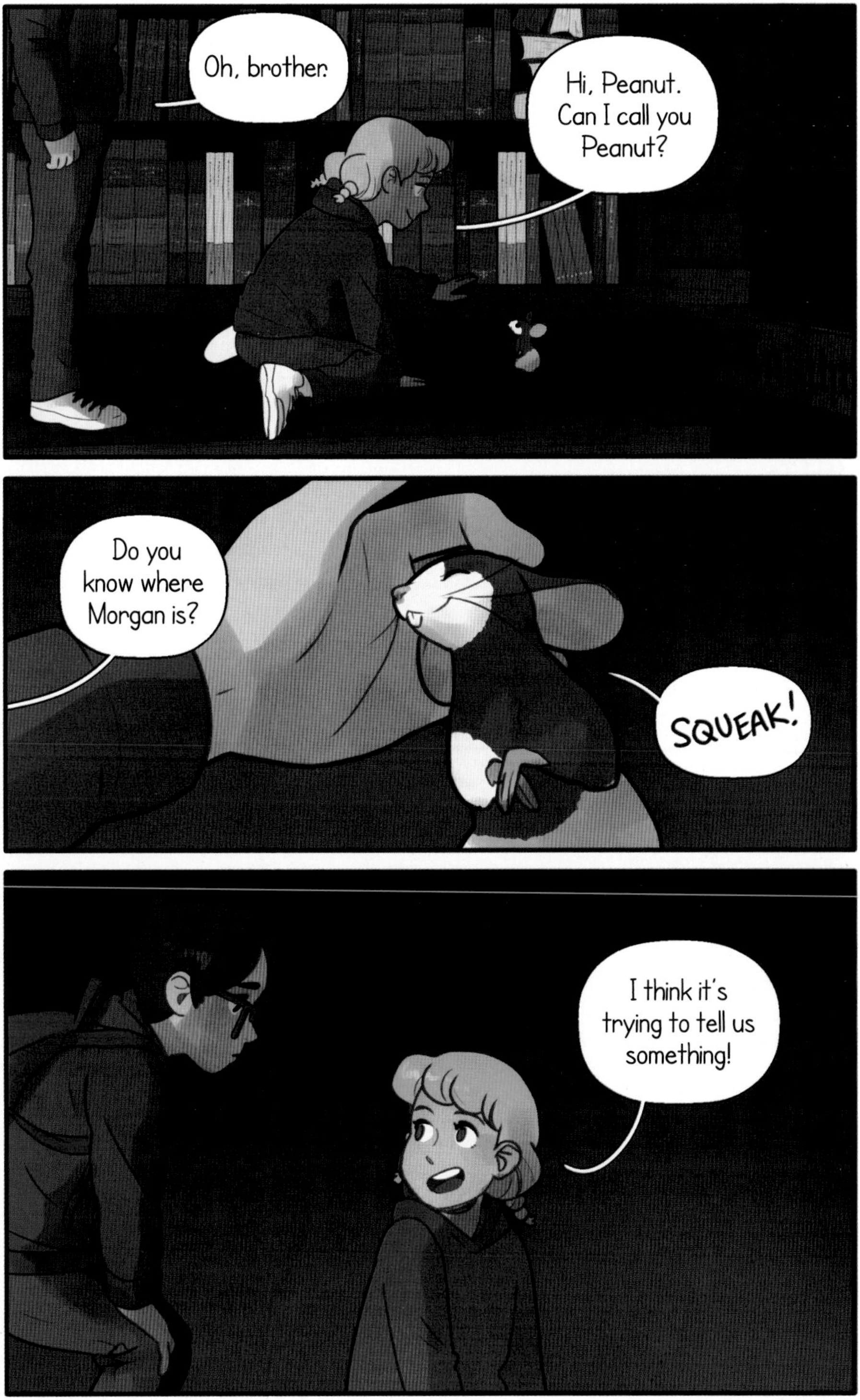
Oh, brother.
Hi, Peanut. Can I call you Peanut?
Do you know where Morgan is?
SQUEAK!
I think it's trying to tell us something!

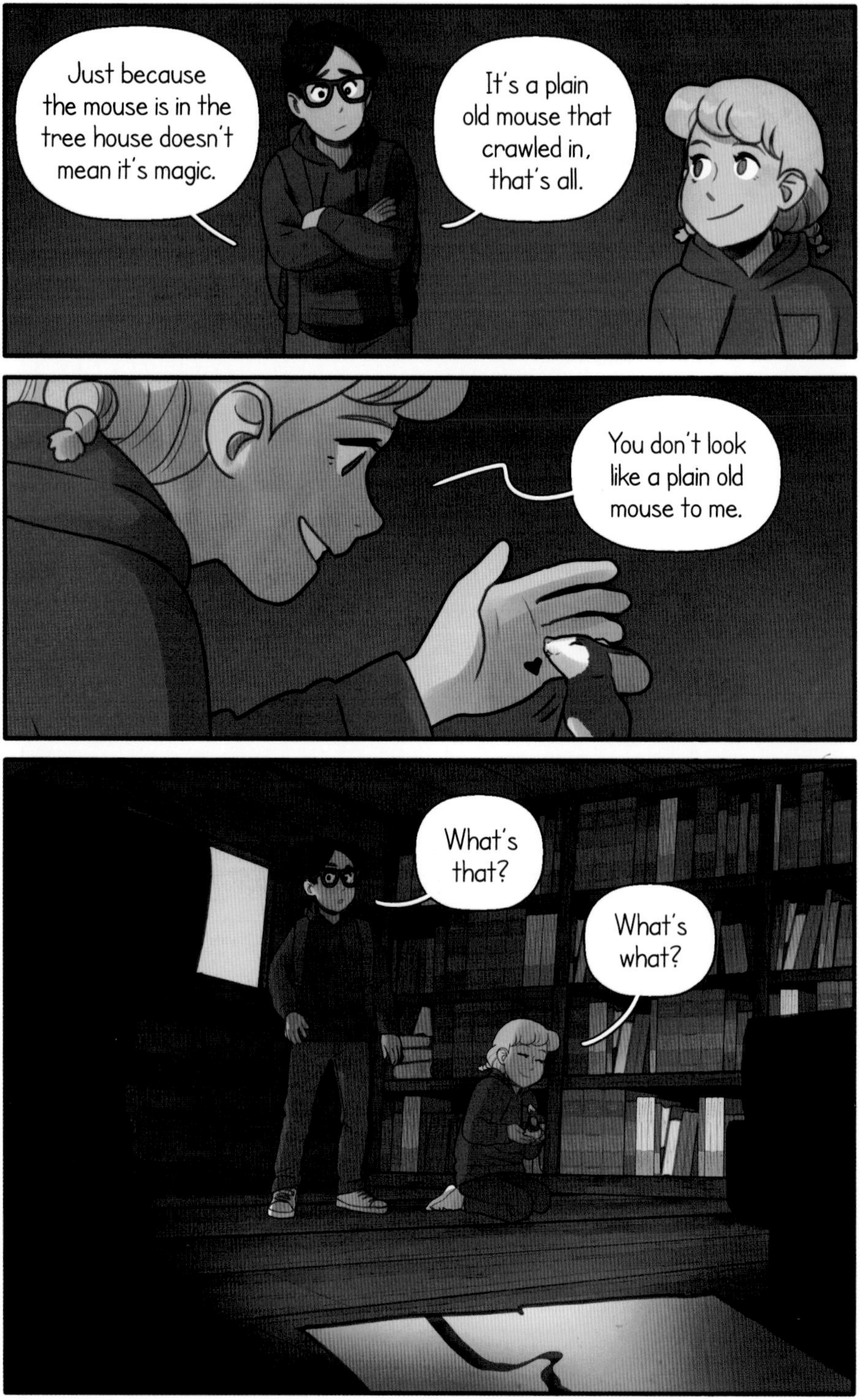
Just because the mouse is in the tree house doesn't mean it's magic.
It's a plain old mouse that crawled in, that's all.
You don't look like a plain old mouse to me.
What's that?
What's what?

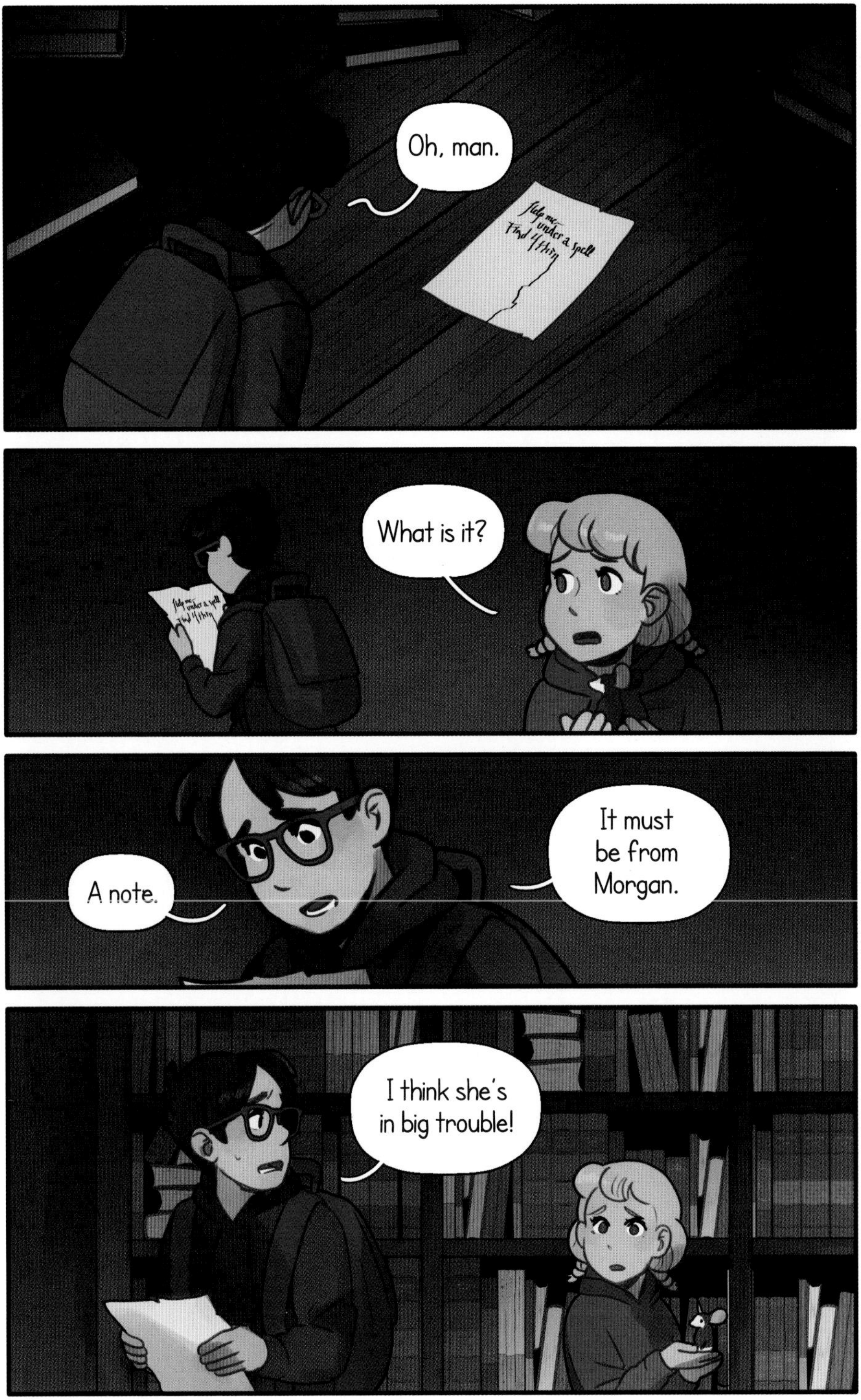
Oh, man.
What is it?
A note.
It must be from Morgan.
I think she's in big trouble!

CHAPTER TWO
The Open Book

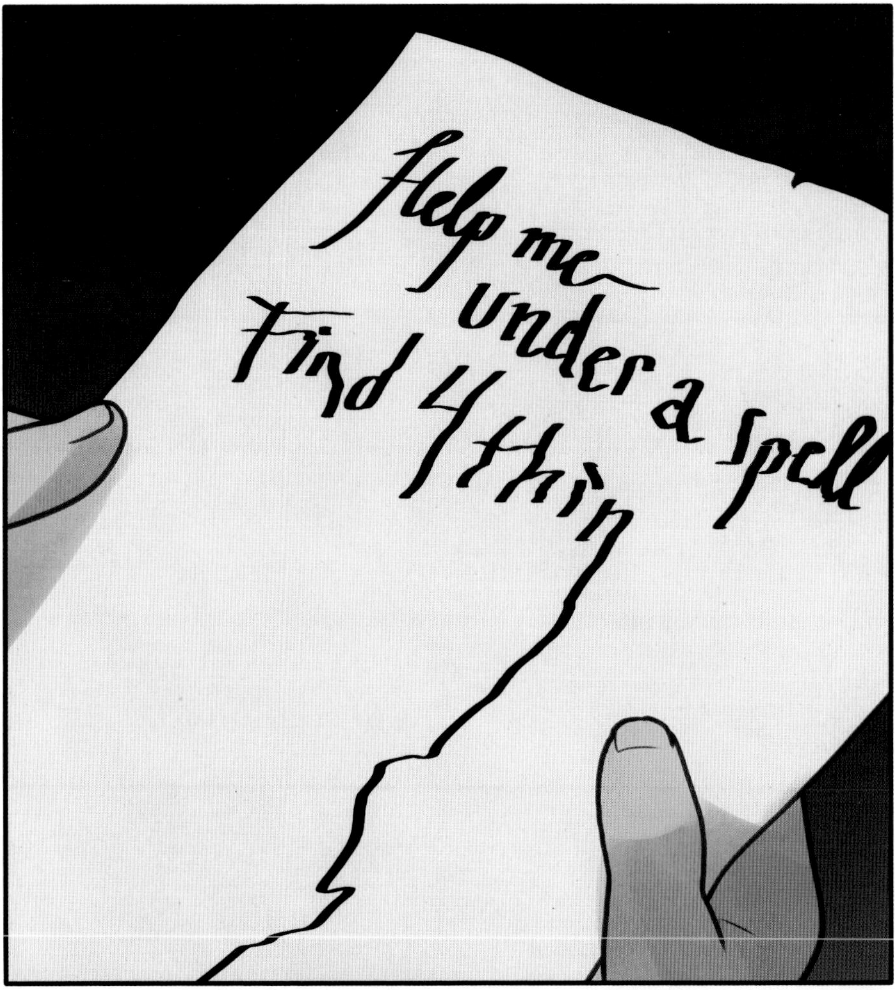
Help me
under a spell
Find 4thin

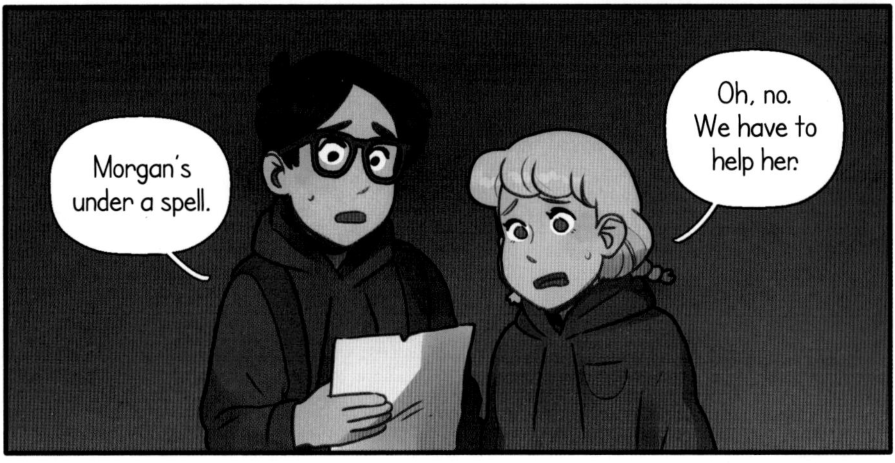
Morgan's under a spell.
Oh, no. We have to help her.

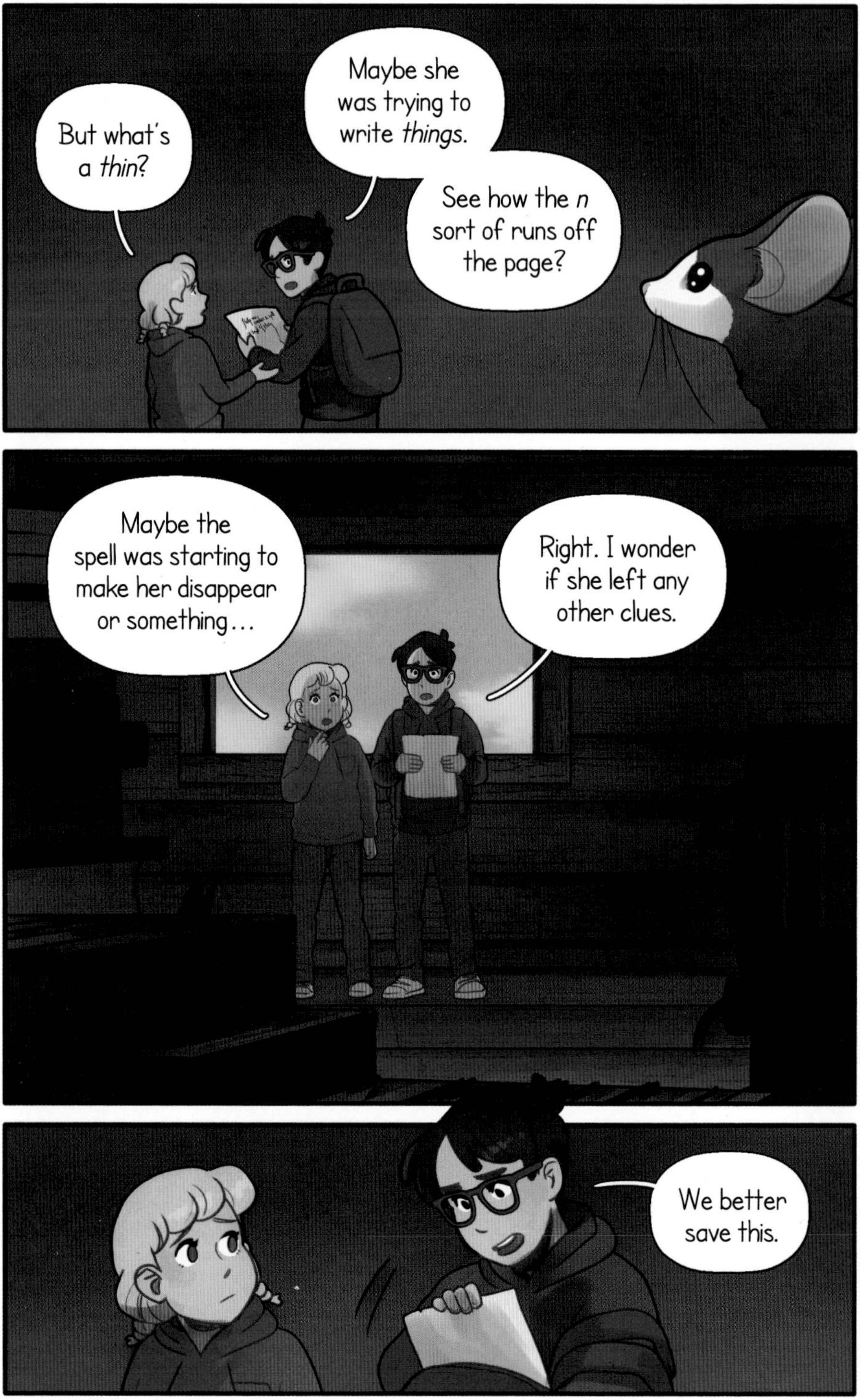
But what's a *thin*?
Maybe she was trying to write *things*.
See how the *n* sort of runs off the page?
Maybe the spell was starting to make her disappear or something...
Right. I wonder if she left any other clues.
We better save this.

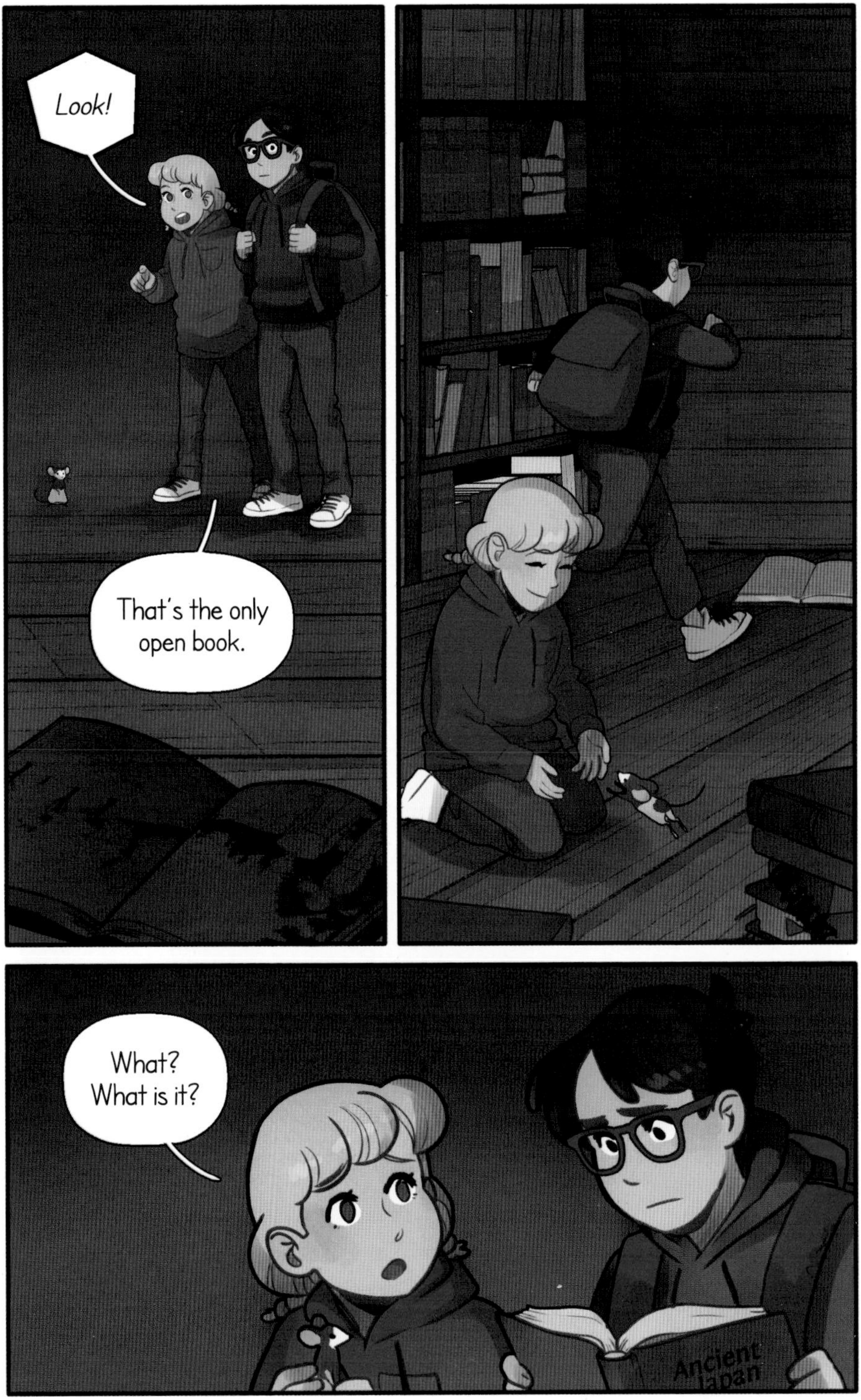
Look!
That's the only open book.
What? What is it?
Ancient Japan

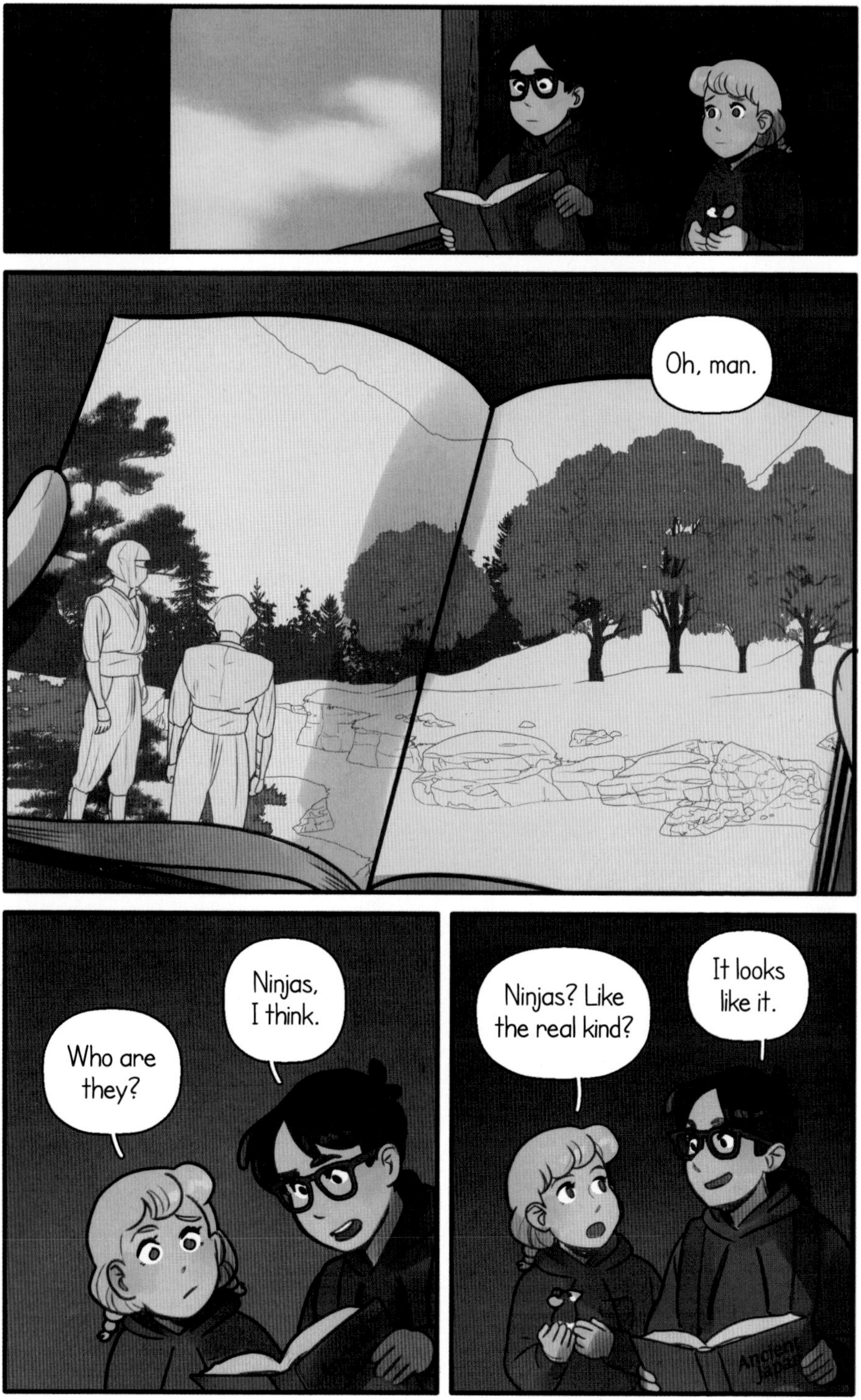
Oh, man.
Who are they?
Ninjas, I think.
Ninjas? Like the real kind?
It looks like it.

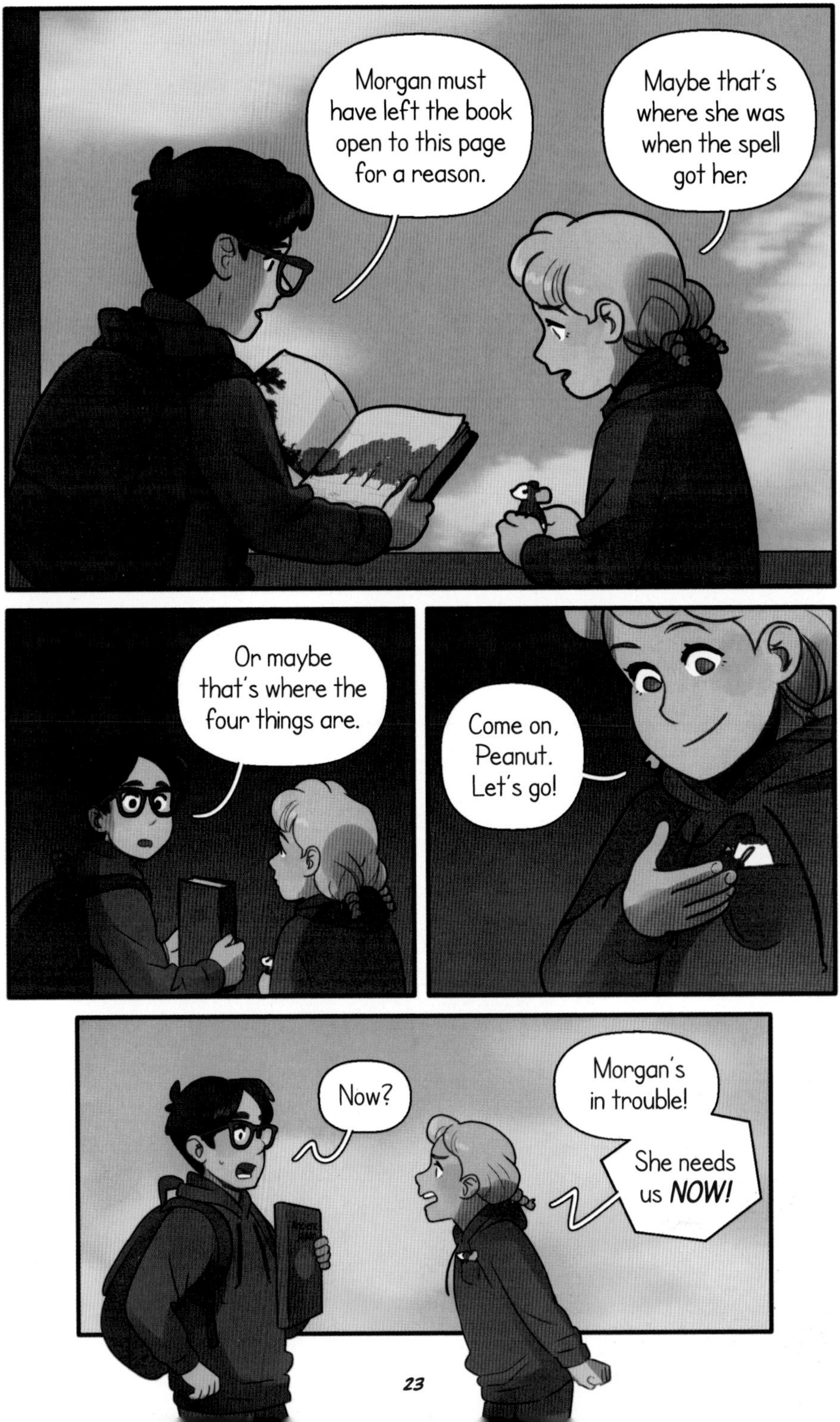
Morgan must have left the book open to this page for a reason.
Maybe that's where she was when the spell got her.
Or maybe that's where the four things are.
Come on, Peanut. Let's go!
Now?
Morgan's in trouble!
She needs us *NOW!*

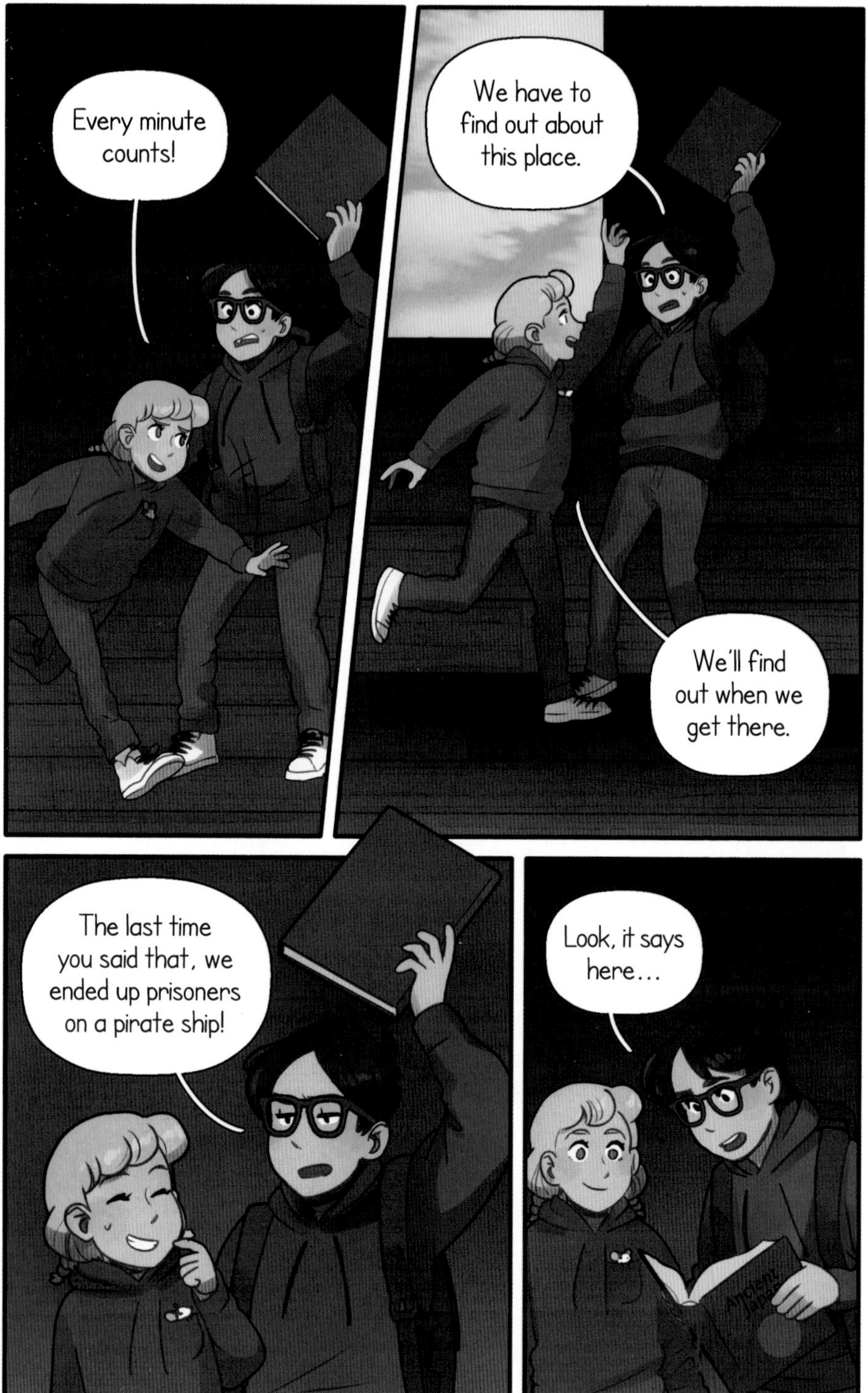
Every minute counts!
We have to find out about this place.
We'll find out when we get there.
The last time you said that, we ended up prisoners on a pirate ship!
Look, it says here...

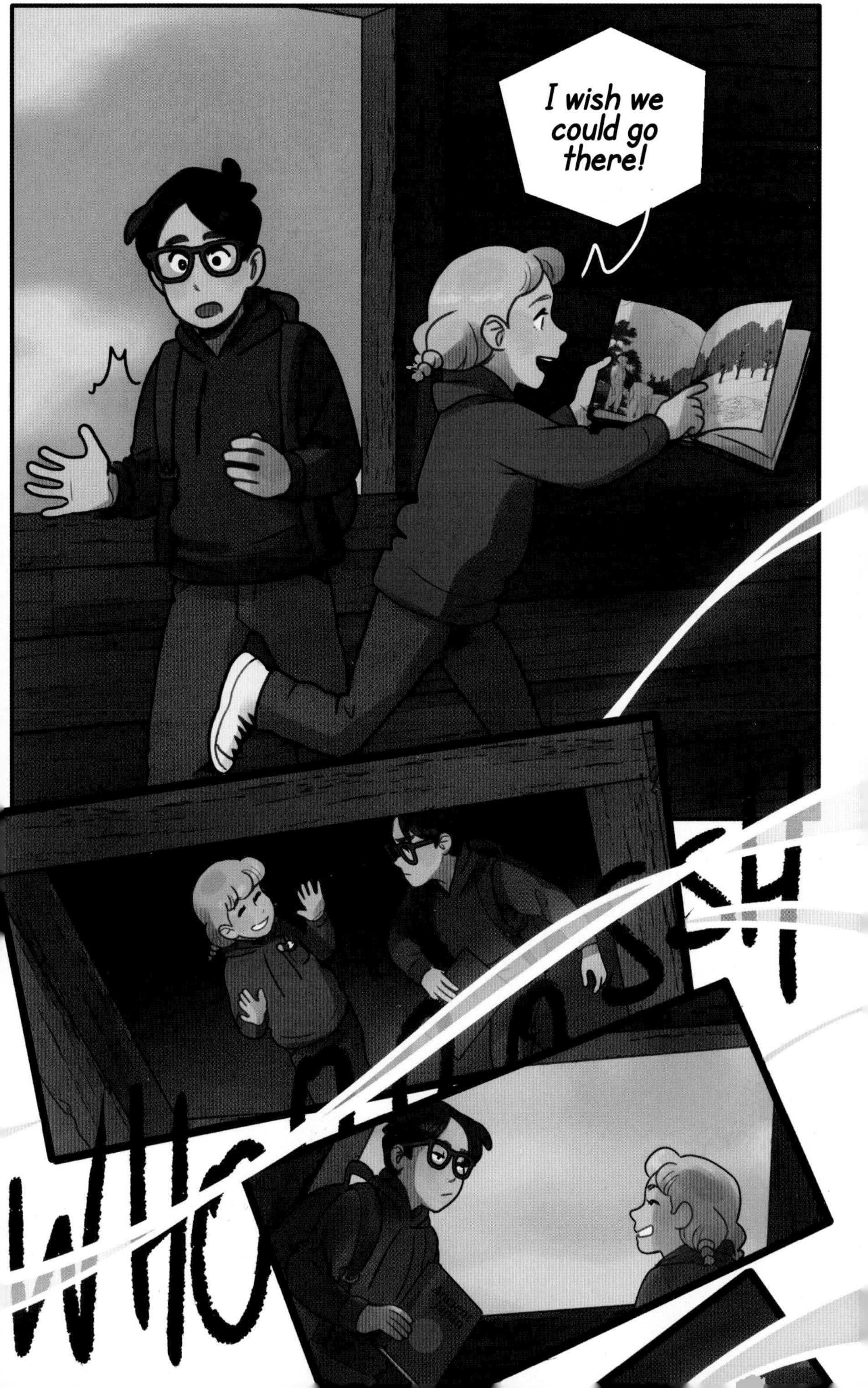
I wish we could go there!

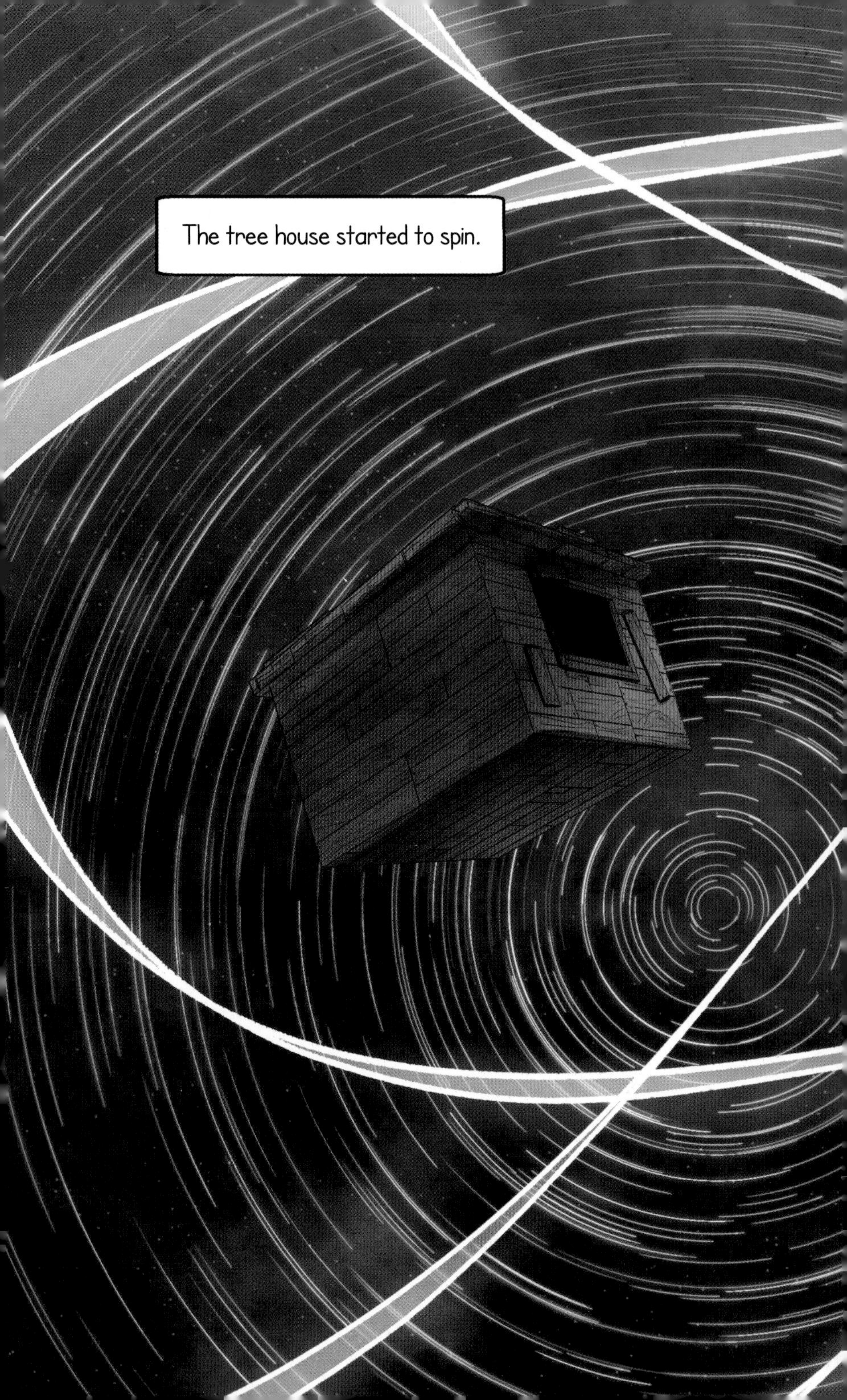
The tree house started to spin.

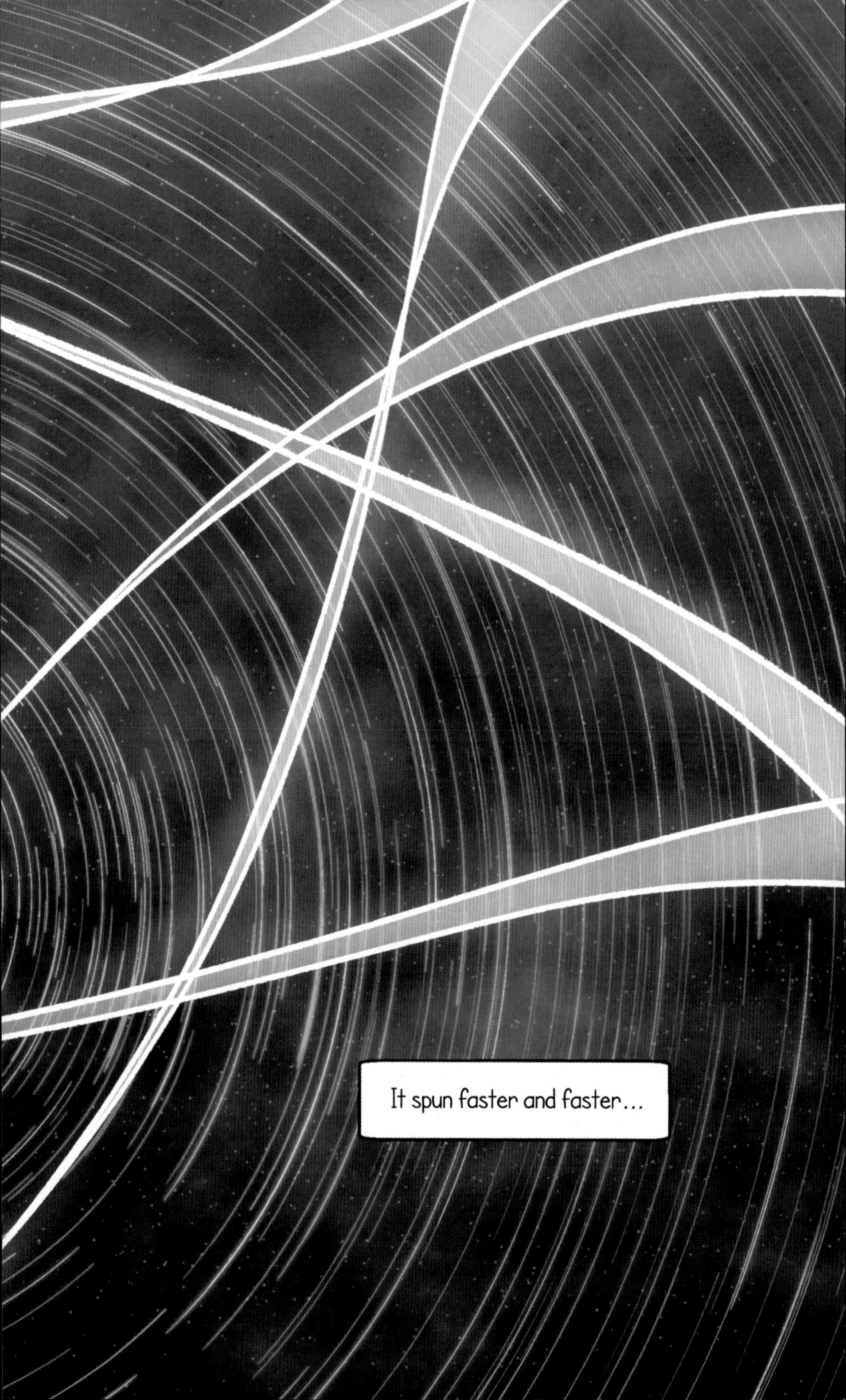
It spun faster and faster…

CHAPTER THREE

E-HY!

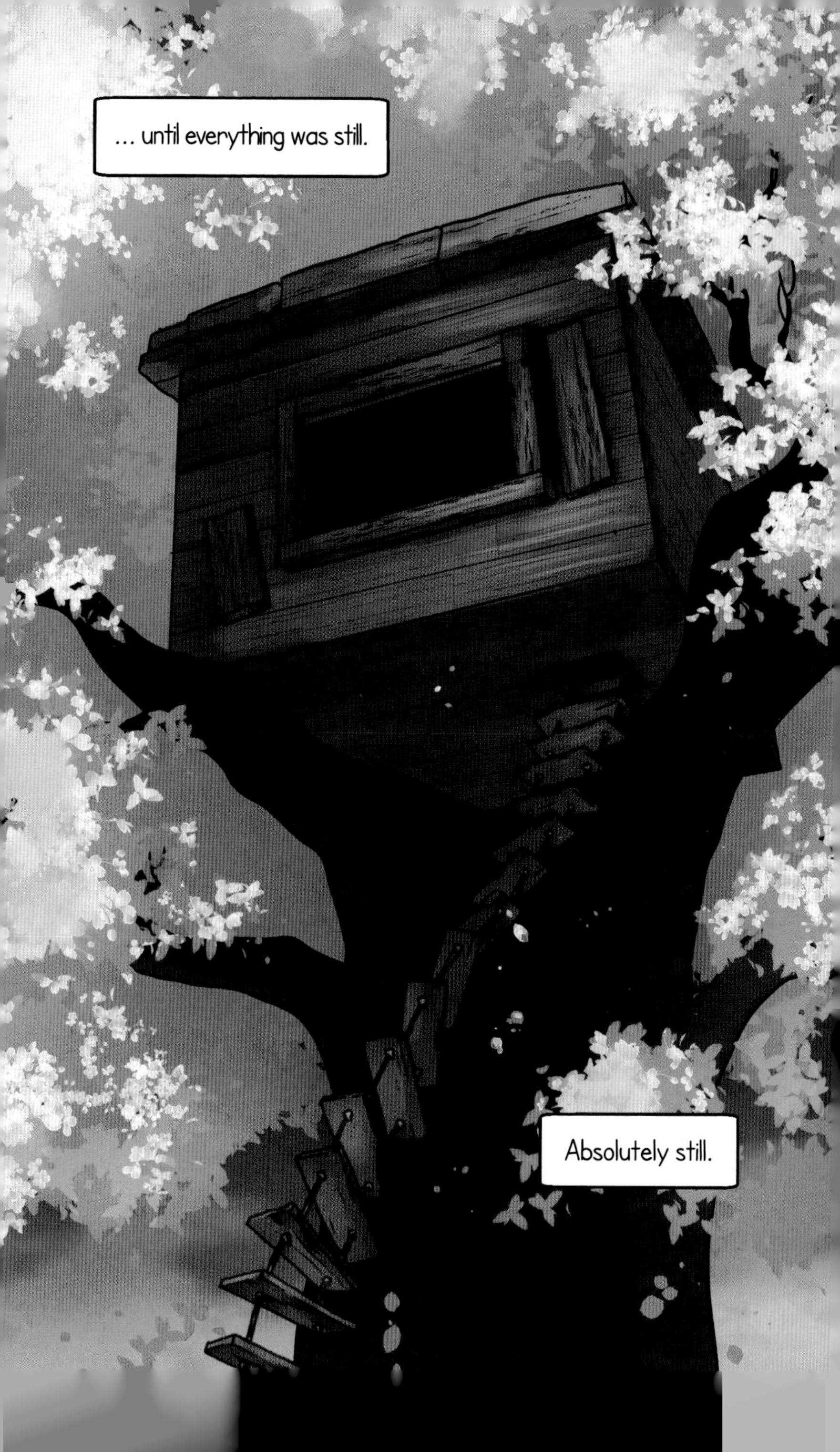
... until everything was still.
Absolutely still.

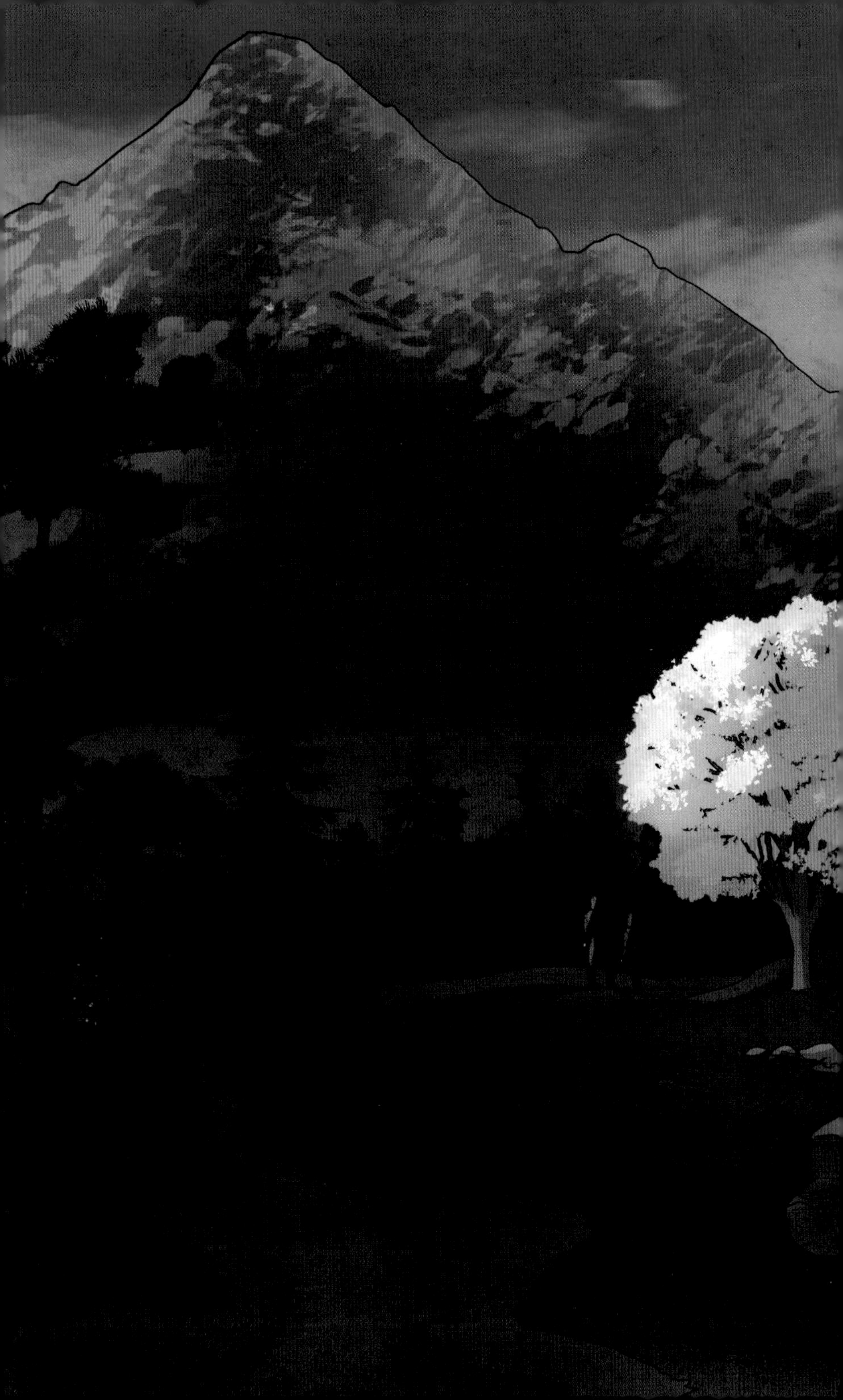

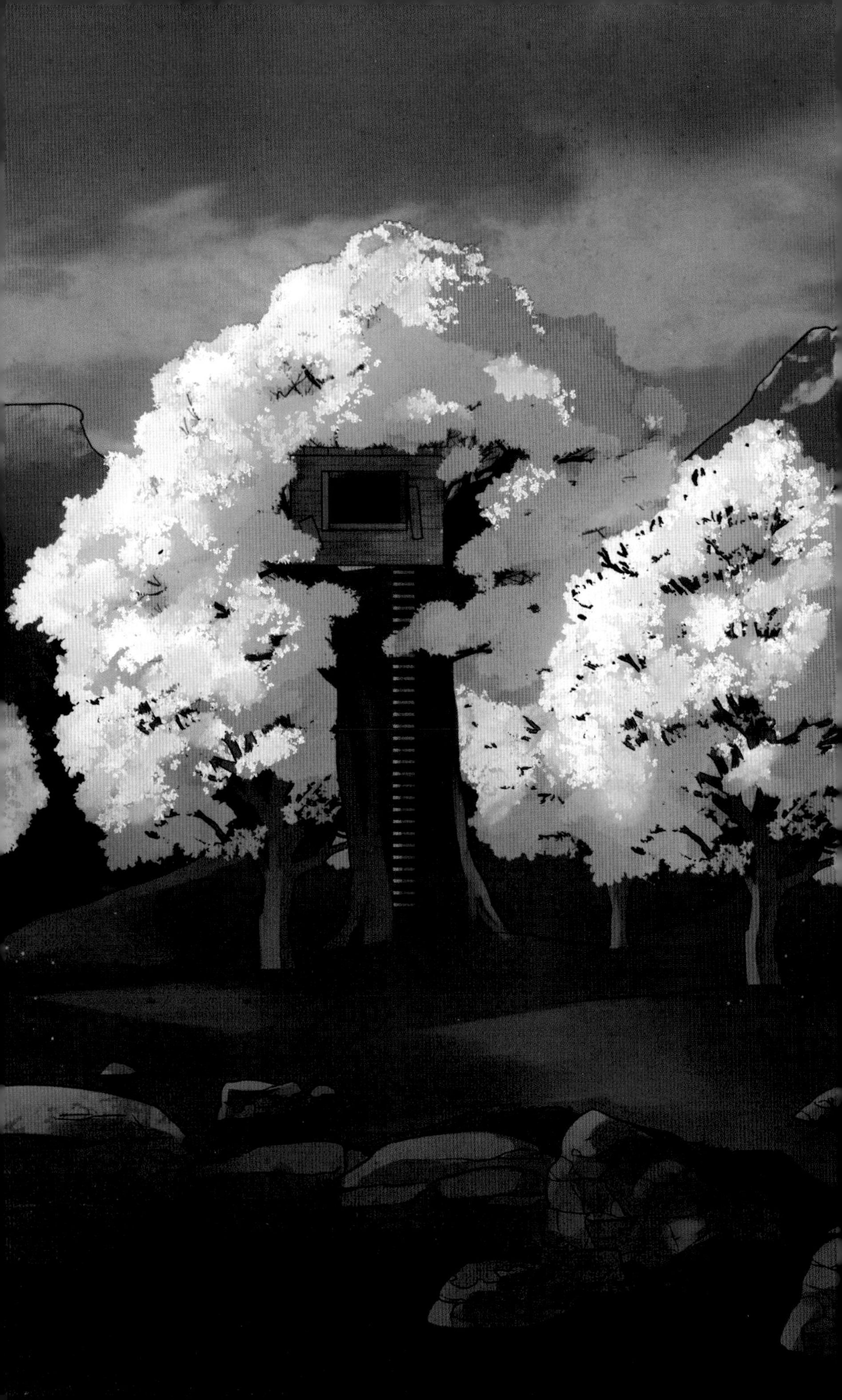

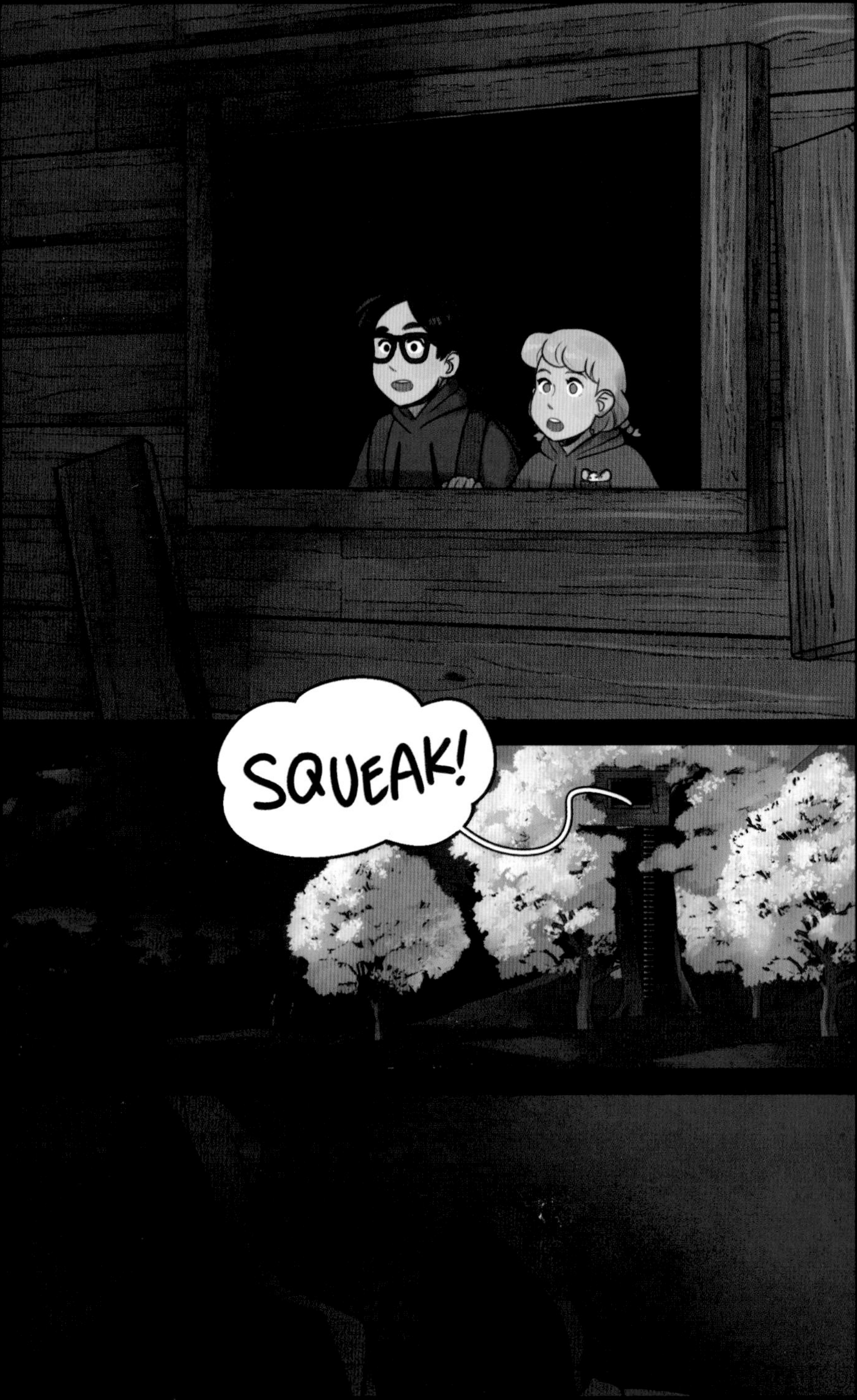
SQUEAK!

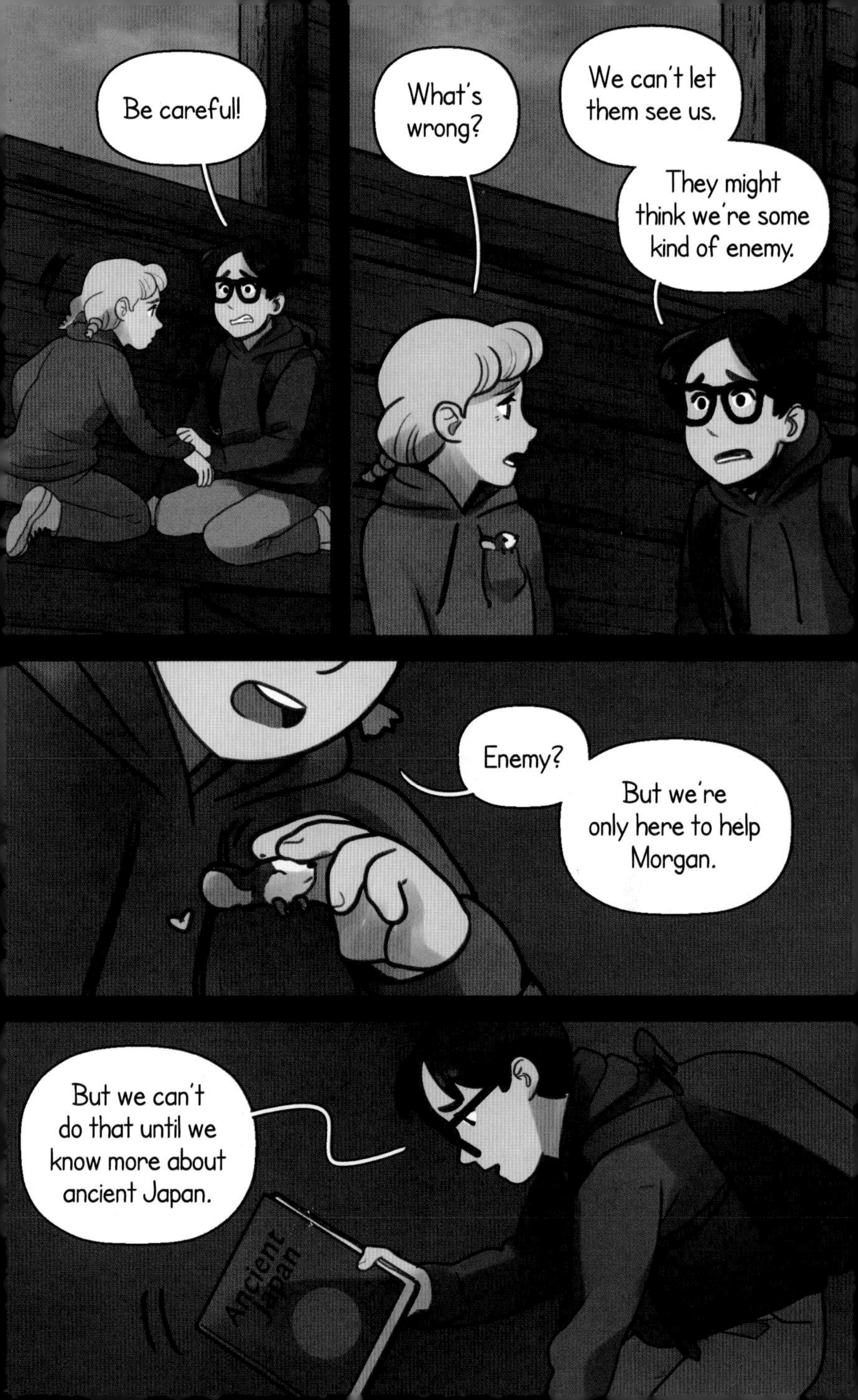
Be careful!
What's wrong?
We can't let them see us.
They might think we're some kind of enemy.
Enemy?
But we're only here to help Morgan.
But we can't do that until we know more about ancient Japan.
Ancient Japan

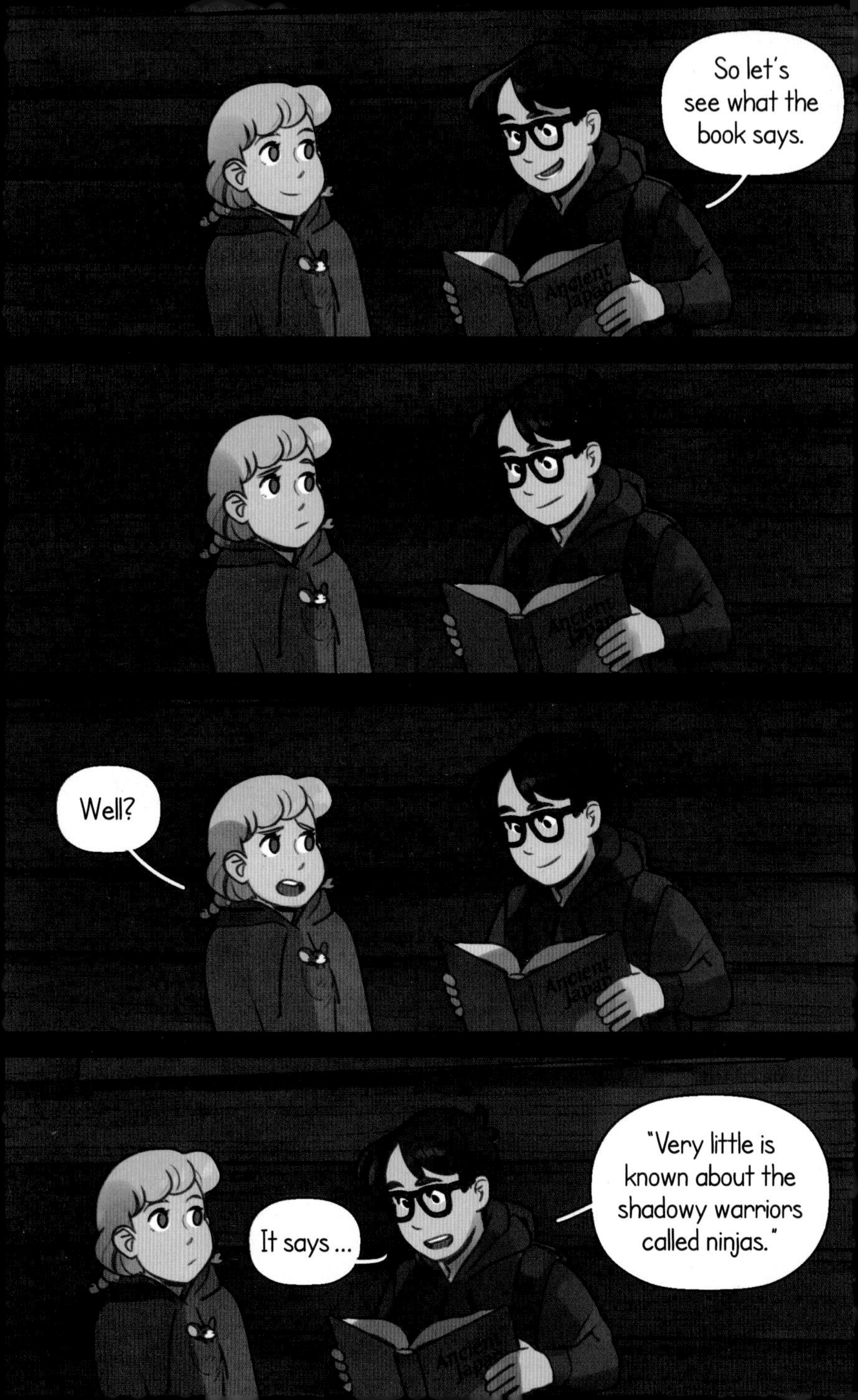
So let's see what the book says.
Ancient Japan
Well?
It says ...
"Very little is known about the shadowy warriors called ninjas."

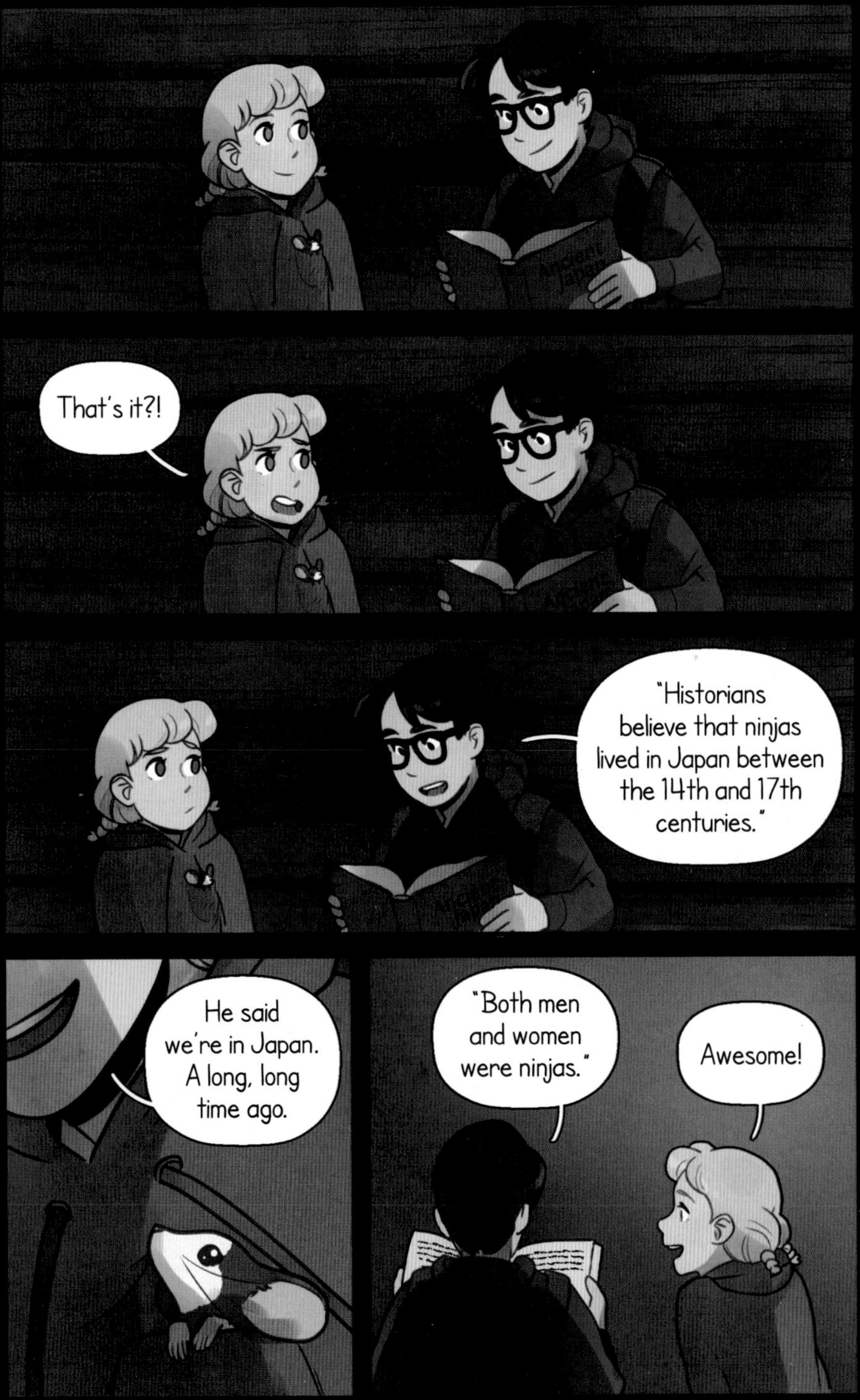
Ancient Japan
That's it?!
"Historians believe that ninjas lived in Japan between the 14th and 17th centuries."
He said we're in Japan. A long, long time ago.
"Both men and women were ninjas."
Awesome!

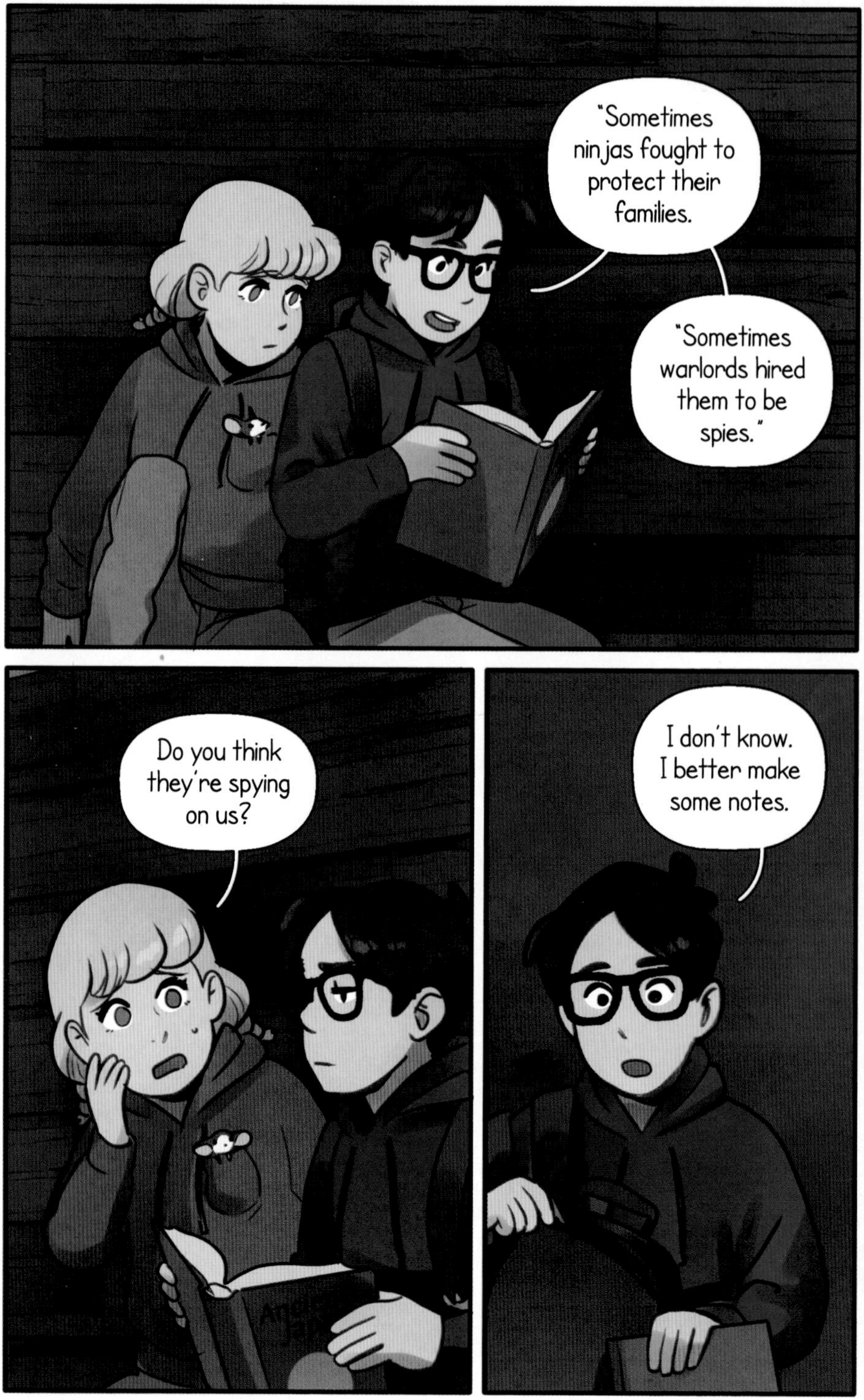
"Sometimes ninjas fought to protect their families.
"Sometimes warlords hired them to be spies."
Do you think they're spying on us?
I don't know. I better make some notes.

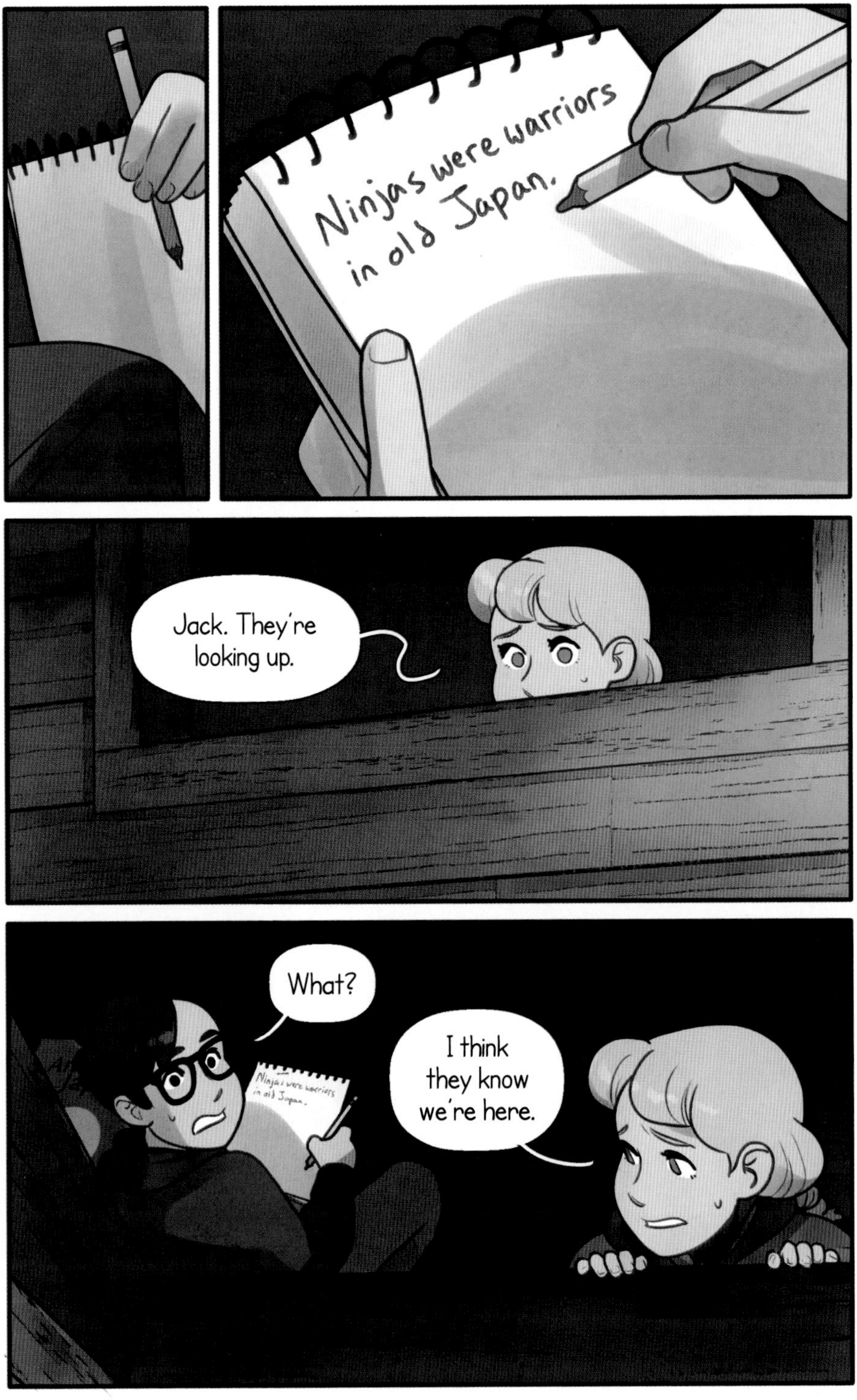
Ninjas were warriors in old Japan.
Jack. They're looking up.
What?
Ninjas were warriors in old Japan.
I think they know we're here.

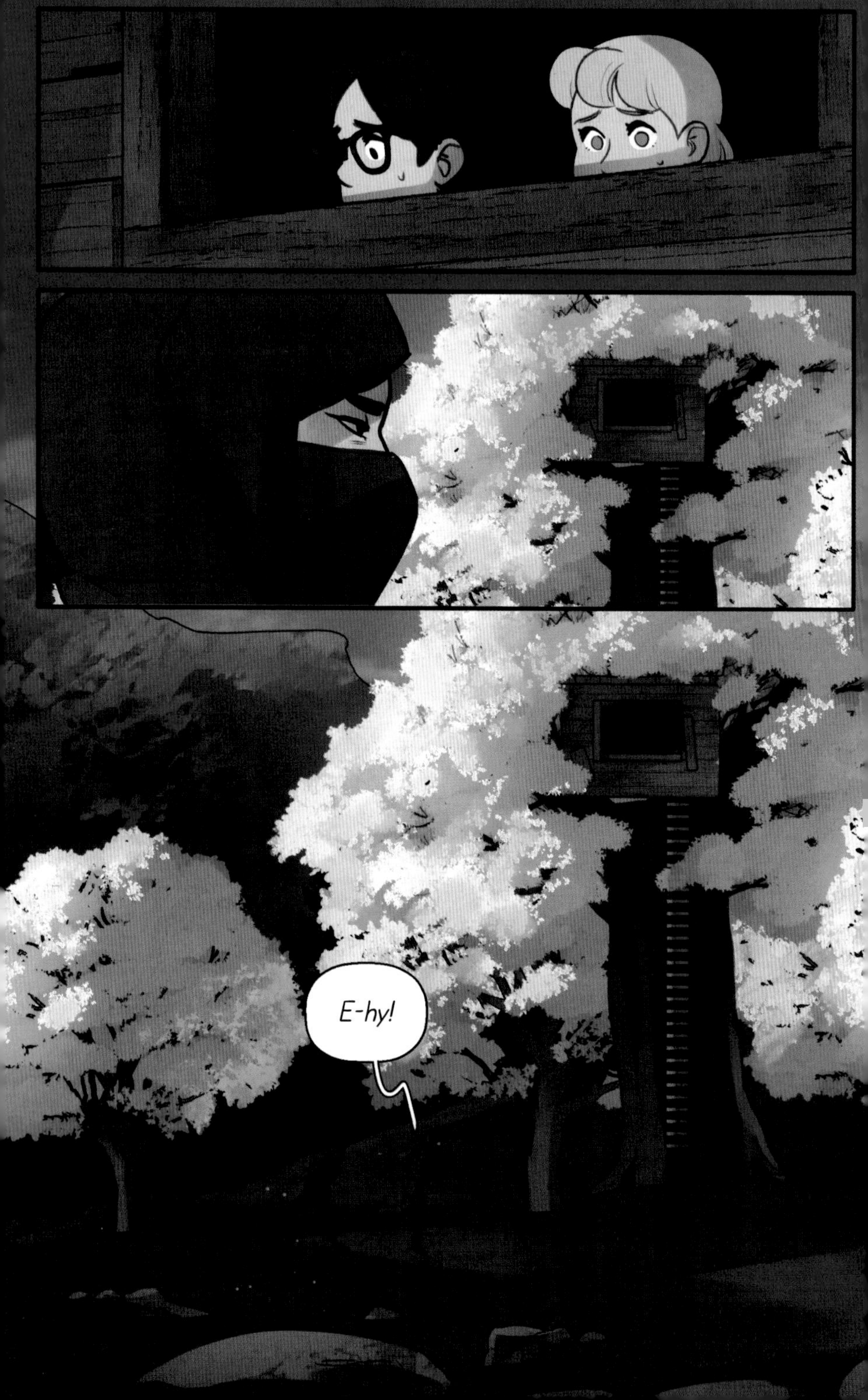
E-hy!

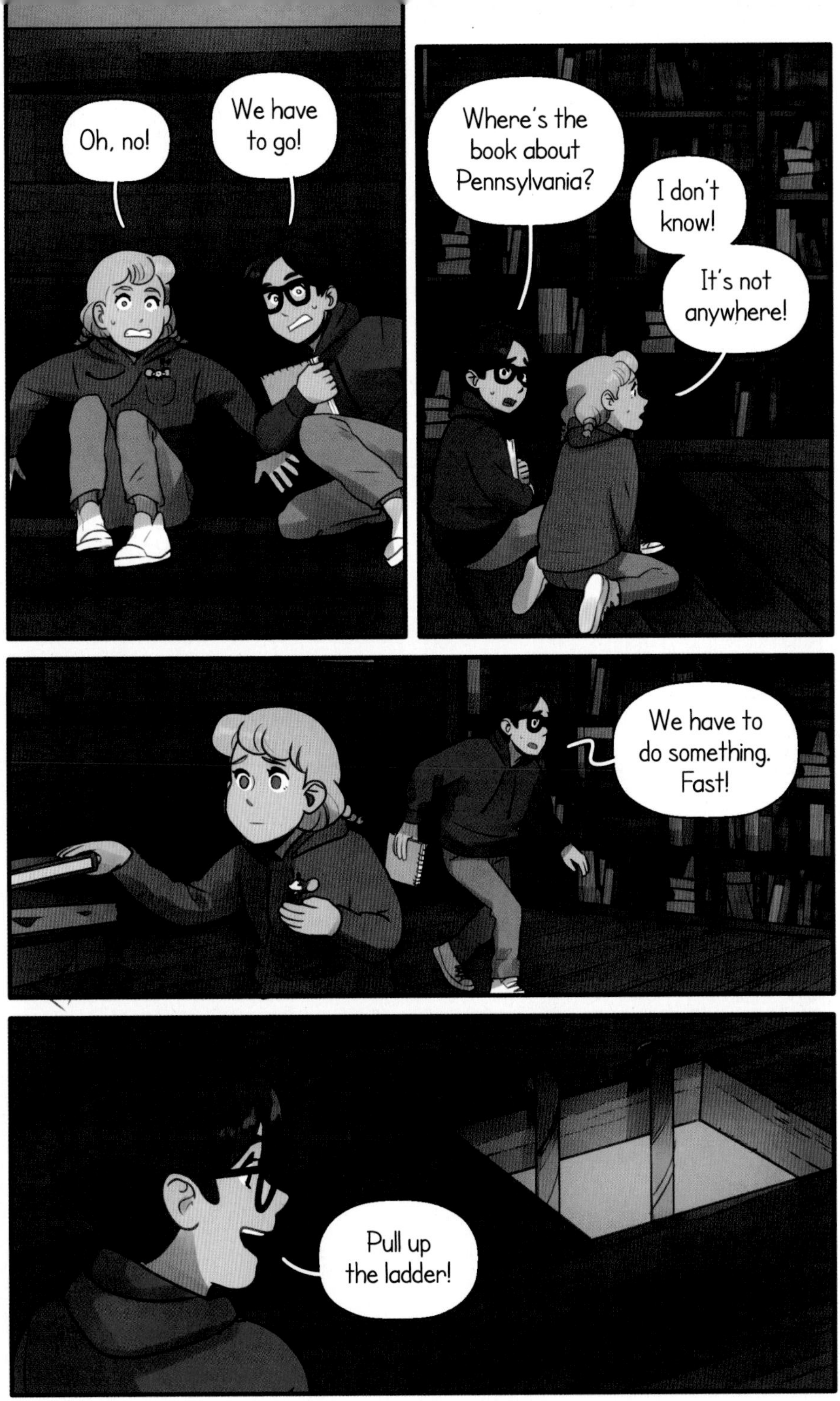
Oh, no!
We have to go!
Where's the book about Pennsylvania?
I don't know!
It's not anywhere!
We have to do something. Fast!
Pull up the ladder!

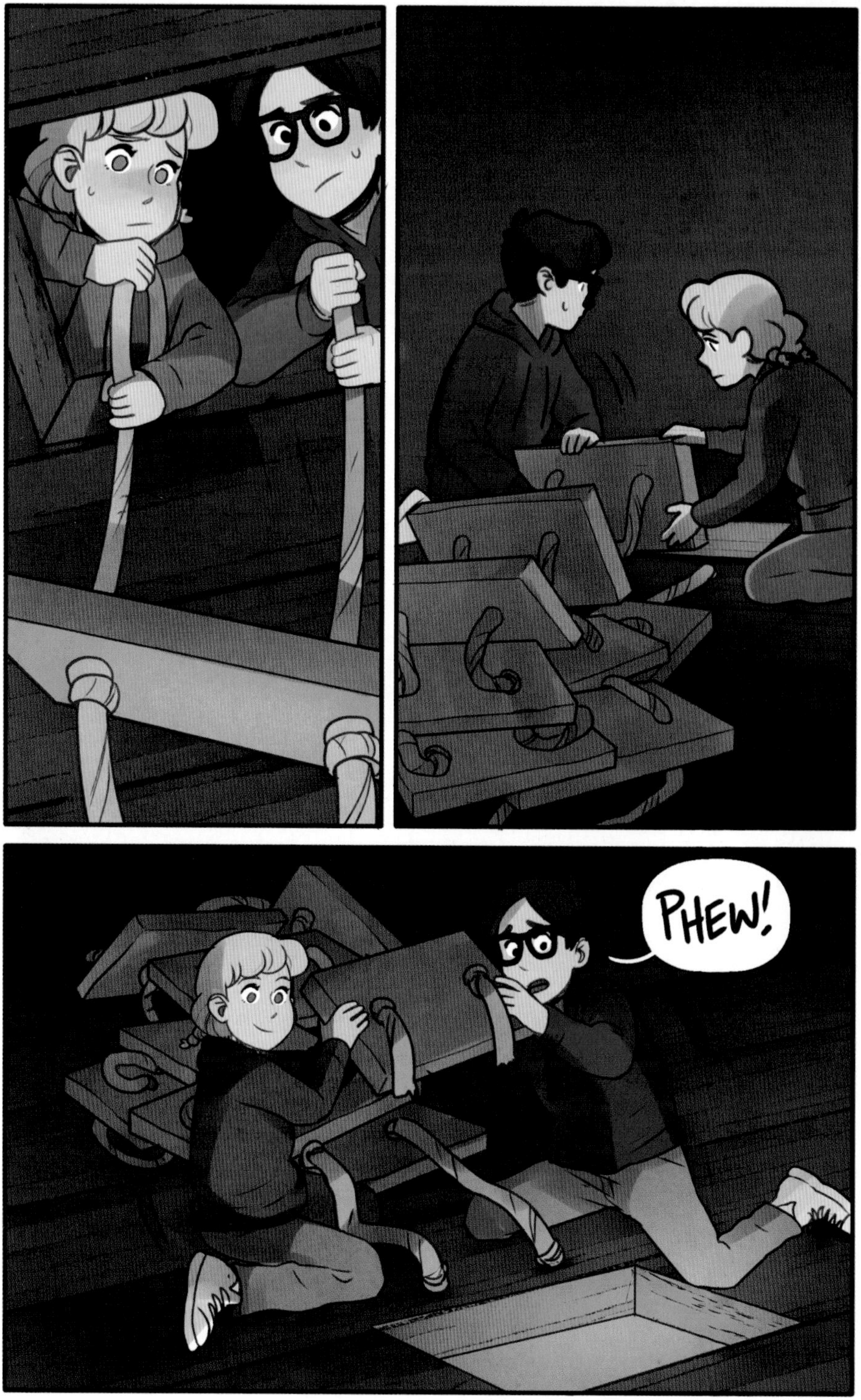
PHEW!

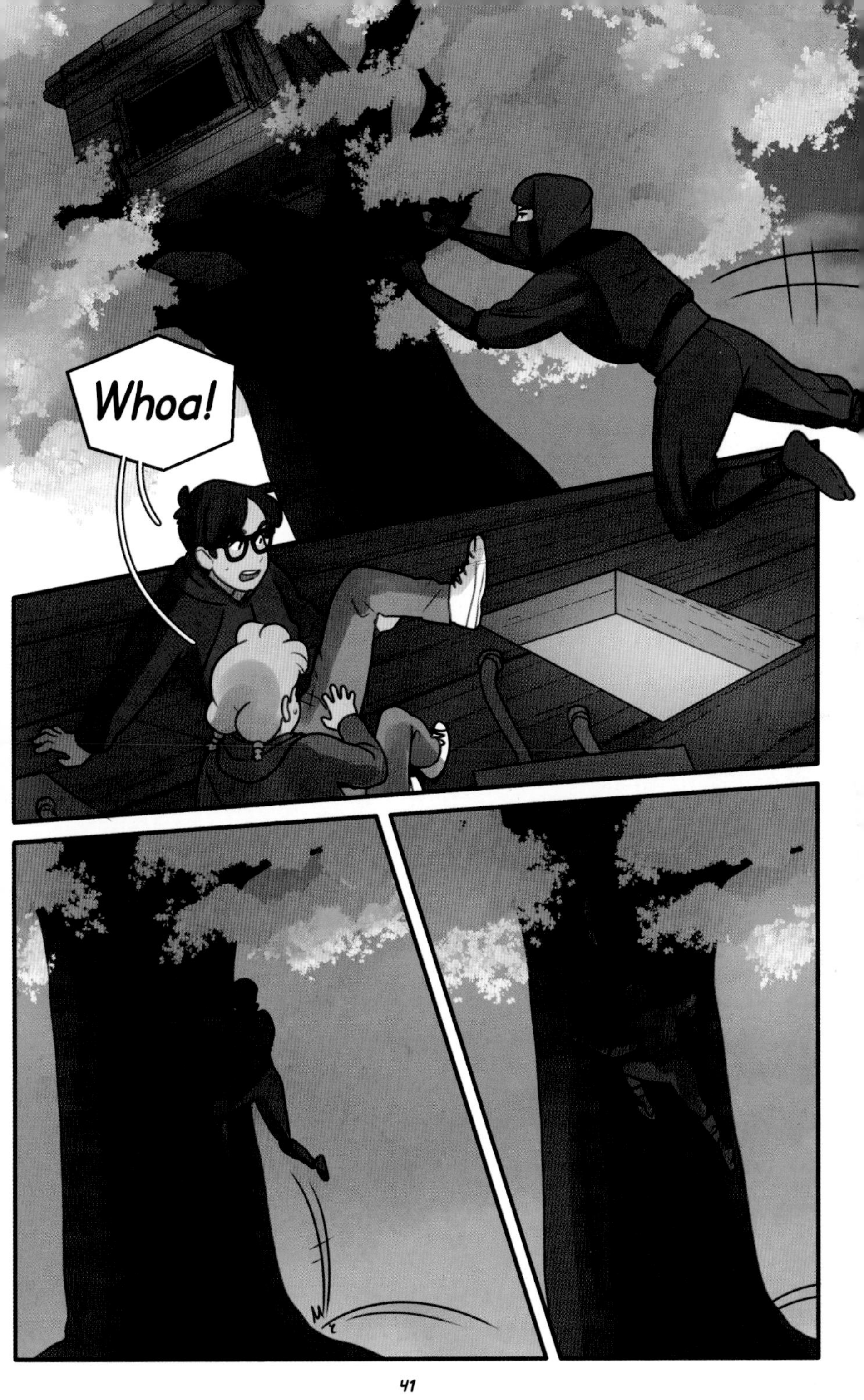
Whoa!

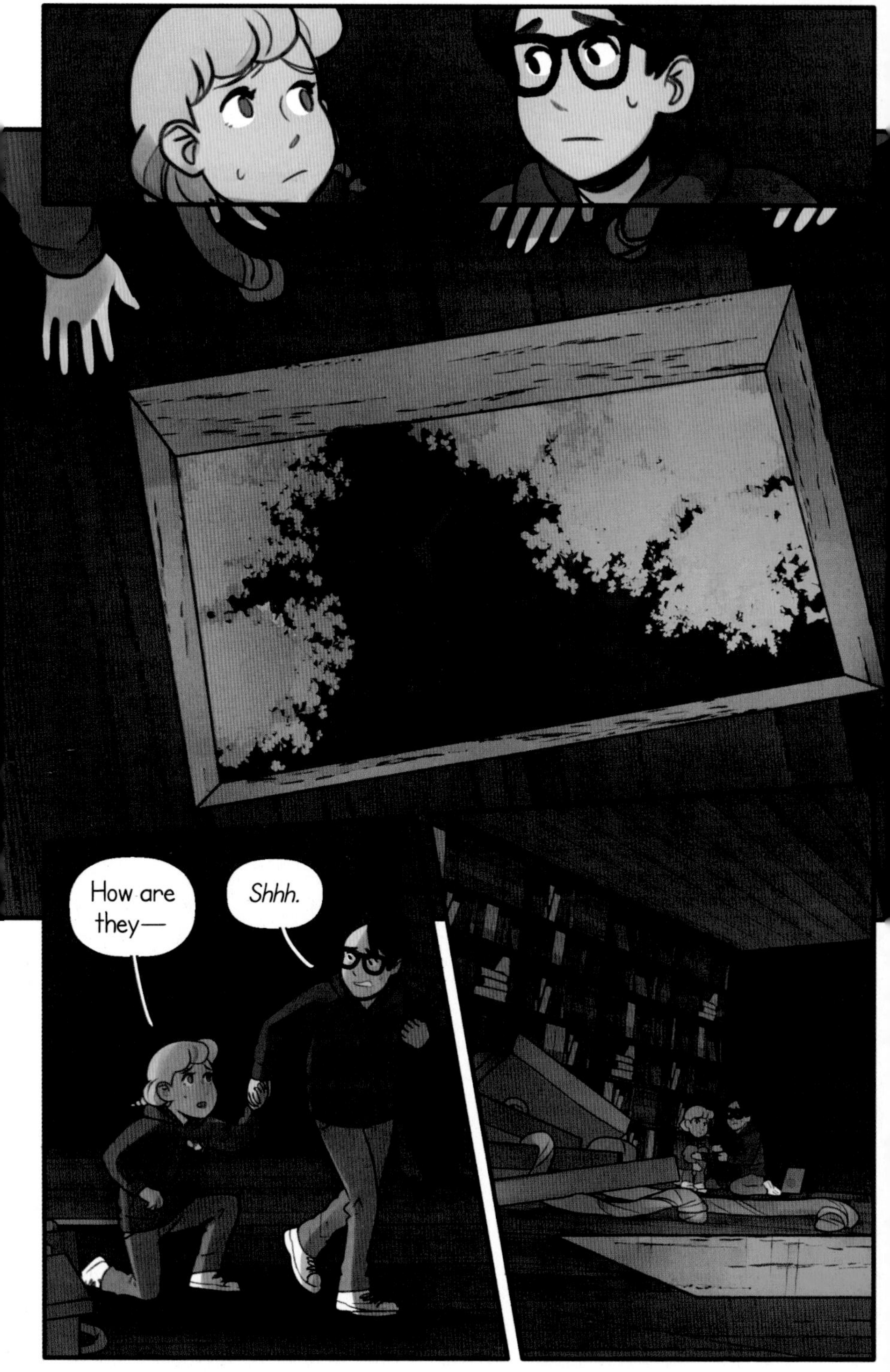
How are they—
Shhh.

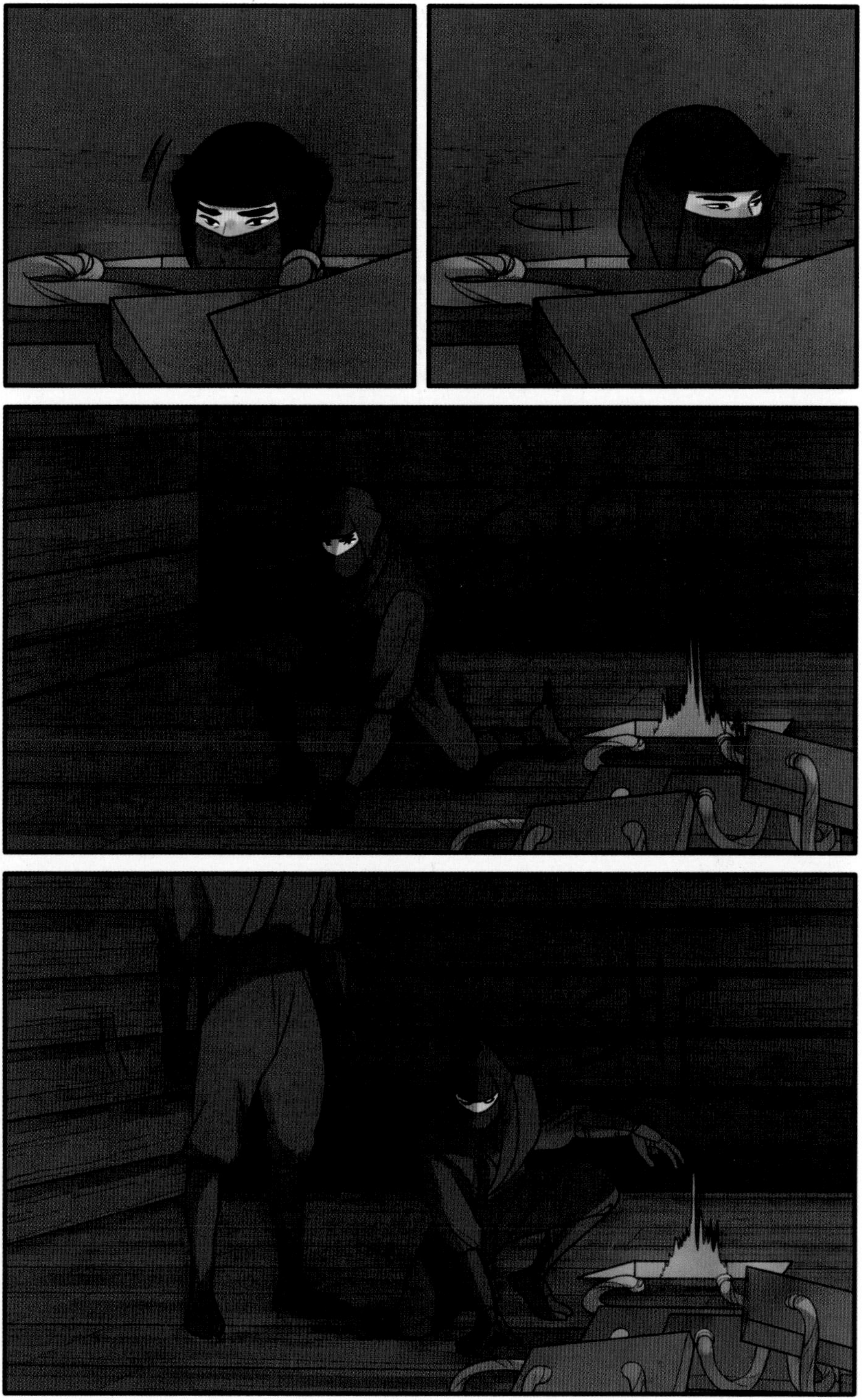

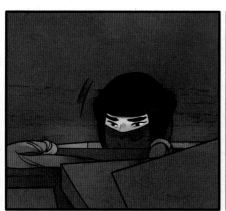

CHAPTER FOUR
Captured

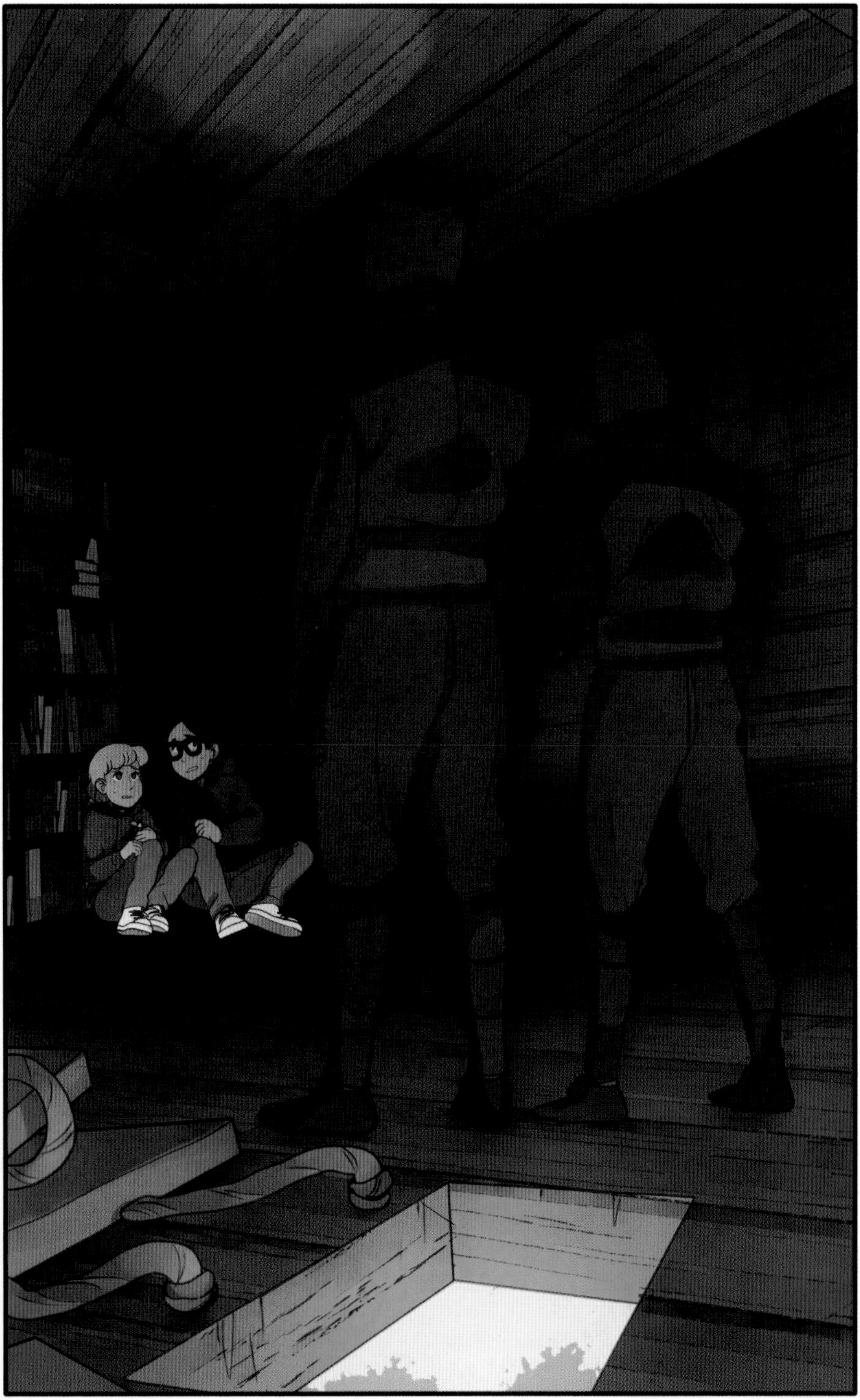

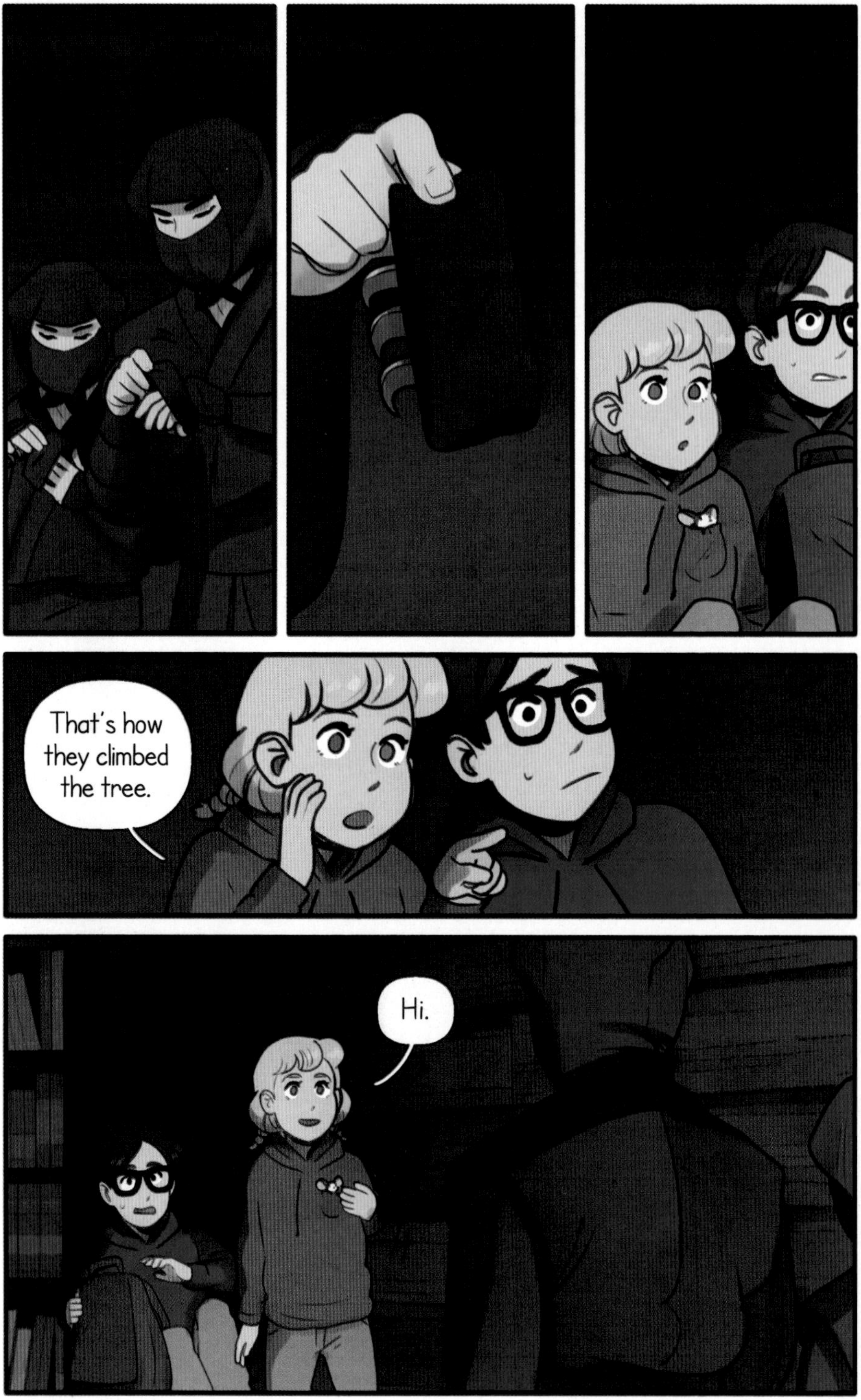
That's how they climbed the tree.
Hi.

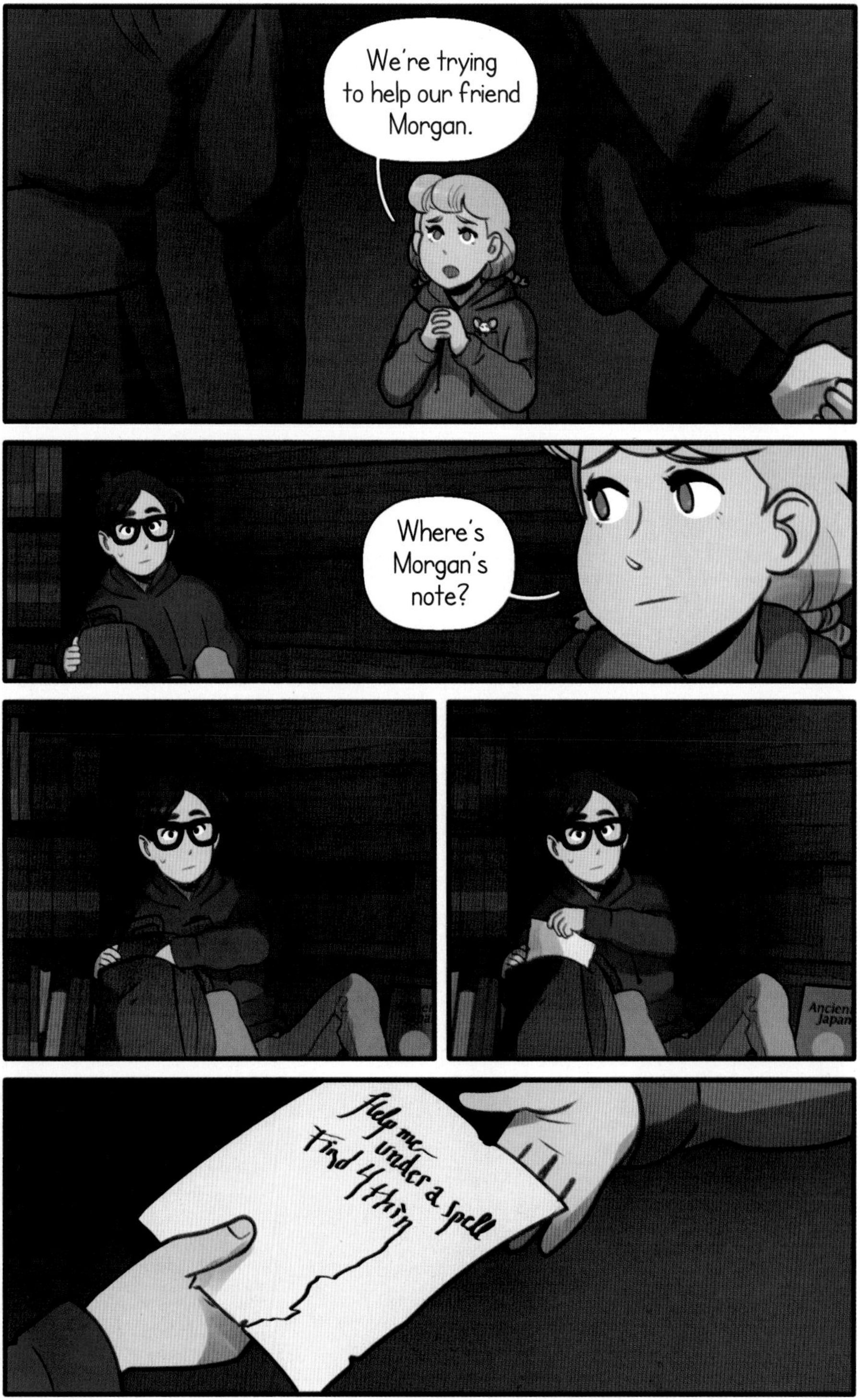
We're trying to help our friend Morgan.
Where's Morgan's note?
Ancient Japan
Help me
under a spell
Find 4 thin

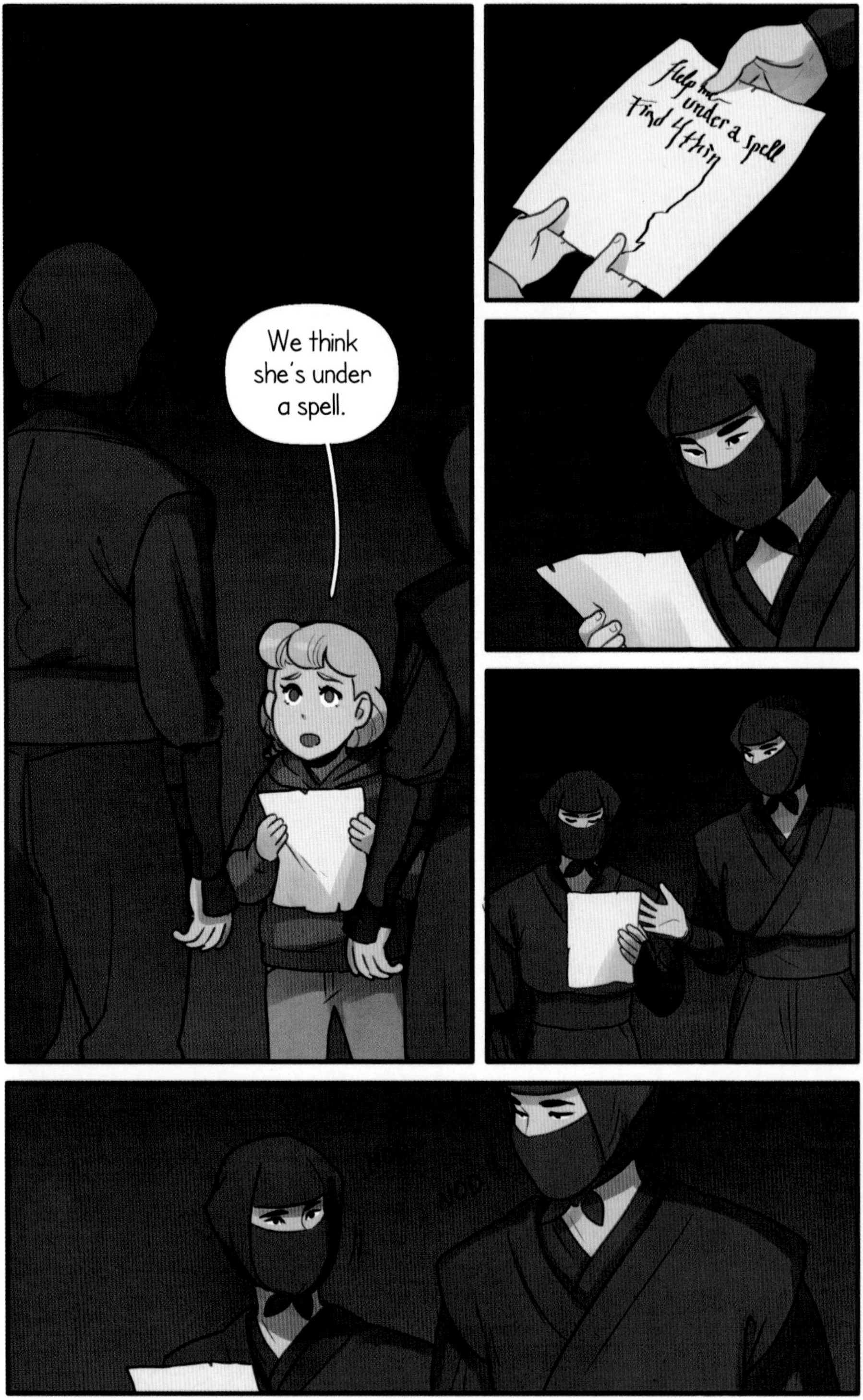
We think she's under a spell.
Help me
under a spell
Find 4 thin

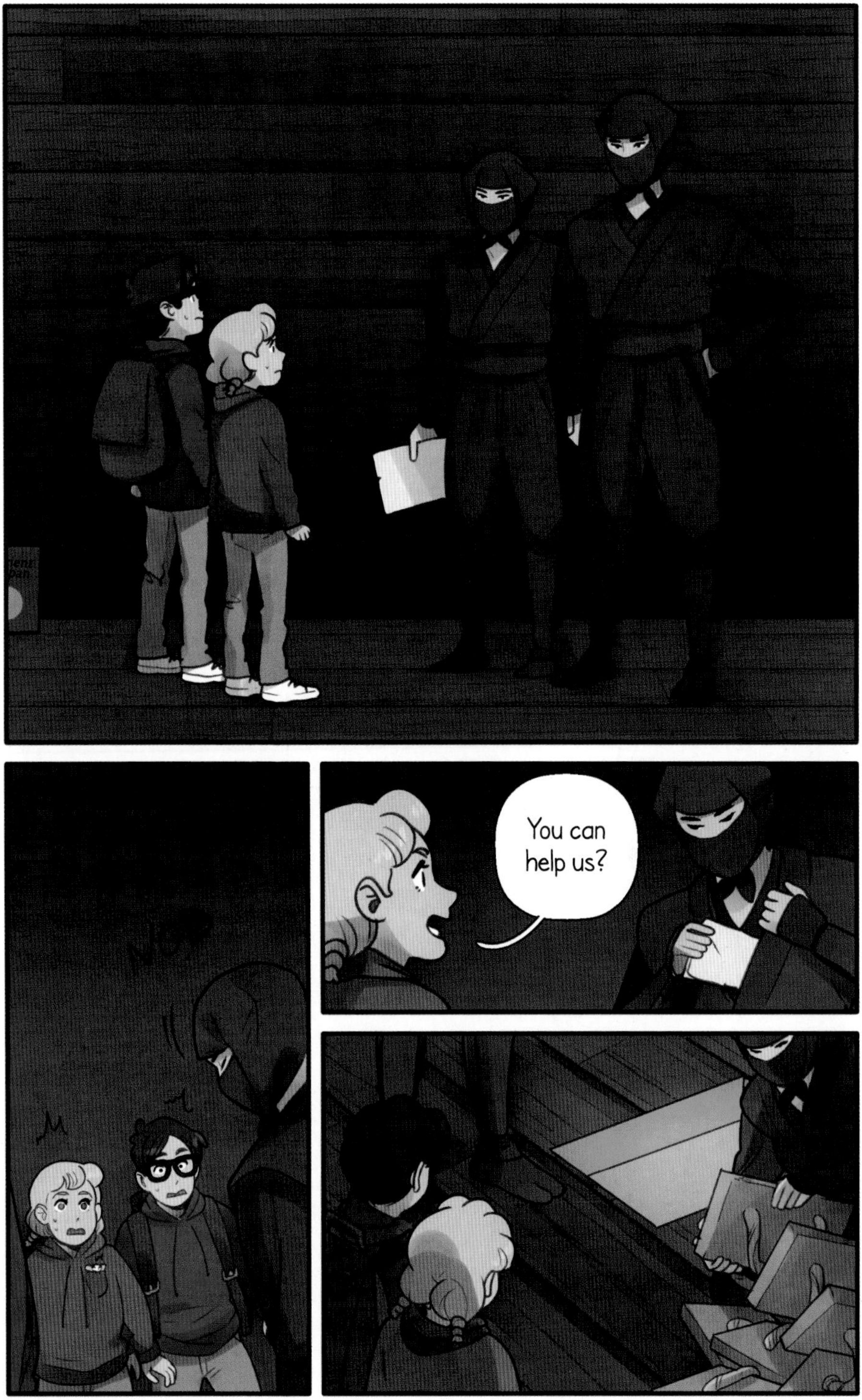
You can help us?

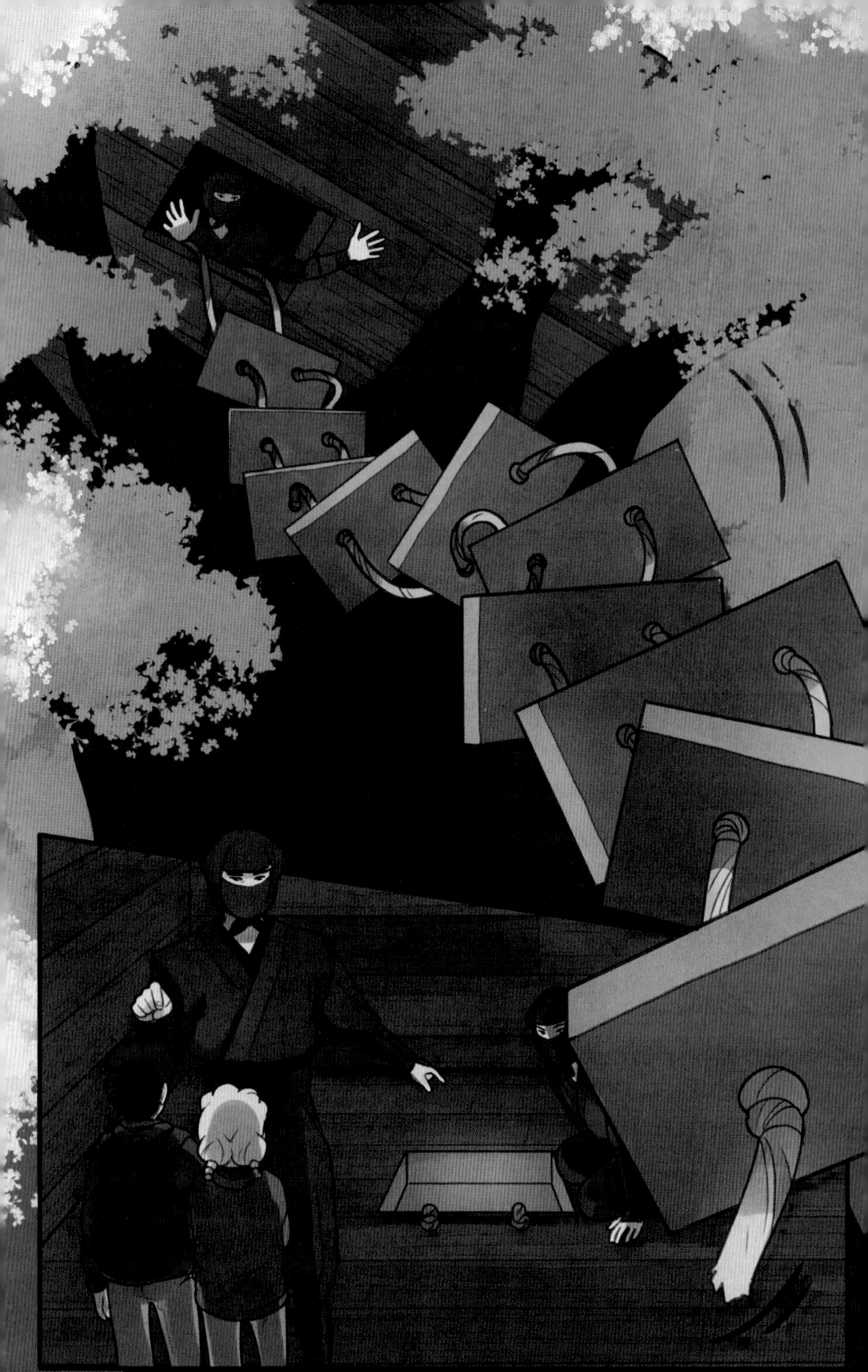

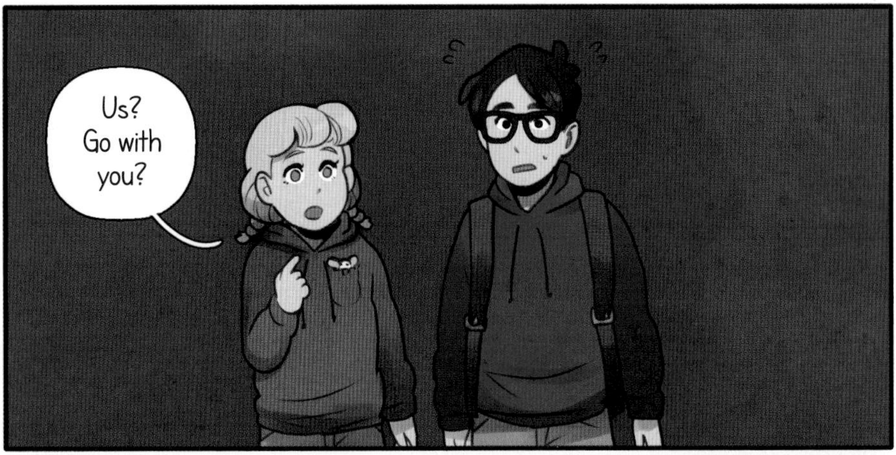
Us? Go with you?

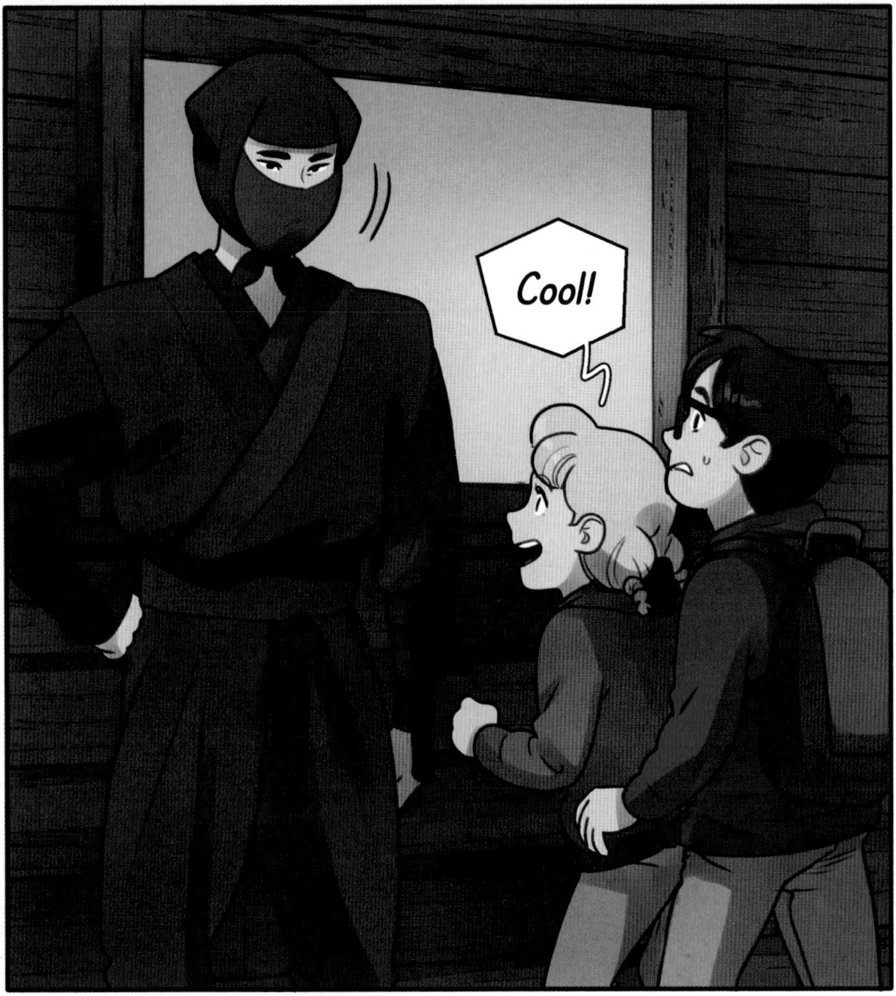
Cool!

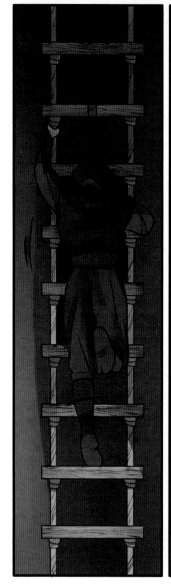

Wow!

They're like
spiders dropping
from webs.

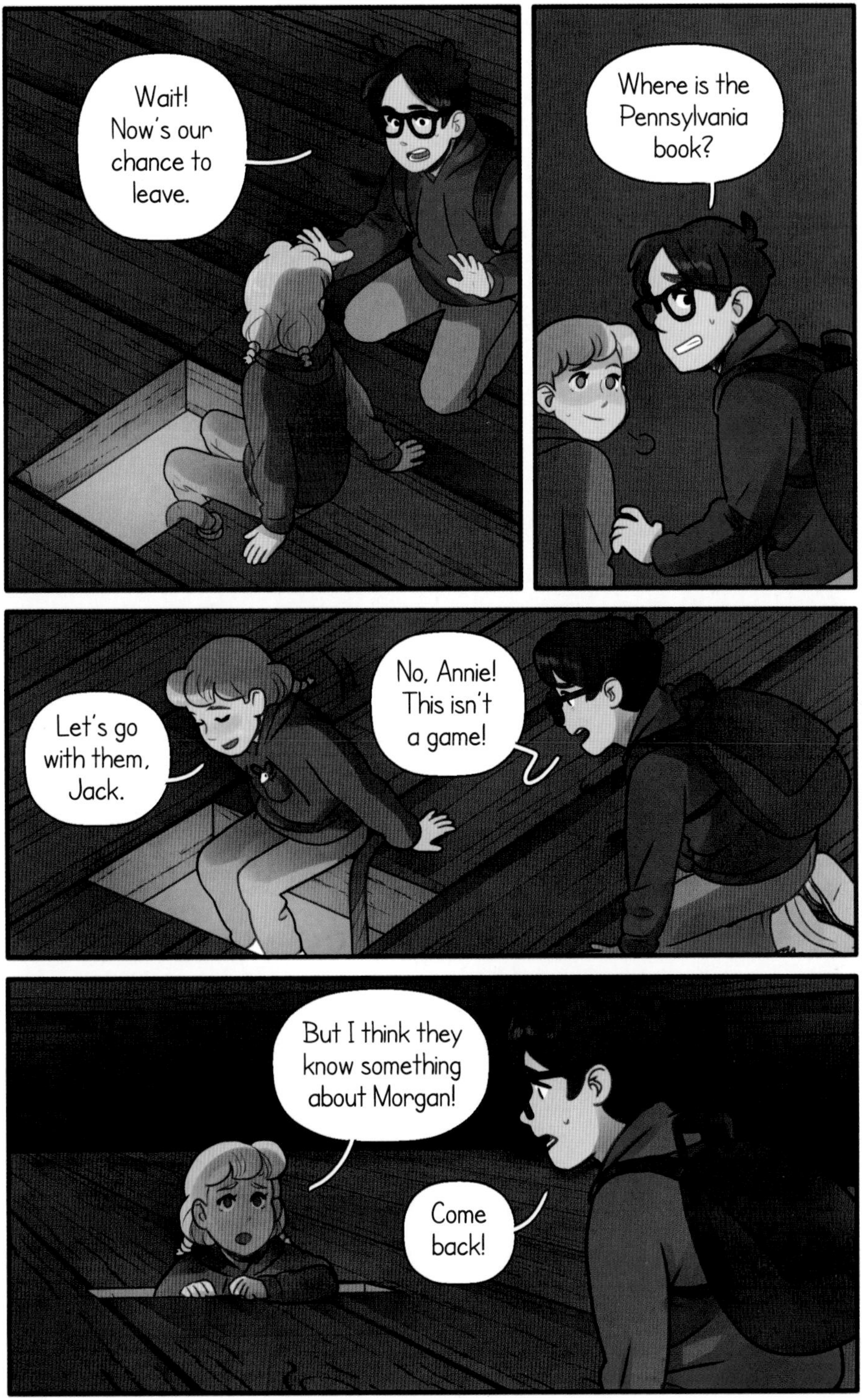
Wait! Now's our chance to leave.
Where is the Pennsylvania book?
Let's go with them, Jack.
No, Annie! This isn't a game!
But I think they know something about Morgan!
Come back!

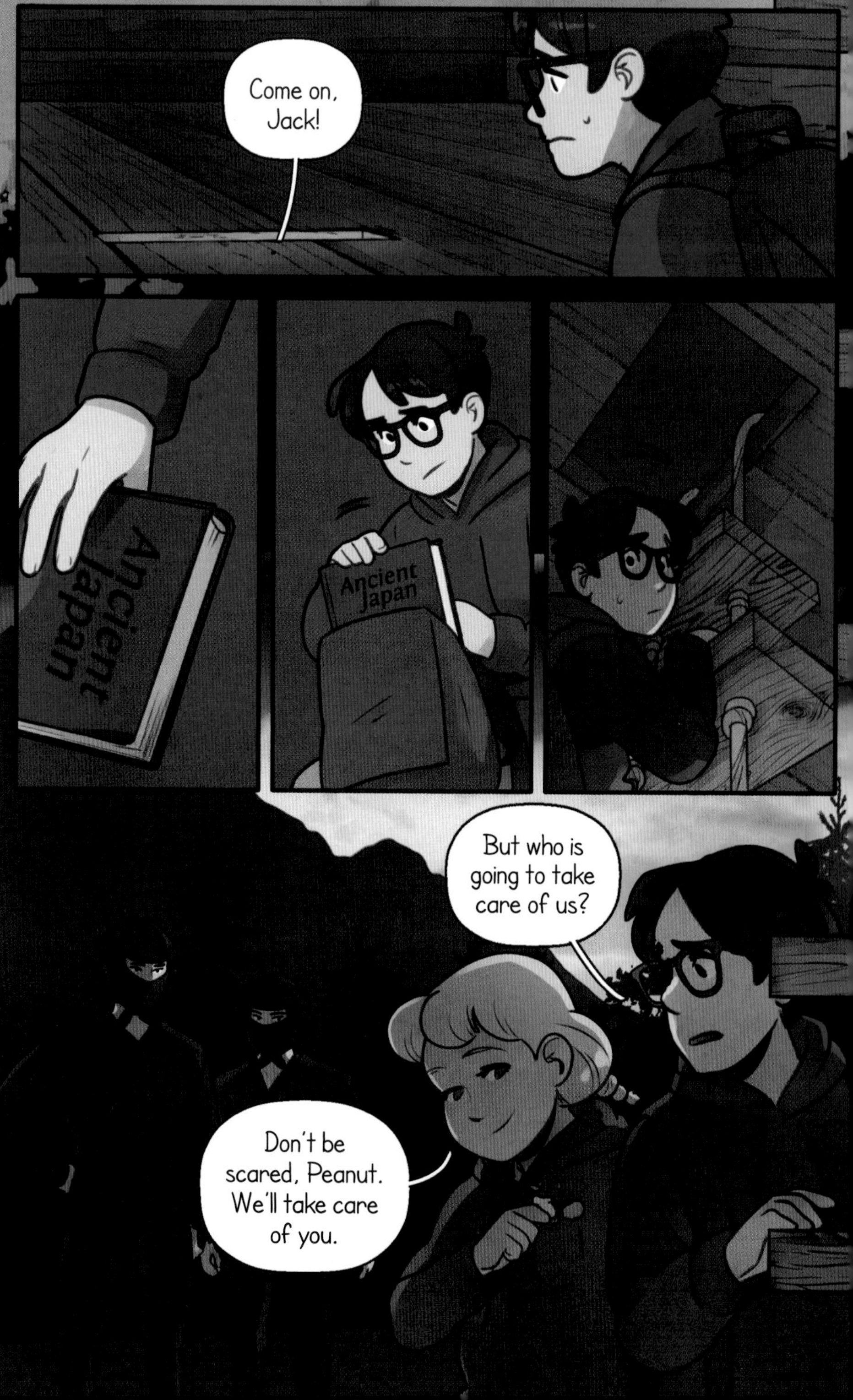

Come on, Jack!
Ancient Japan
Ancient Japan
But who is going to take care of us?
Don't be scared, Peanut. We'll take care of you.

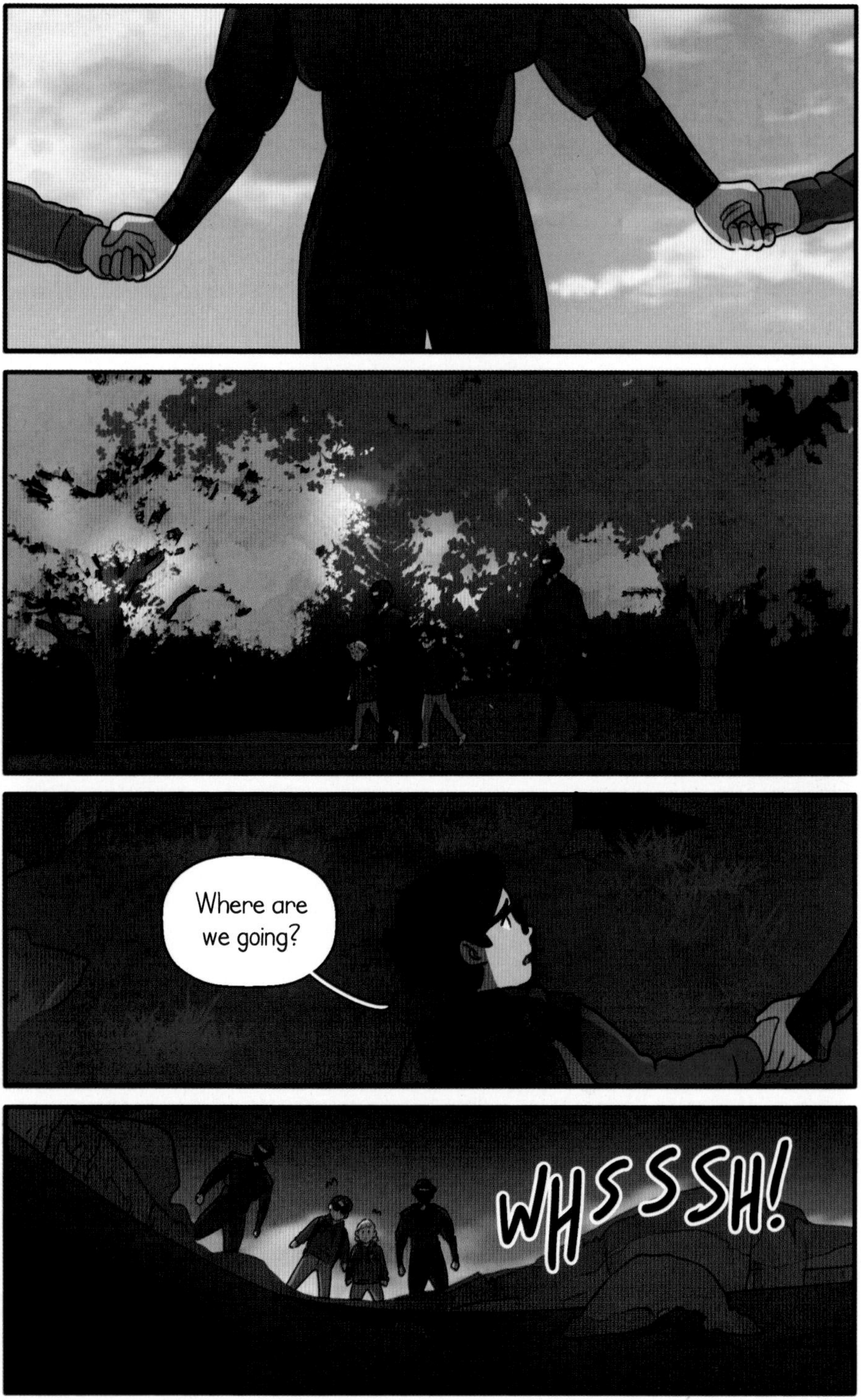
Where are we going?
WHSSSH!

You want us to cross it?

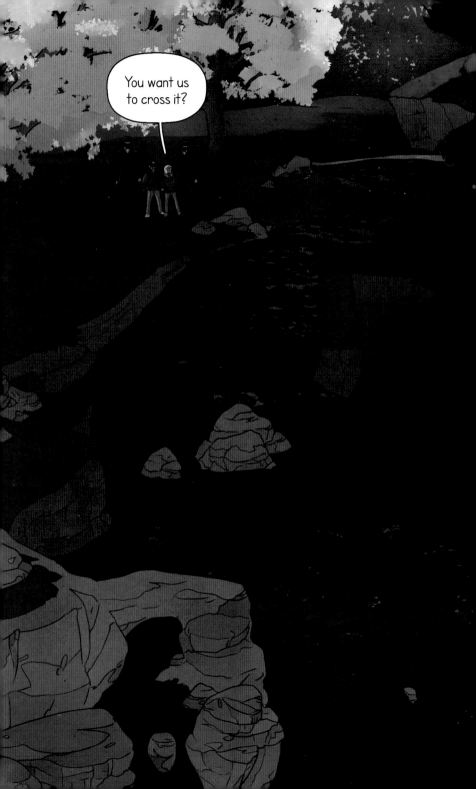

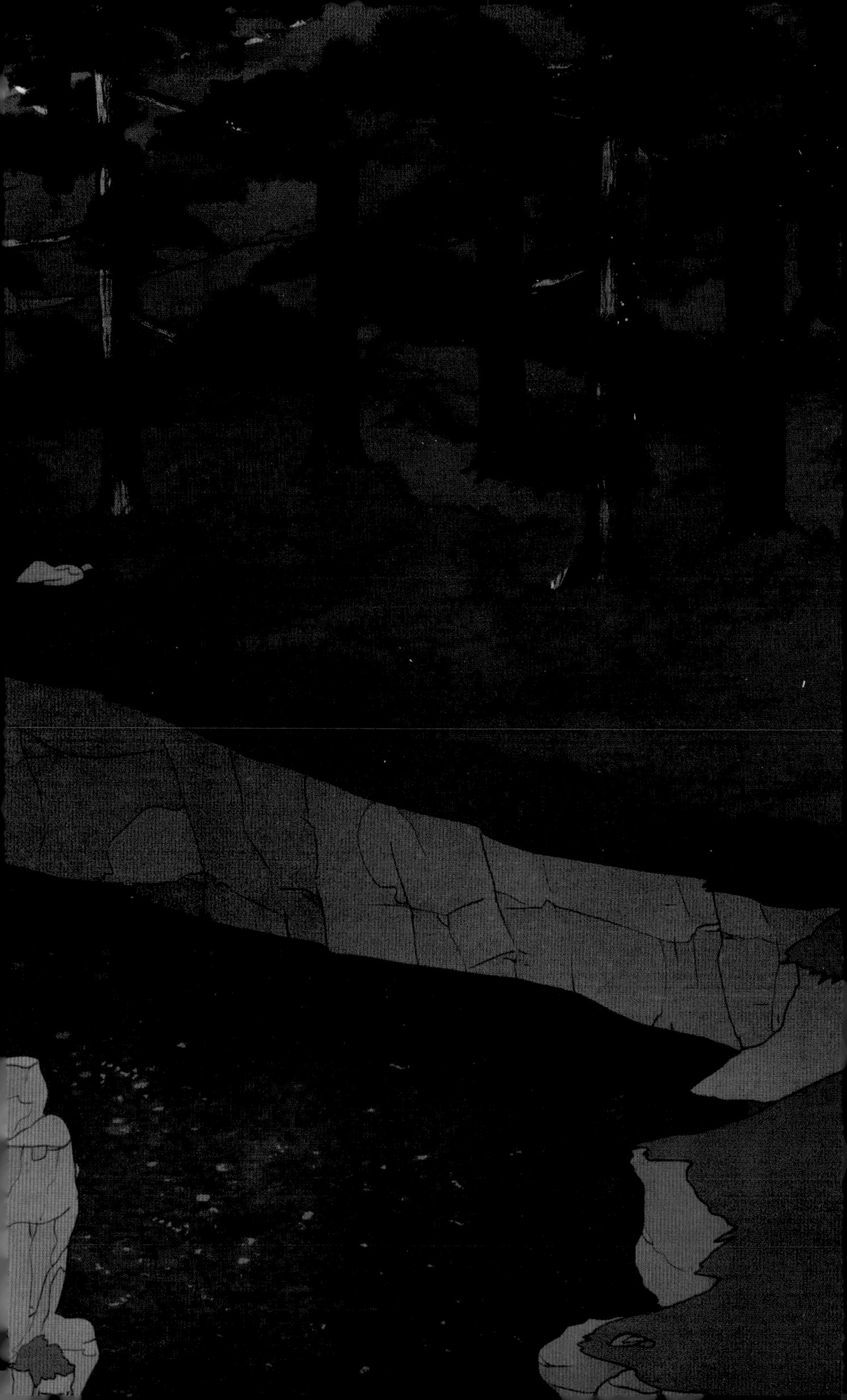

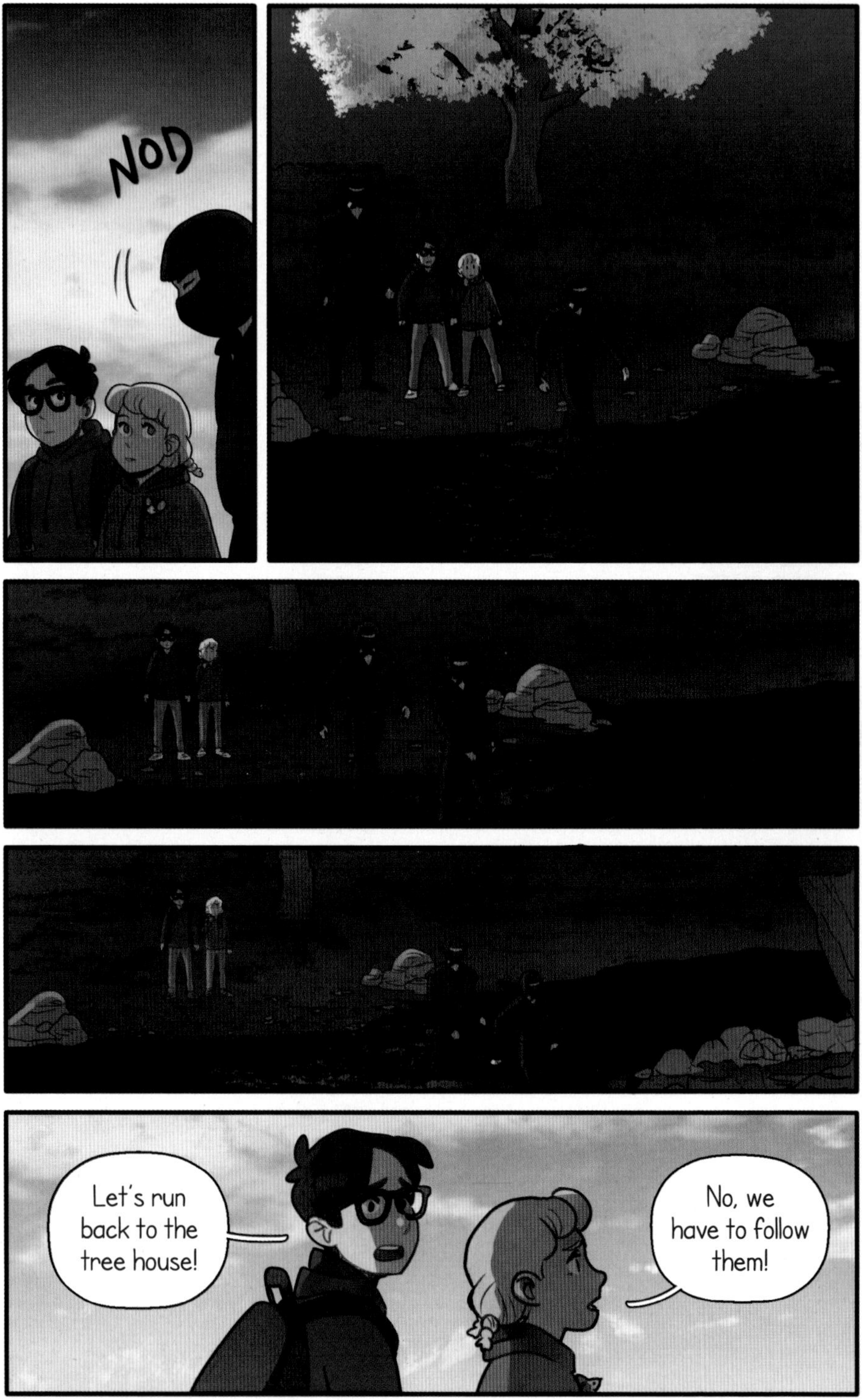
NOD
Let's run back to the tree house!
No, we have to follow them!

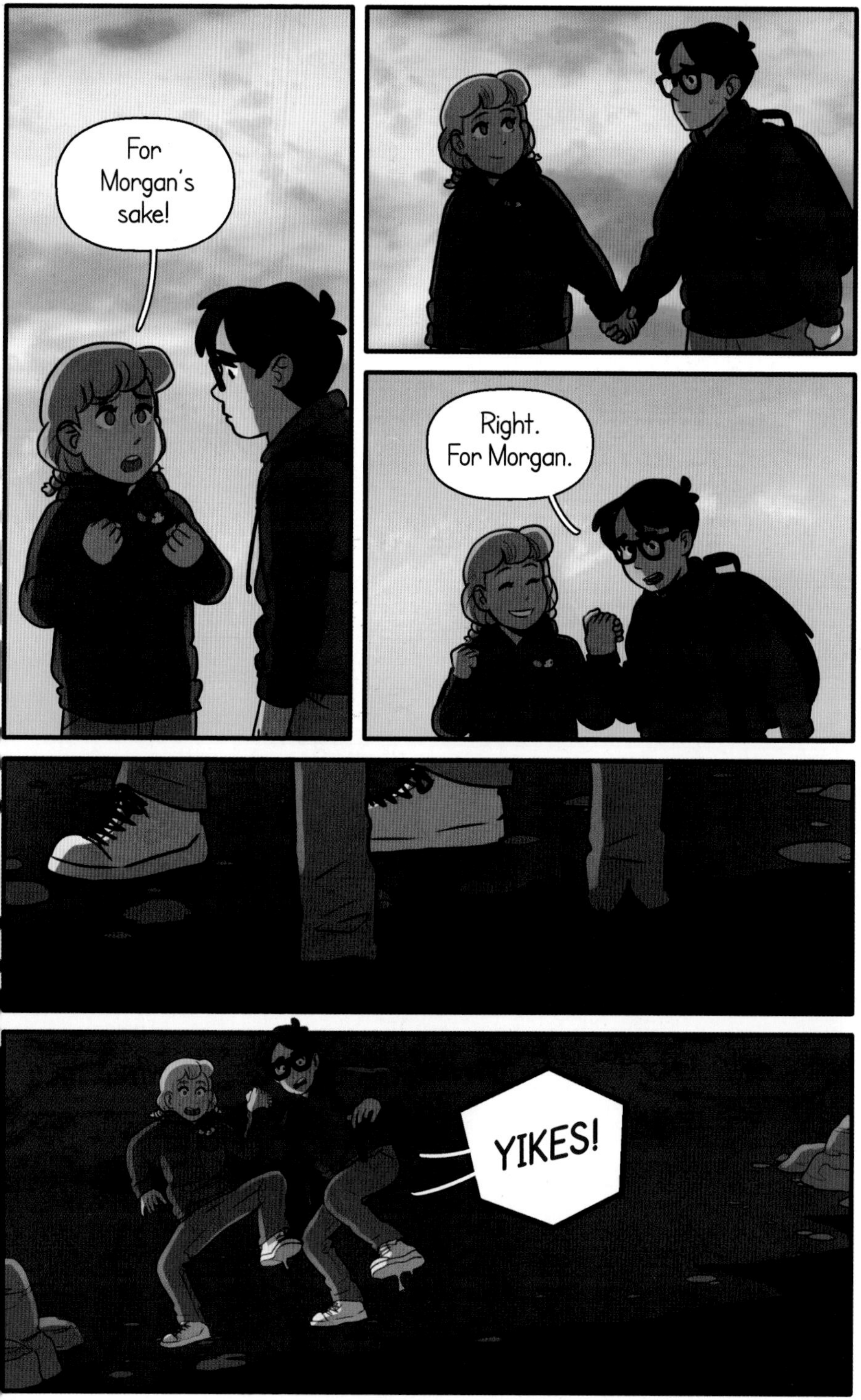
For Morgan's sake!
Right. For Morgan.
YIKES!

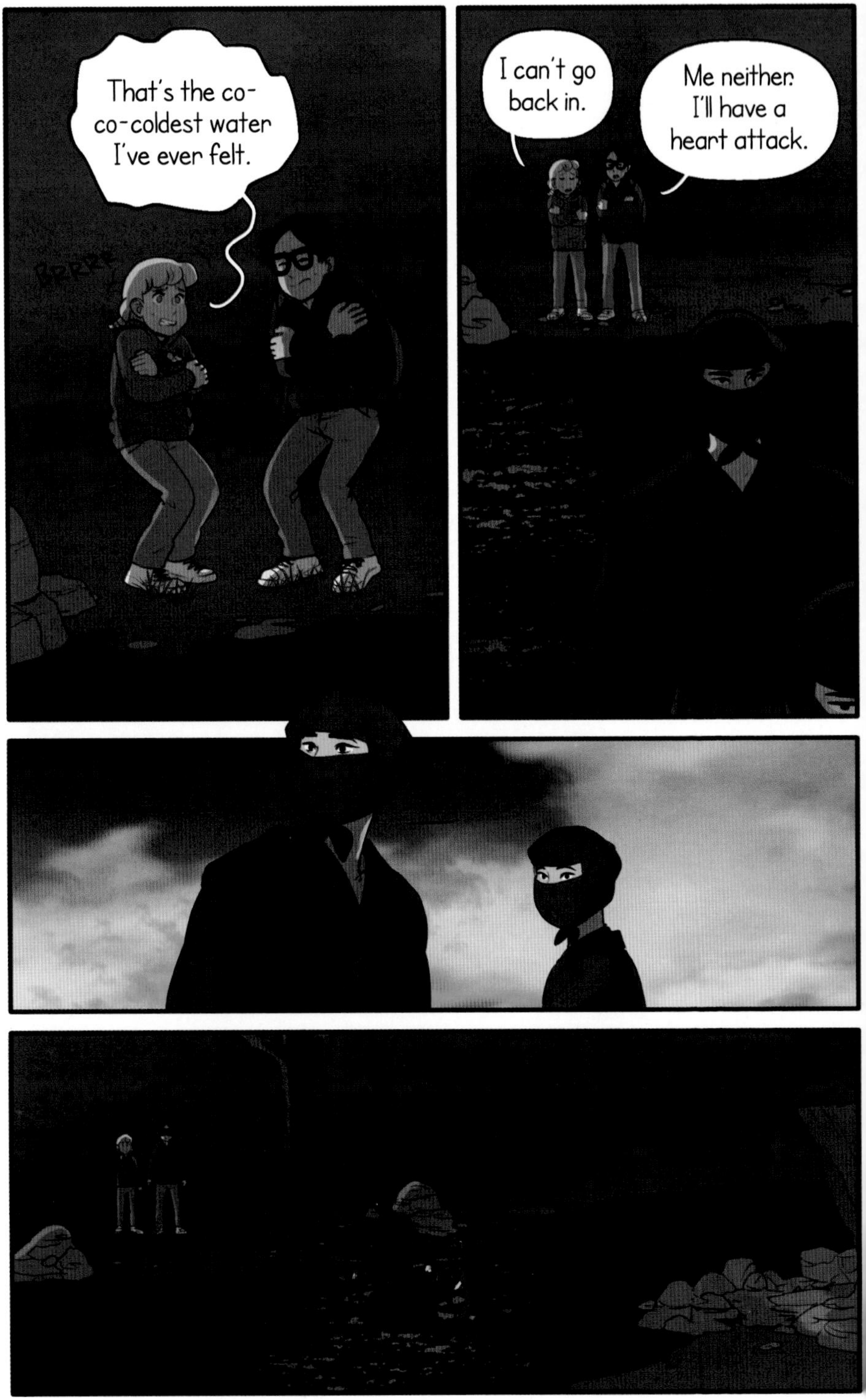
BRRRR
That's the co-co-coldest water I've ever felt.
I can't go back in.
Me neither. I'll have a heart attack.

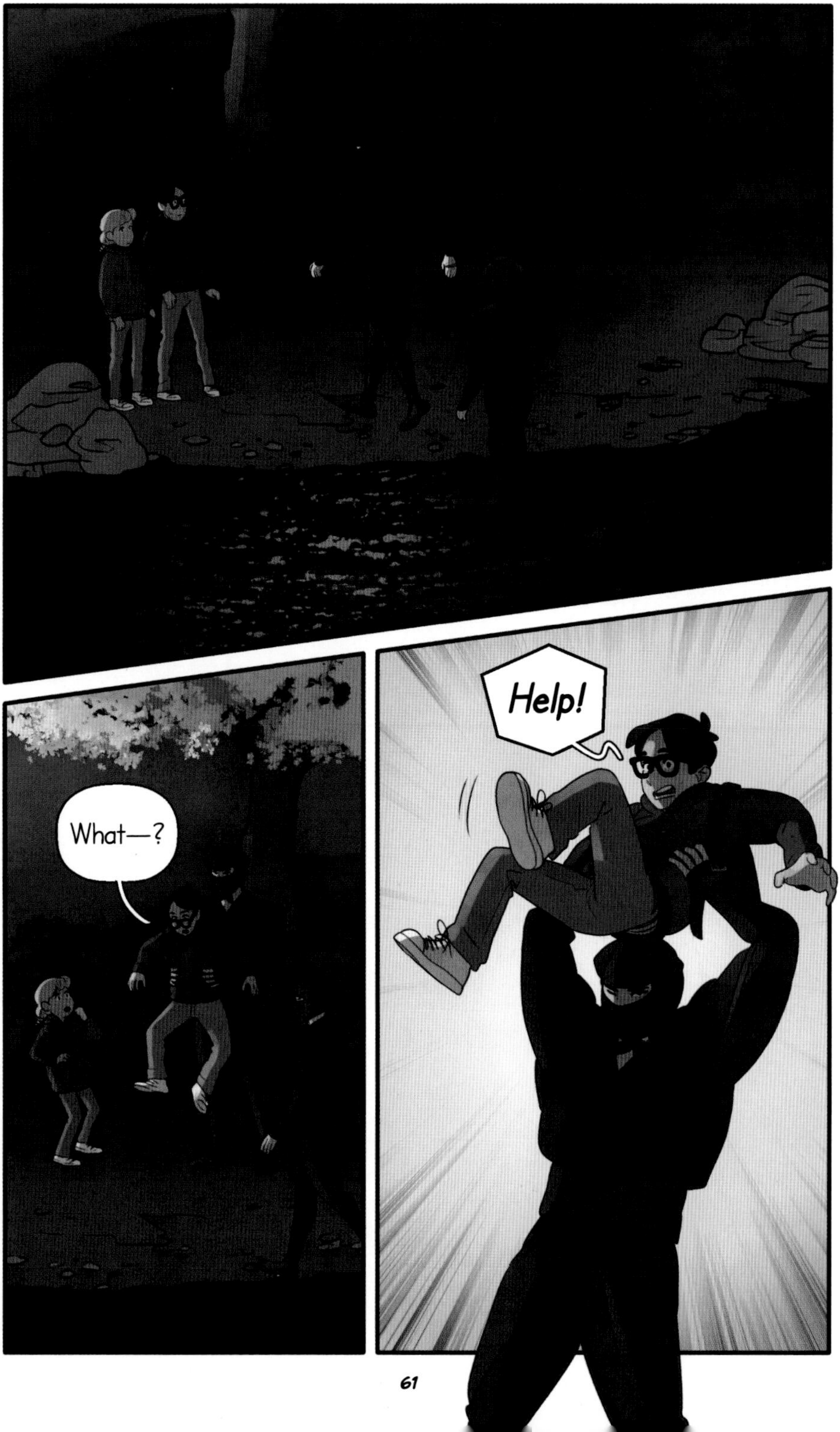
What—?
Help!

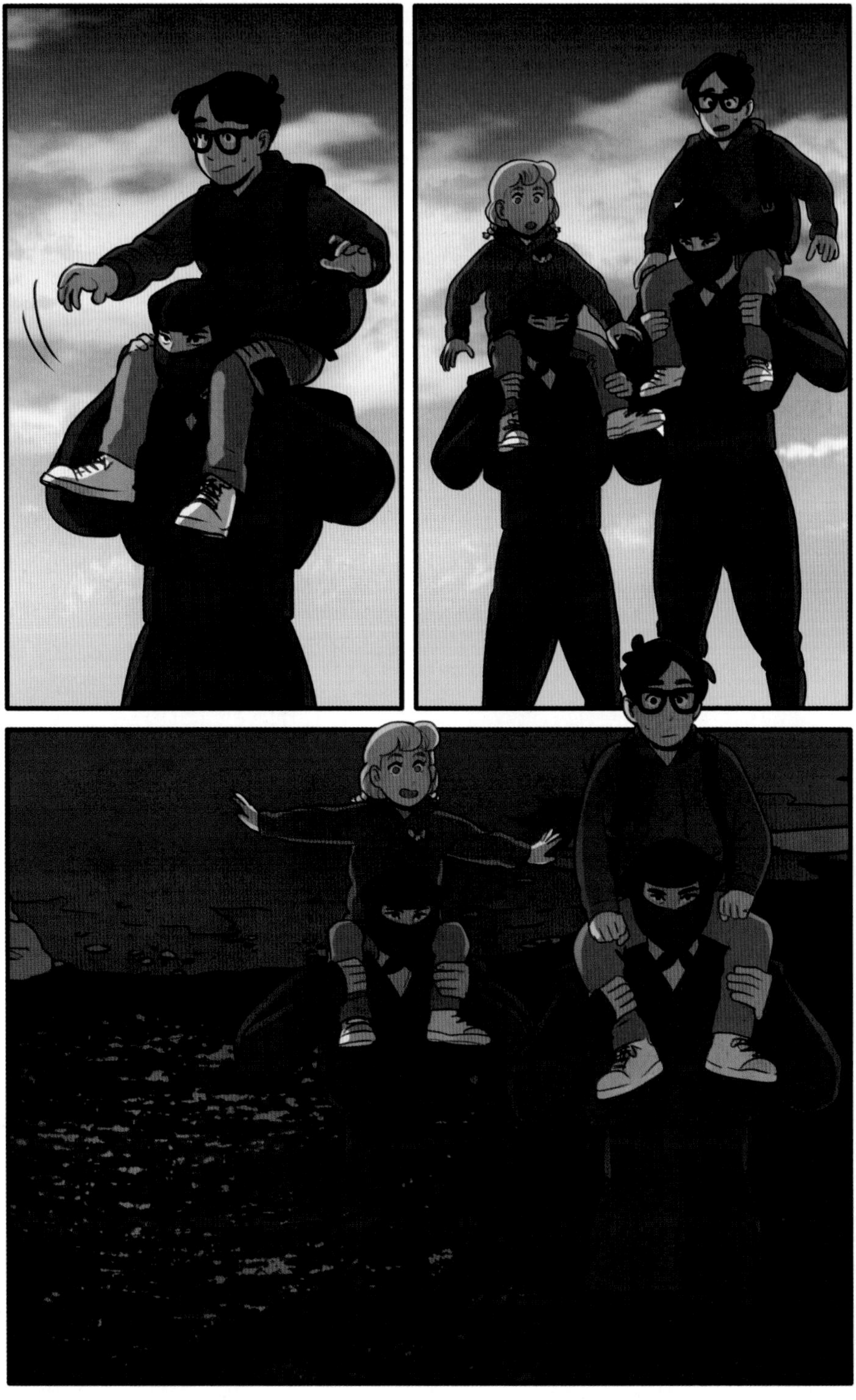

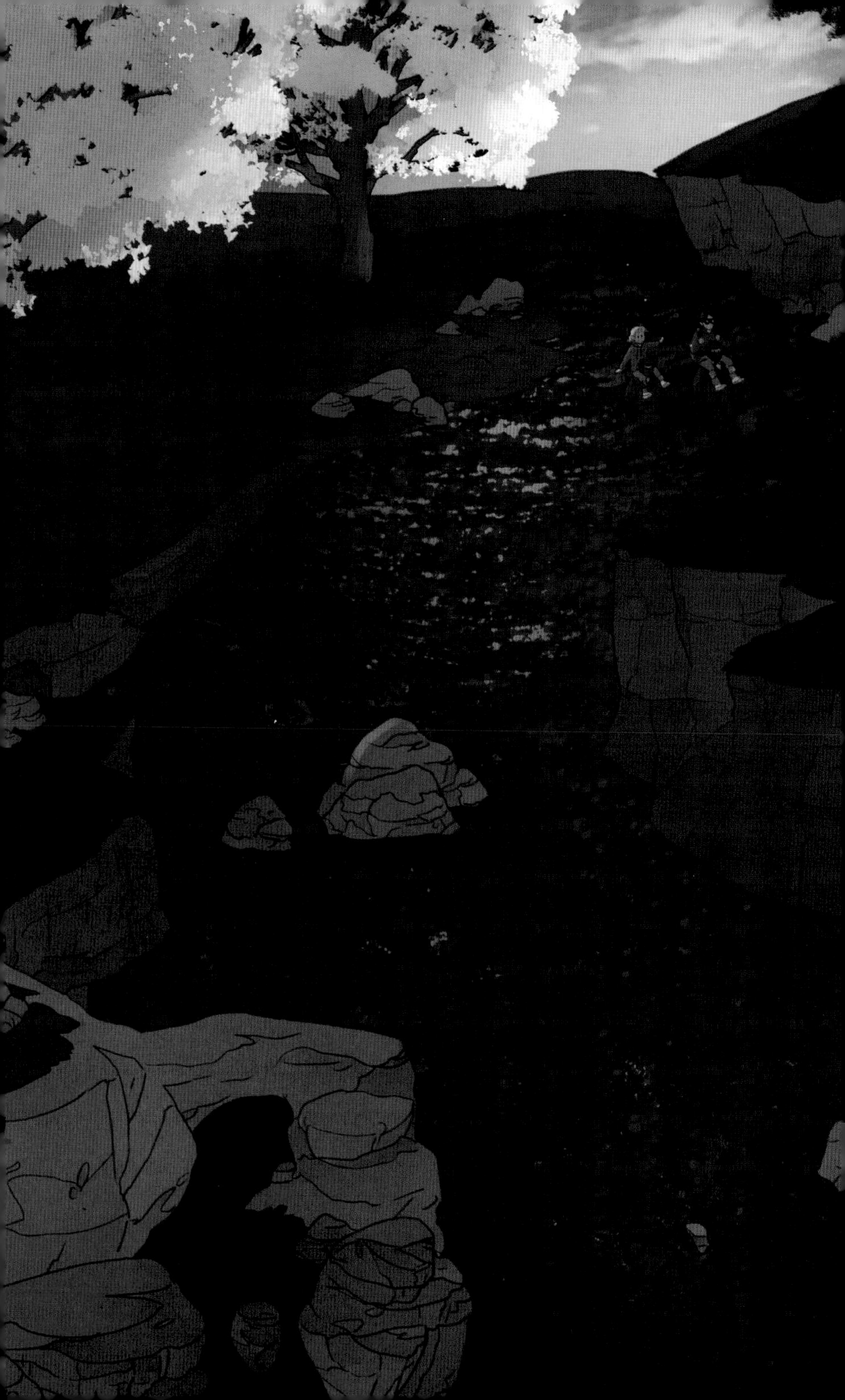

CHAPTER FIVE
Flames in the Mist

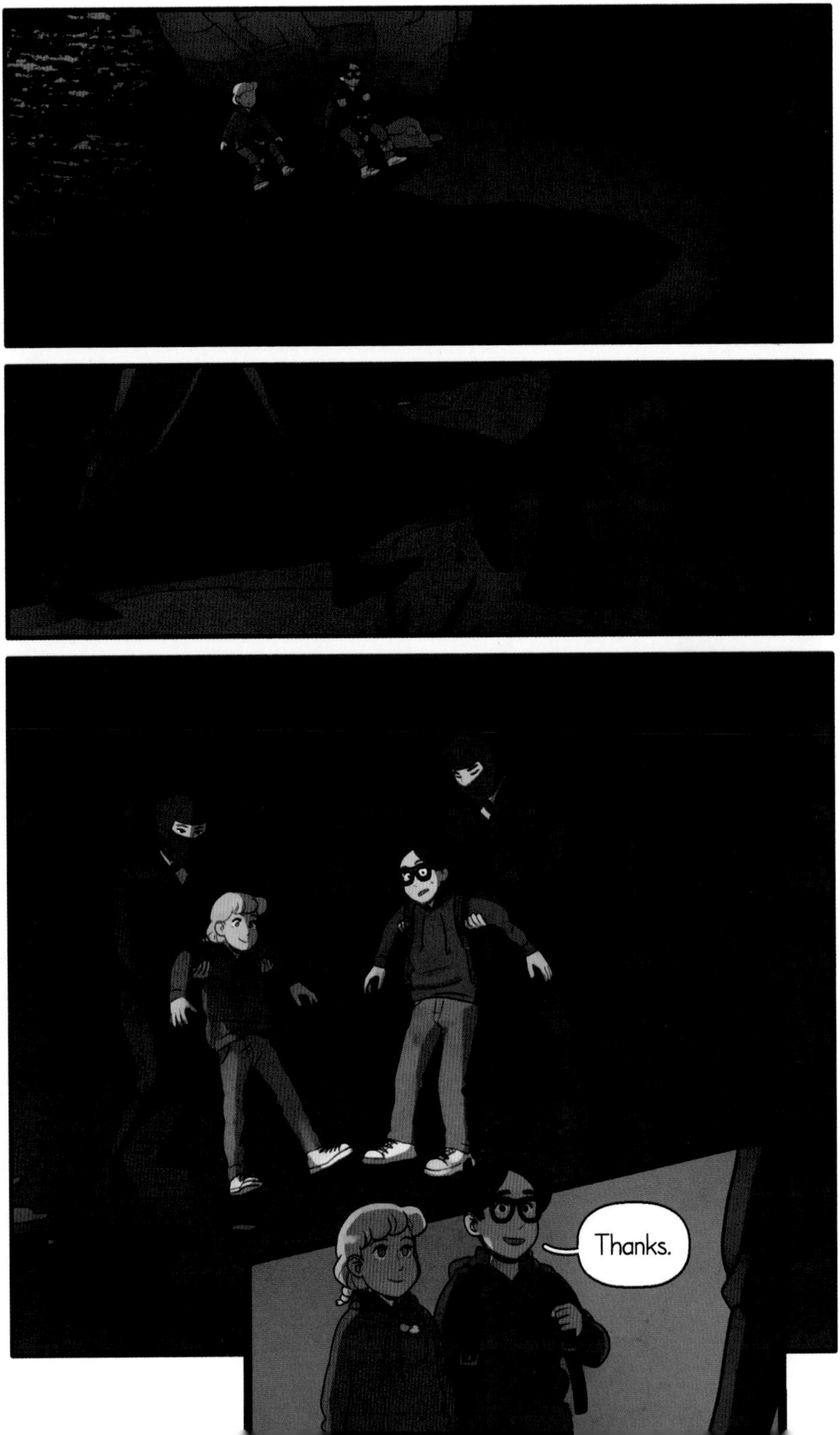
Thanks.

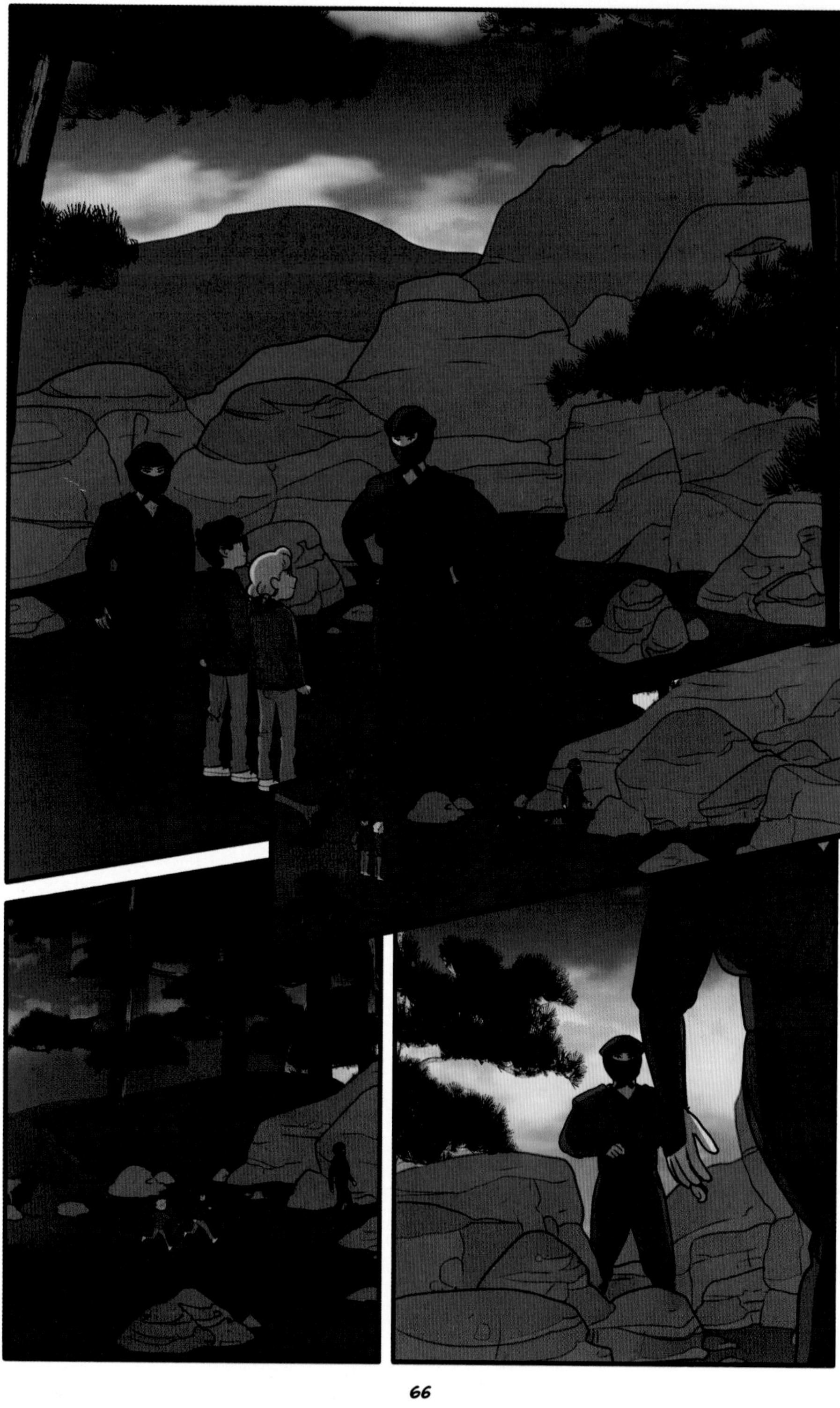

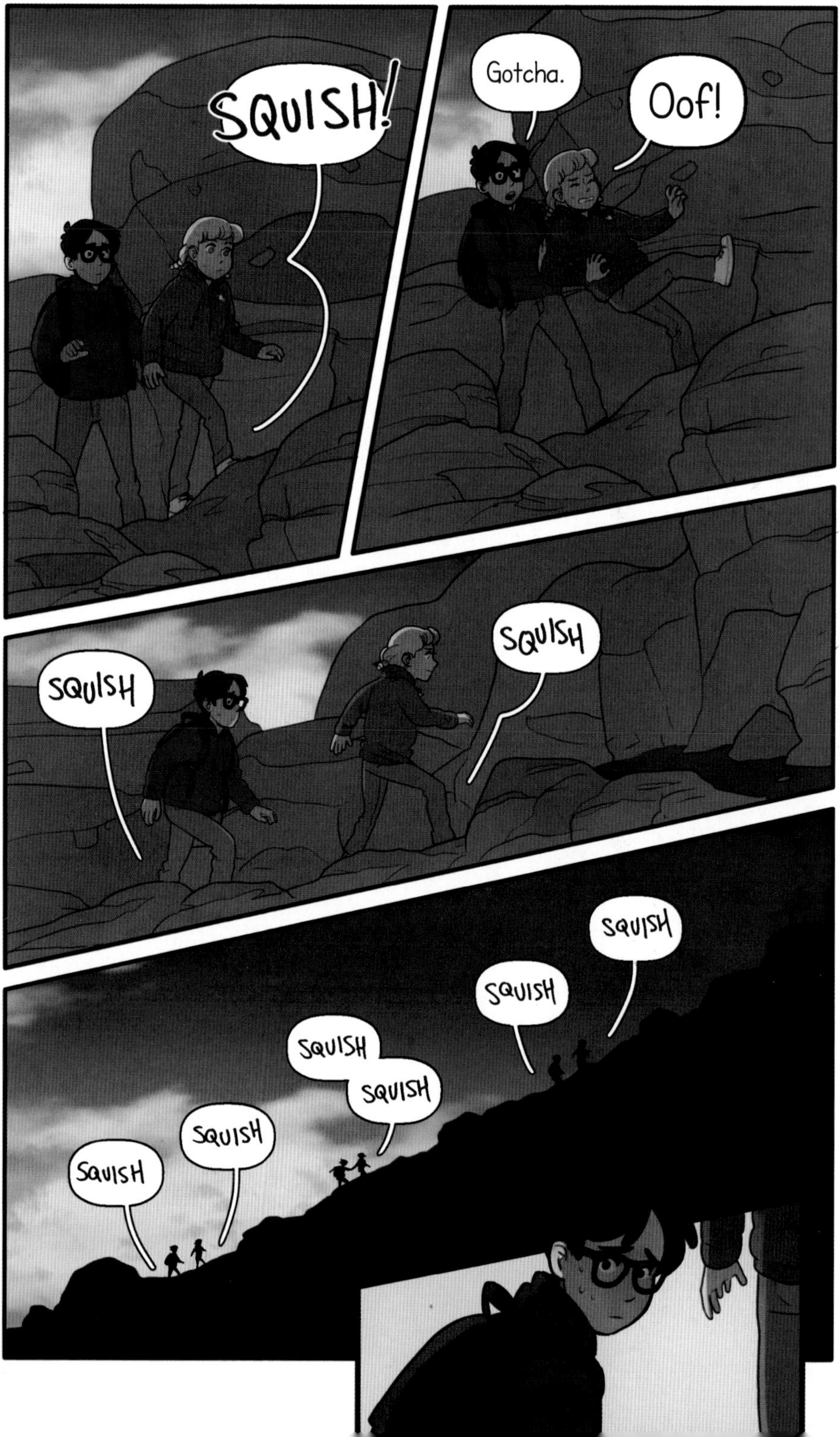
SQUISH!
Gotcha.
Oof!
SQUISH
SQUISH
SQUISH
SQUISH
SQUISH
SQUISH
SQUISH
SQUISH

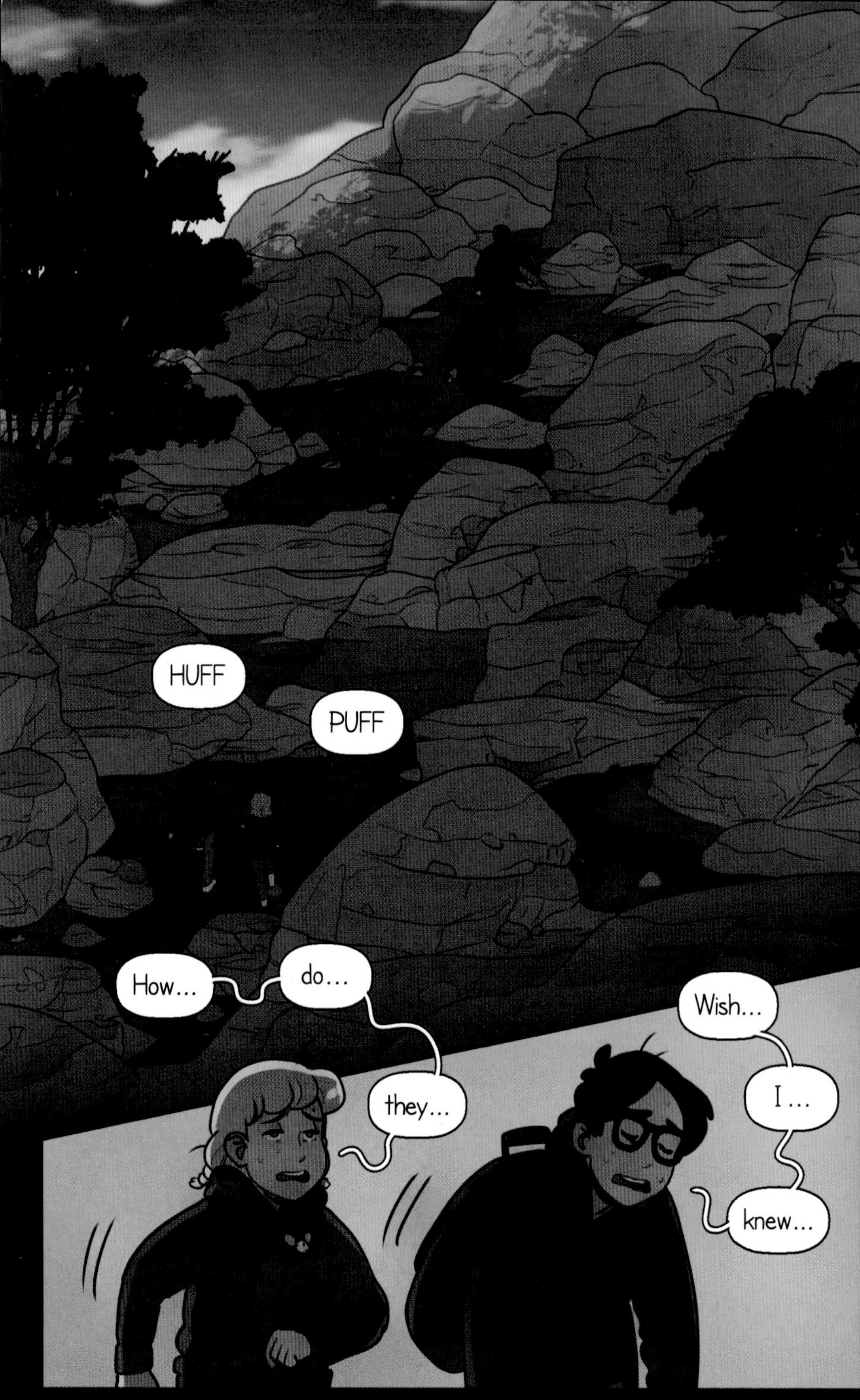
HUFF
PUFF
How...
do...
they...
Wish...
I...
knew...

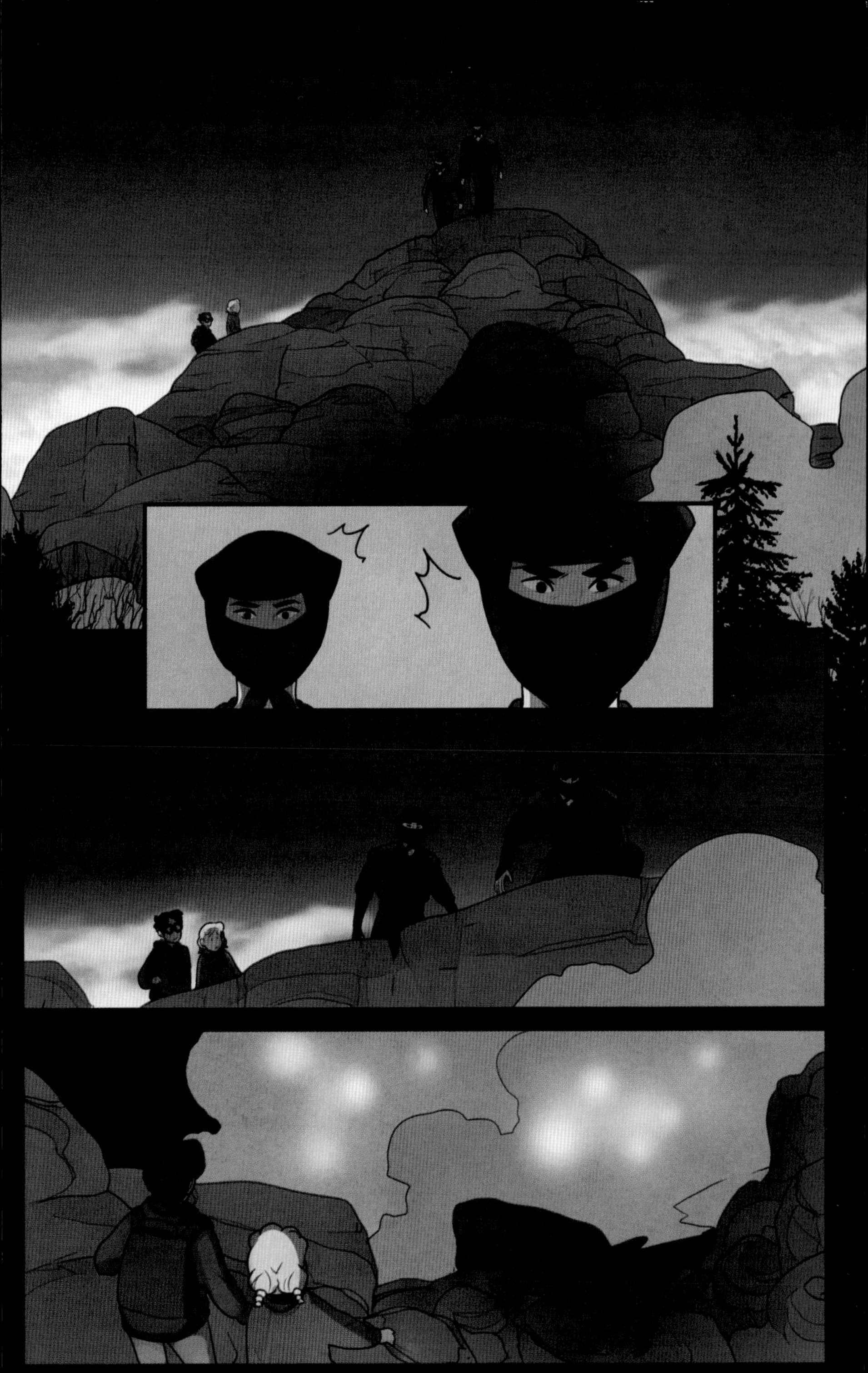

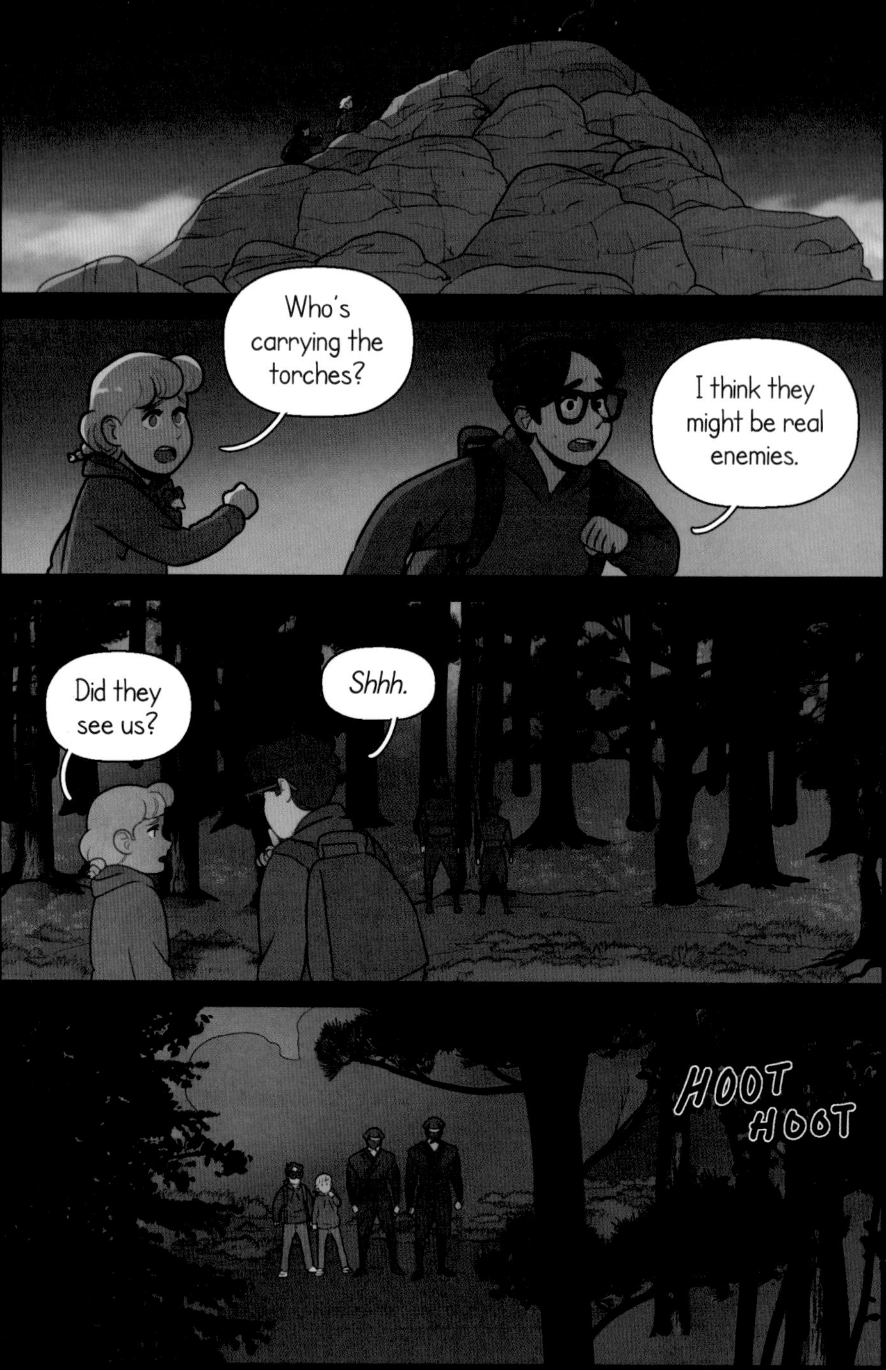
Who's carrying the torches?
I think they might be real enemies.
Did they see us?
Shhh.
HOOT HOOT

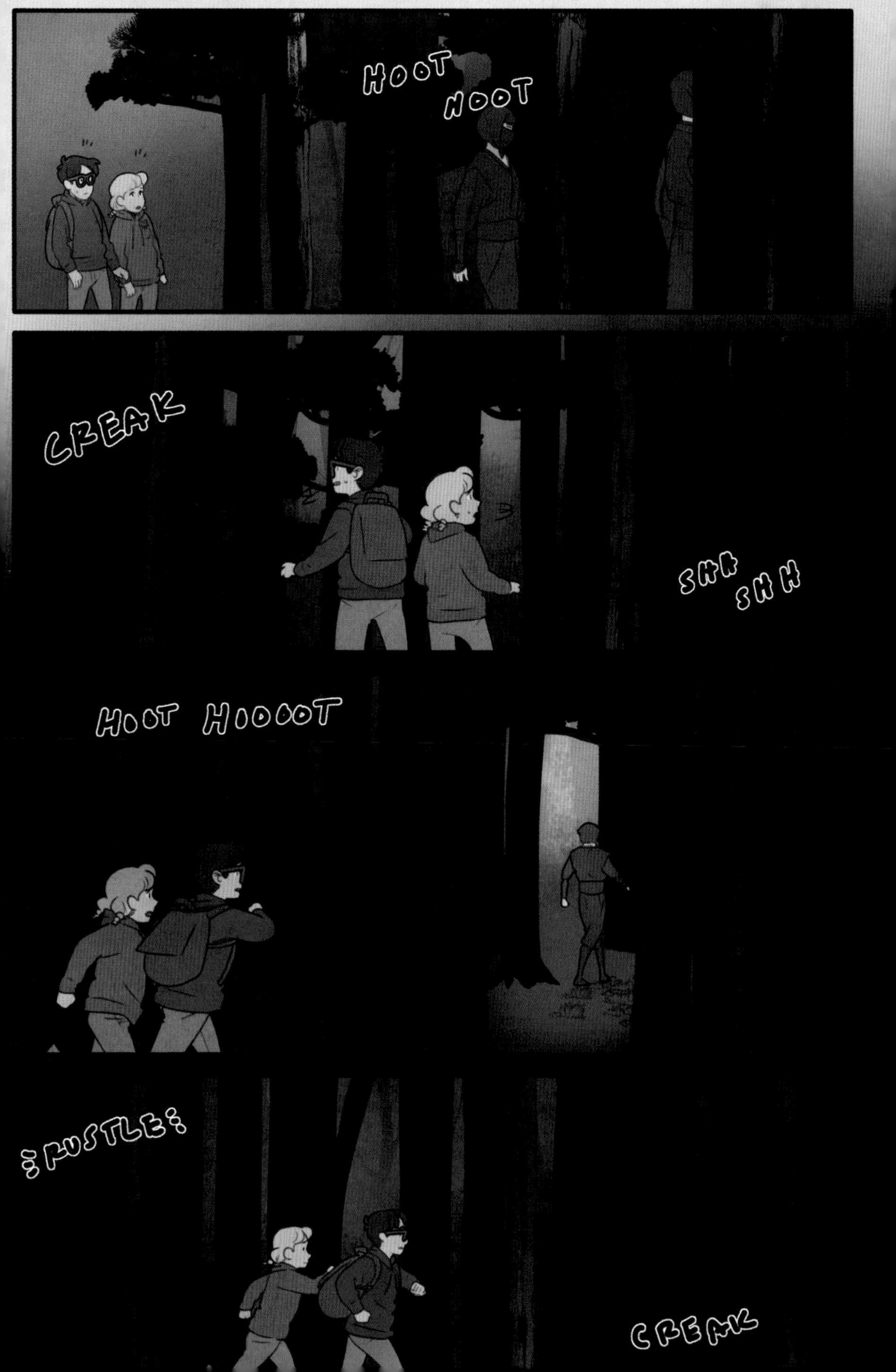
HOOT
HOOT
CREAK
SHH
SHH
HOOT HOOOOT
:RUSTLE:
CREAK

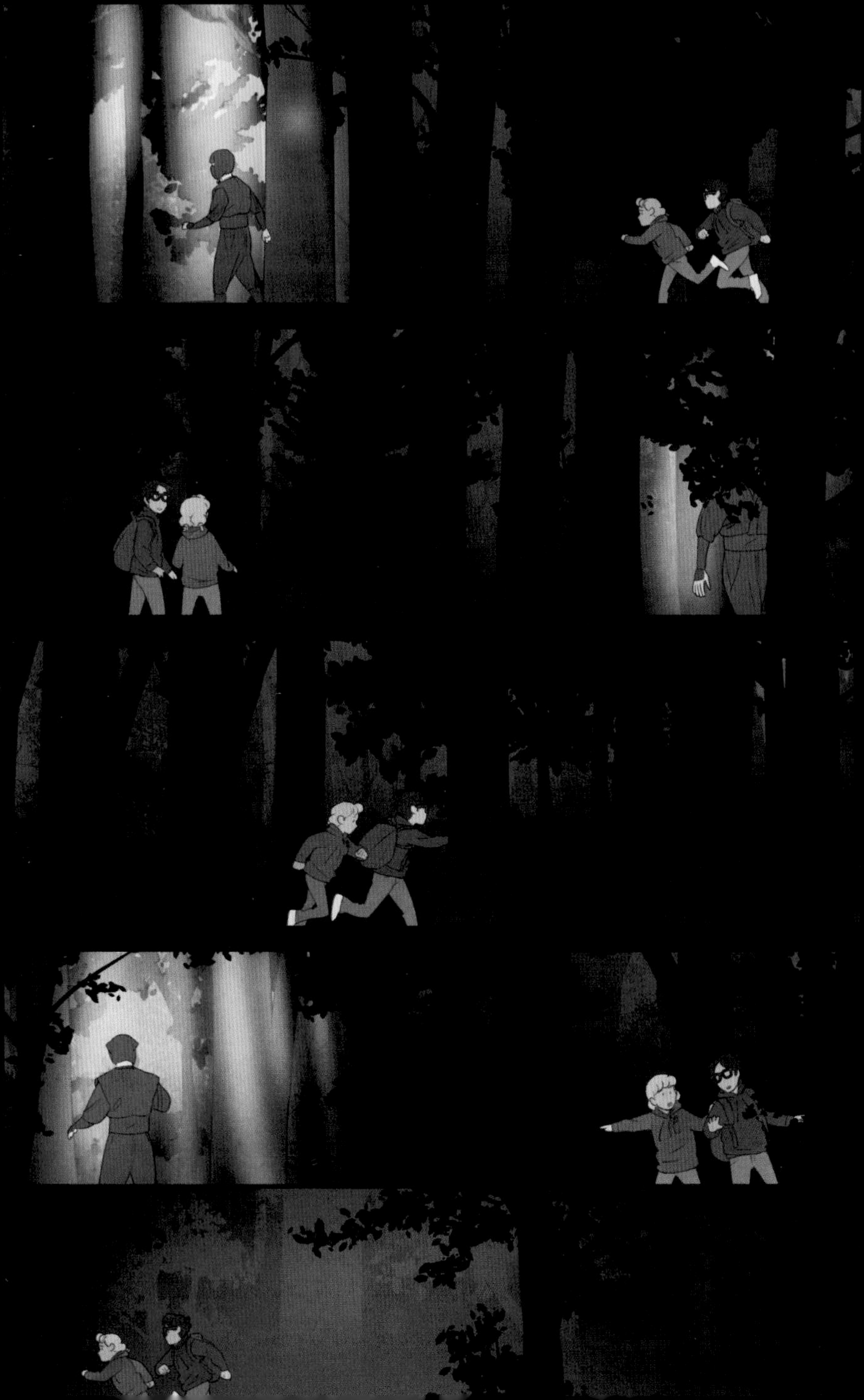

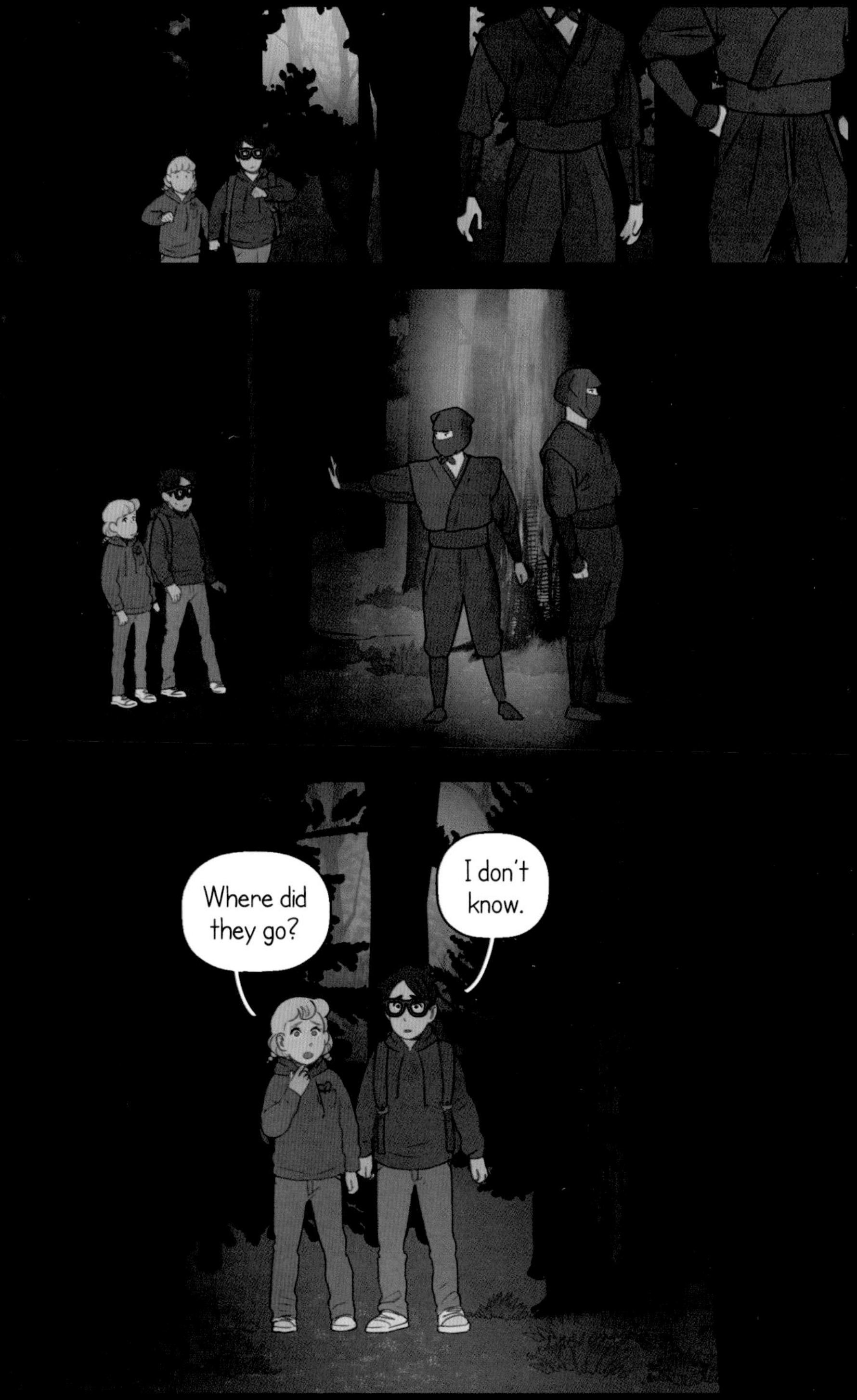
Where did they go?
I don't know.

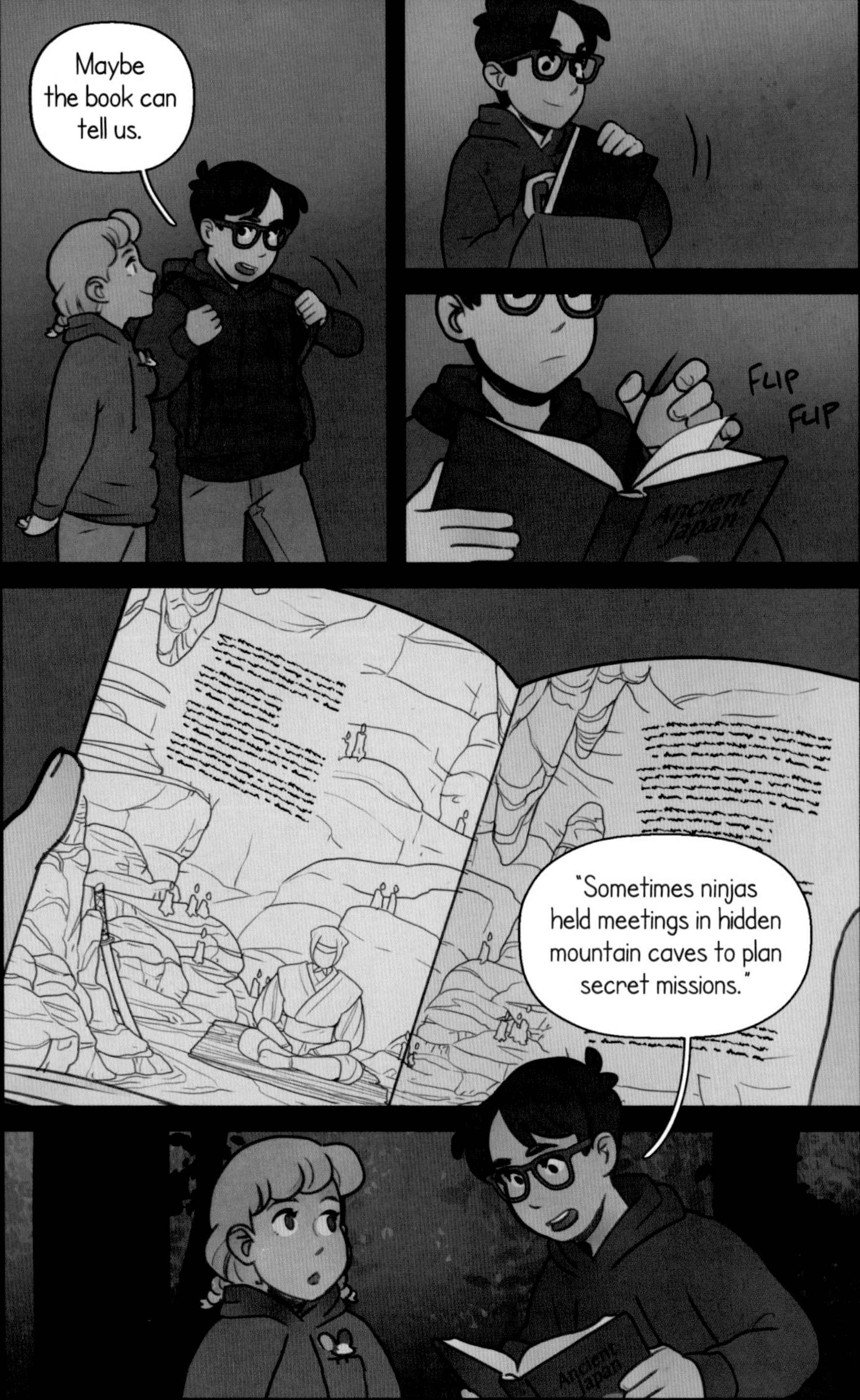
Maybe the book can tell us.
FLIP
FLIP
Ancient Japan
"Sometimes ninjas held meetings in hidden mountain caves to plan secret missions."
Ancient Japan

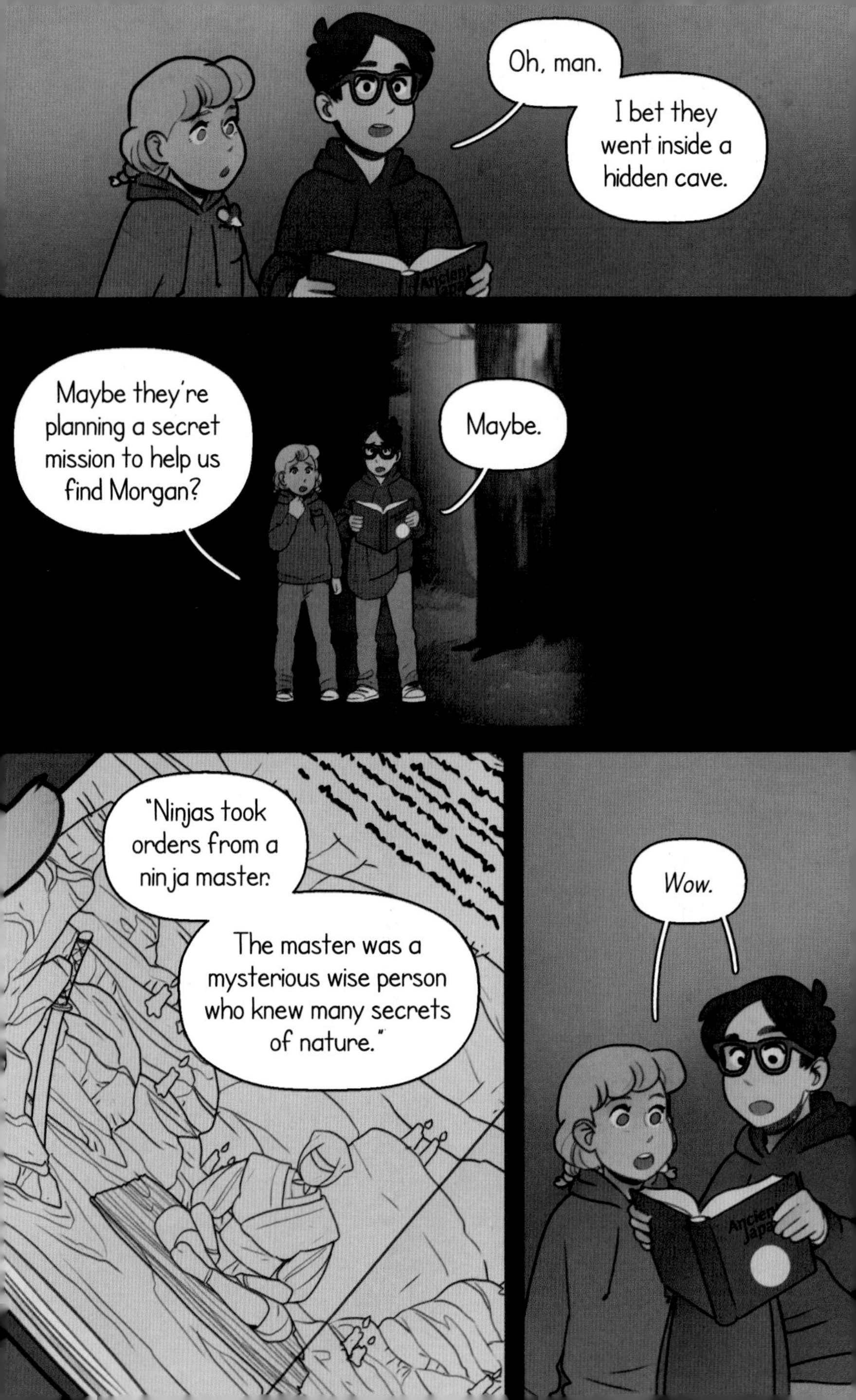
Oh, man.
I bet they went inside a hidden cave.
Maybe they're planning a secret mission to help us find Morgan?
Maybe.
"Ninjas took orders from a ninja master.
The master was a mysterious wise person who knew many secrets of nature."
Wow.

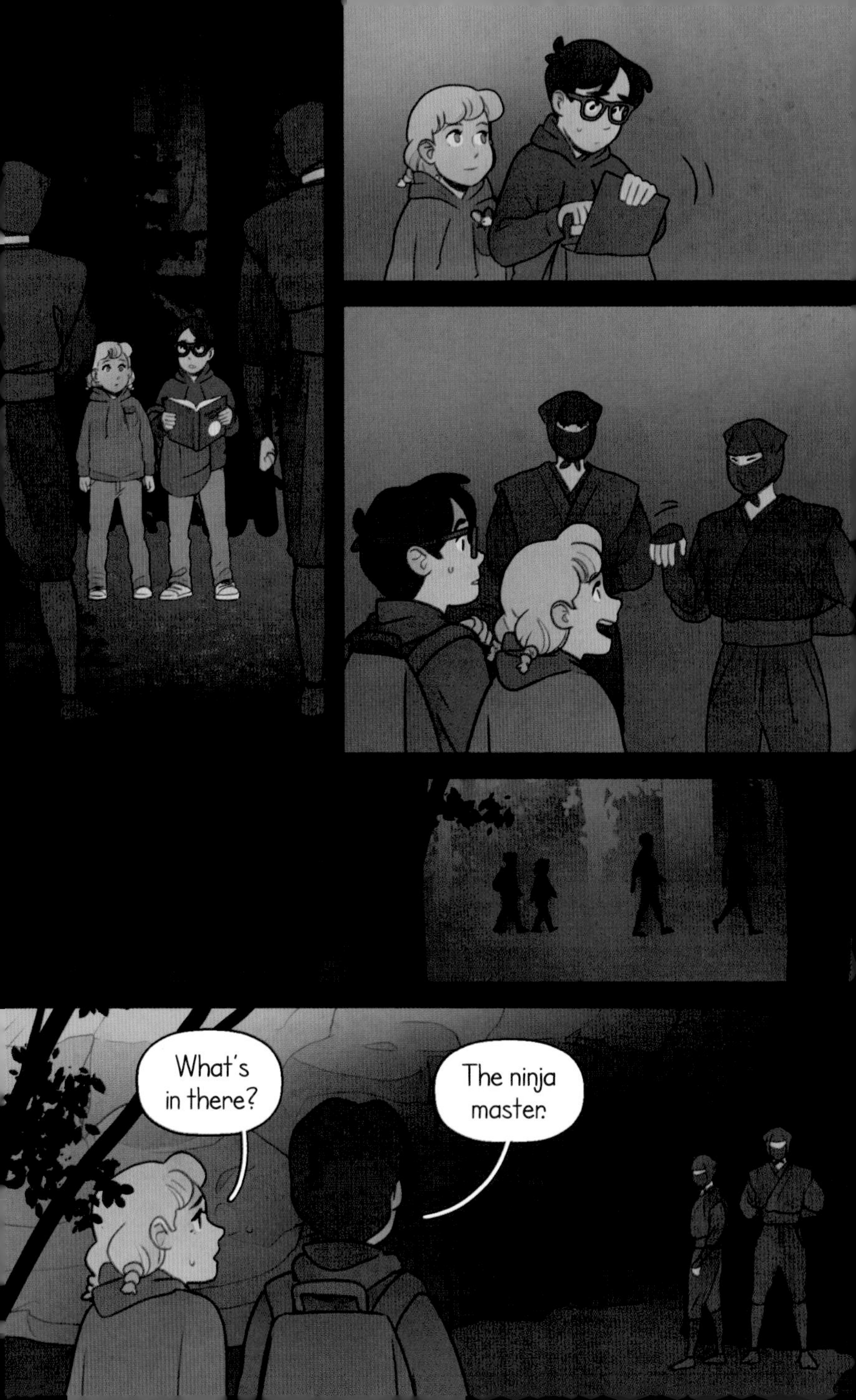
What's in there?
The ninja master.

CHAPTER SIX
Shadow Warrior

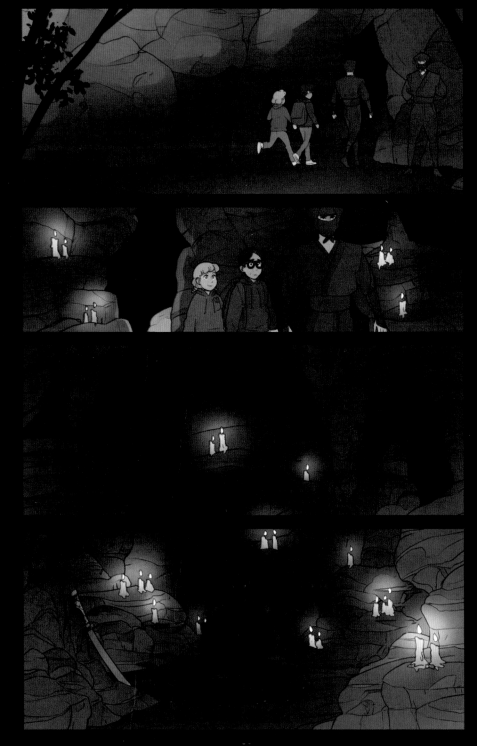

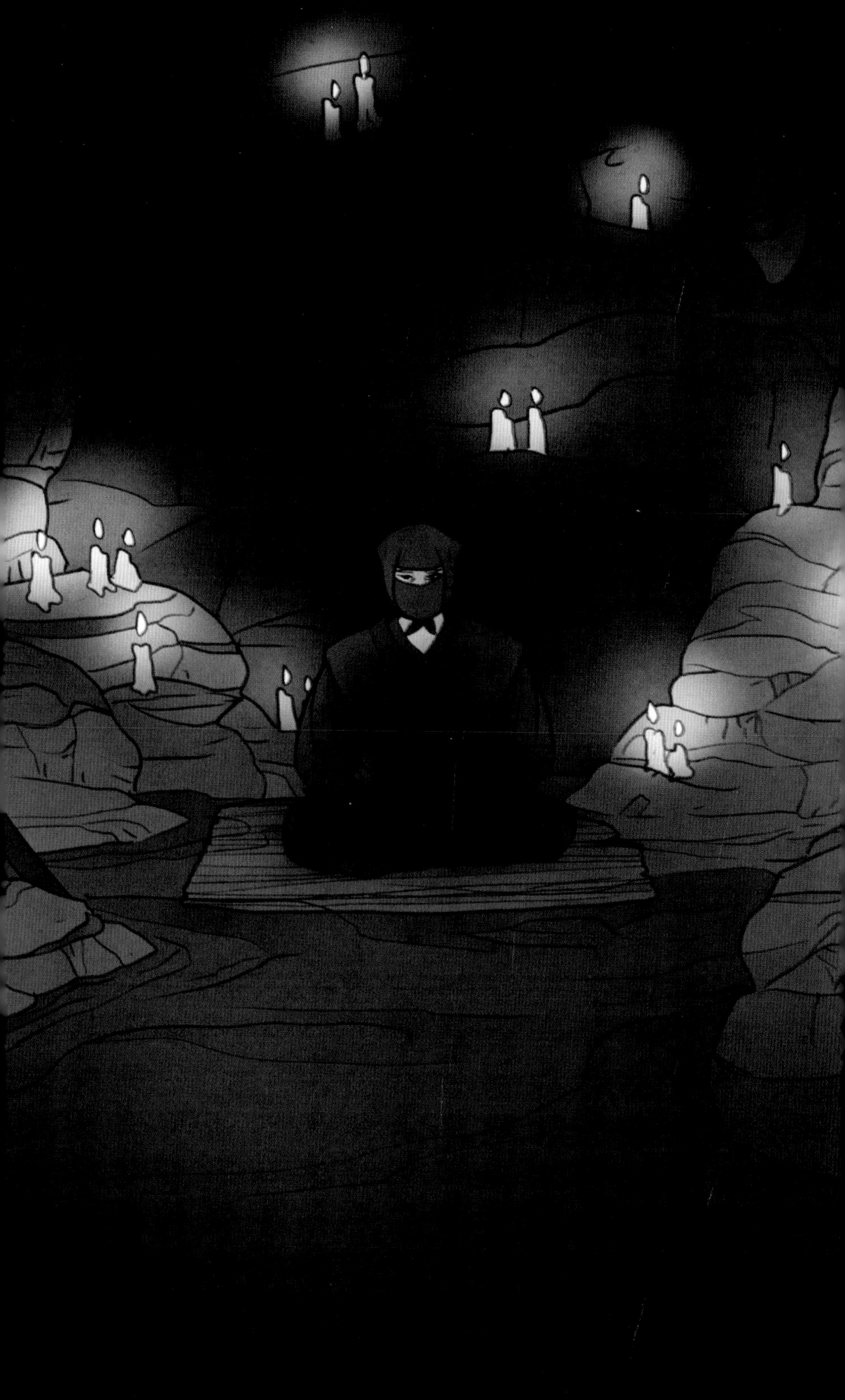

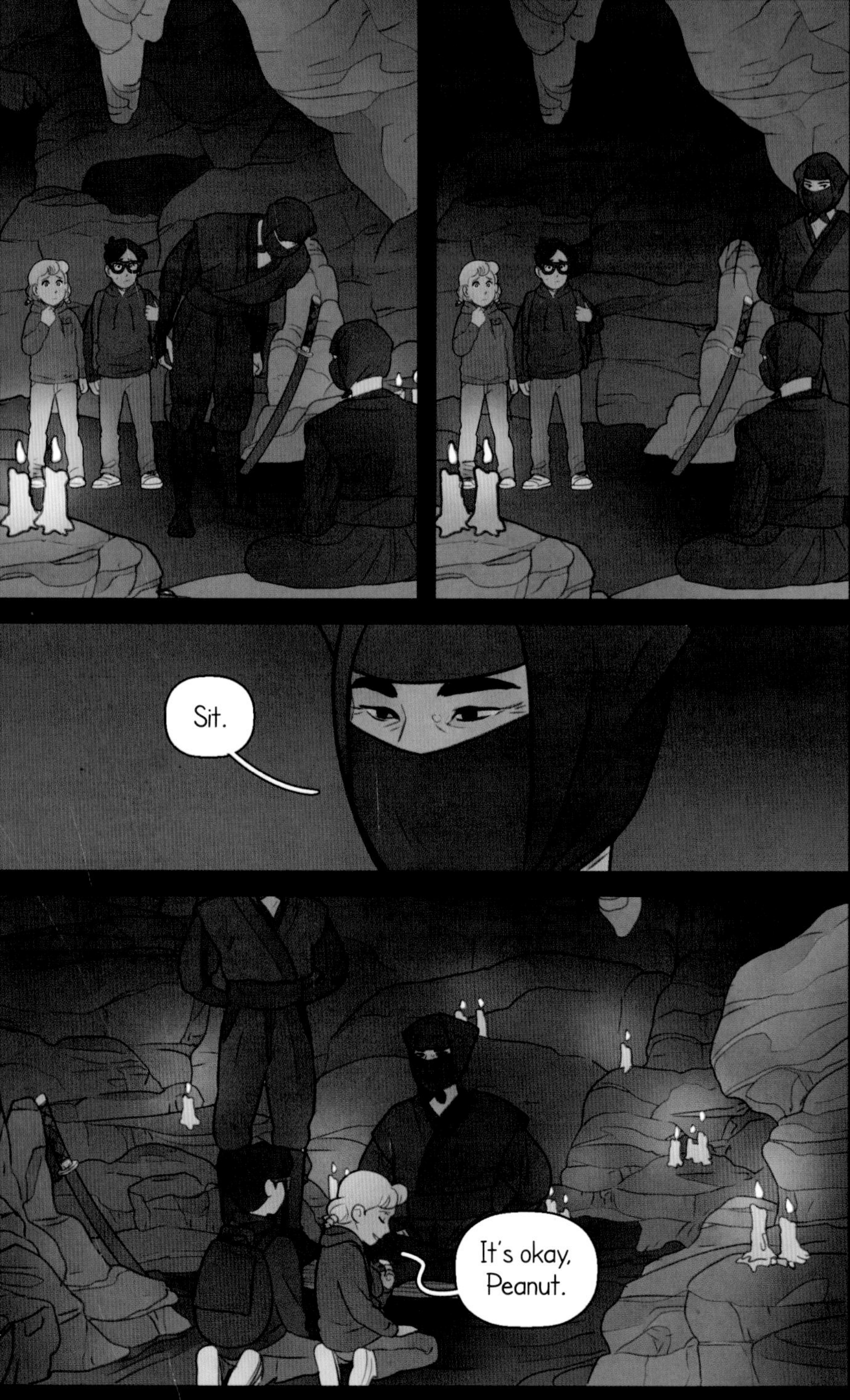
Sit.
It's okay, Peanut.

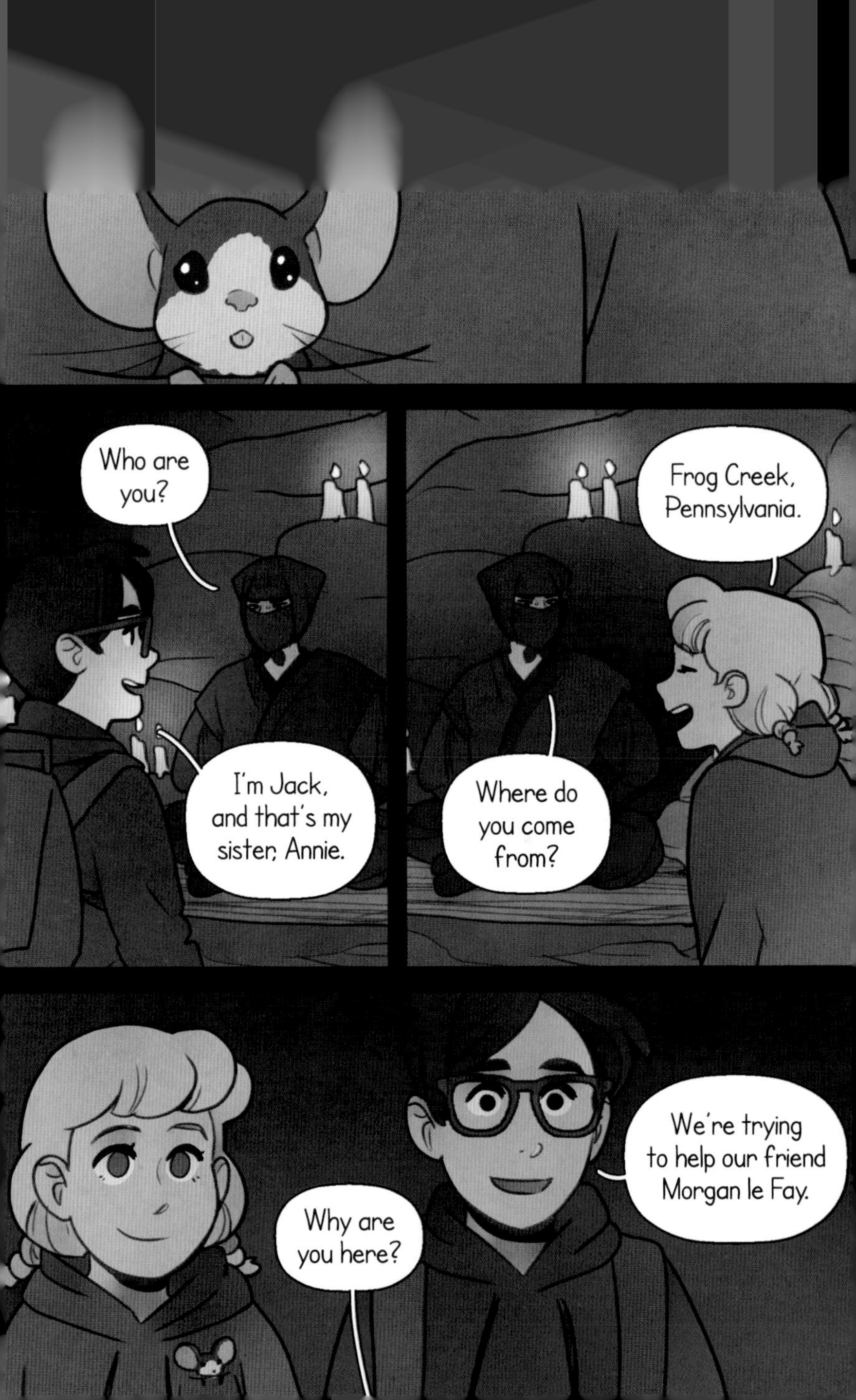
Who are you?
I'm Jack, and that's my sister, Annie.
Where do you come from?
Frog Creek, Pennsylvania.
Why are you here?
We're trying to help our friend Morgan le Fay.

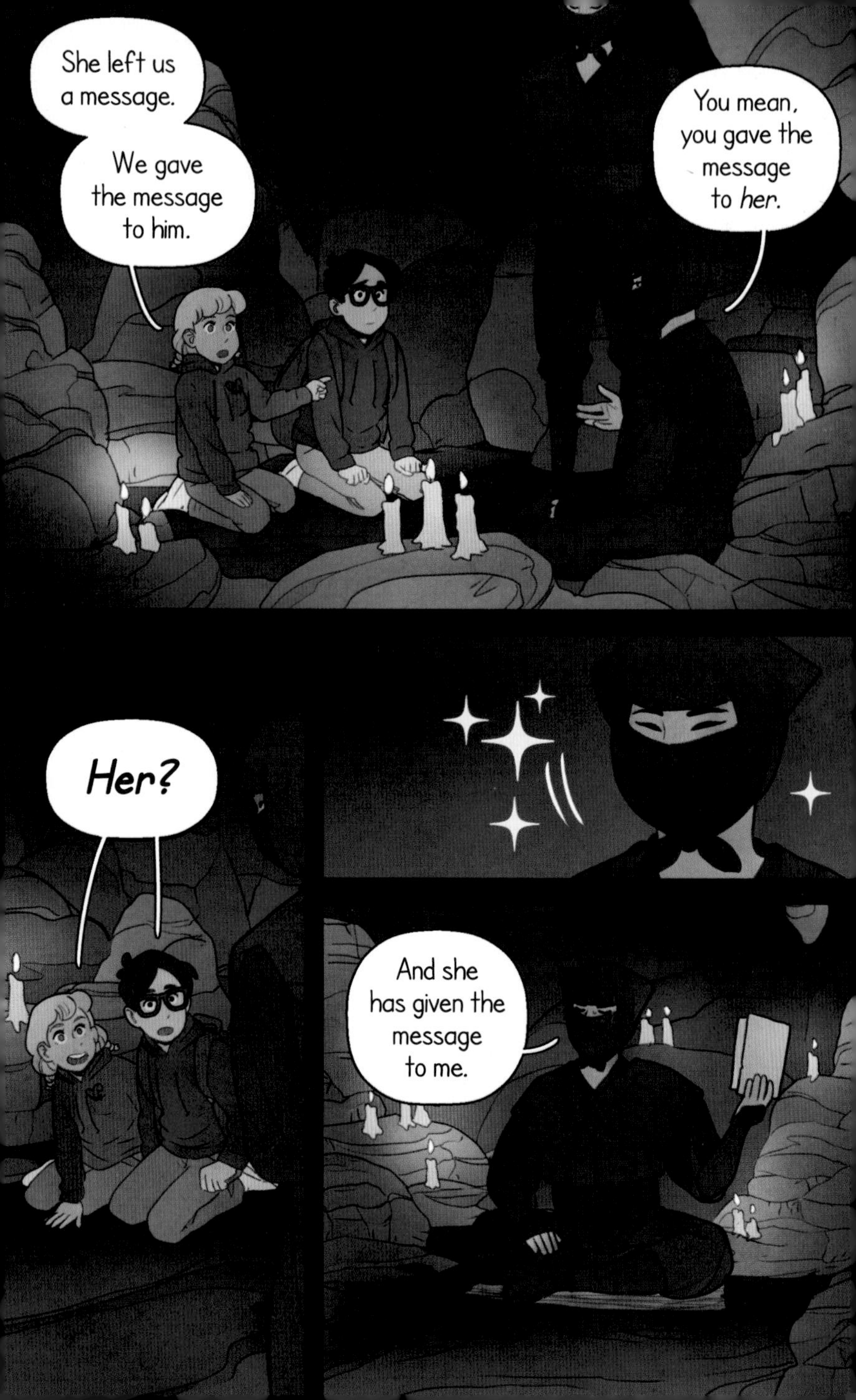
She left us a message.
We gave the message to him.
You mean, you gave the message to *her*.
Her?
And she has given the message to me.

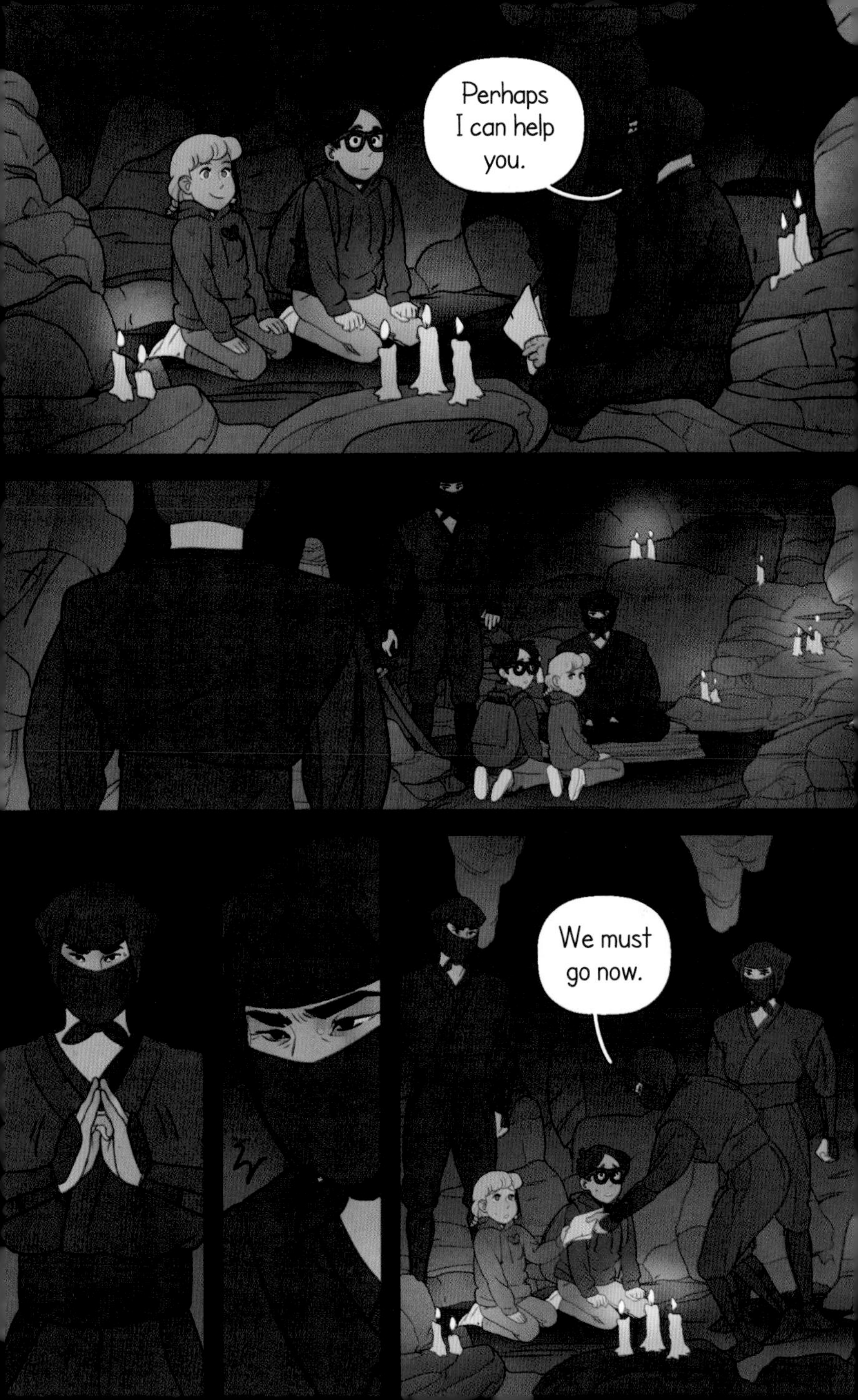
Perhaps I can help you.
We must go now.

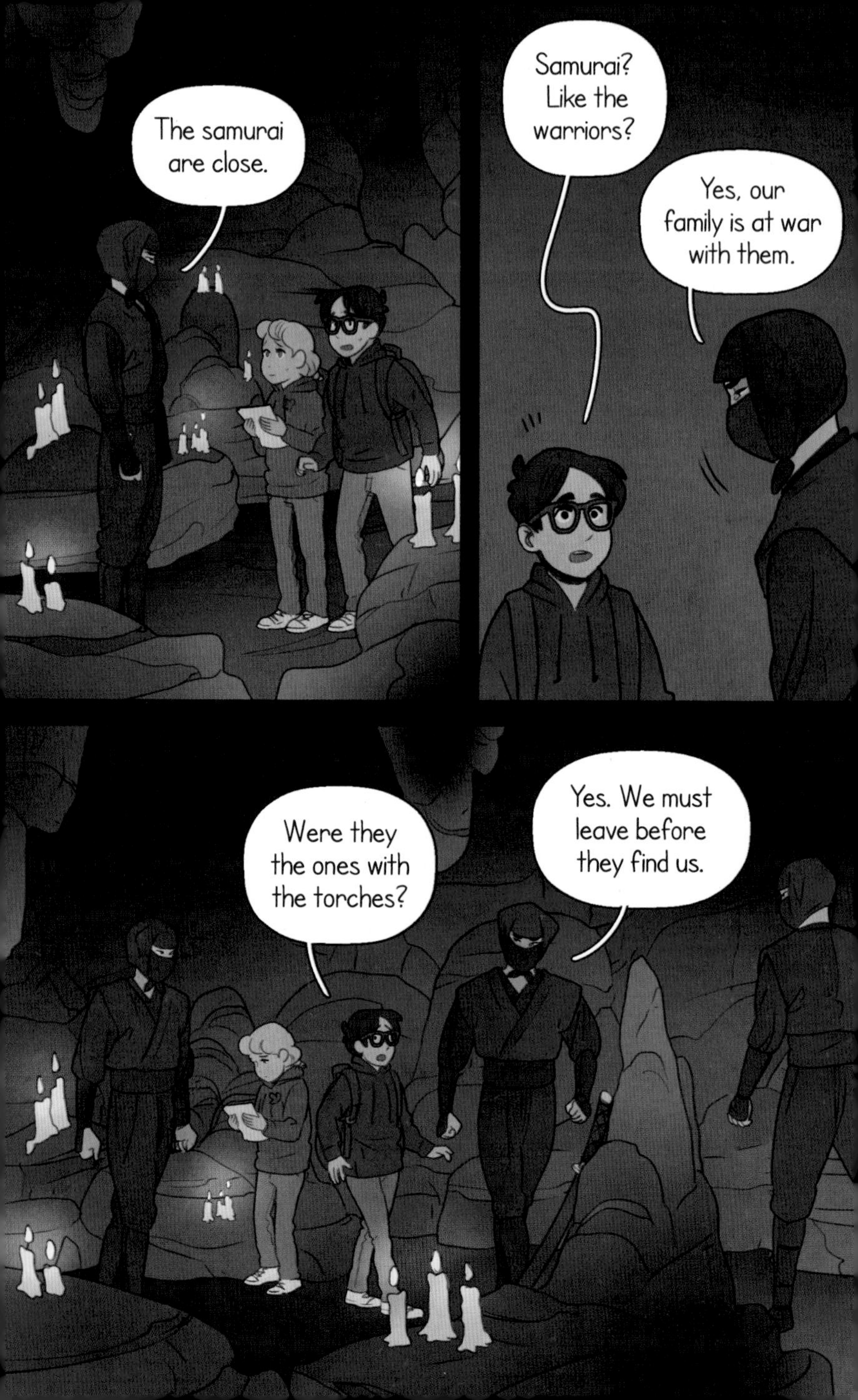
The samurai are close.
Samurai? Like the warriors?
Yes, our family is at war with them.
Were they the ones with the torches?
Yes. We must leave before they find us.

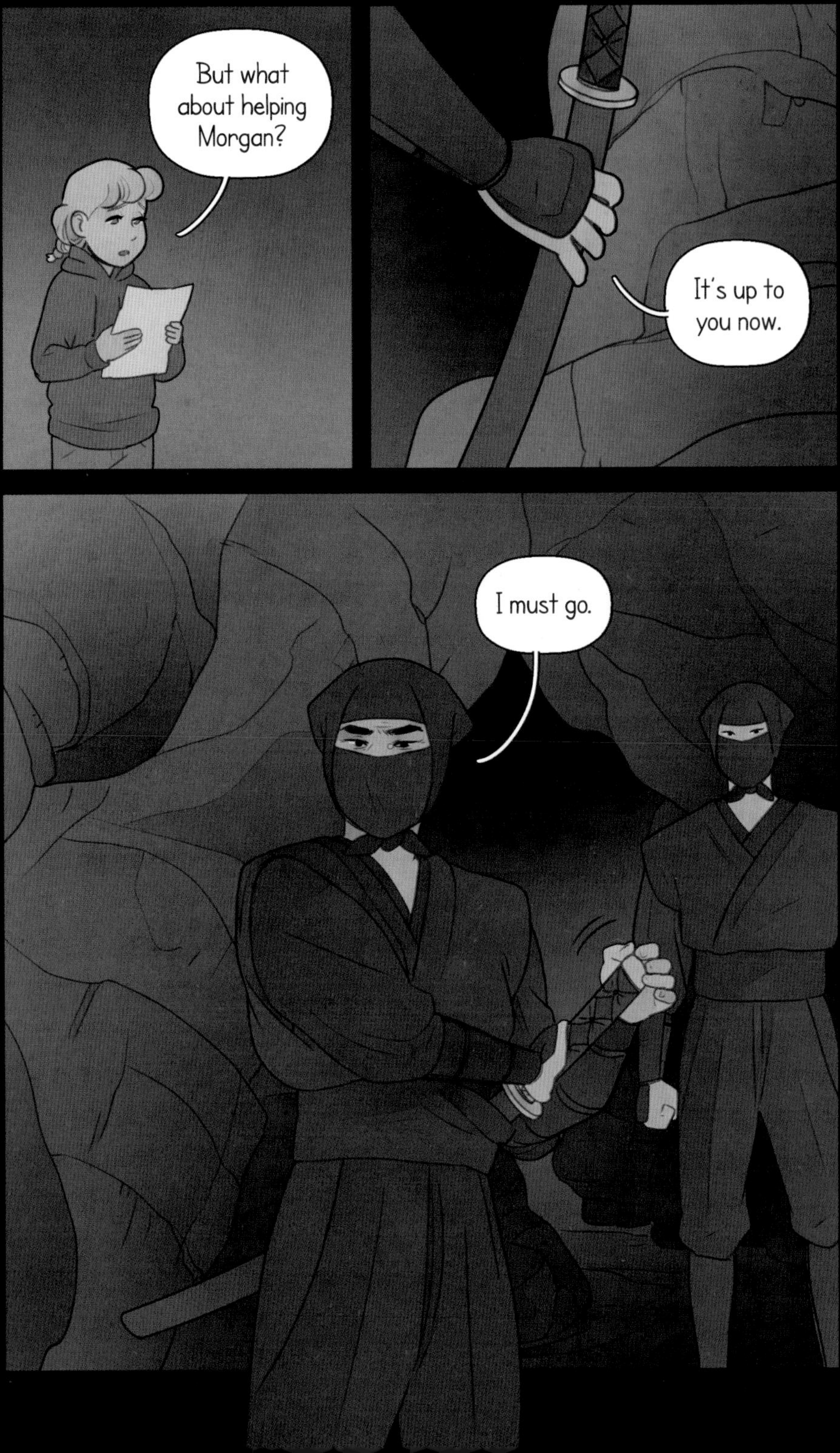
But what about helping Morgan?
It's up to you now.
I must go.

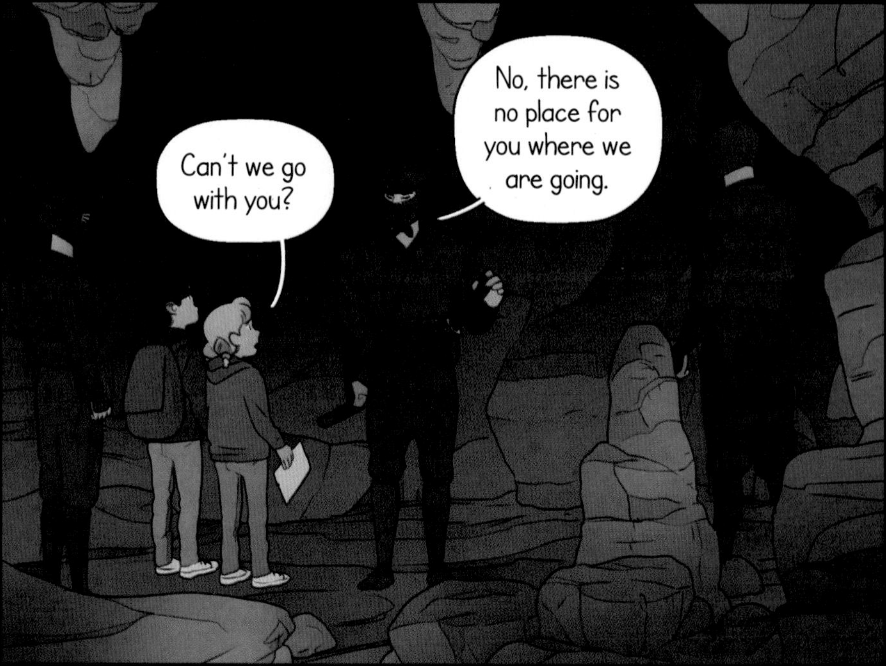
Can't we go with you?
No, there is no place for you where we are going.

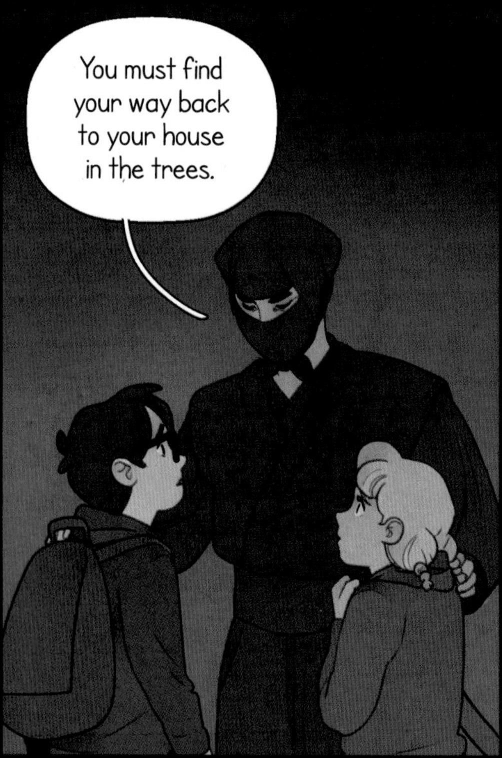
You must find your way back to your house in the trees.

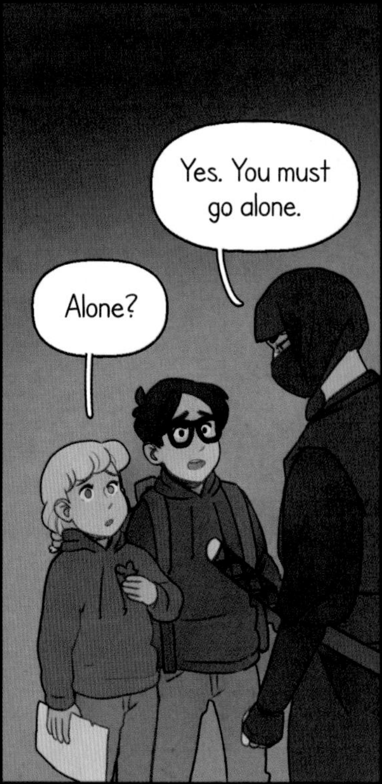
Alone?
Yes. You must go alone.

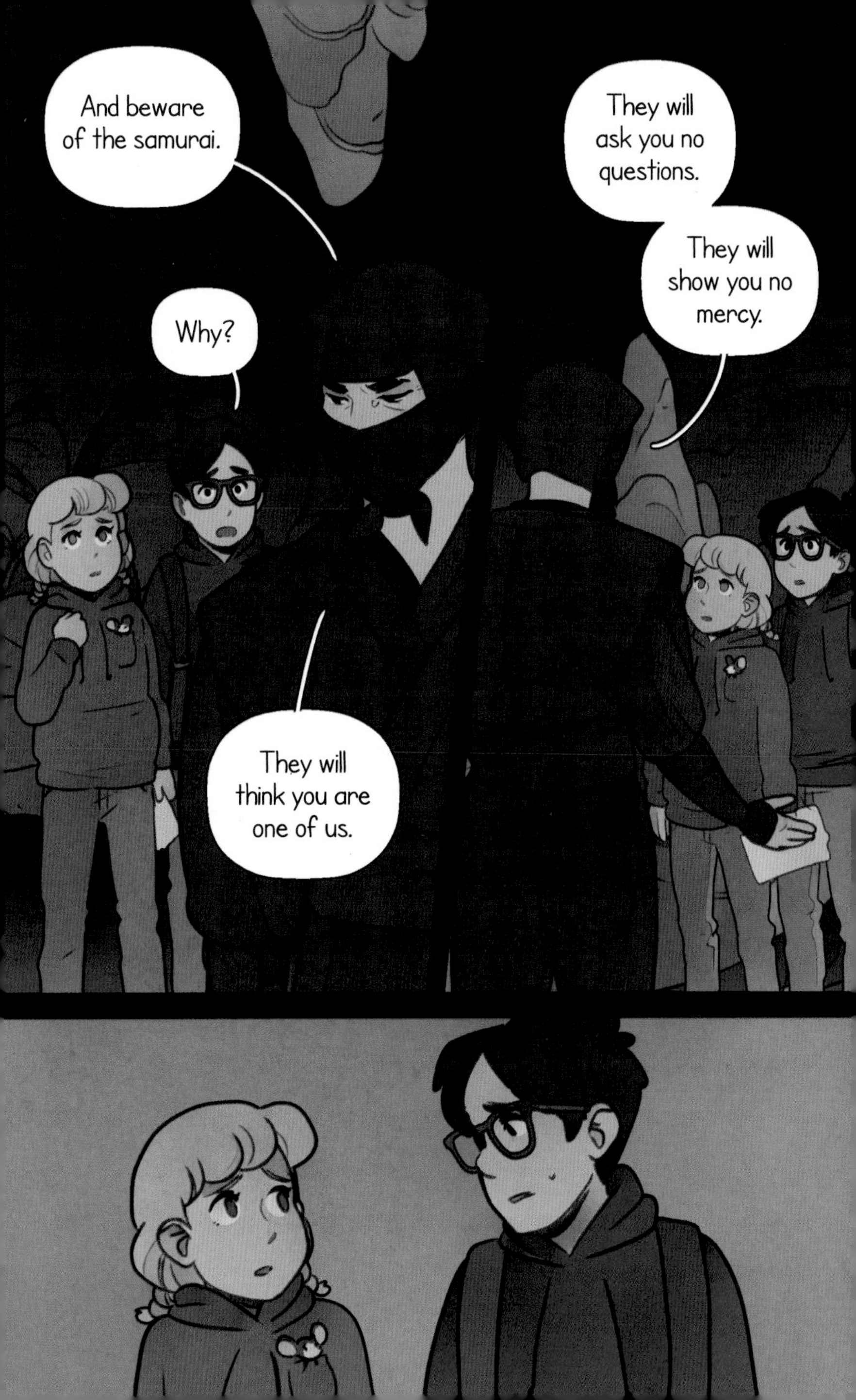
And beware of the samurai.
They will ask you no questions.
Why?
They will show you no mercy.
They will think you are one of us.

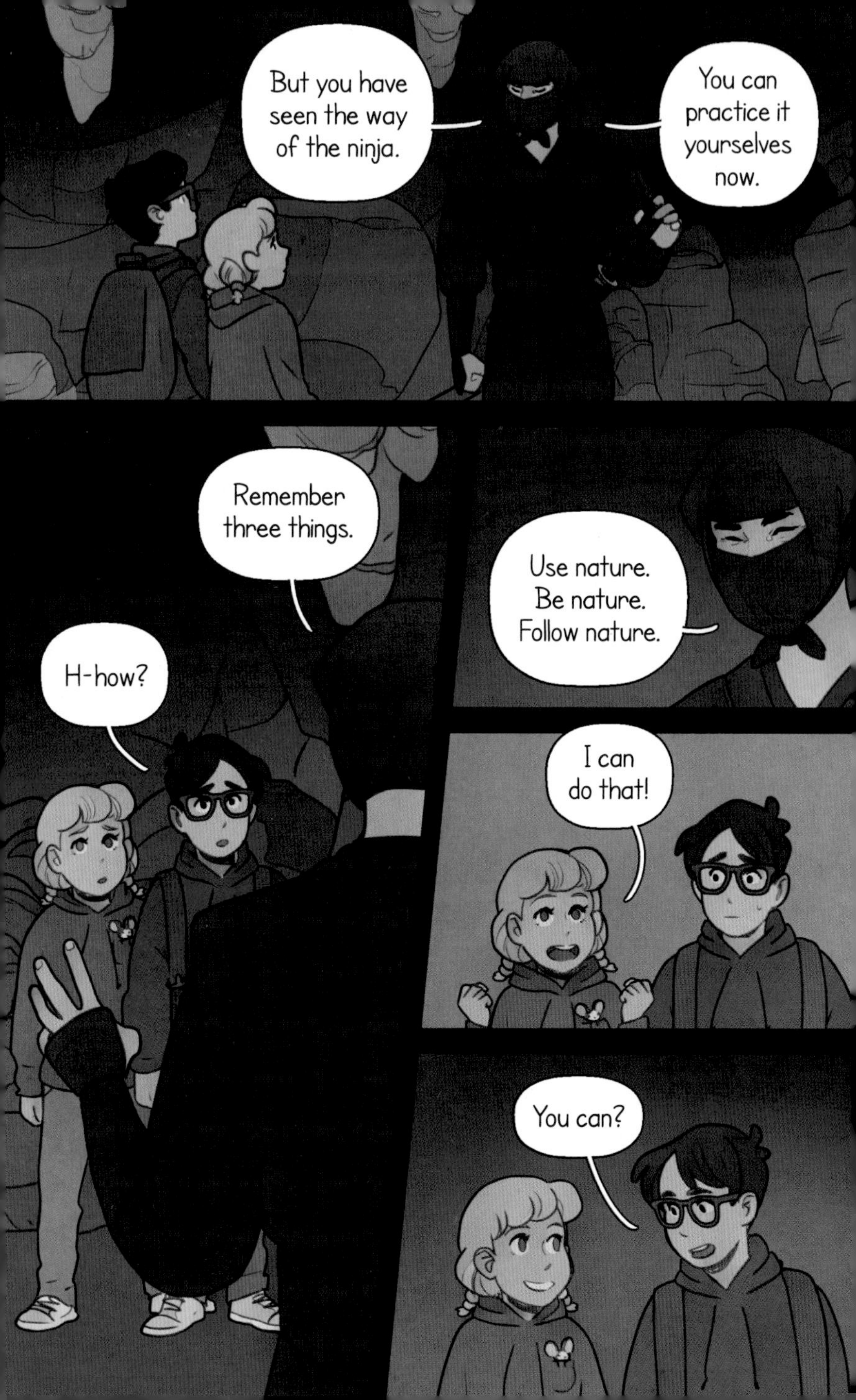
But you have seen the way of the ninja.
You can practice it yourselves now.
Remember three things.
Use nature. Be nature. Follow nature.
H-how?
I can do that!
You can?

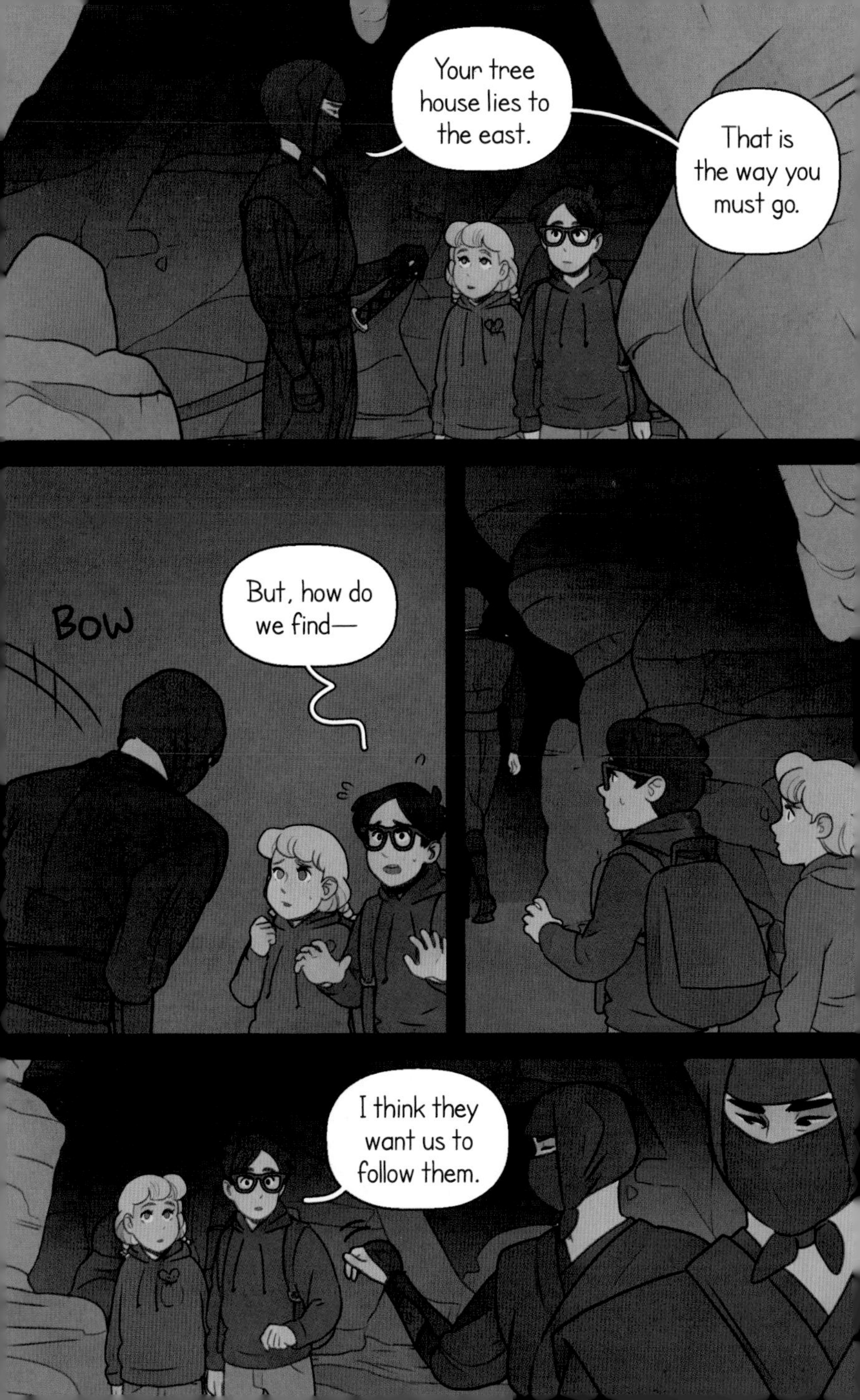
Your tree house lies to the east.
That is the way you must go.
BOW
But, how do we find—
I think they want us to follow them.

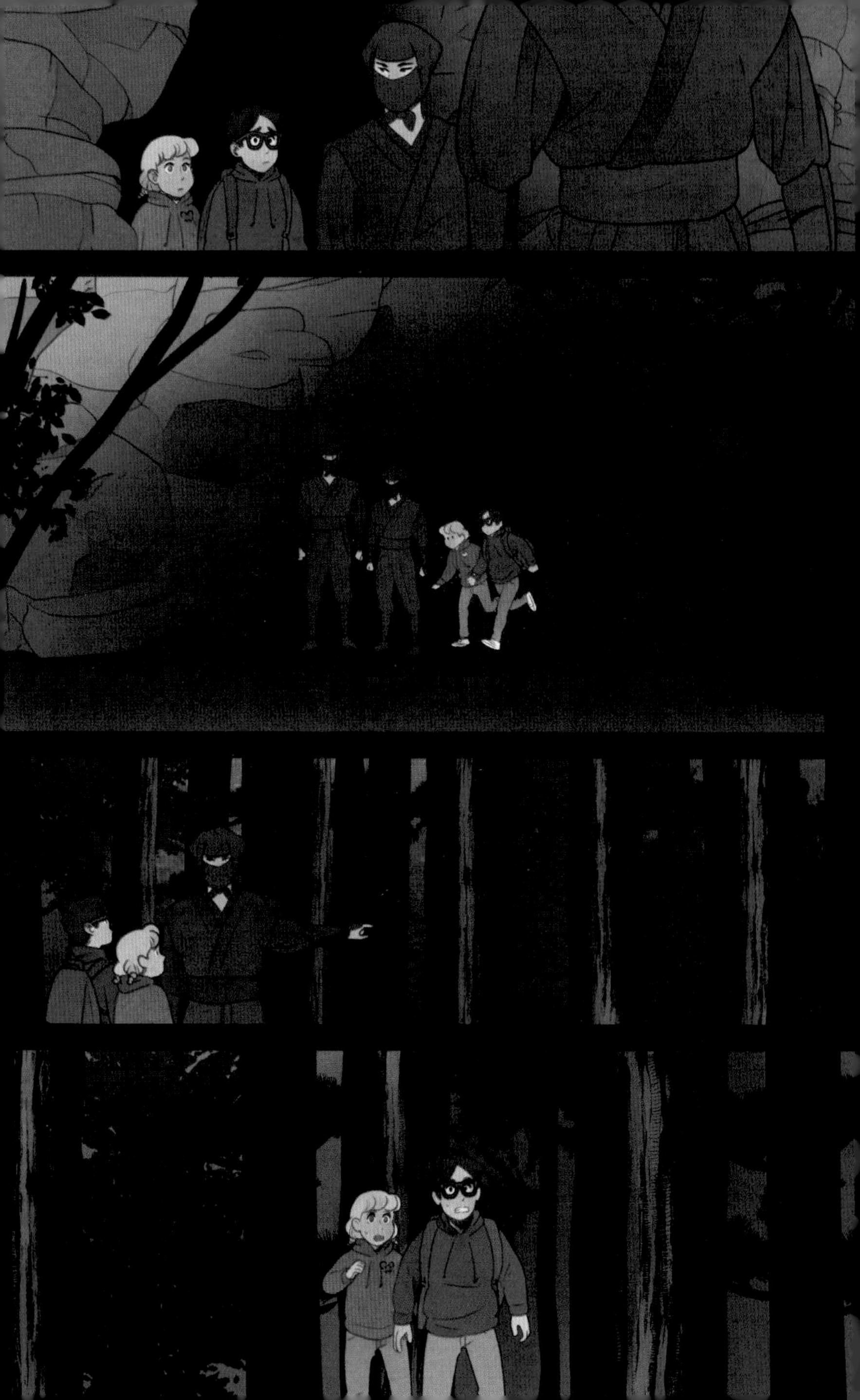

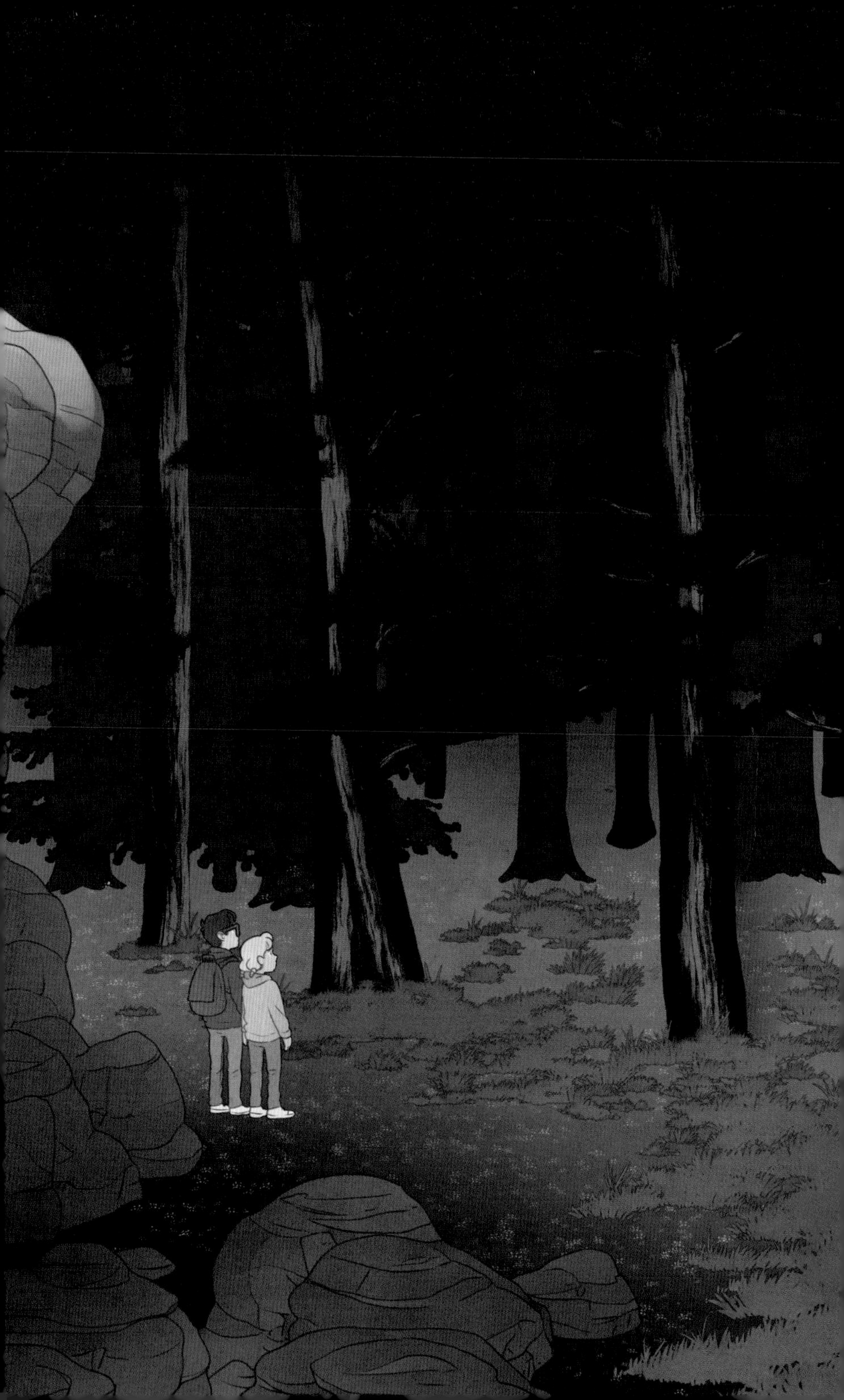

CHAPTER SEVEN
To the East

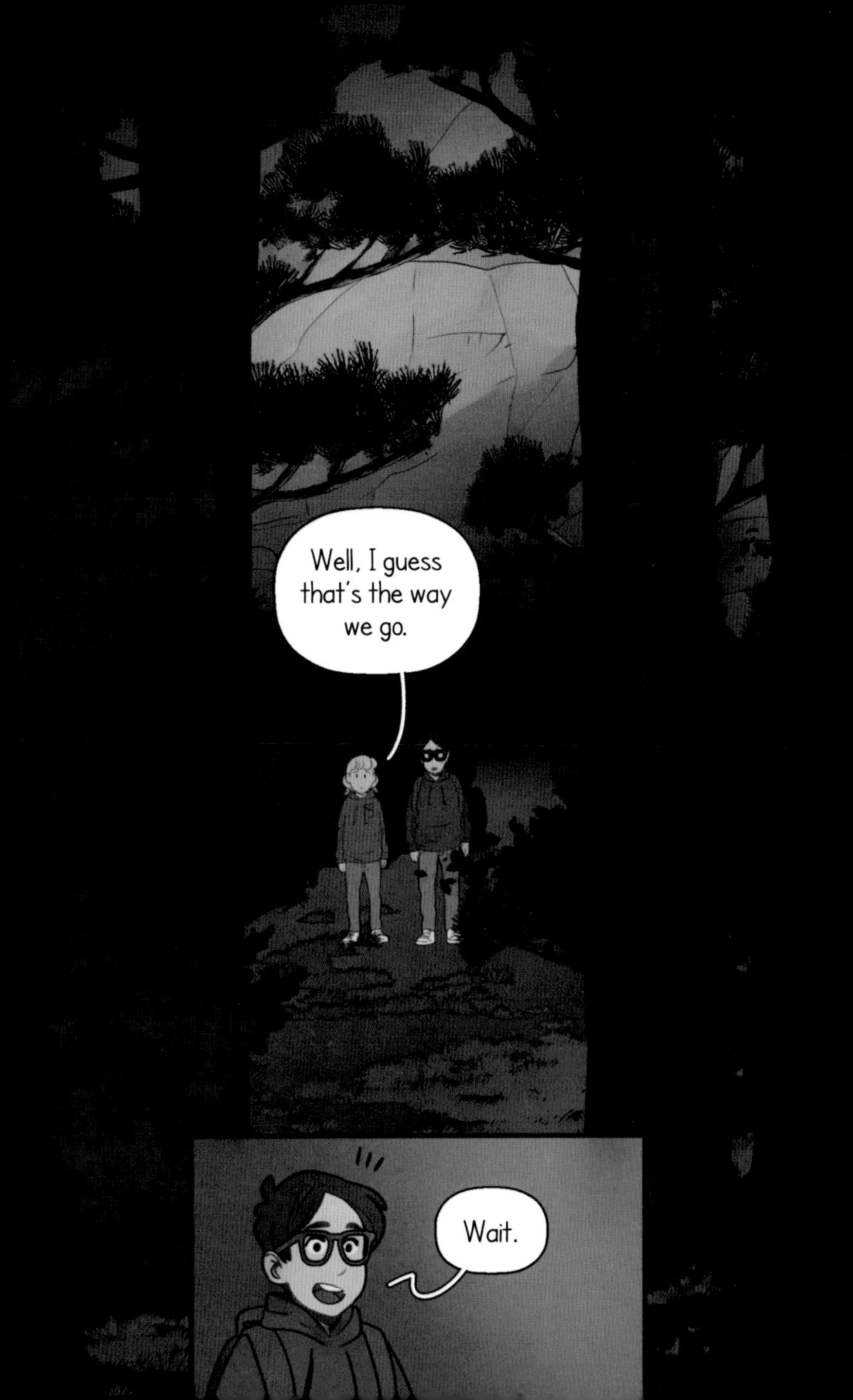
Well, I guess that's the way we go.
Wait.

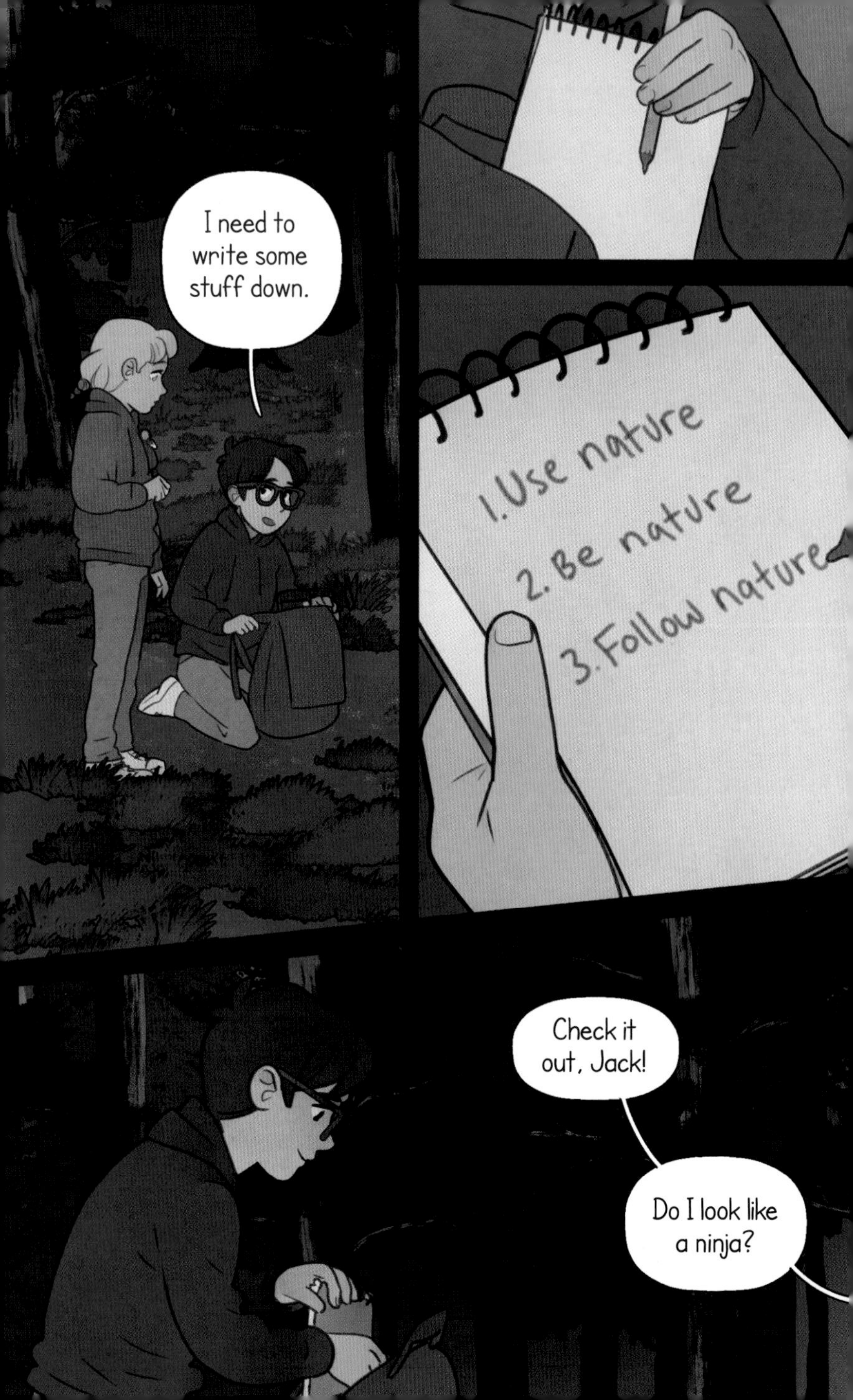
I need to write some stuff down.
1. Use nature
2. Be nature
3. Follow nature
Check it out, Jack!
Do I look like a ninja?

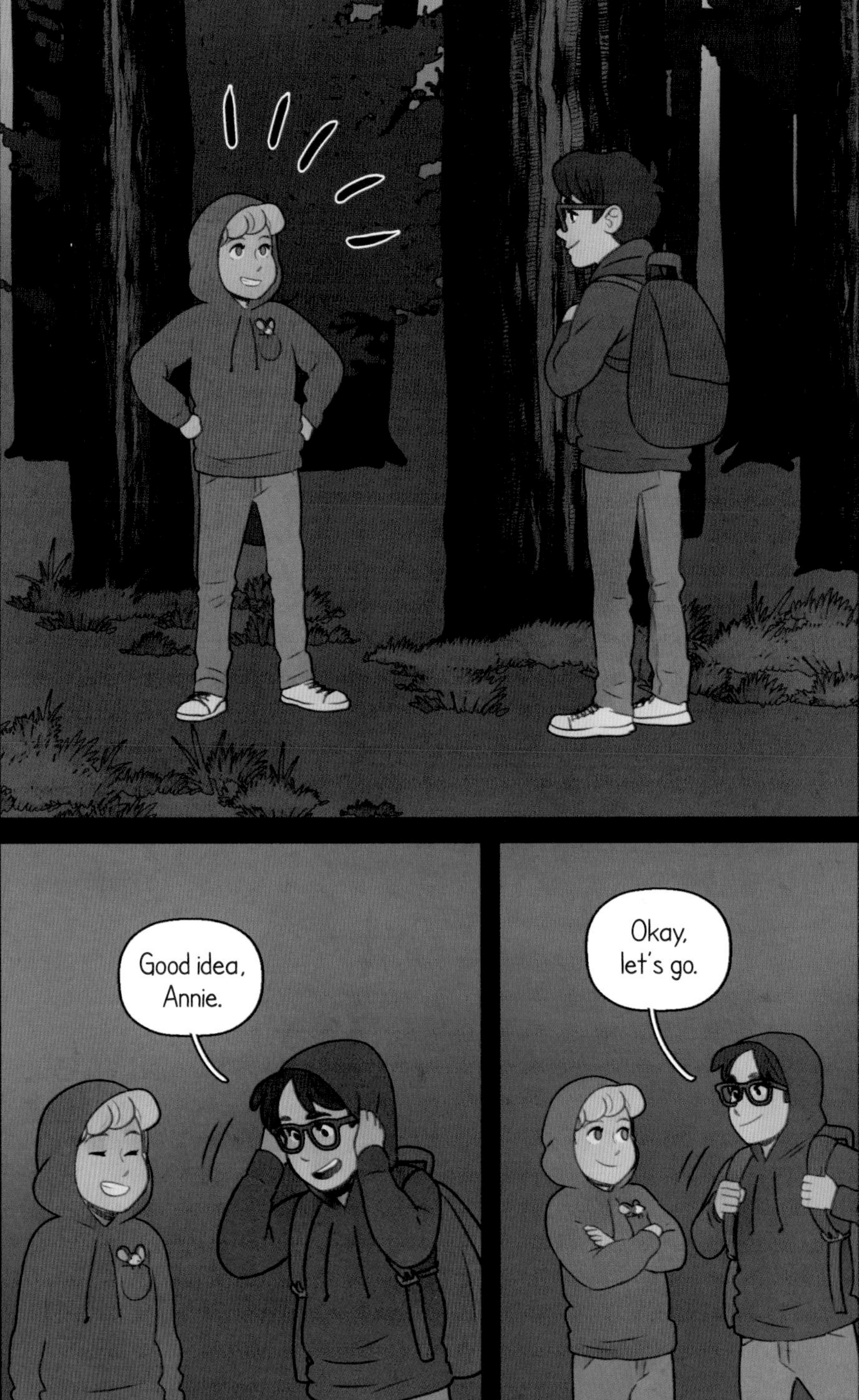
Good idea, Annie.
Okay, let's go.

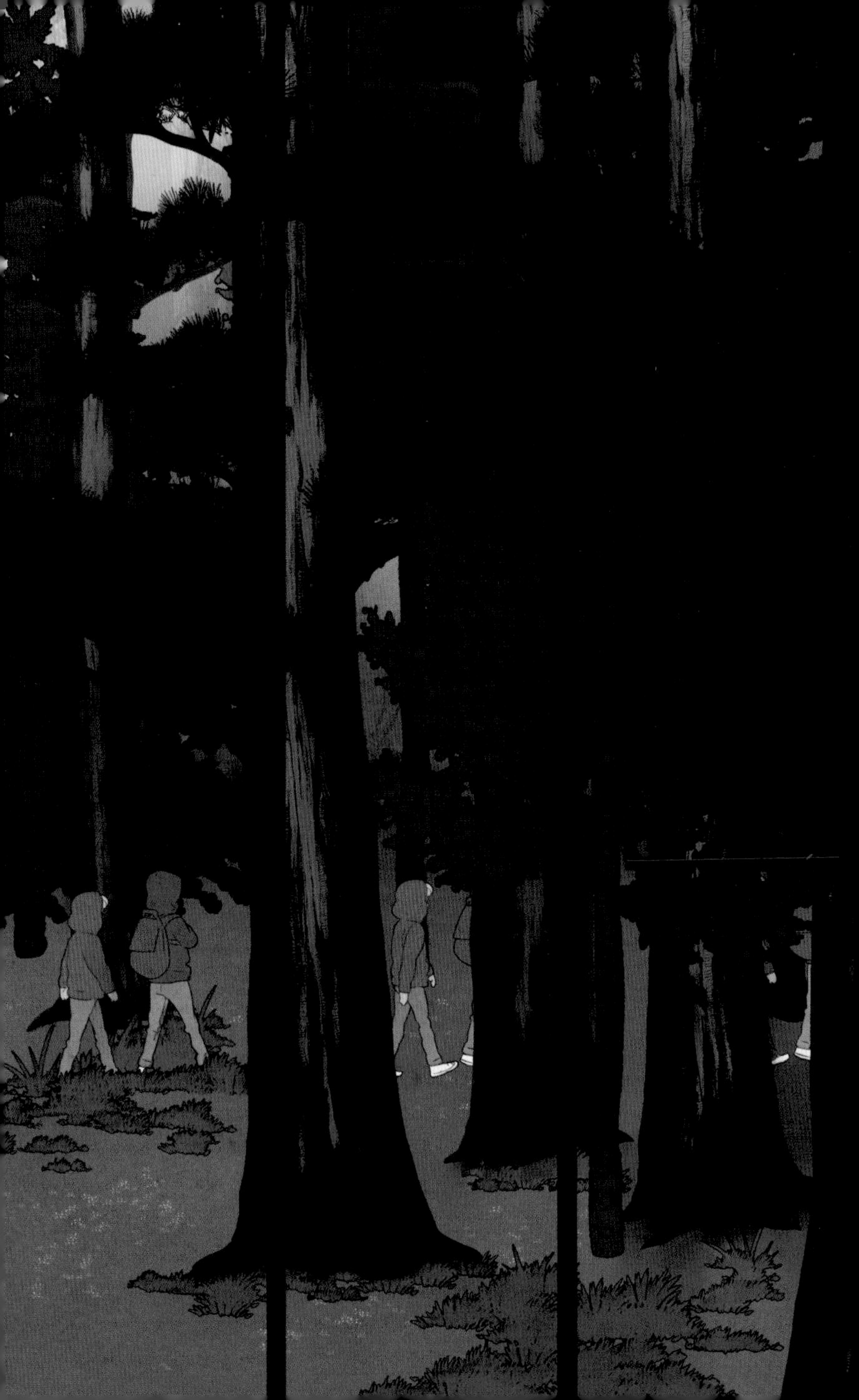

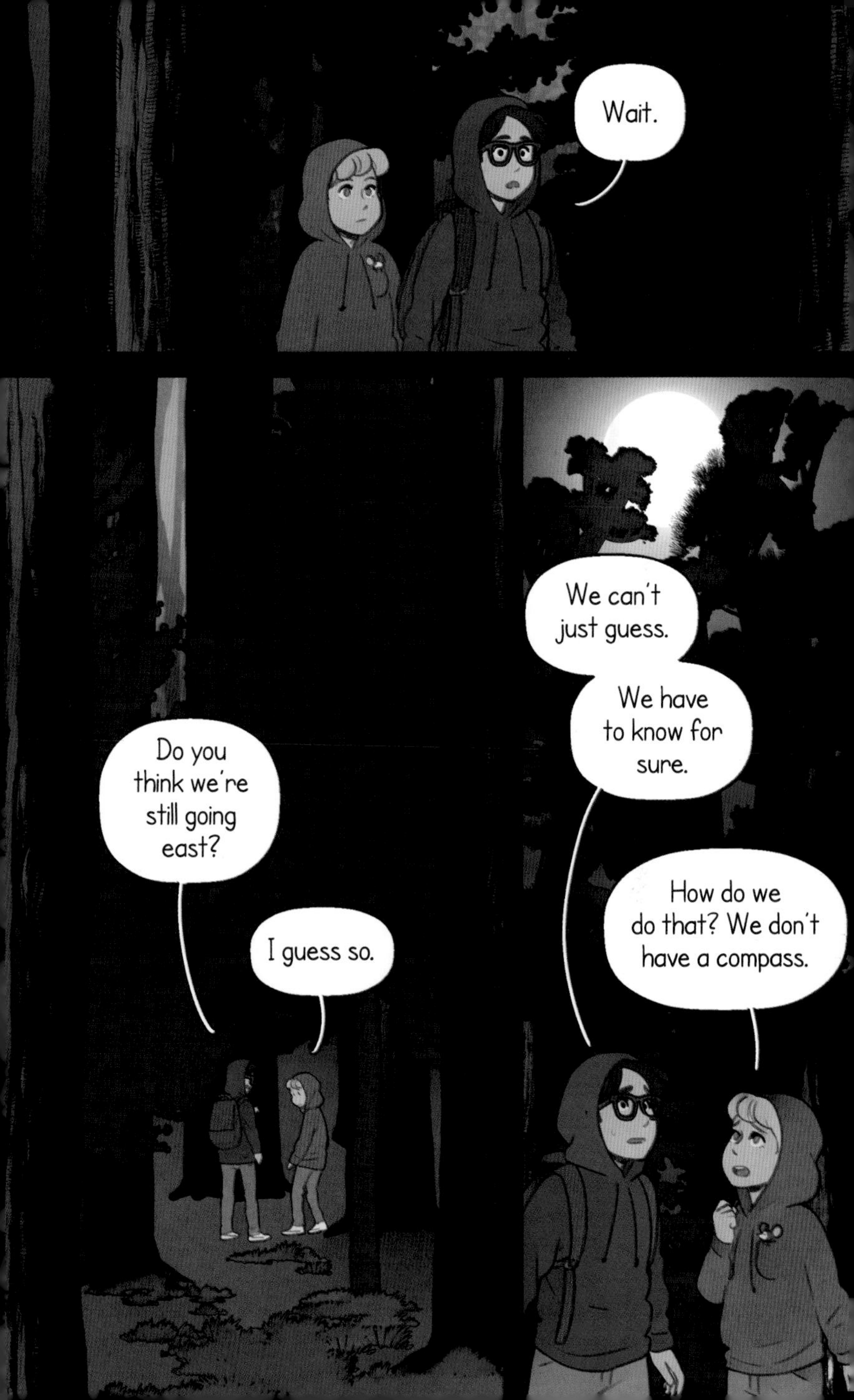
Wait.
Do you think we're still going east?
I guess so.
We can't just guess.
We have to know for sure.
How do we do that? We don't have a compass.

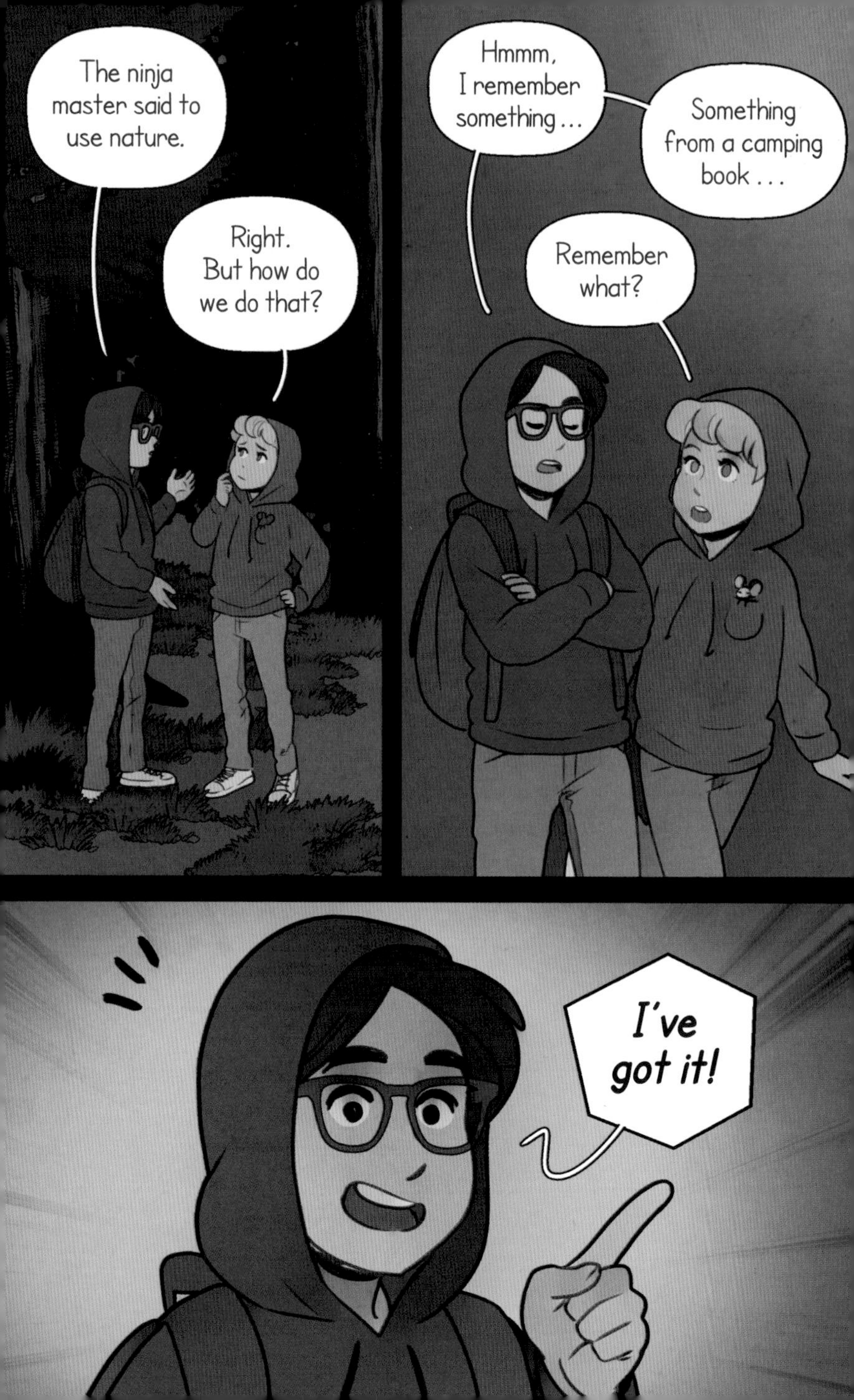
The ninja master said to use nature.
Right. But how do we do that?
Hmmm, I remember something...
Something from a camping book . . .
Remember what?
I've got it!

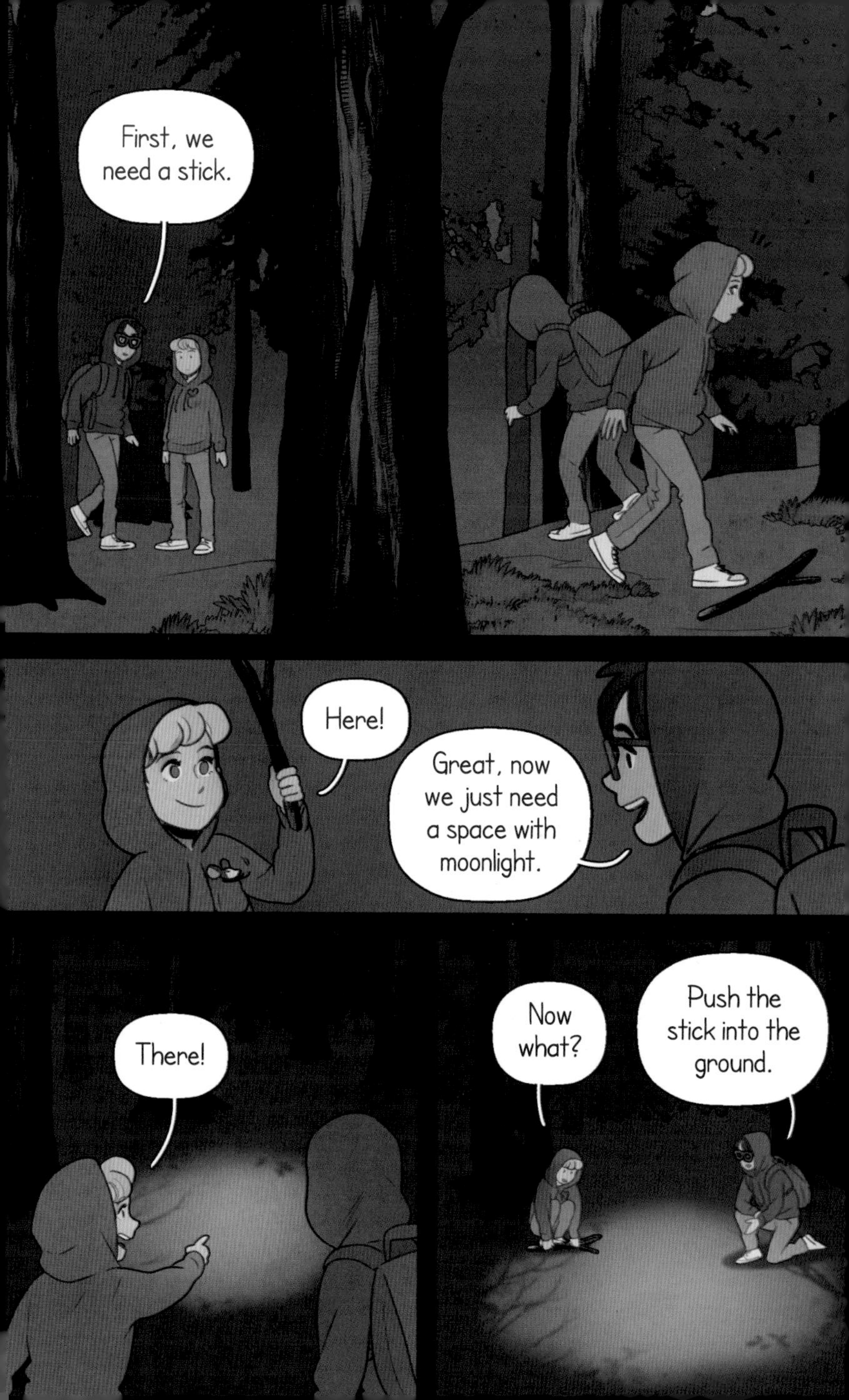
First, we need a stick.
Here!
Great, now we just need a space with moonlight.
There!
Now what?
Push the stick into the ground.

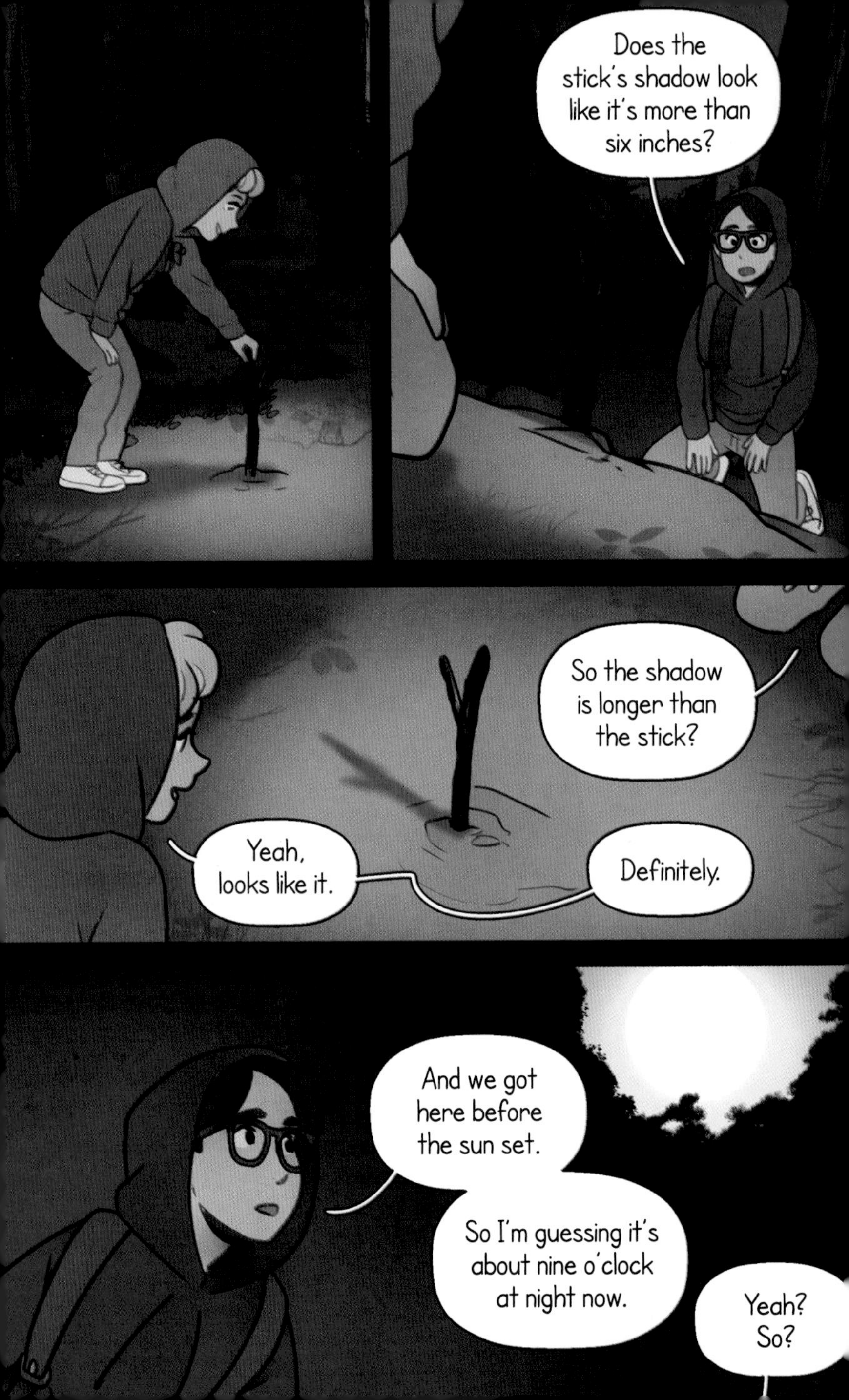
Does the stick's shadow look like it's more than six inches?
So the shadow is longer than the stick?
Yeah, looks like it.
Definitely.
And we got here before the sun set.
So I'm guessing it's about nine o'clock at night now.
Yeah? So?

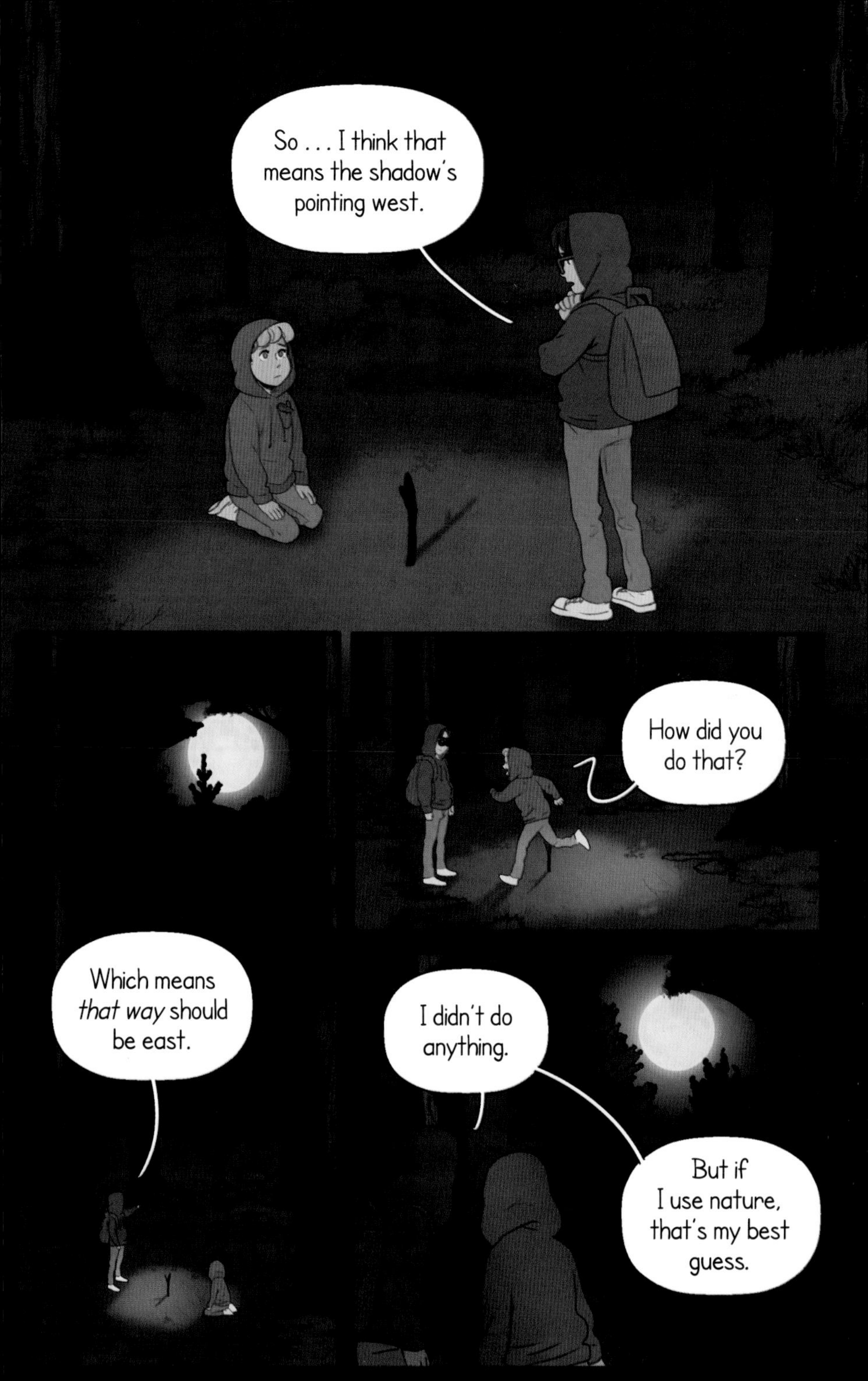
So . . . I think that means the shadow's pointing west.
How did you do that?
Which means *that way* should be east.
I didn't do anything.
But if I use nature, that's my best guess.

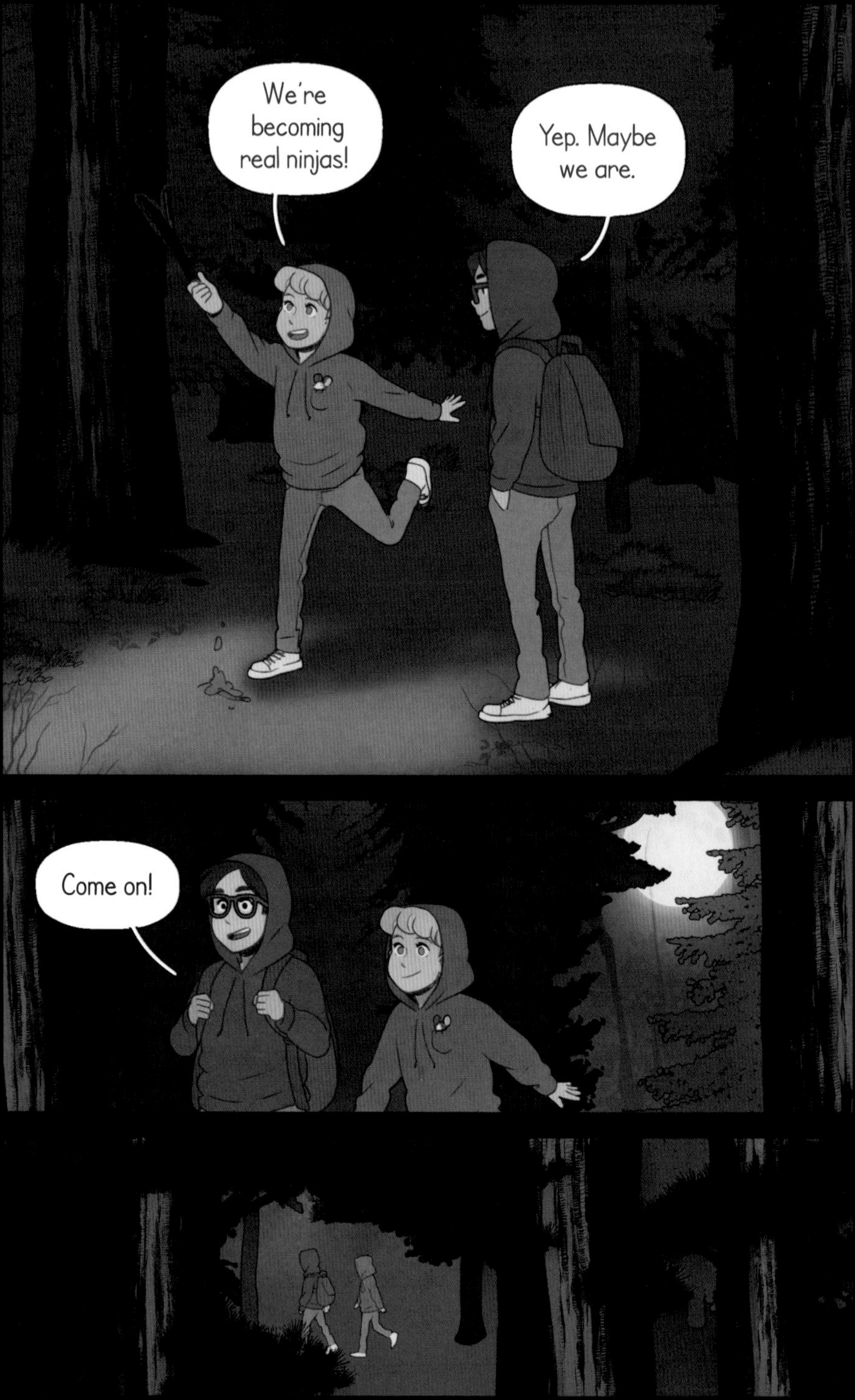
We're becoming real ninjas!
Yep. Maybe we are.
Come on!

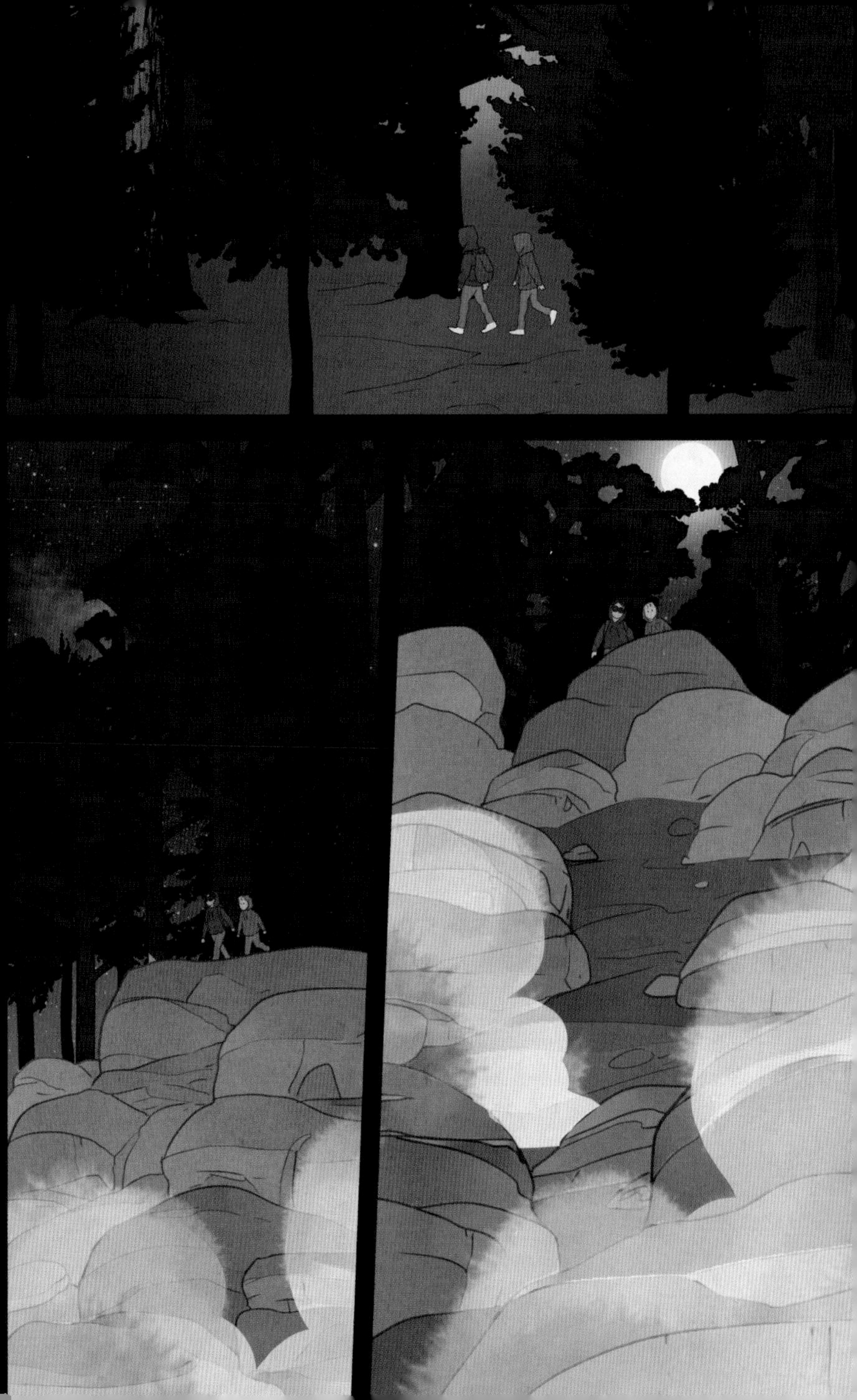

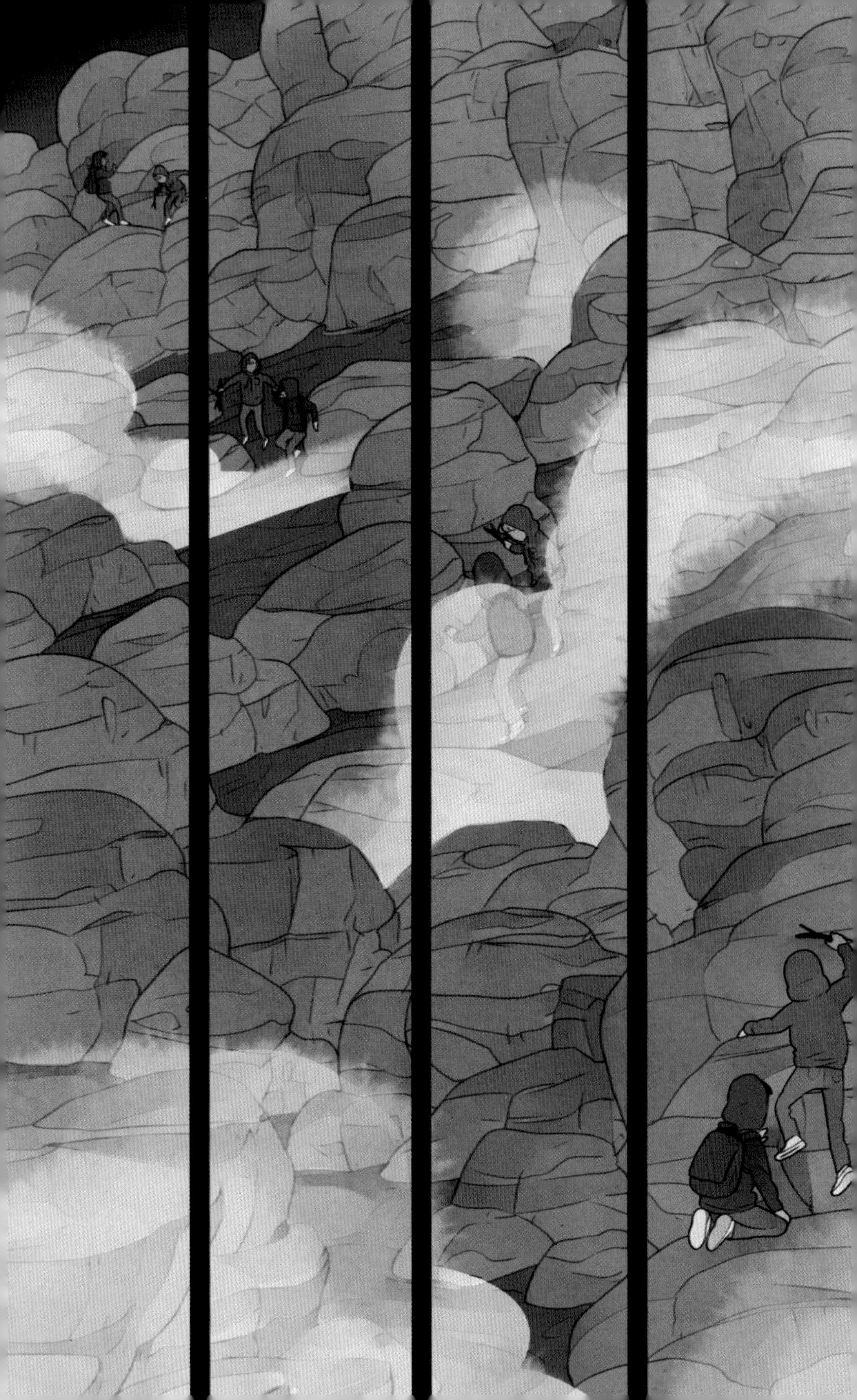

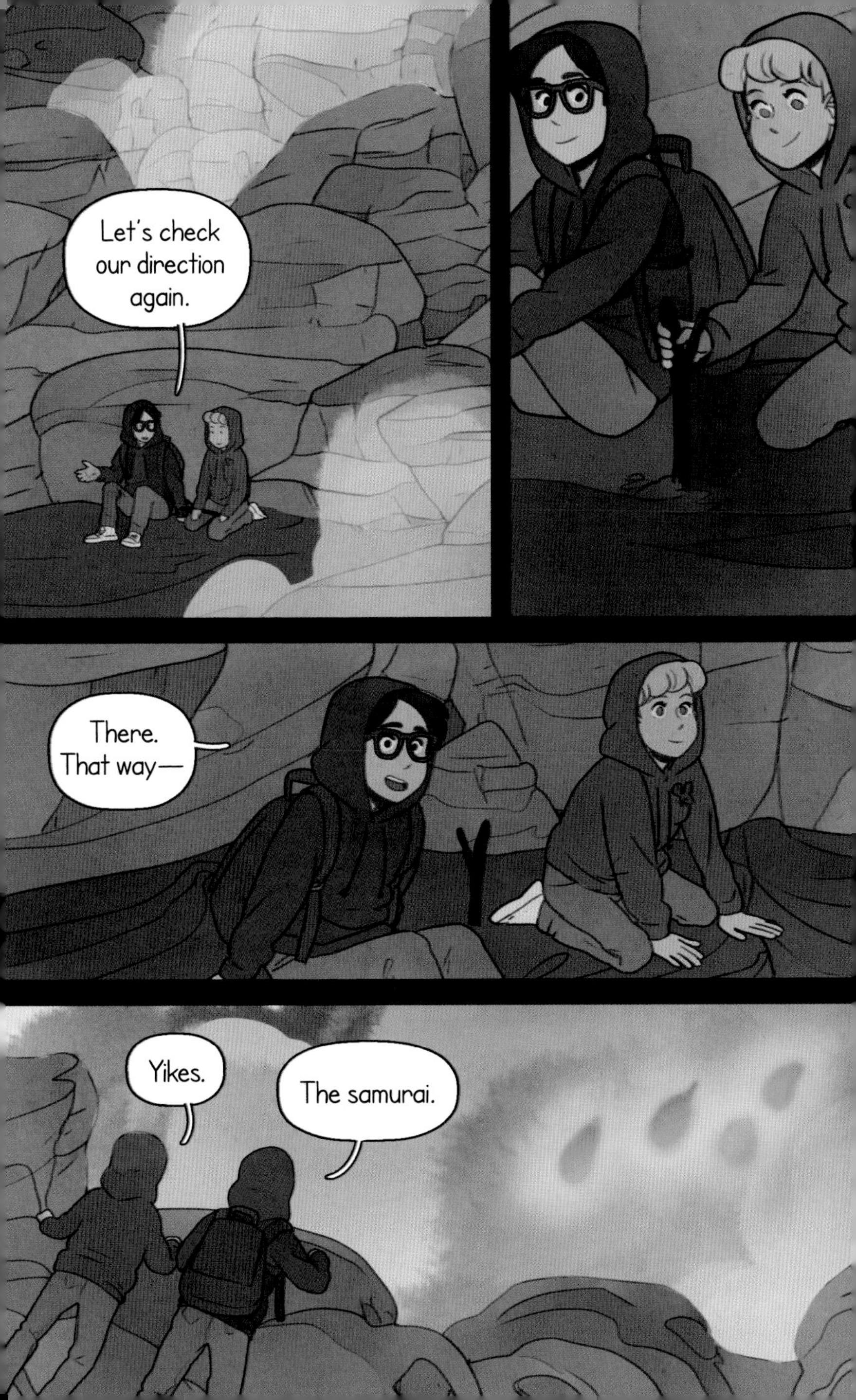
Let's check our direction again.
There. That way—
Yikes.
The samurai.

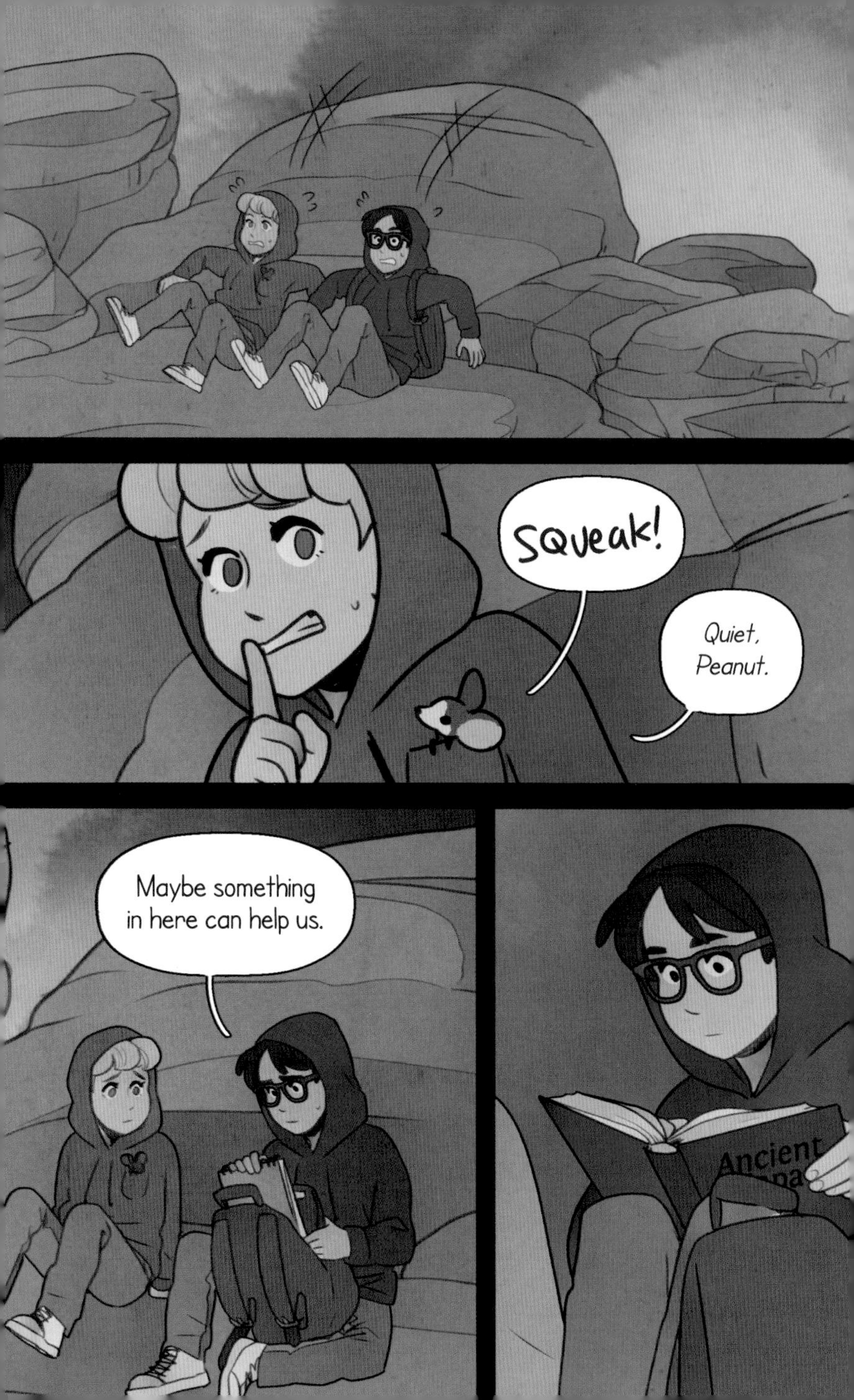
SQUEAK!
Quiet, Peanut.
Maybe something in here can help us.
Ancient

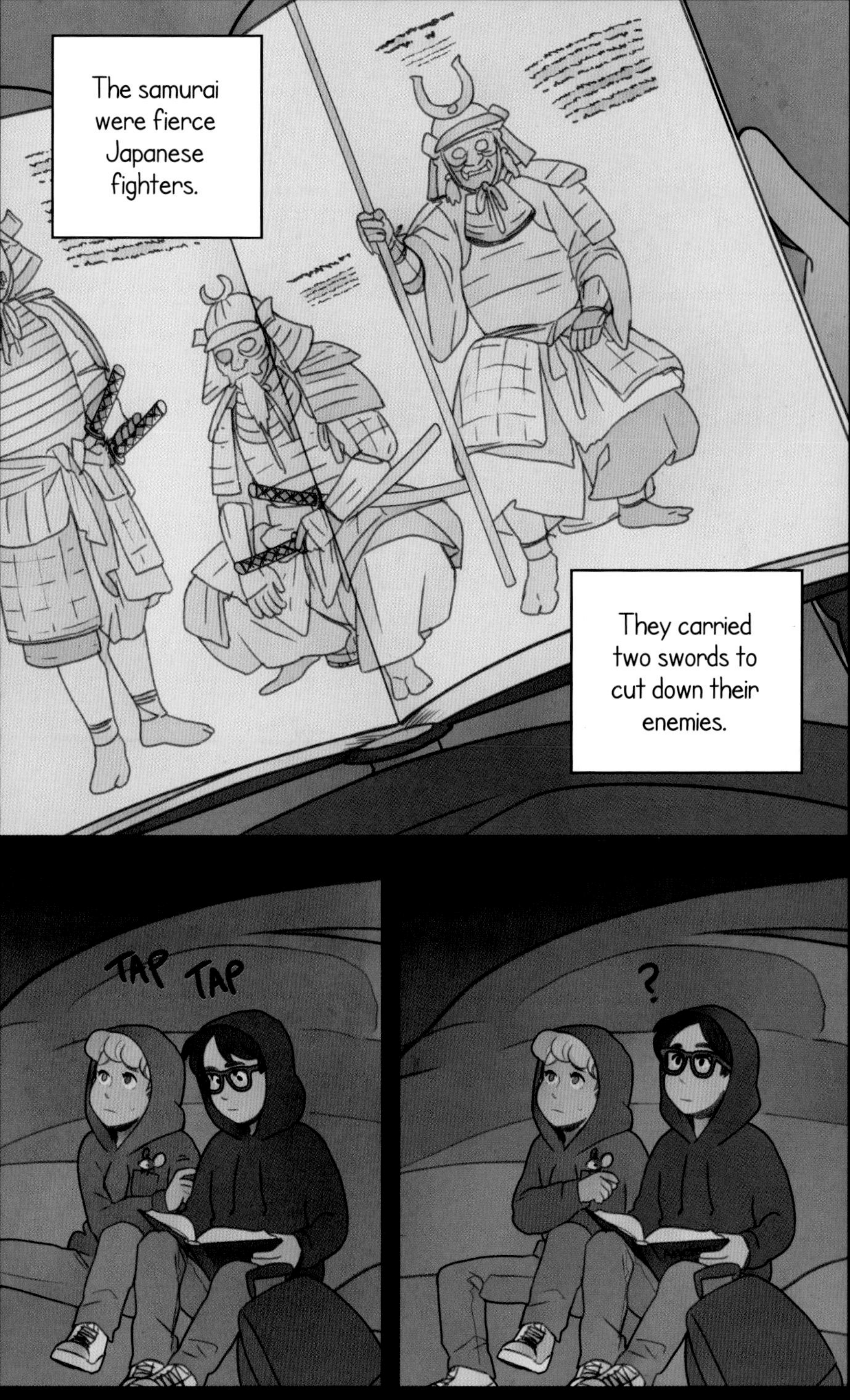
The samurai were fierce Japanese fighters.
They carried two swords to cut down their enemies.
TAP TAP
?

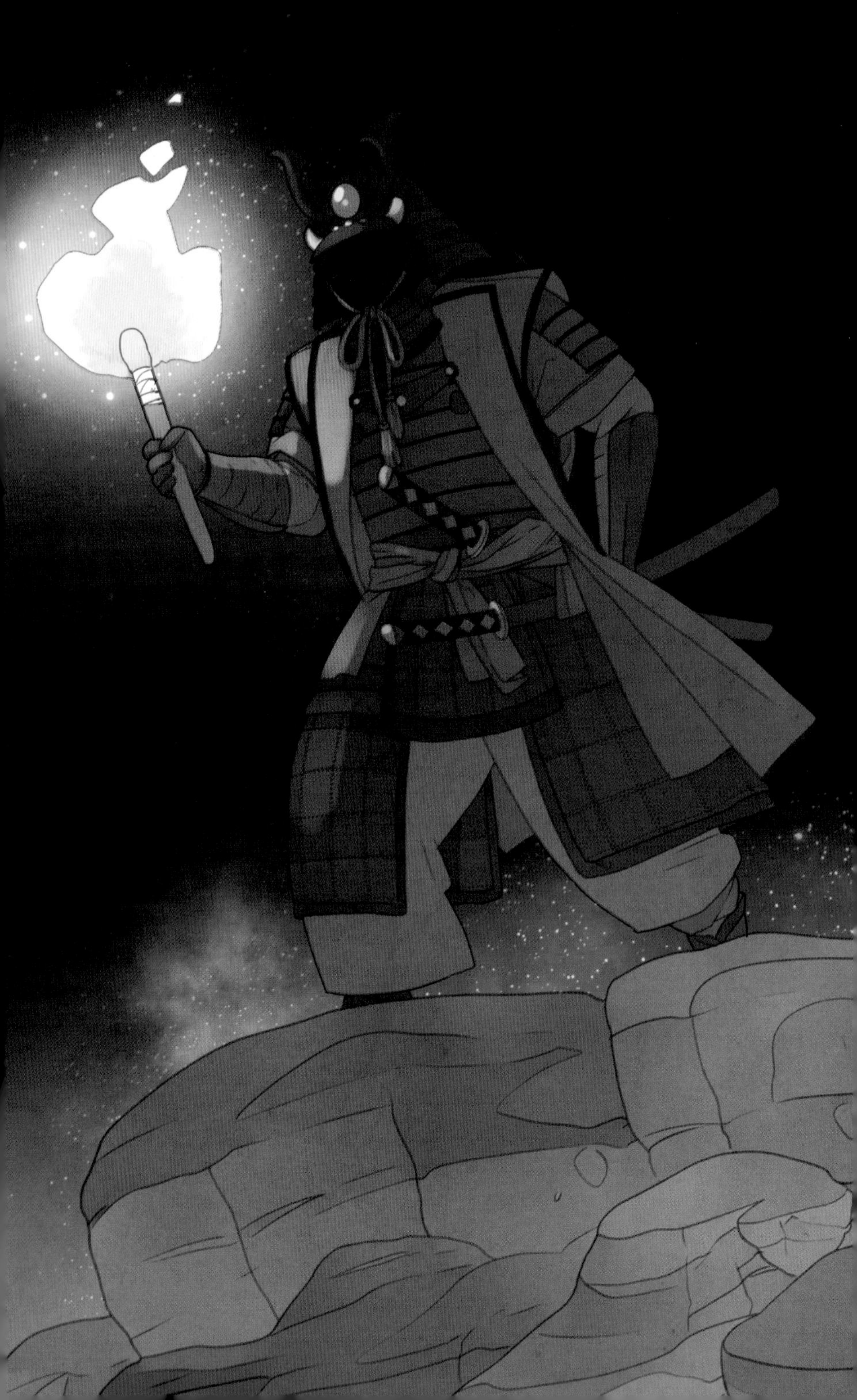

CHAPTER EIGHT
Dragon Water

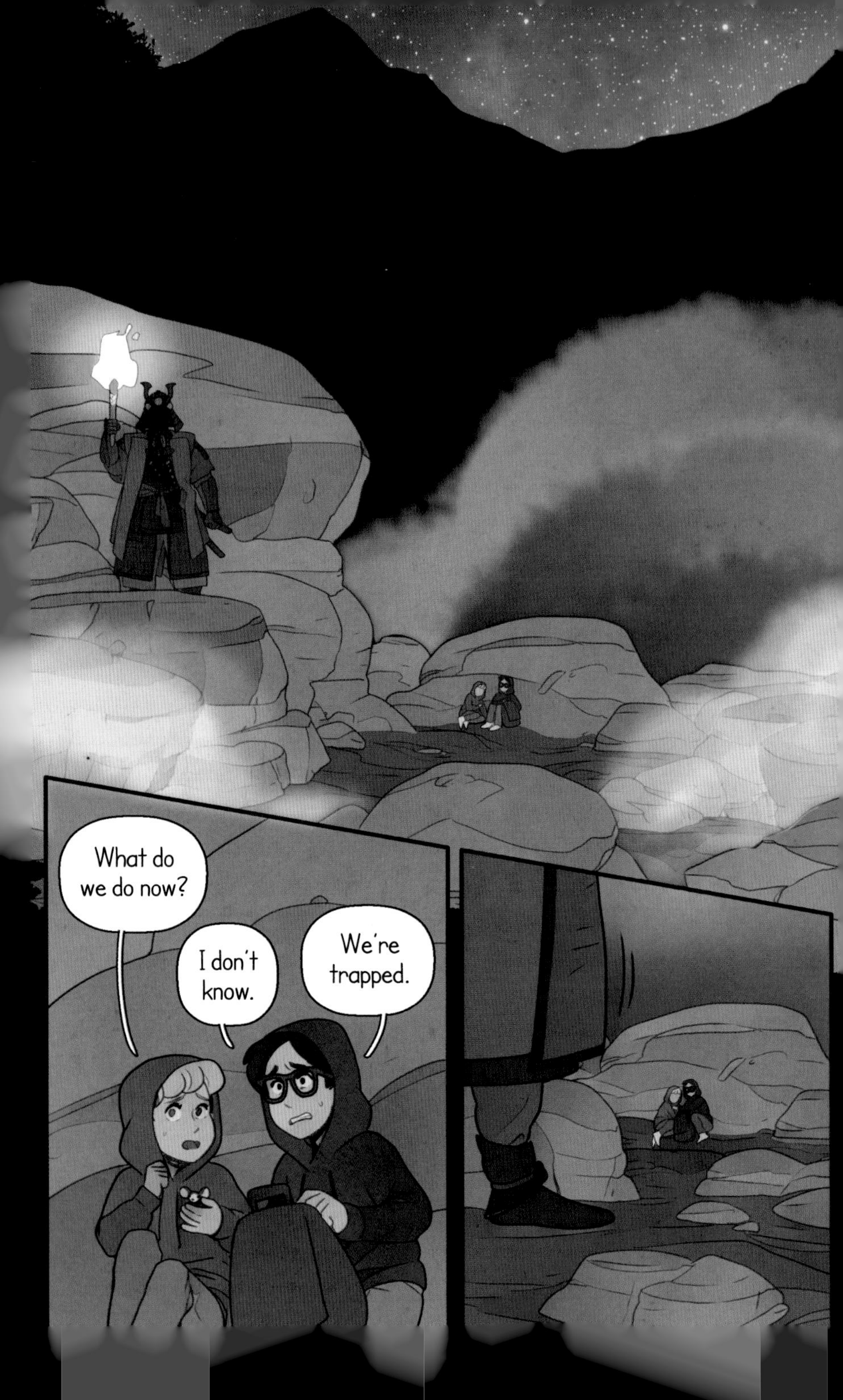
What do we do now?
I don't know.
We're trapped.

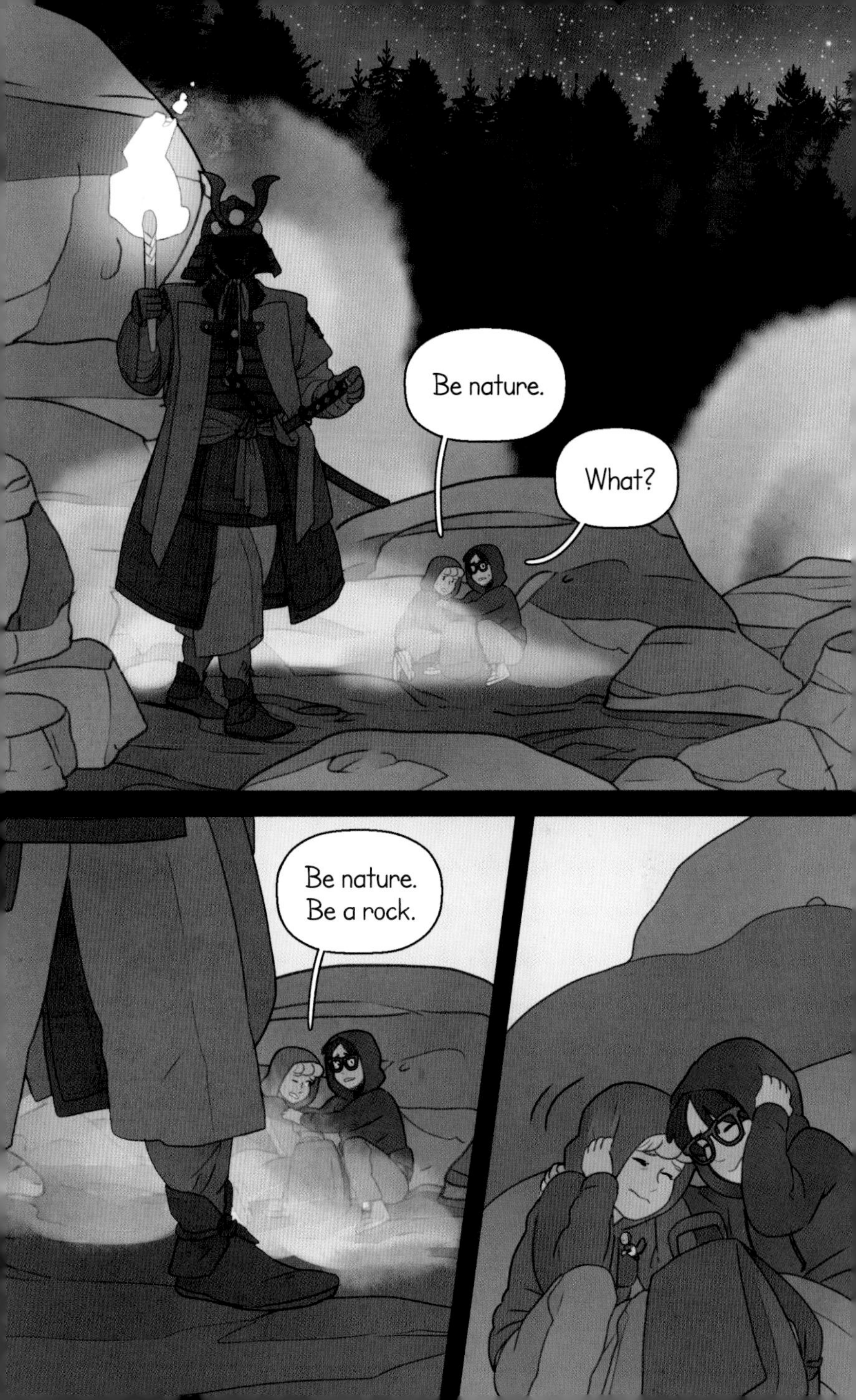
Be nature.
What?
Be nature.
Be a rock.

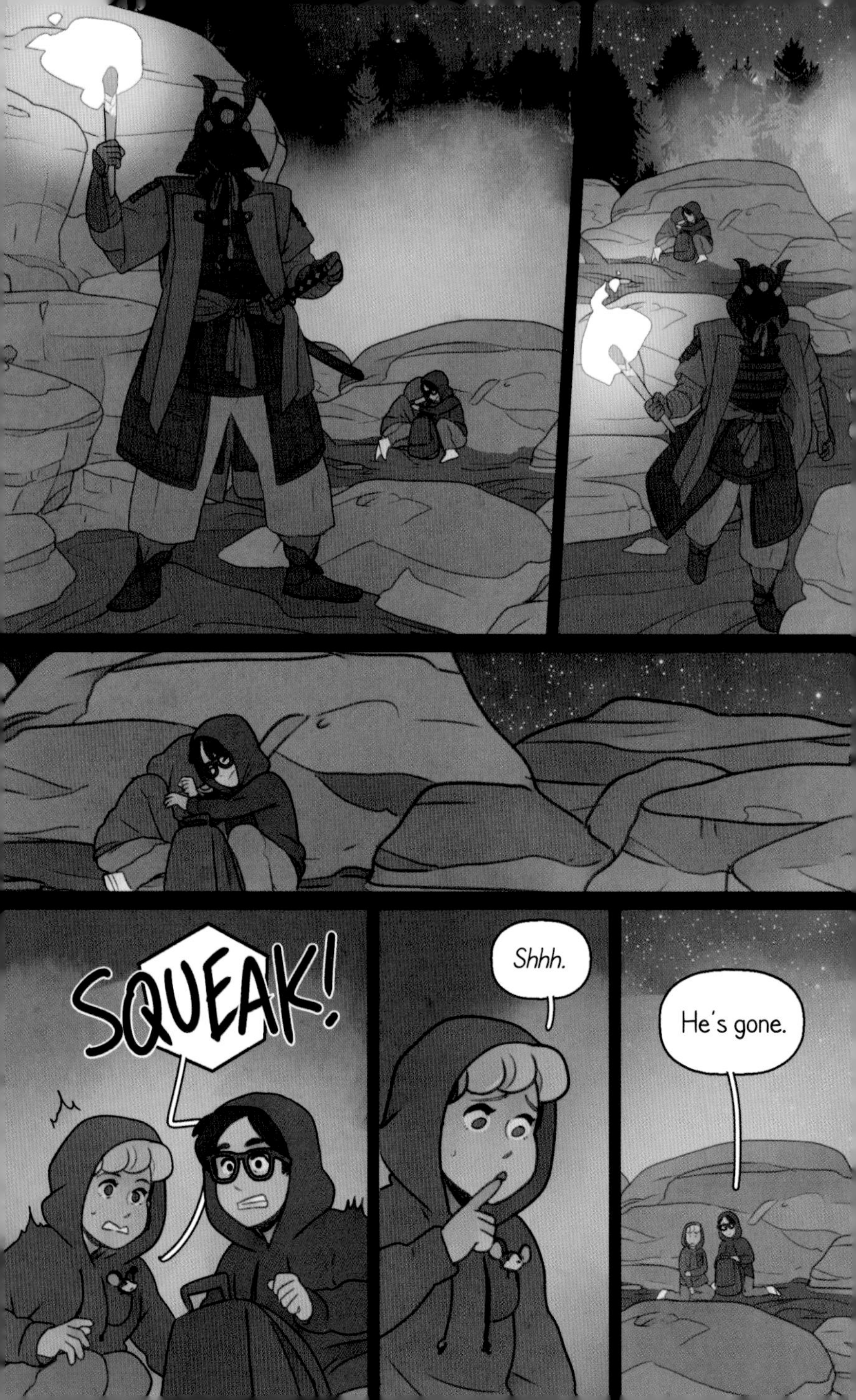
SQUEAK!
Shhh.
He's gone.

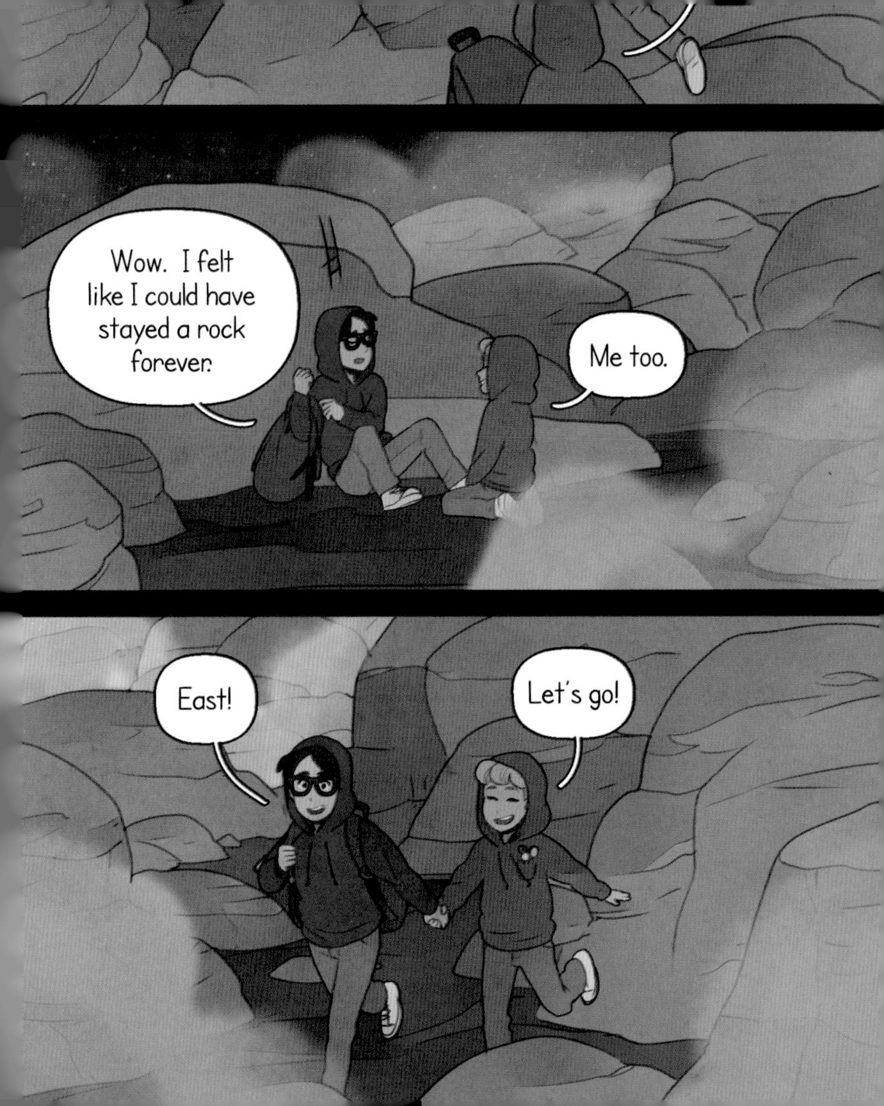
Wow. I felt like I could have stayed a rock forever.
Me too.
East!
Let's go!

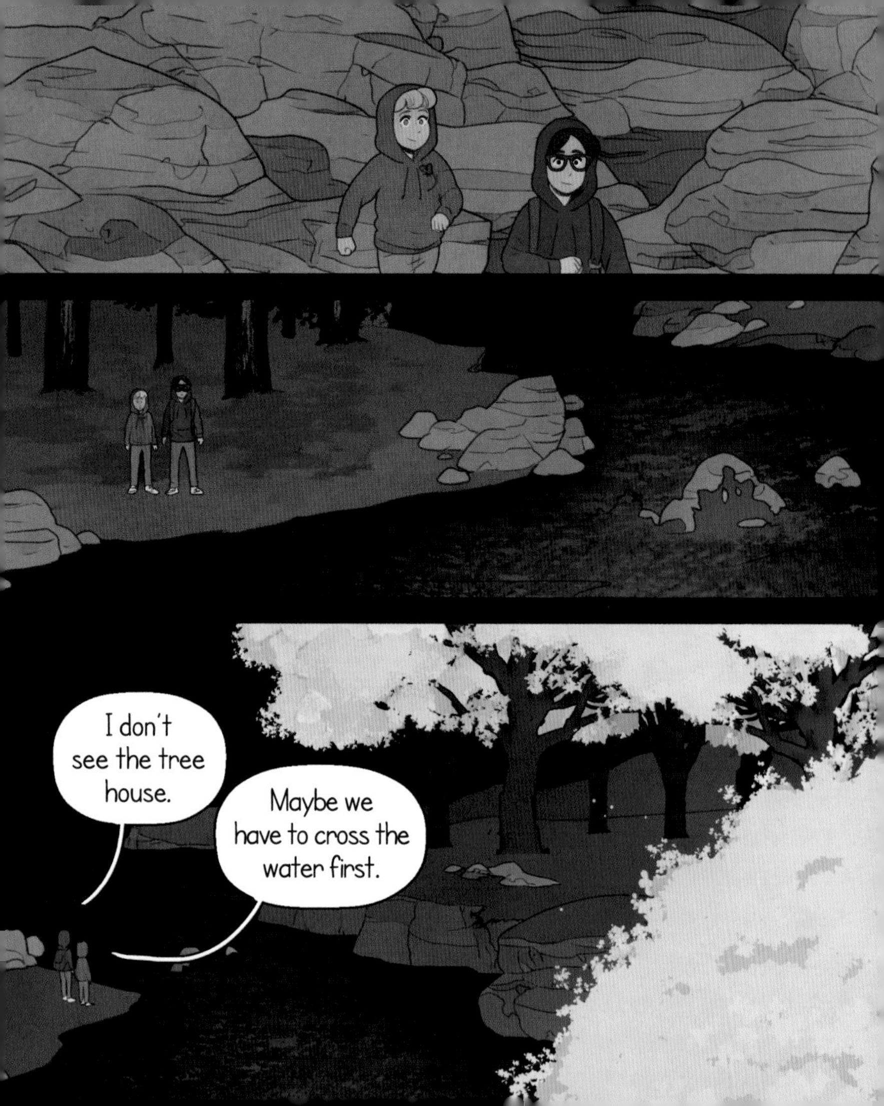
I don't see the tree house.
Maybe we have to cross the water first.

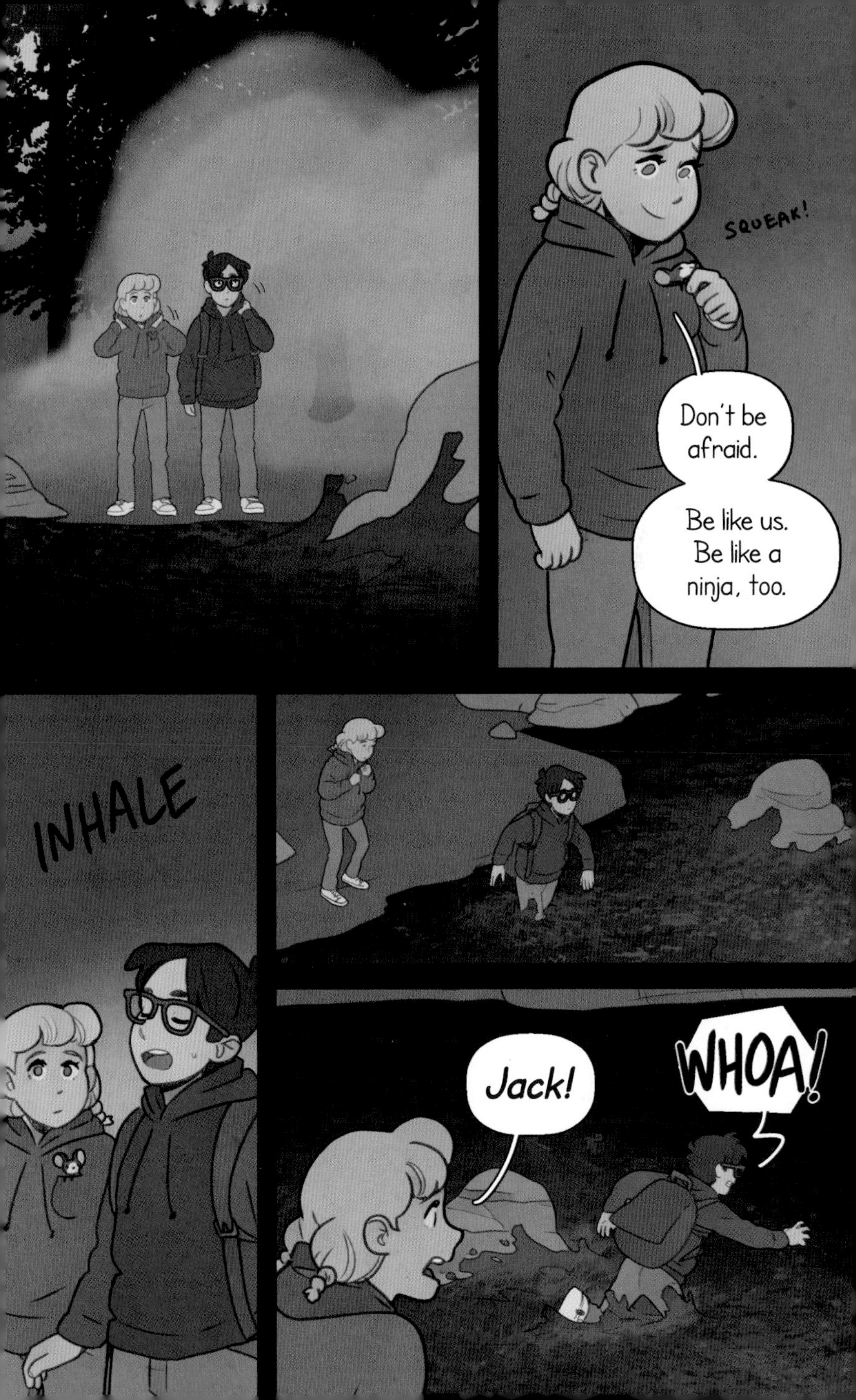
SQUEAK!
Don't be afraid.
Be like us. Be like a ninja, too.
INHALE
Jack!
WHOA!

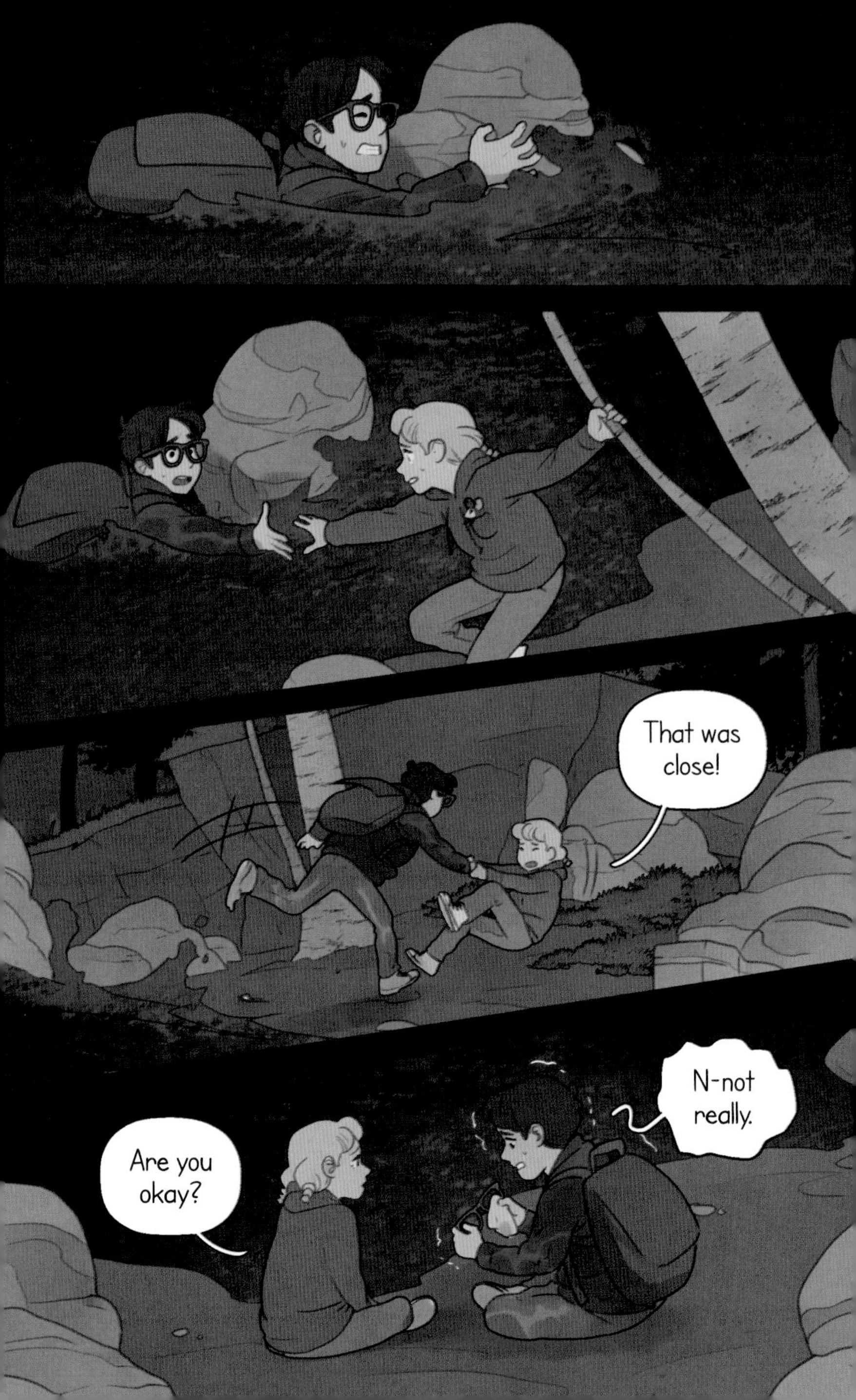
That was close!
Are you okay?
N-not really.

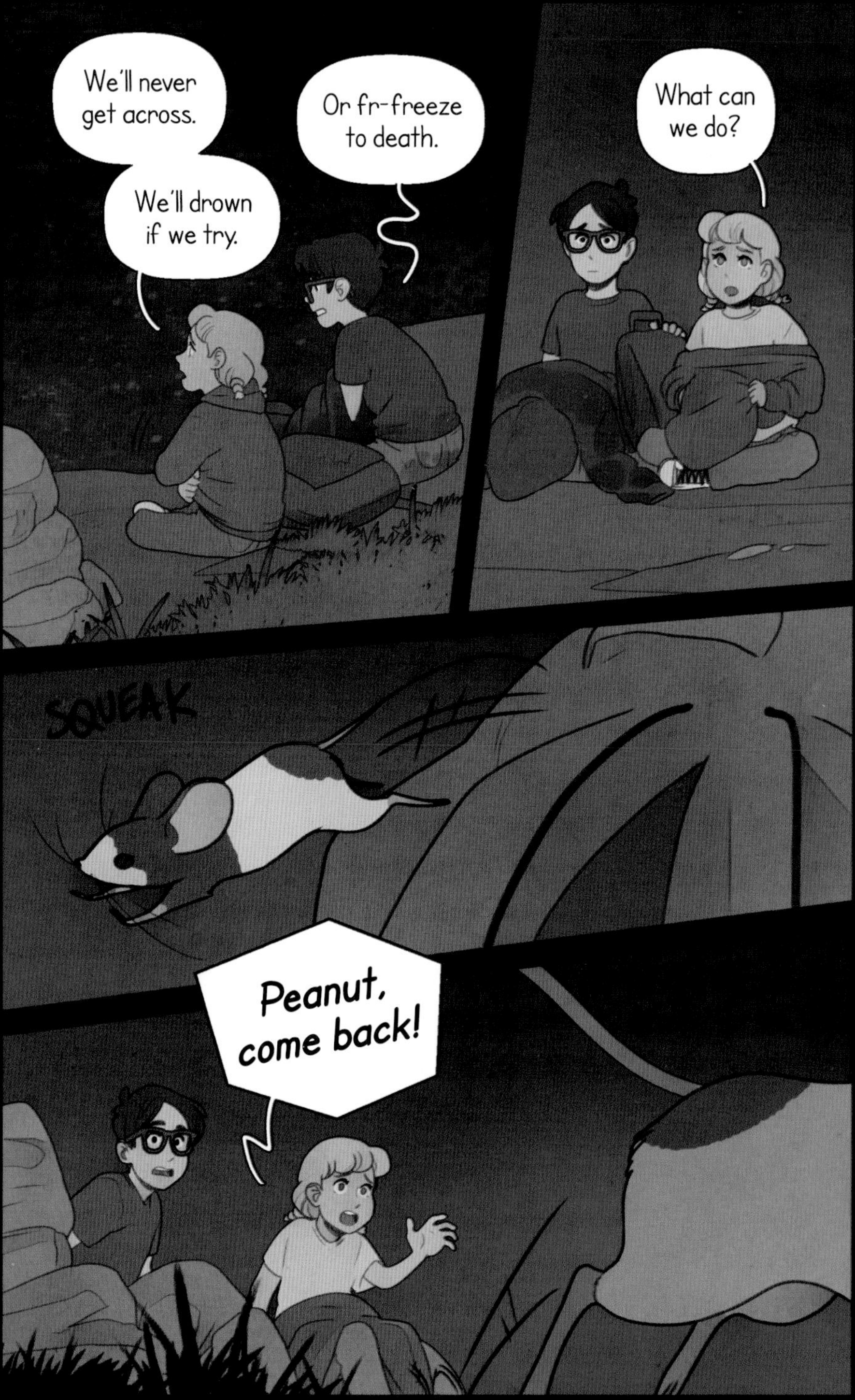
We'll never get across.
We'll drown if we try.
Or fr-freeze to death.
What can we do?
SQUEAK
Peanut, come back!

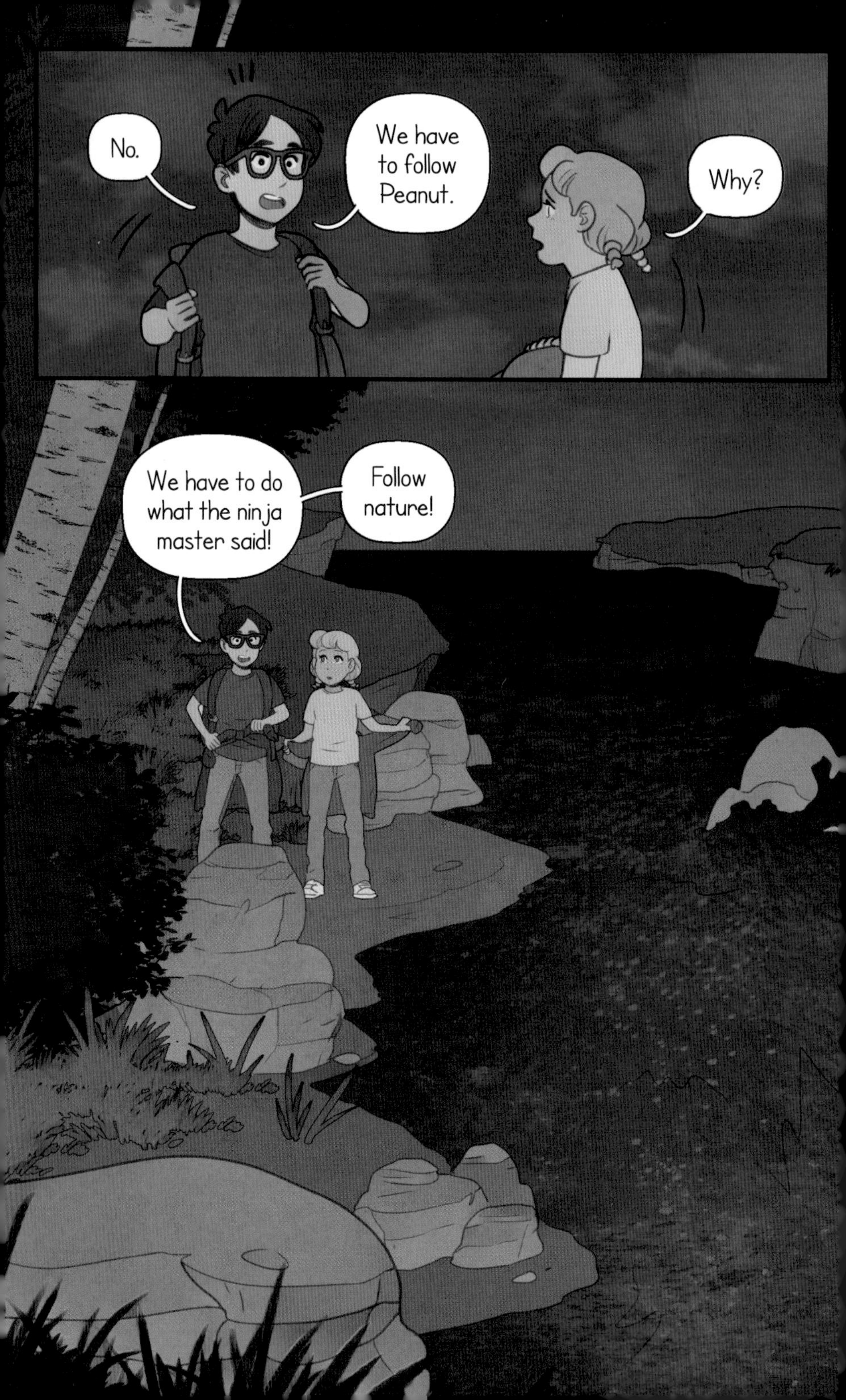
No.
We have to follow Peanut.
Why?
We have to do what the ninja master said!
Follow nature!

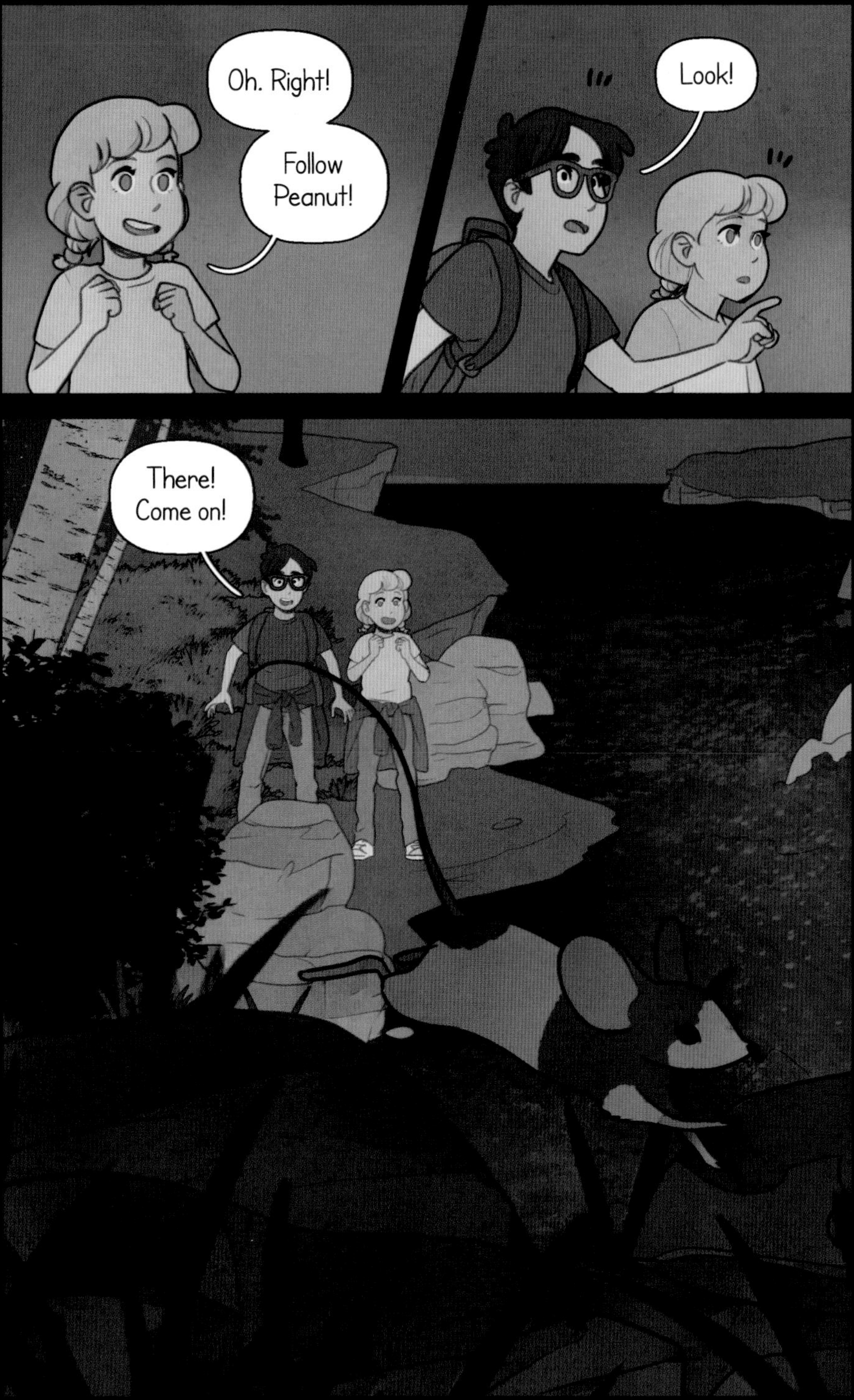
Oh. Right!
Follow Peanut!
Look!
There! Come on!

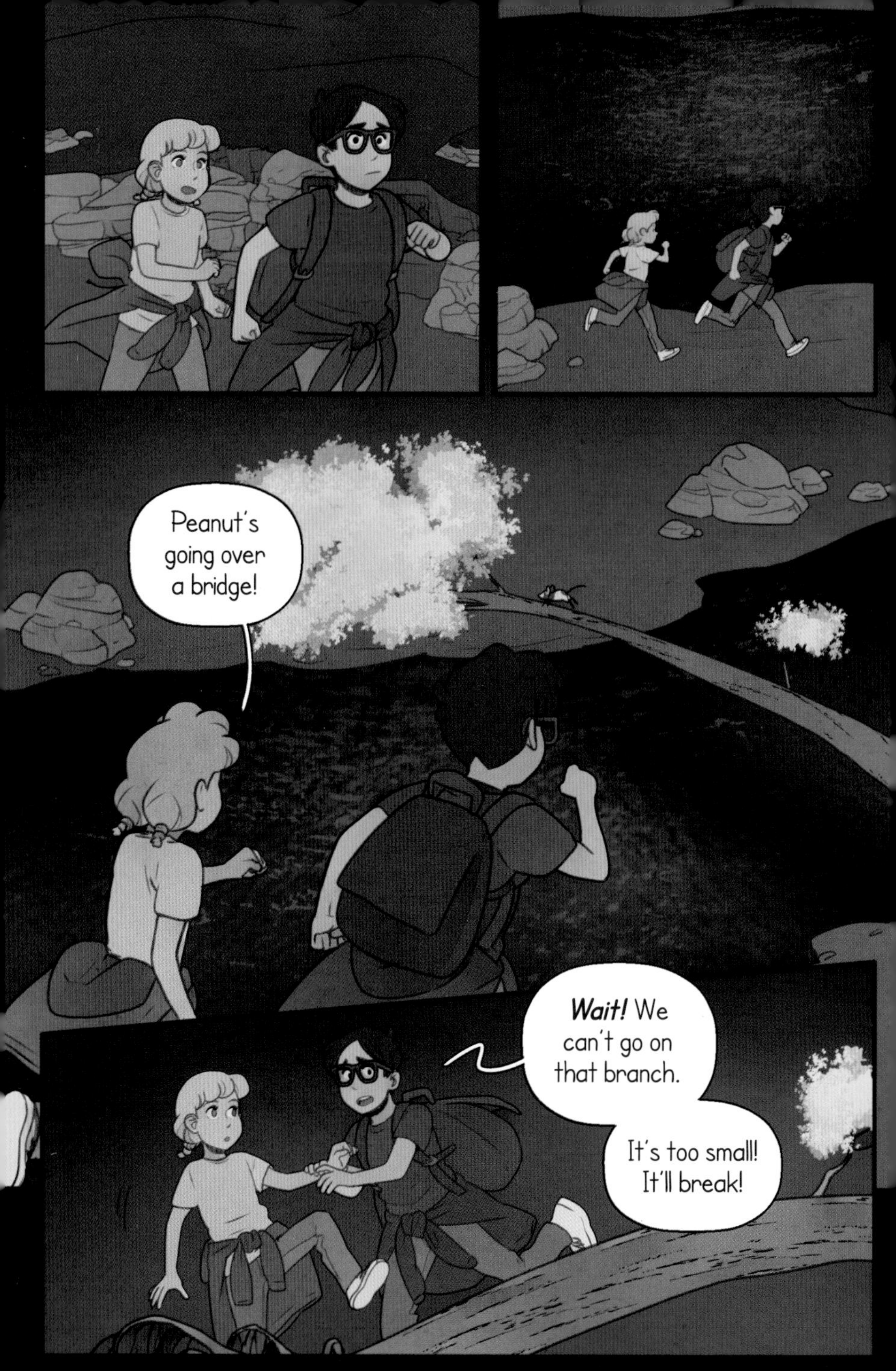
Peanut's going over a bridge!
Wait! We can't go on that branch.
It's too small! It'll break!

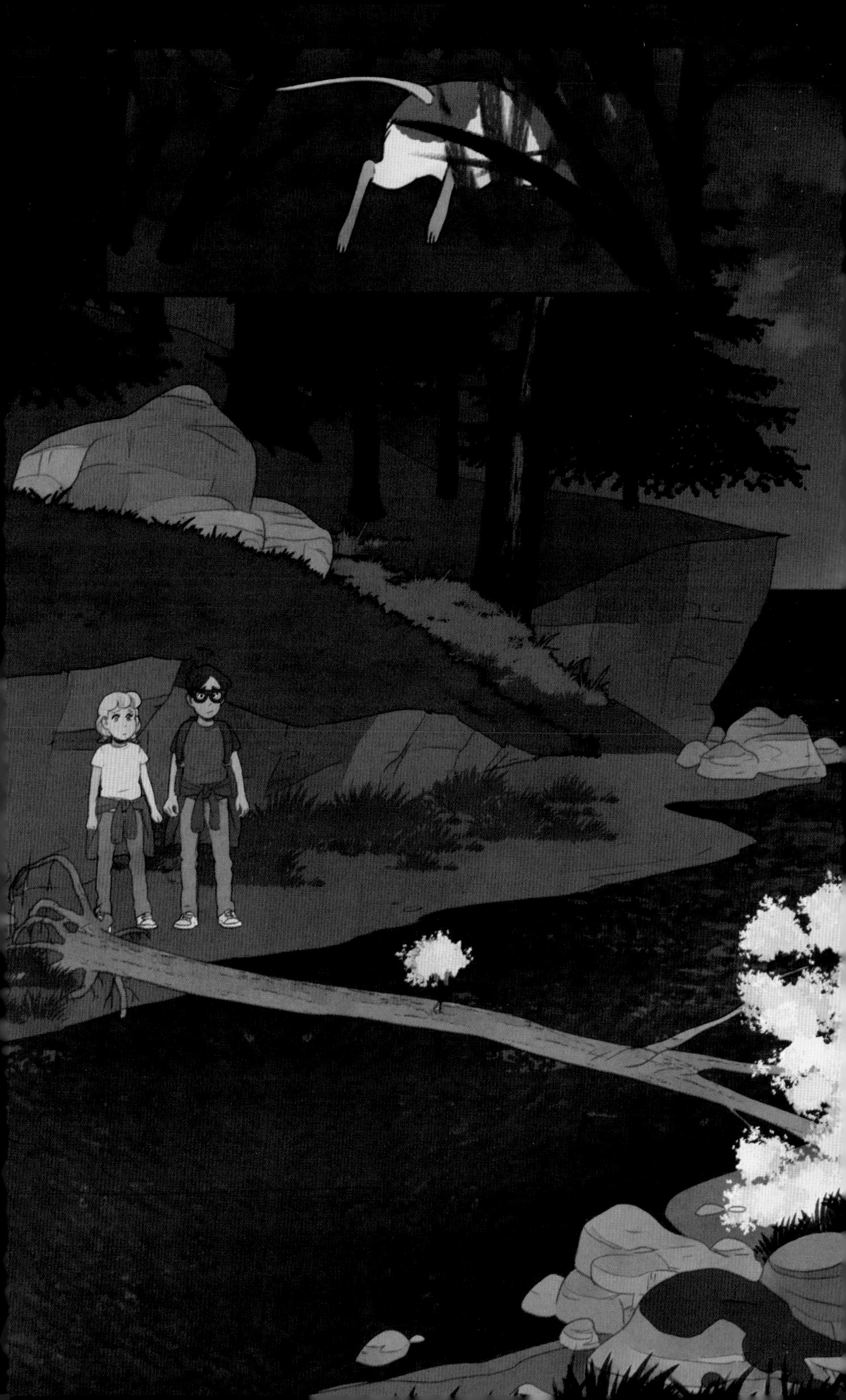

CHAPTER NINE
Mouse-Walk

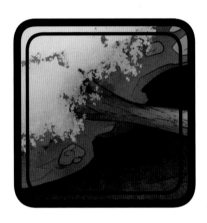

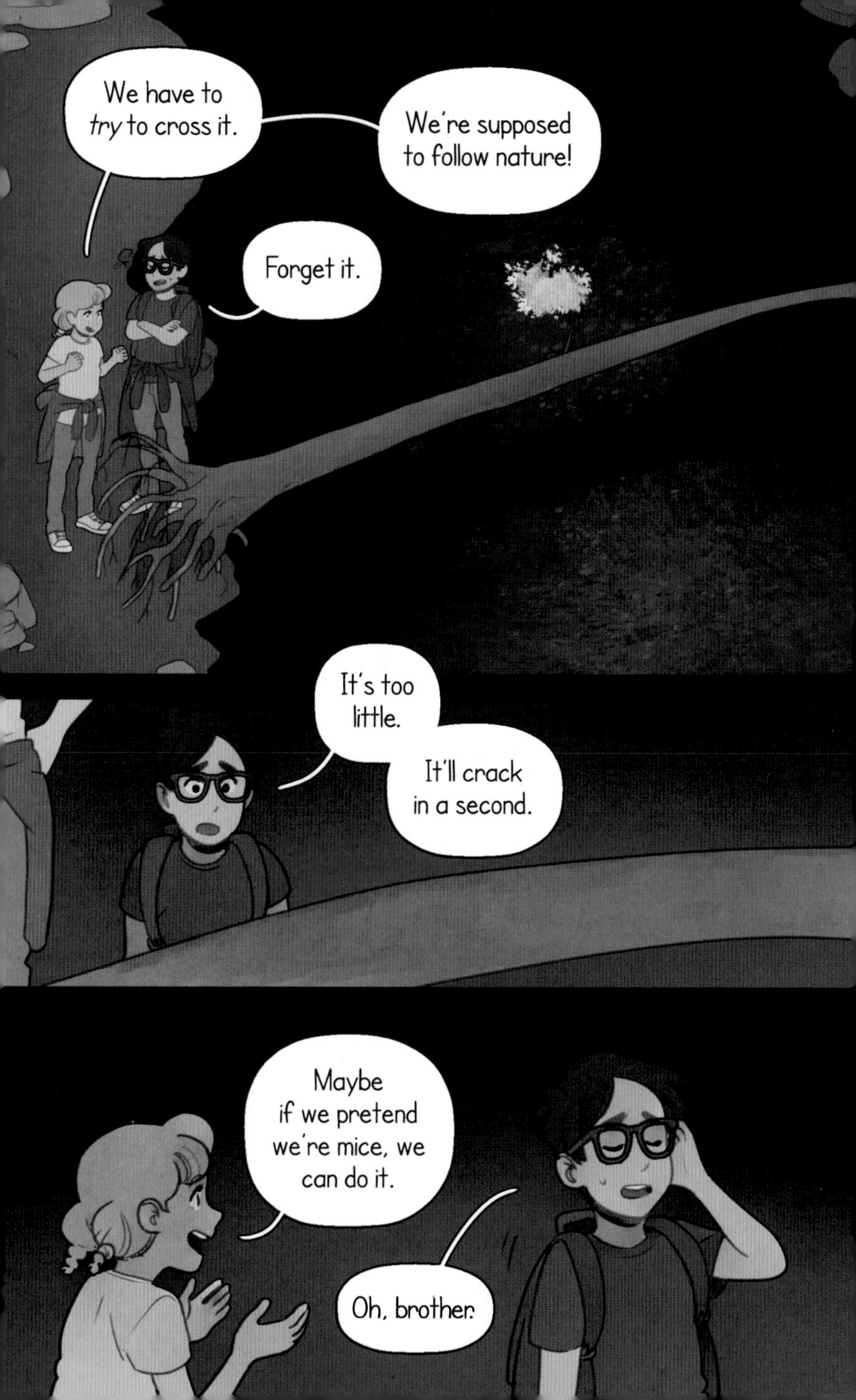
We have to *try* to cross it.
We're supposed to follow nature!
Forget it.
It's too little.
It'll crack in a second.
Maybe if we pretend we're mice, we can do it.
Oh, brother.

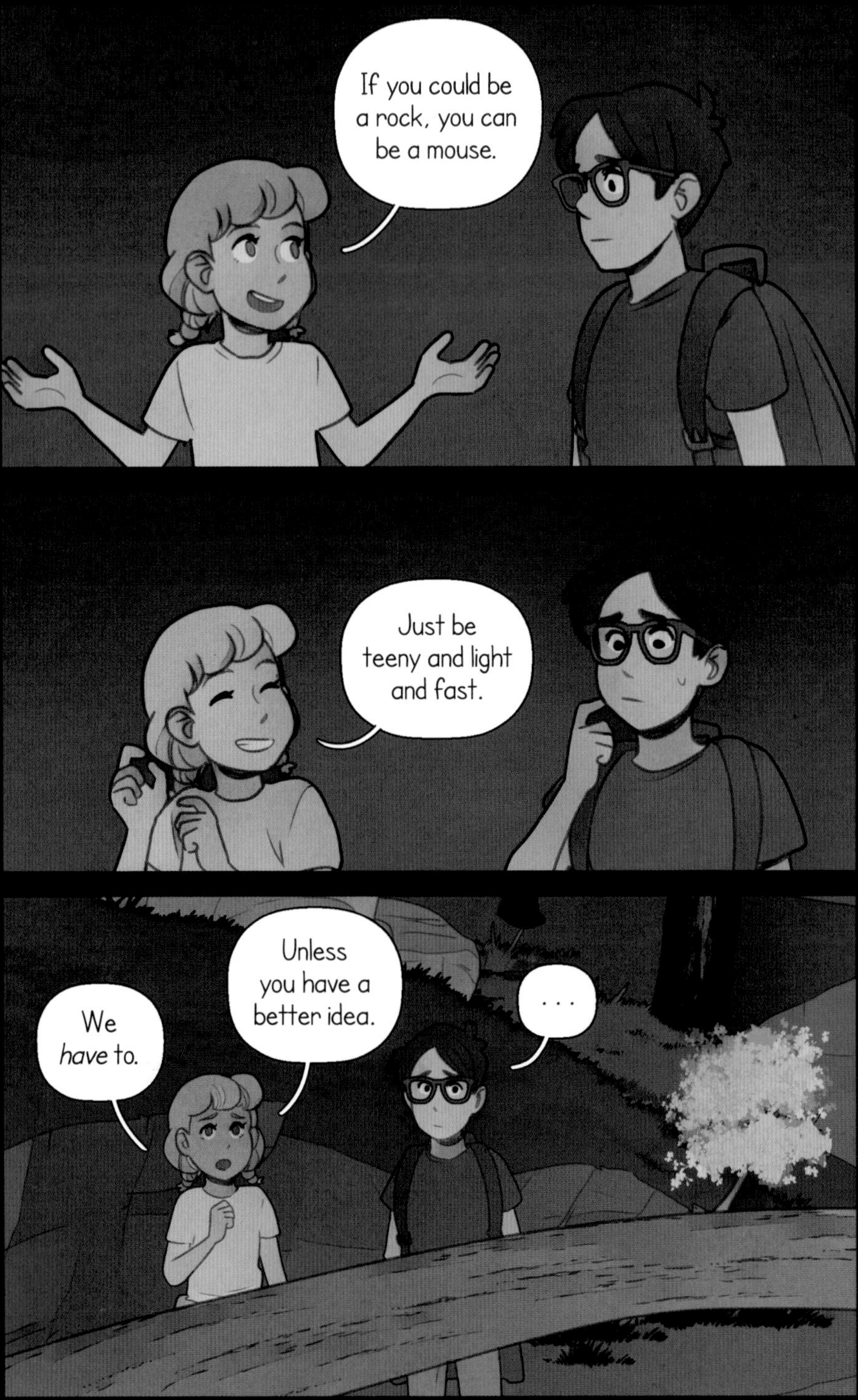
If you could be a rock, you can be a mouse.
Just be teeny and light and fast.
We *have* to.
Unless you have a better idea.
. . .

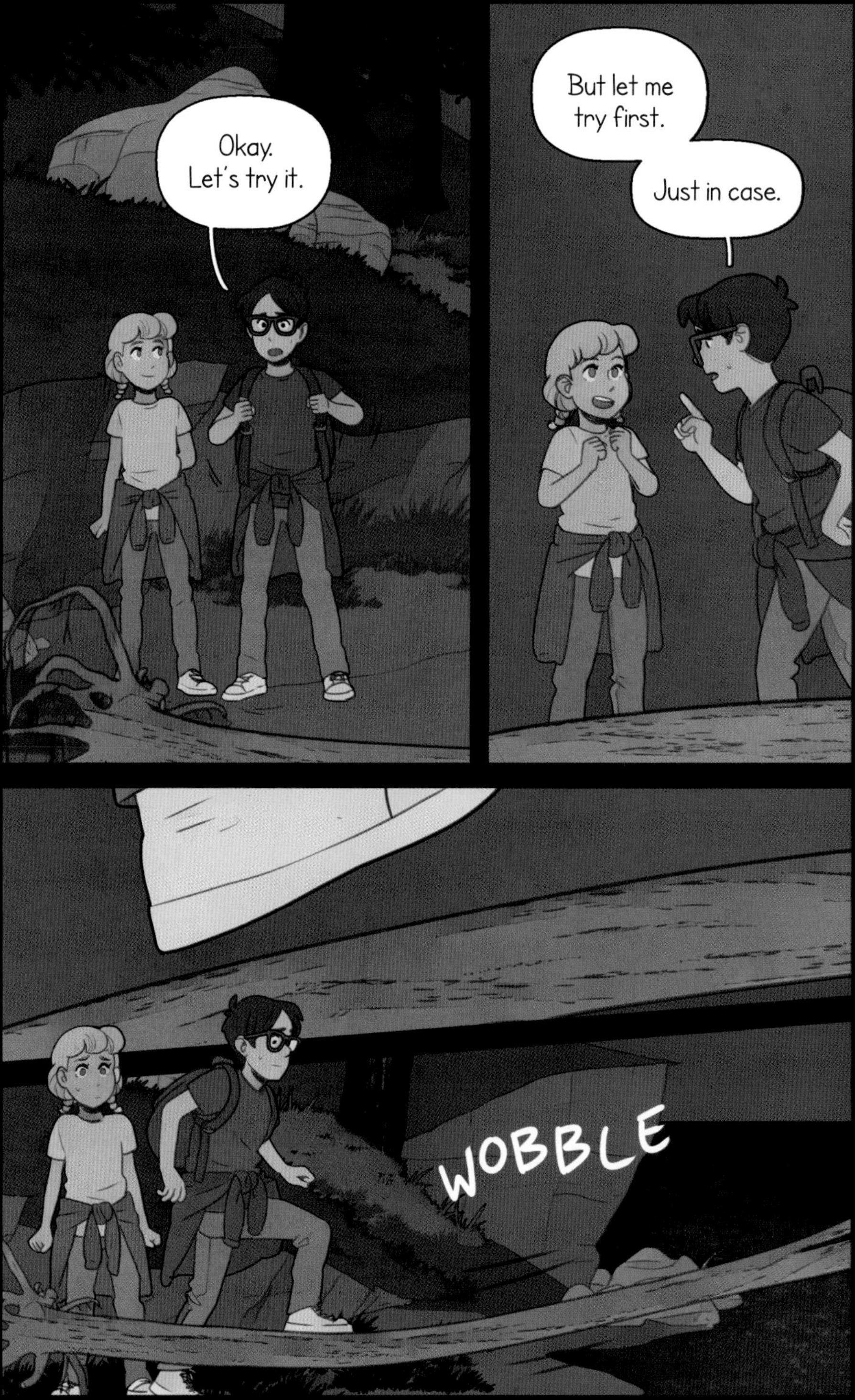
Okay.
Let's try it.
But let me
try first.
Just in case.
WOBBLE

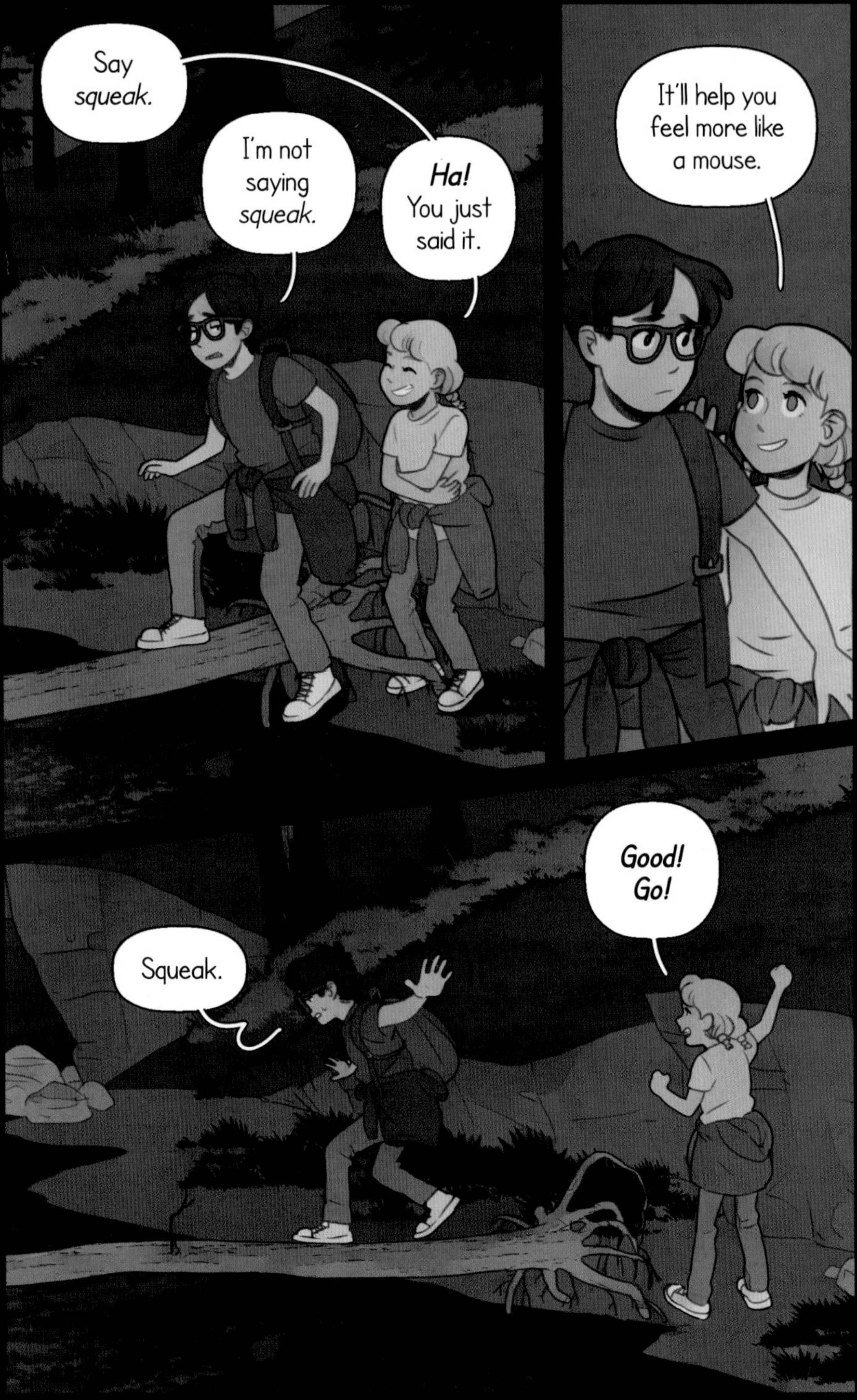
Say *squeak.*
I'm not saying *squeak.*
Ha! You just said it.
It'll help you feel more like a mouse.
Squeak.
Good! Go!

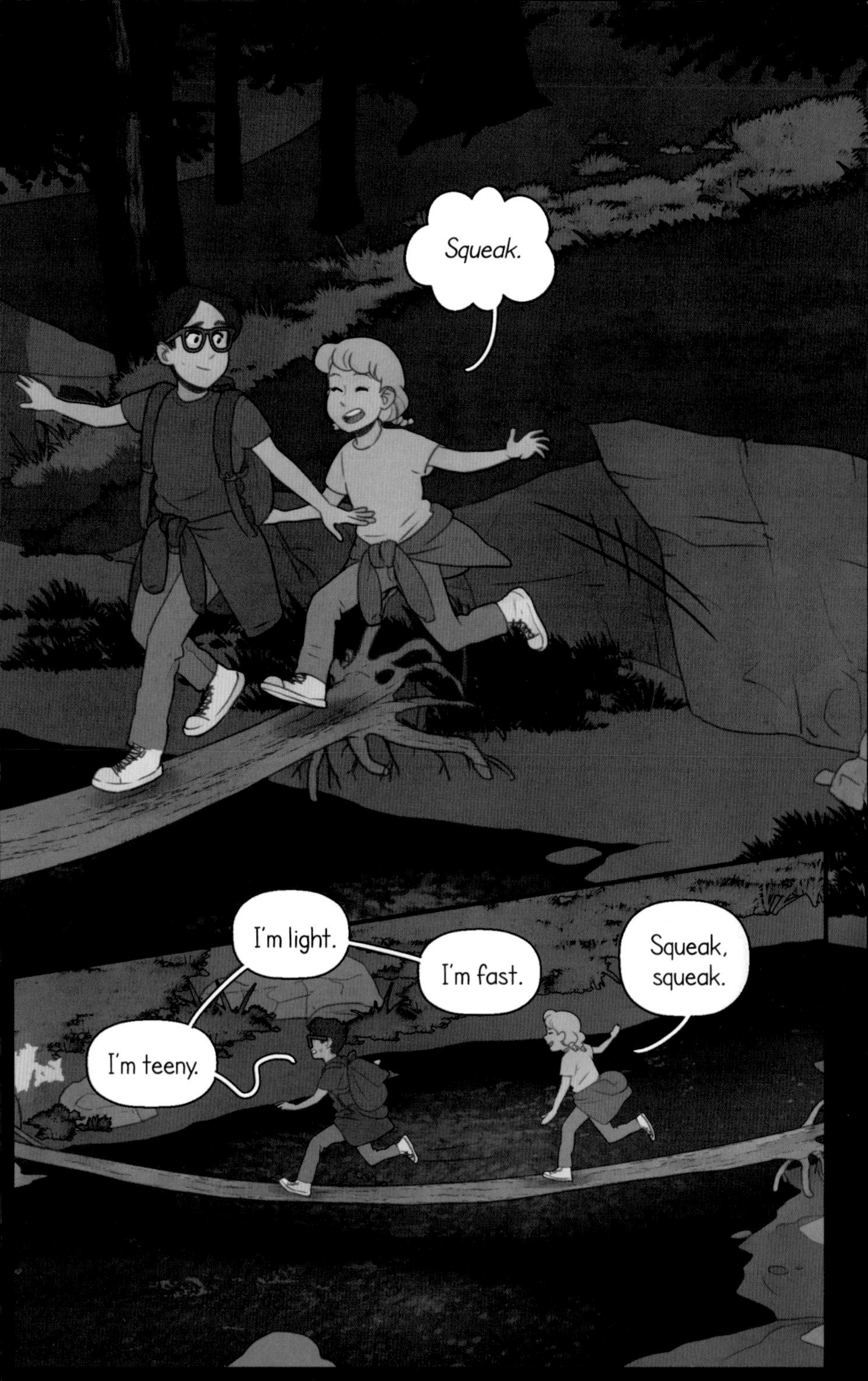
Squeak.
I'm light.
I'm fast.
I'm teeny.
Squeak,
squeak.

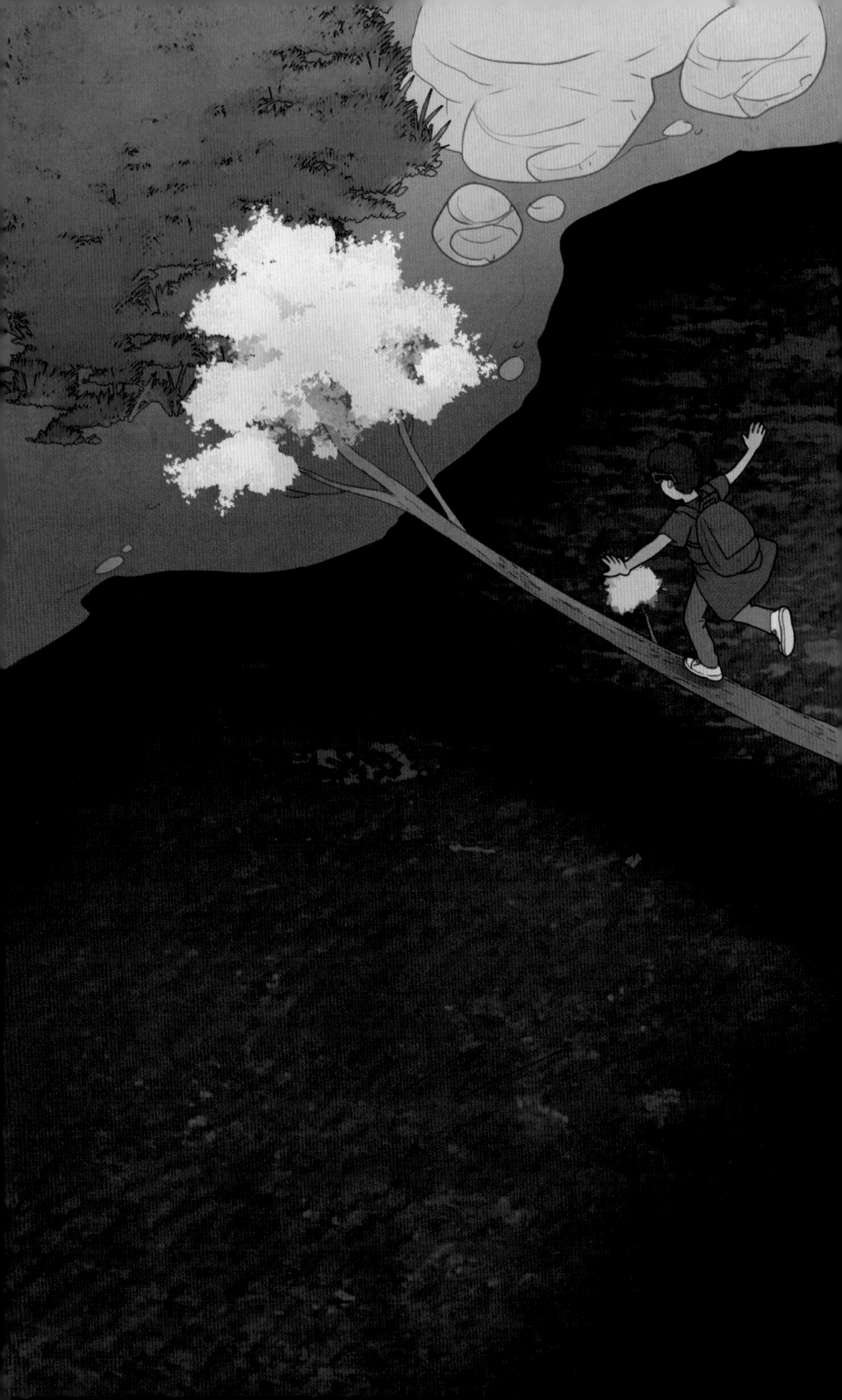

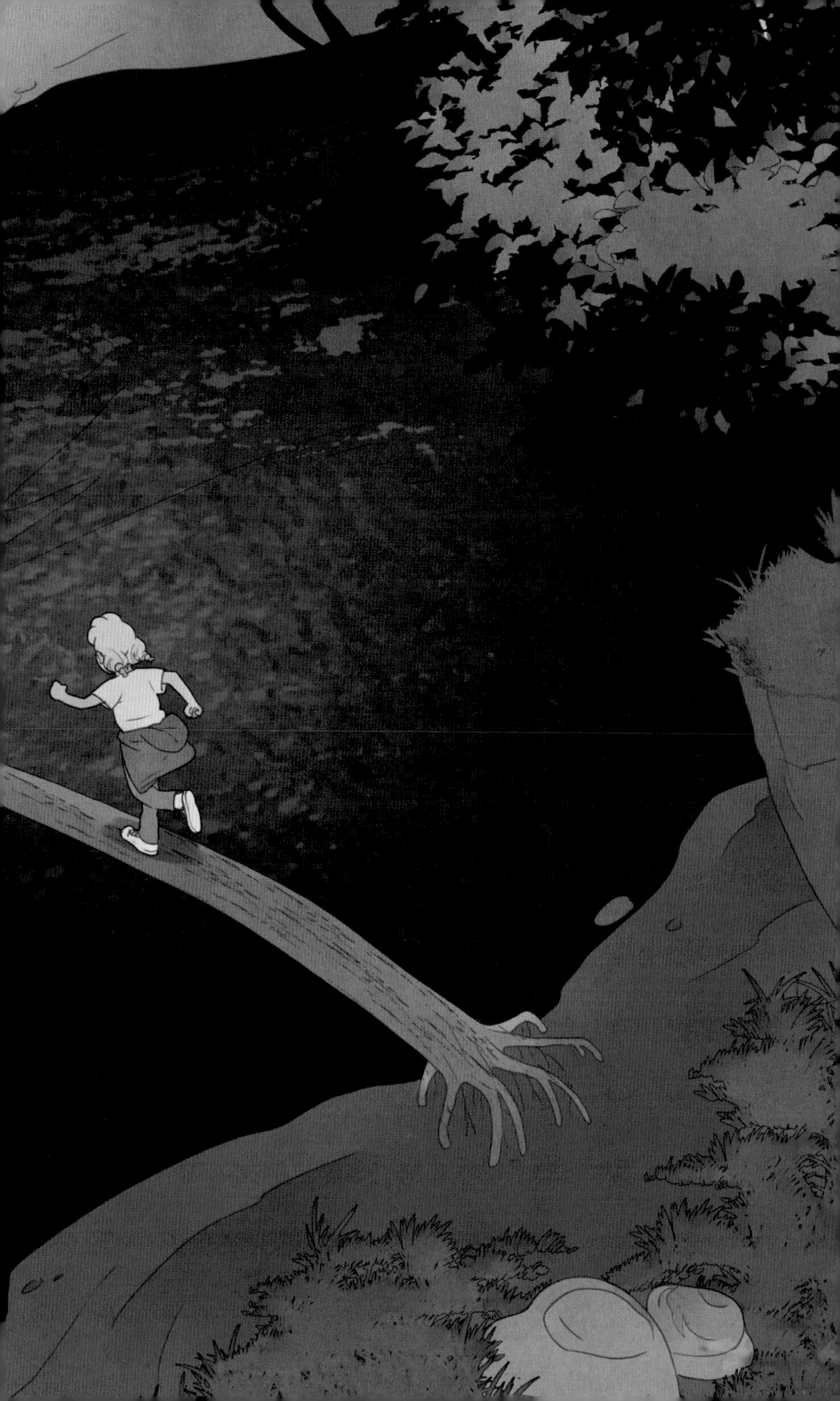

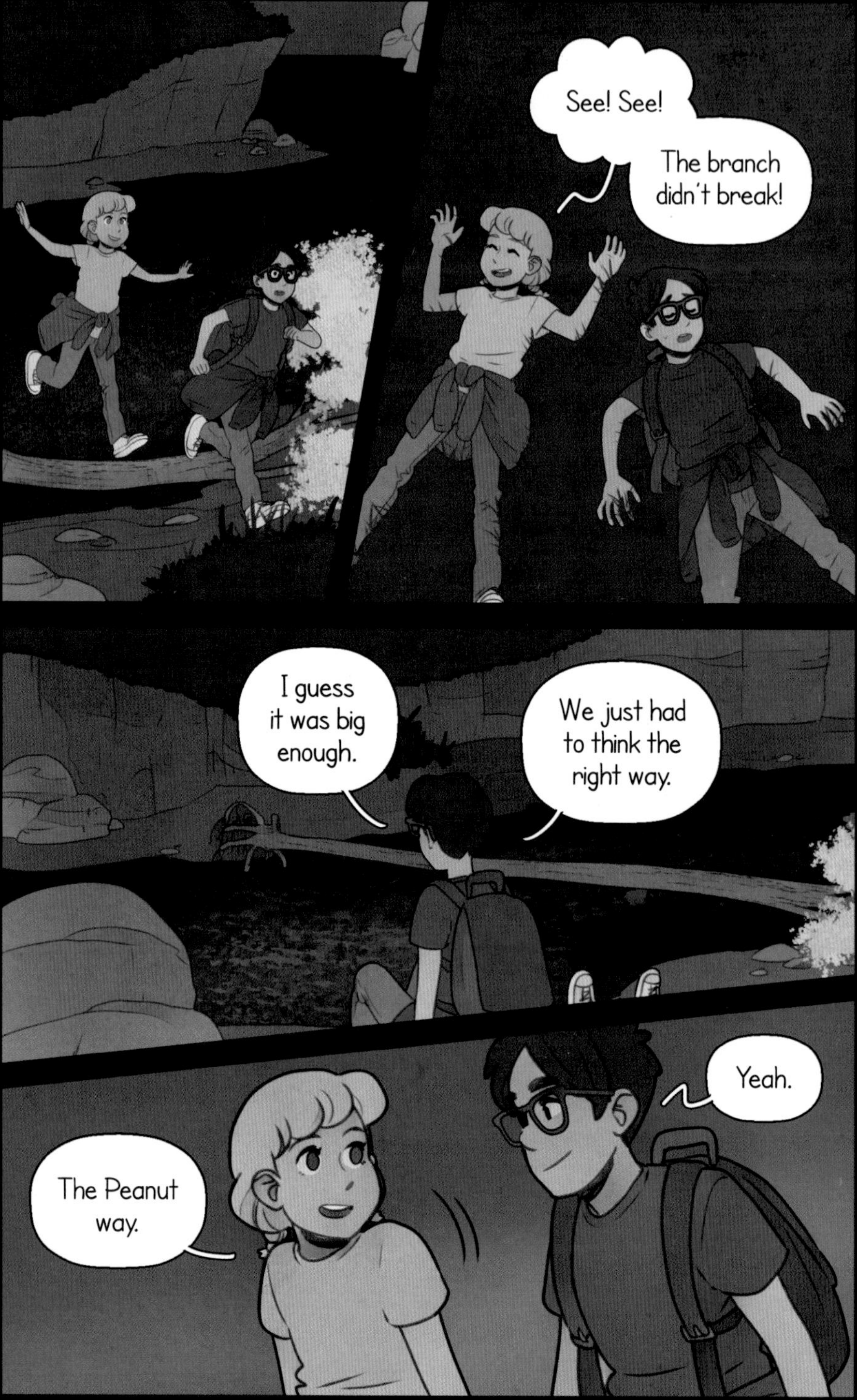
See! See!
The branch didn't break!
I guess it was big enough.
We just had to think the right way.
The Peanut way.
Yeah.

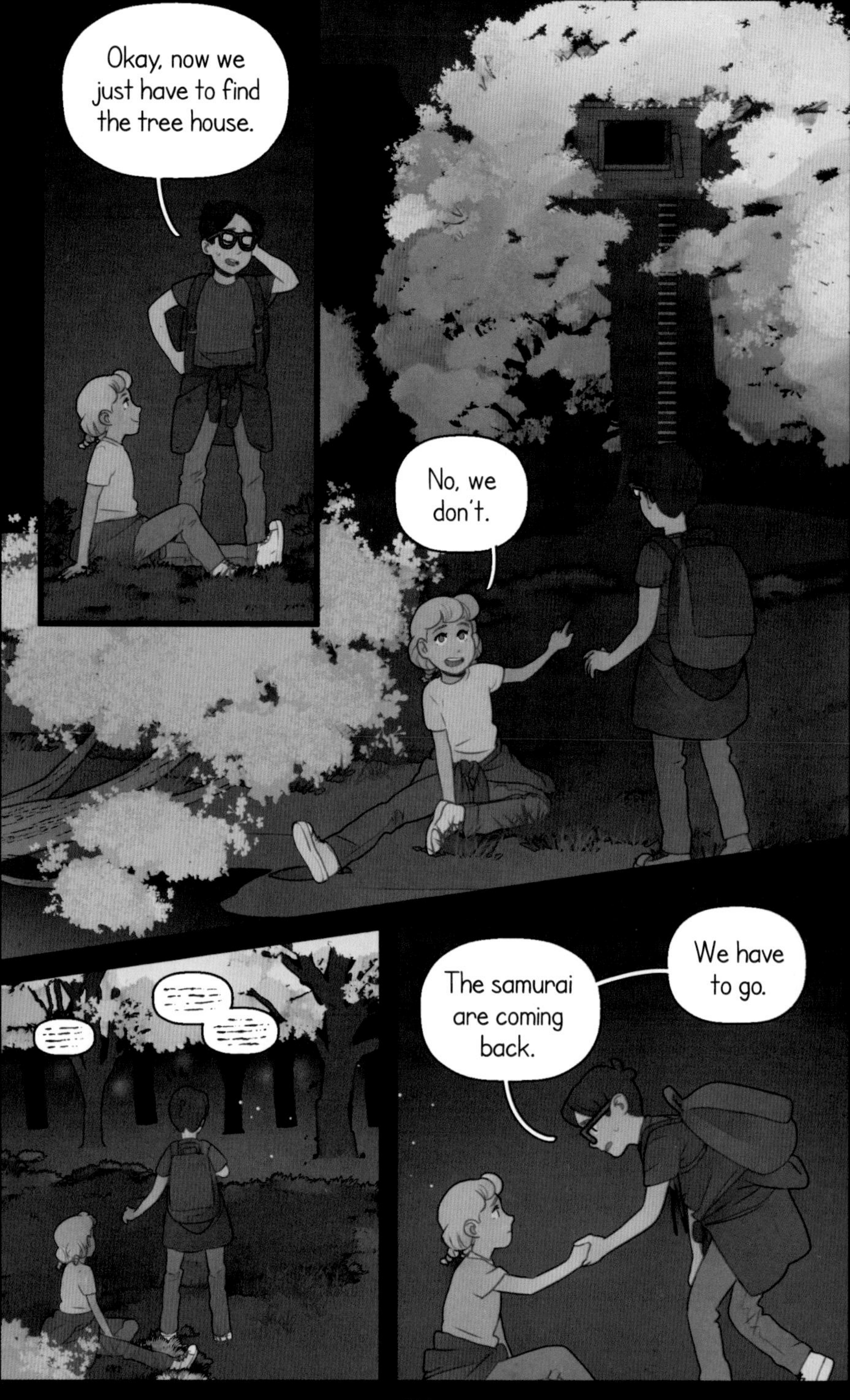

Okay, now we just have to find the tree house.
No, we don't.
The samurai are coming back.
We have to go.

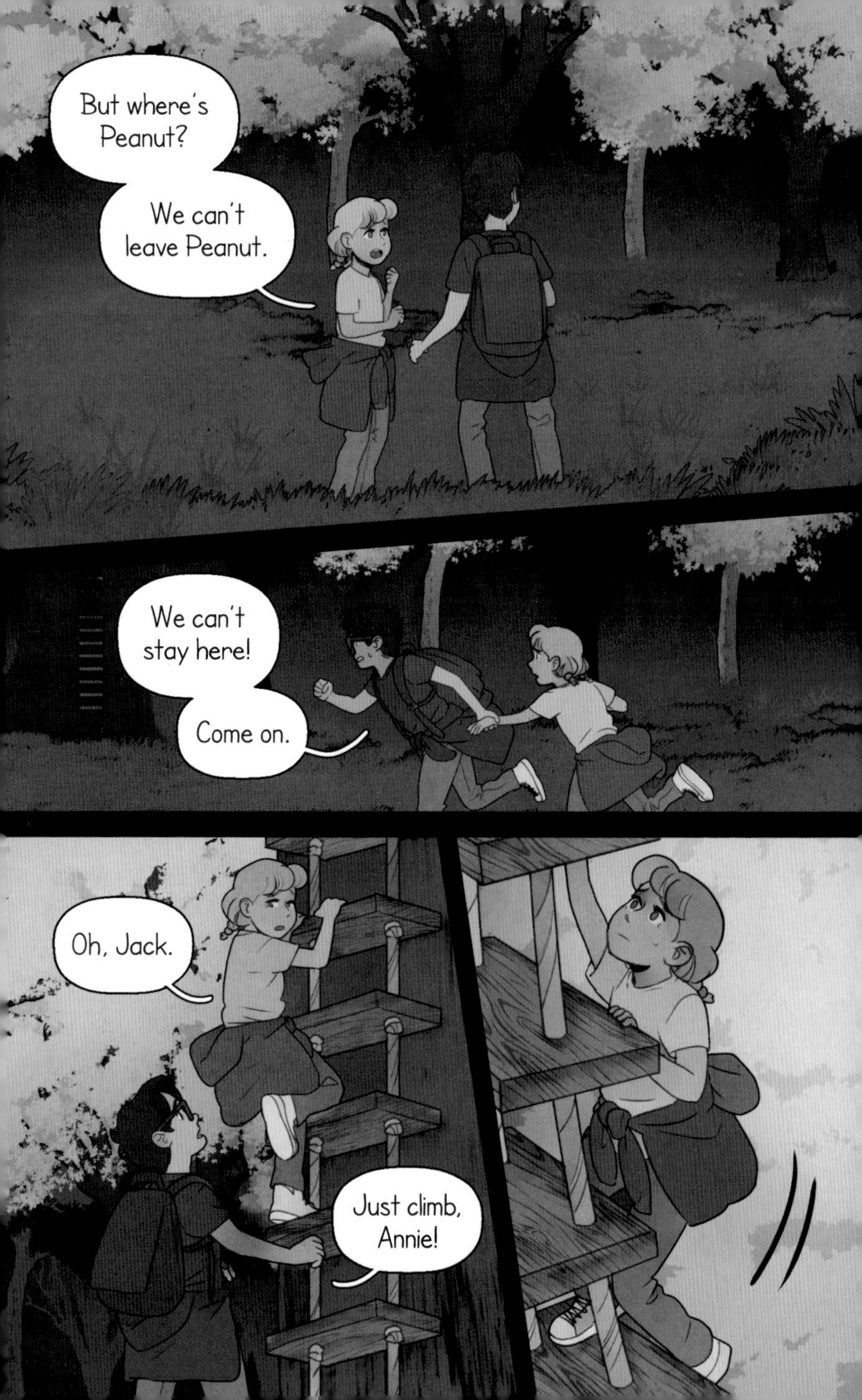
But where's Peanut?
We can't leave Peanut.
We can't stay here!
Come on.
Oh, Jack.
Just climb, Annie!

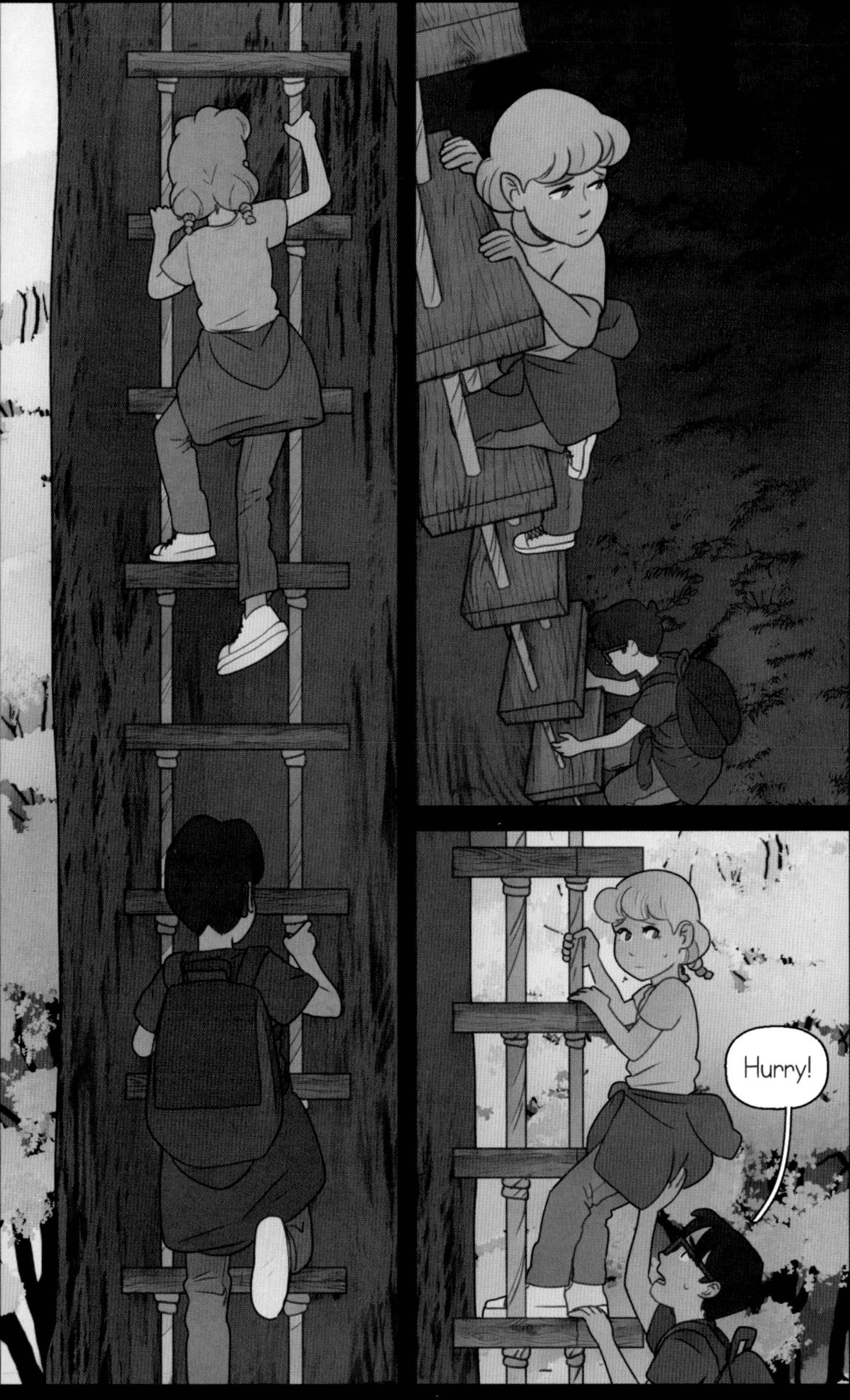
Hurry!

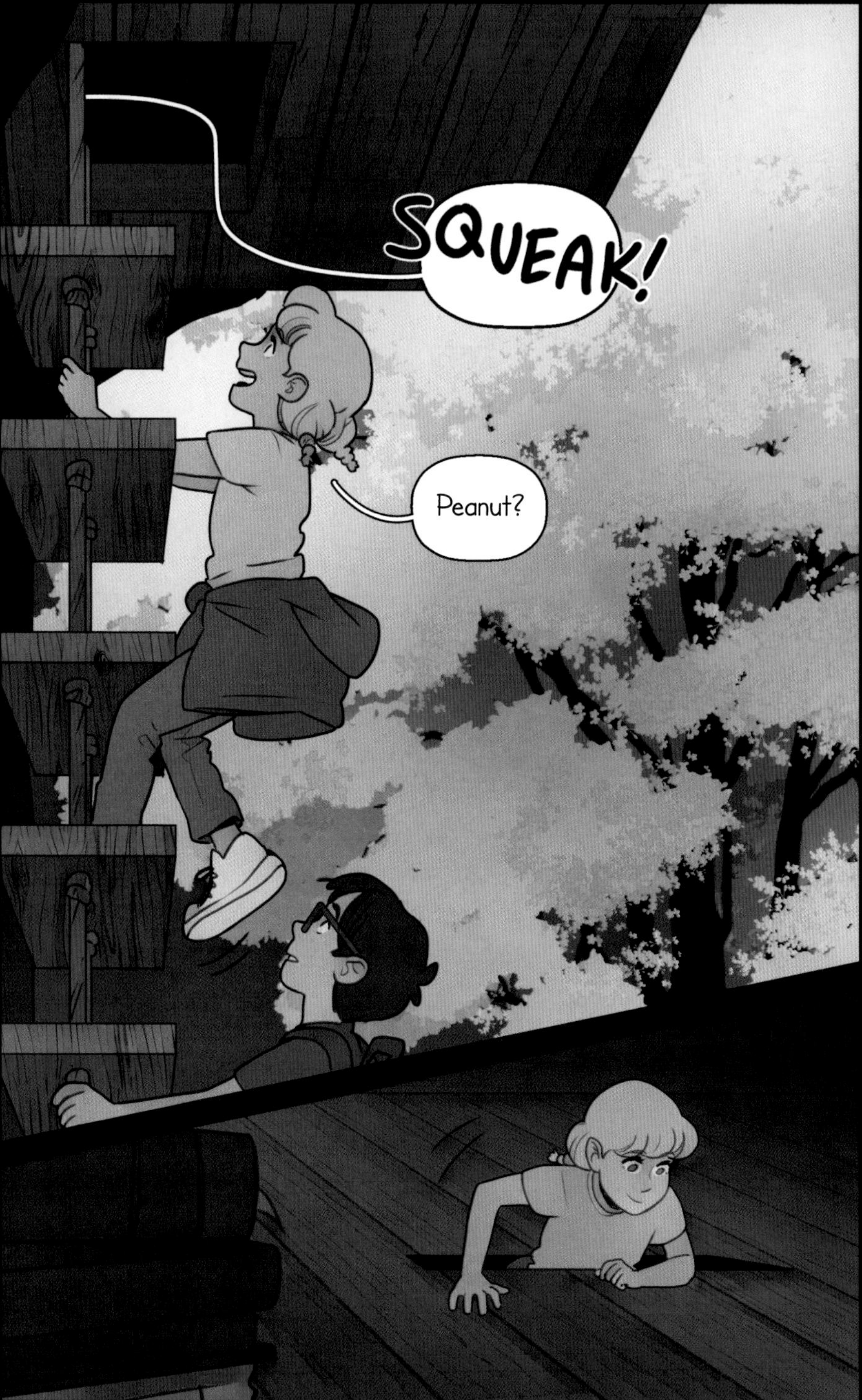
SQUEAK!
Peanut?

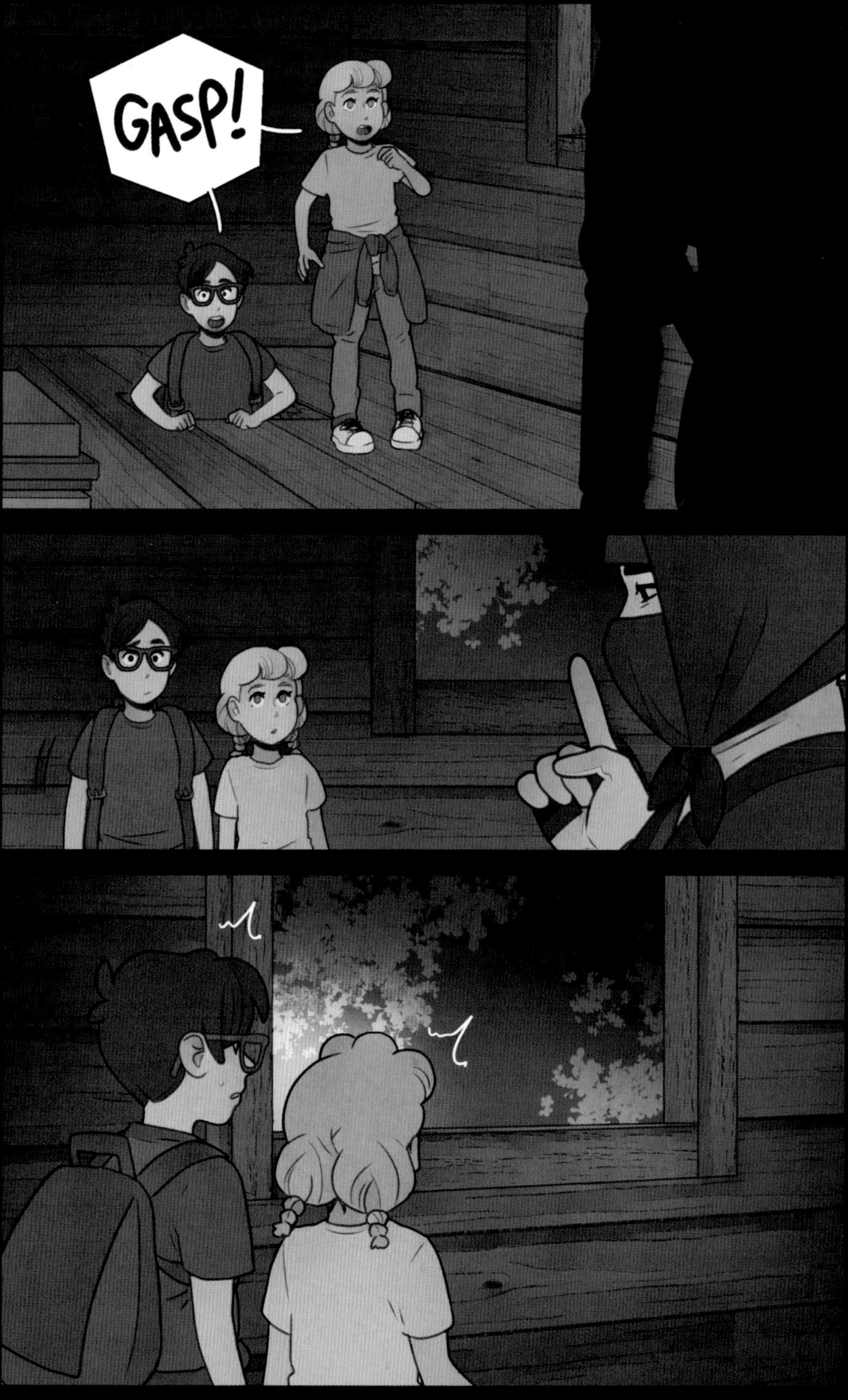
GASP!

CHAPTER TEN
'Night, Peanut

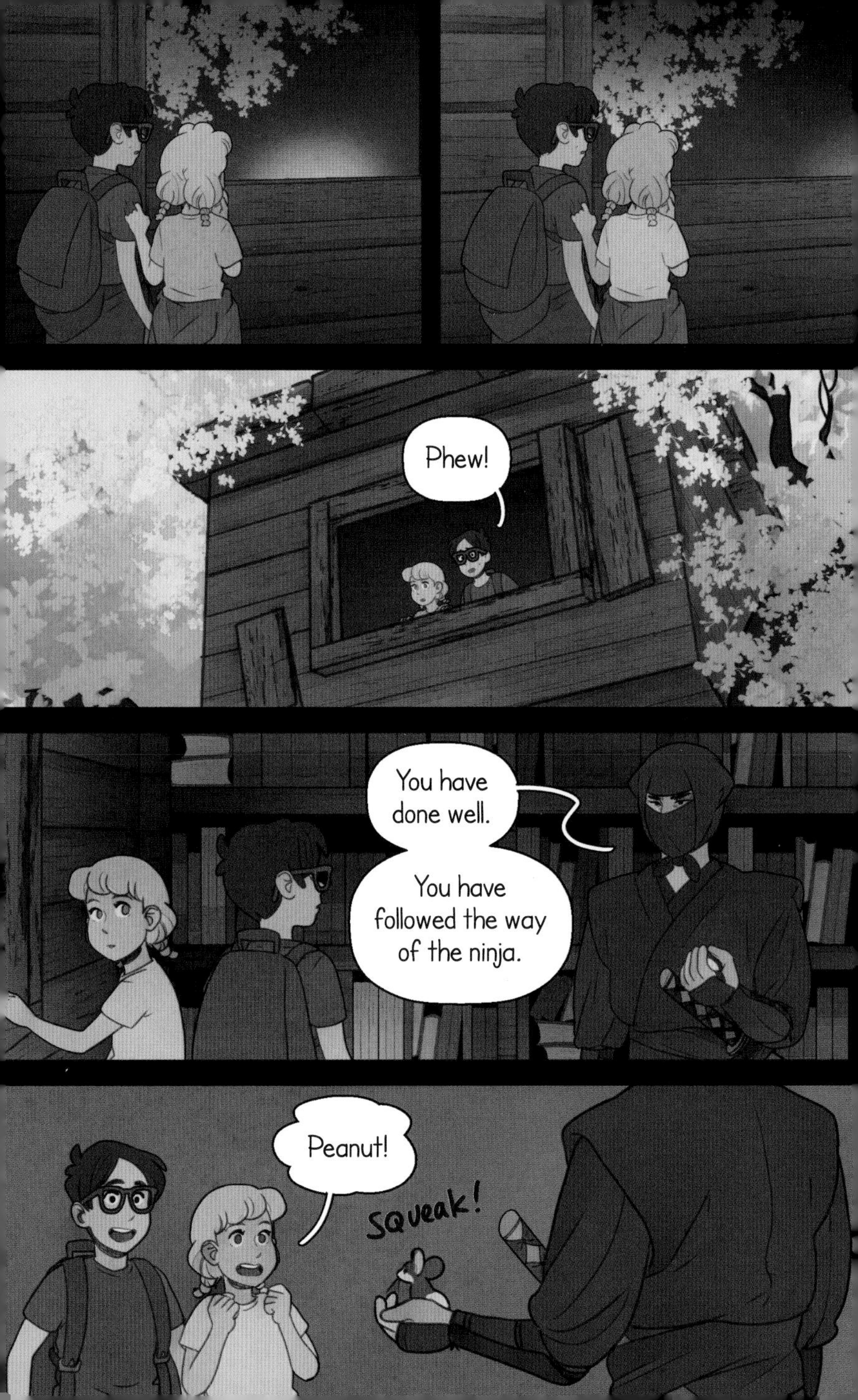
Phew!
You have done well.
You have followed the way of the ninja.
Peanut!
Squeak!

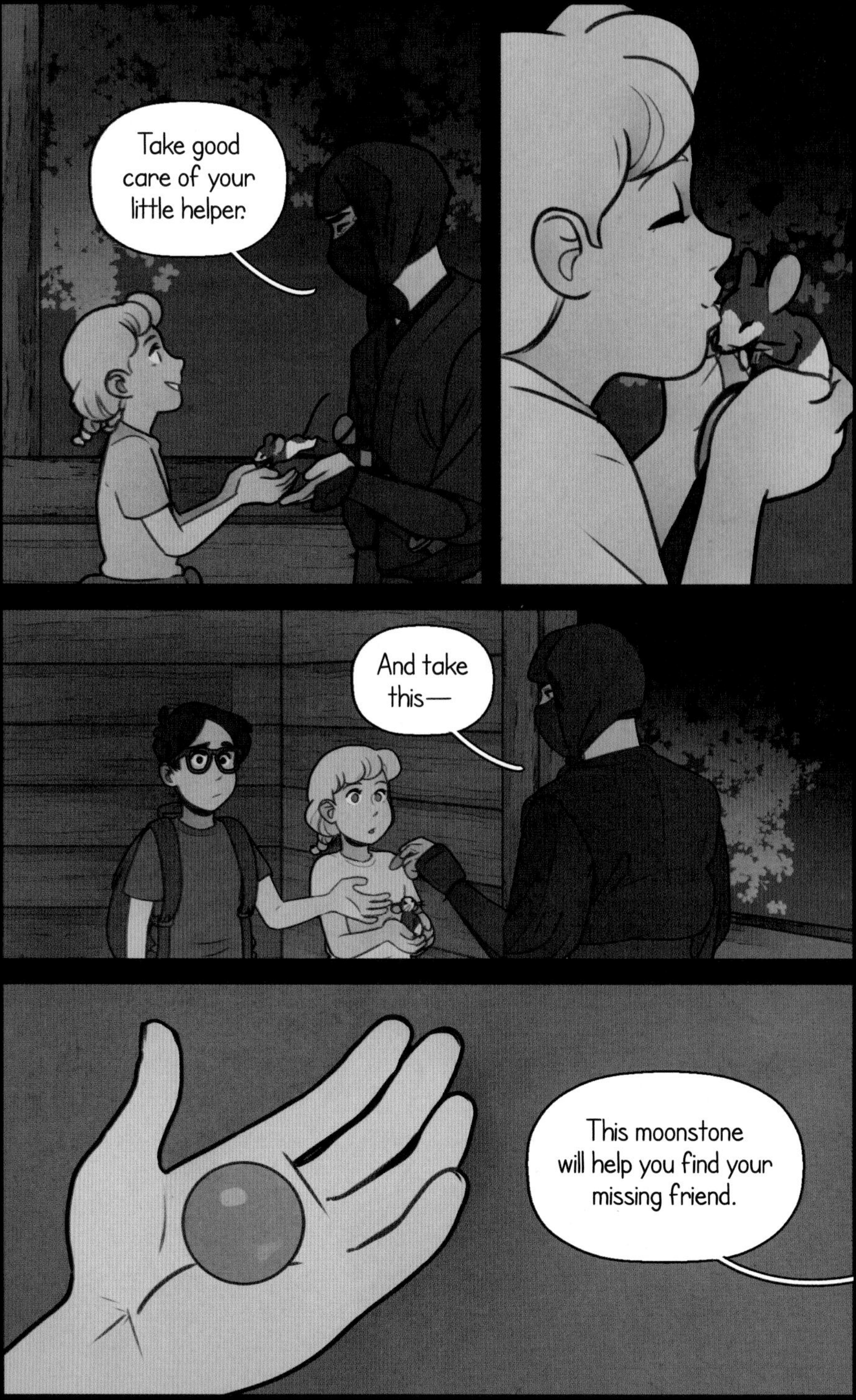
Take good care of your little helper.
And take this—
This moonstone will help you find your missing friend.

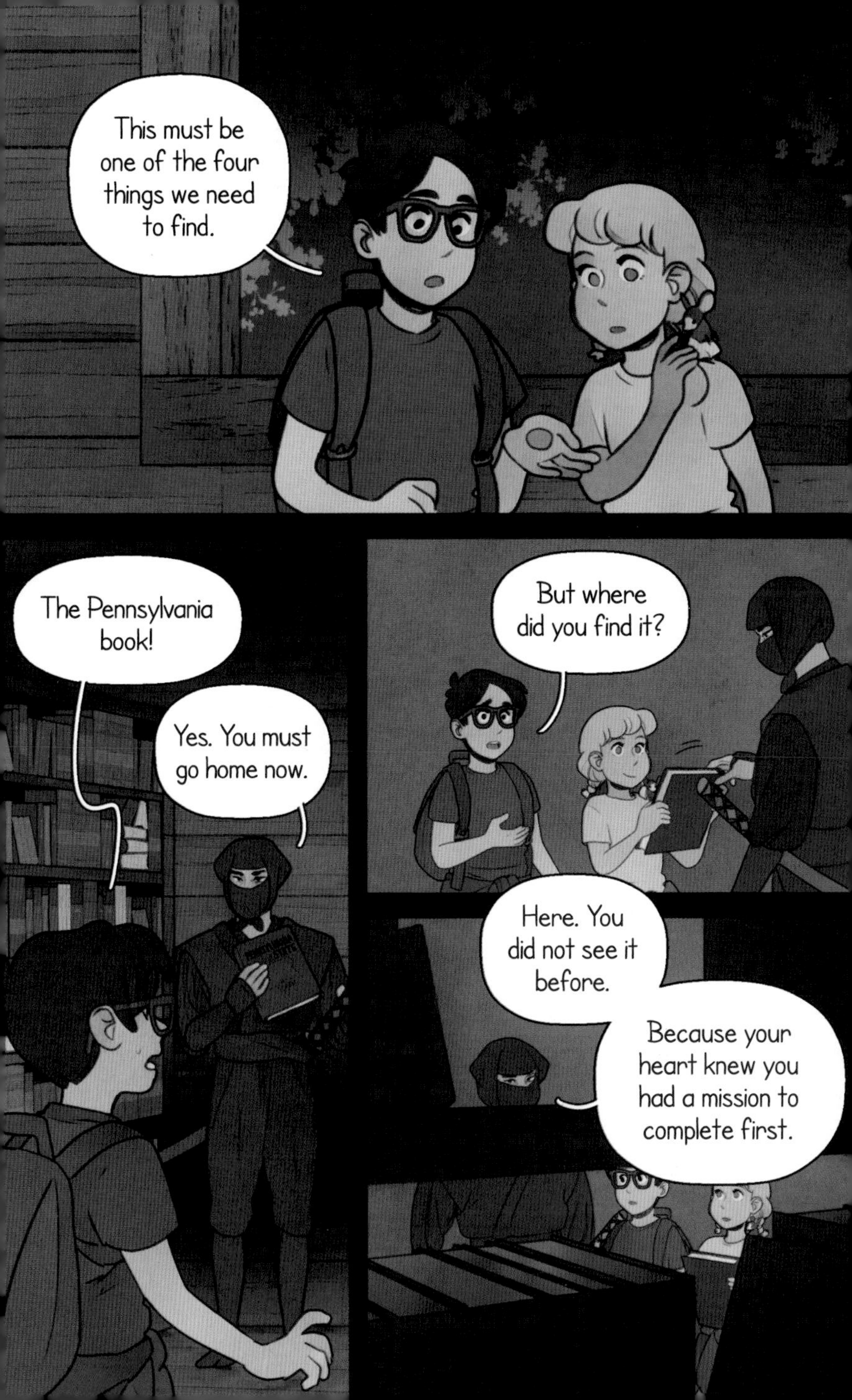
This must be one of the four things we need to find.
The Pennsylvania book!
Yes. You must go home now.
But where did you find it?
Here. You did not see it before.
Because your heart knew you had a mission to complete first.

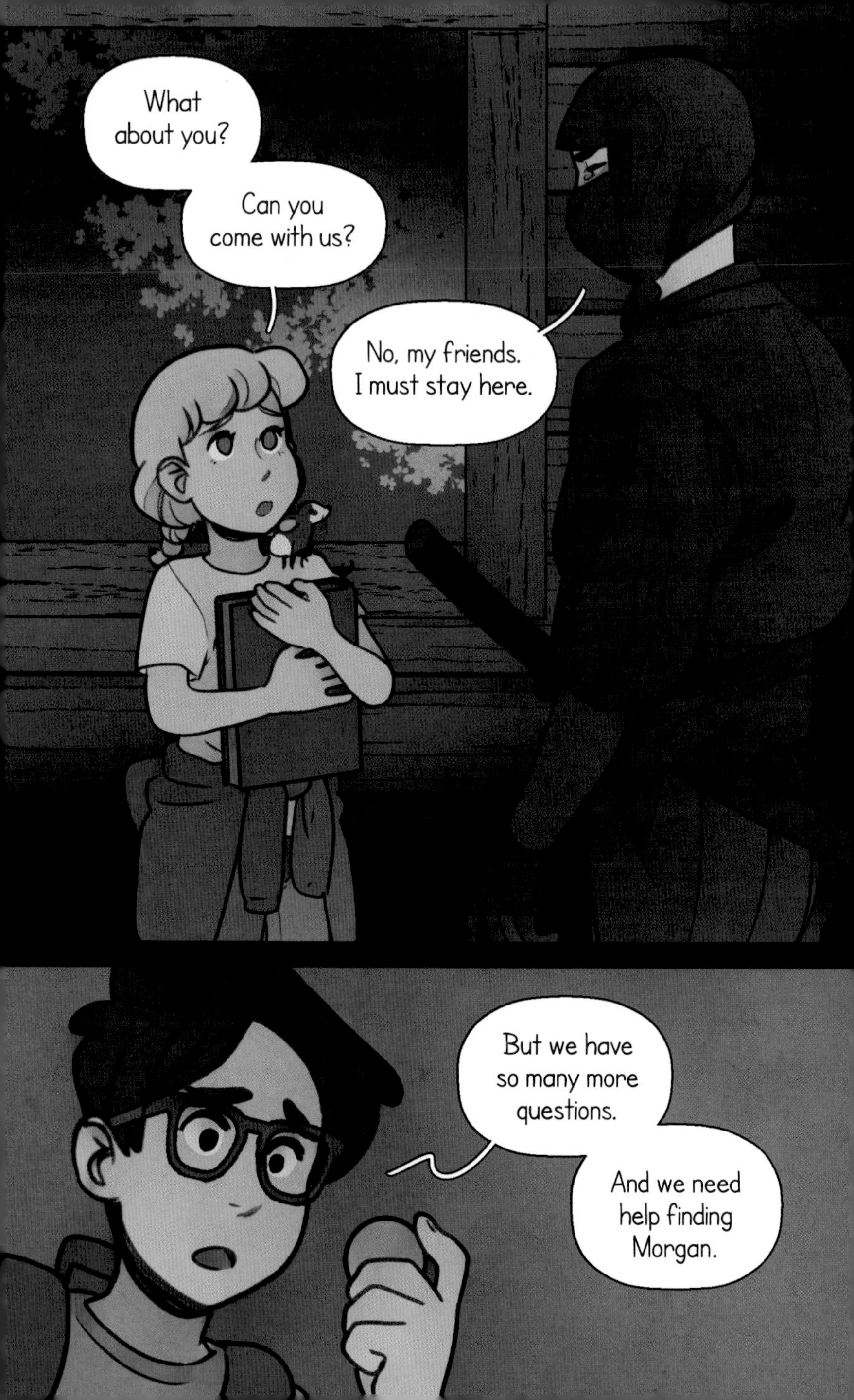
What about you?
Can you come with us?
No, my friends. I must stay here.
But we have so many more questions.
And we need help finding Morgan.

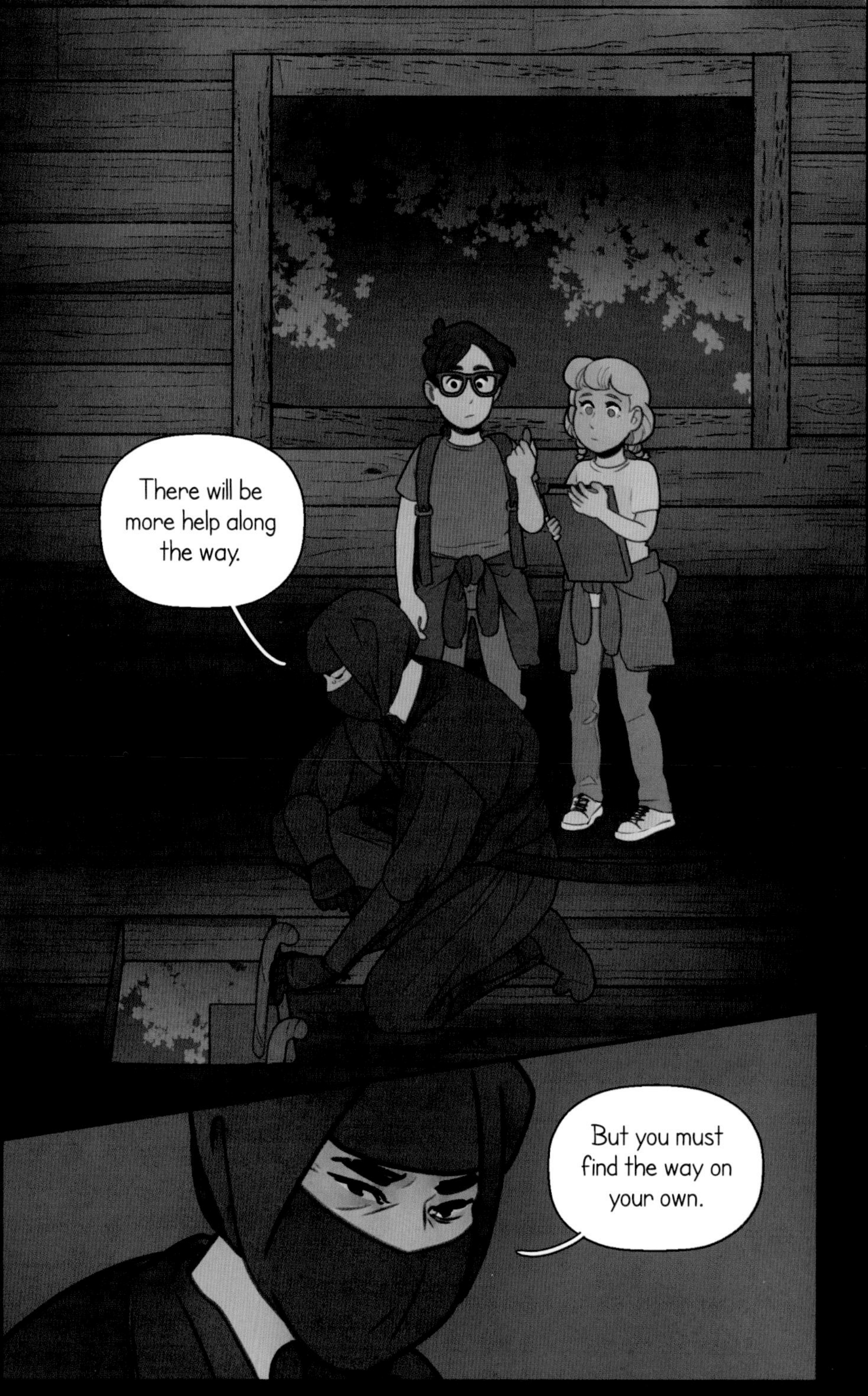
There will be more help along the way.
But you must find the way on your own.

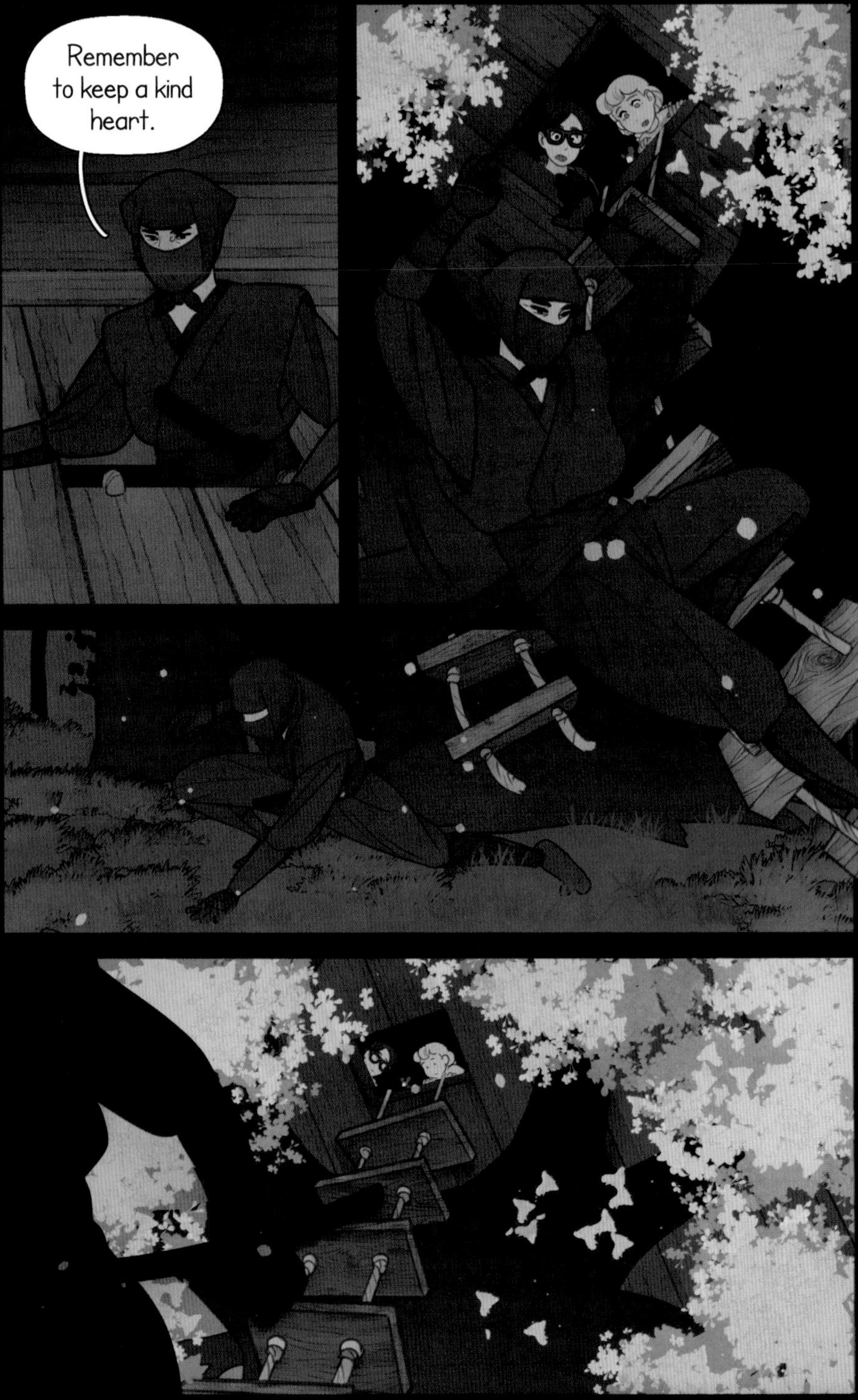
Remember to keep a kind heart.

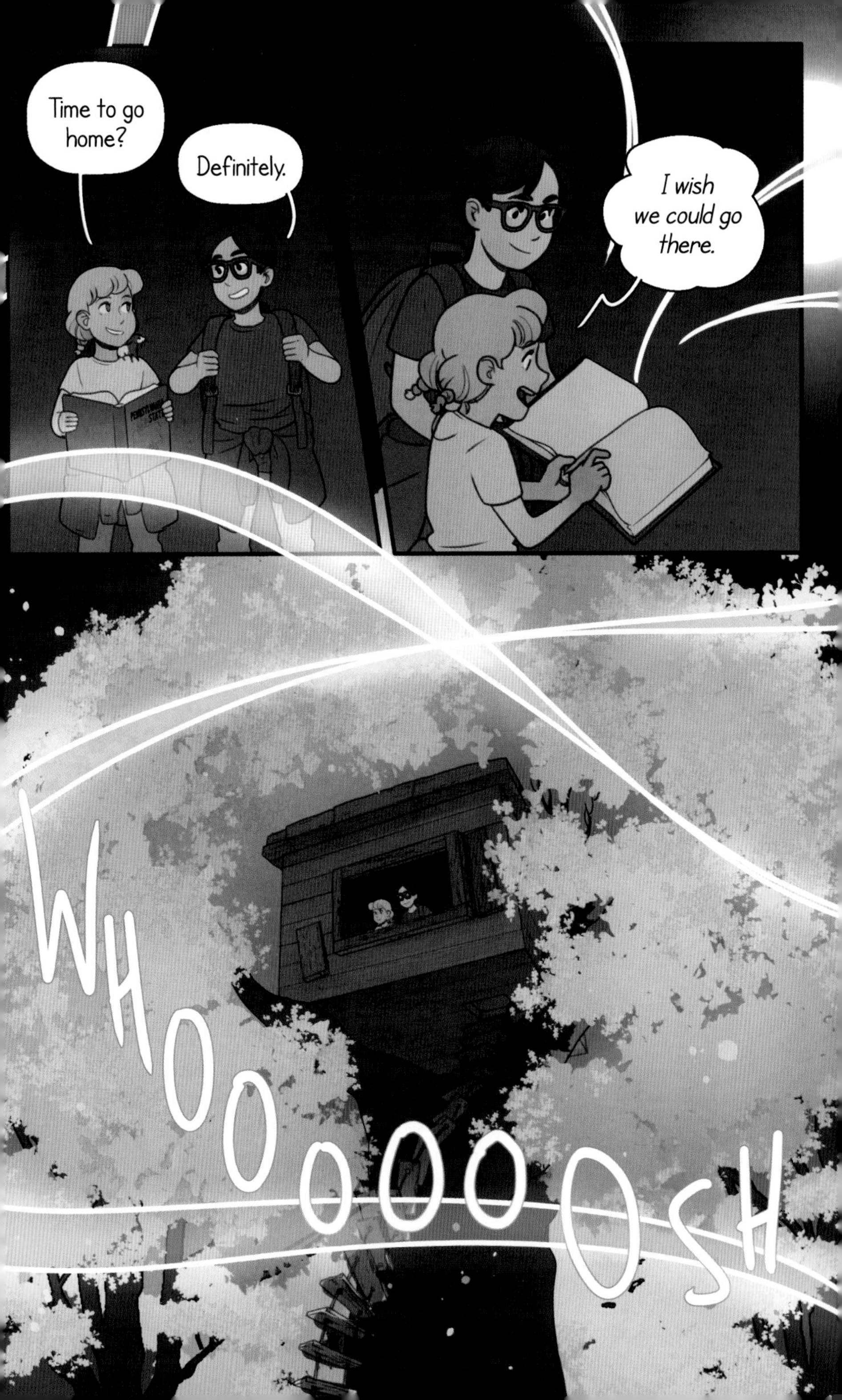

Time to go home?
Definitely.
PENNSYLVANIA STATE
I wish we could go there.
WHOOOOOOOSH

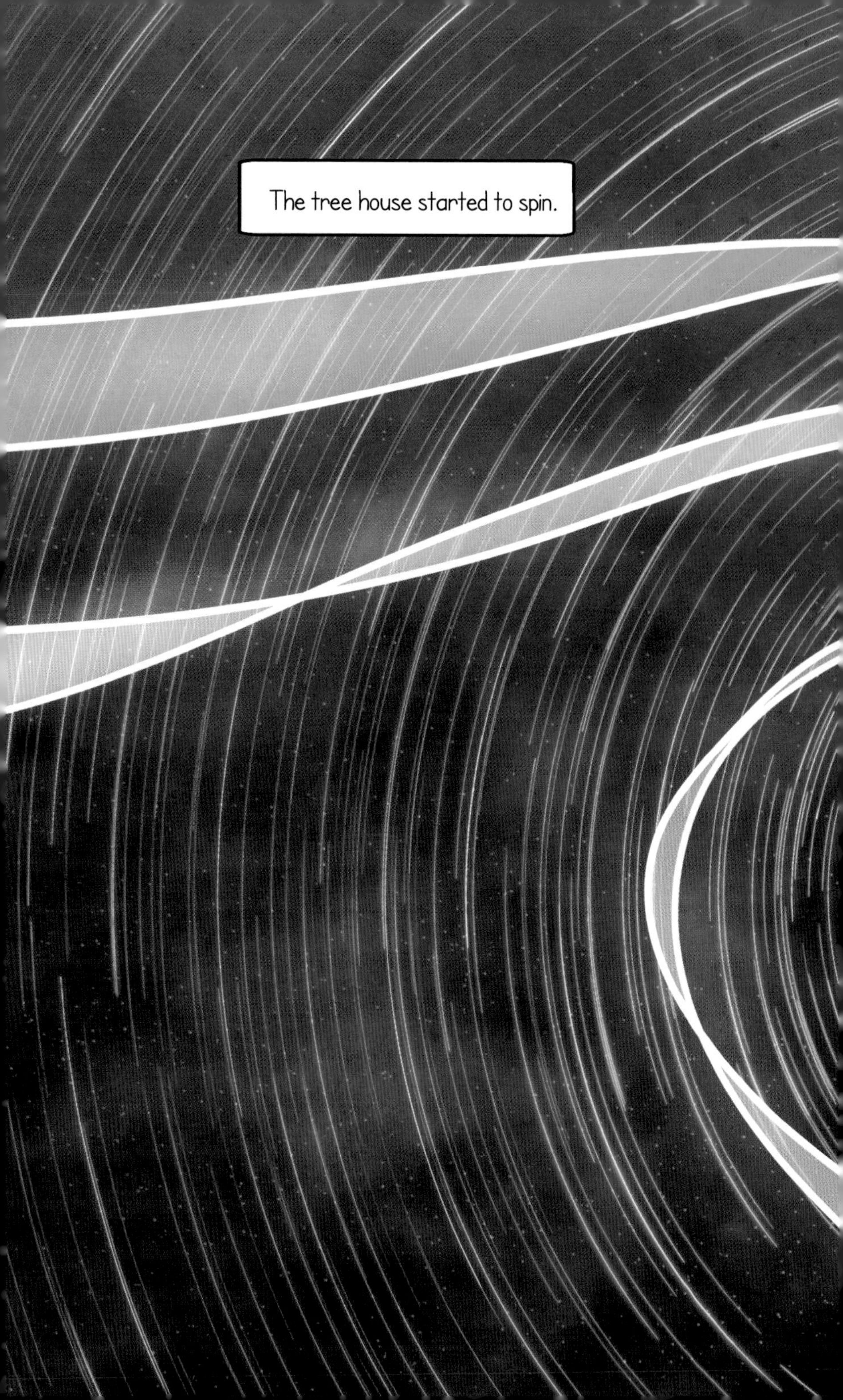
The tree house started to spin.

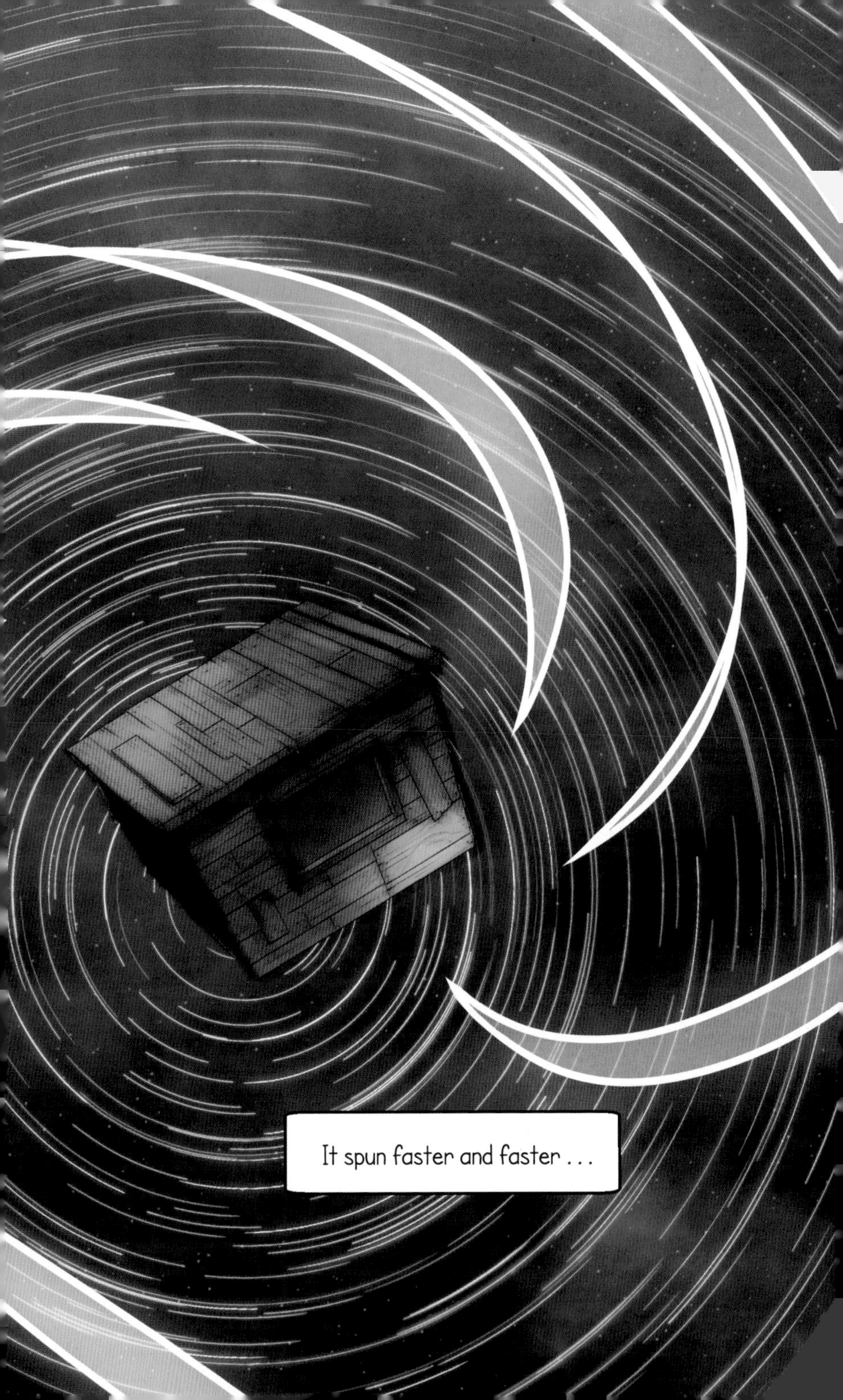
It spun faster and faster . . .

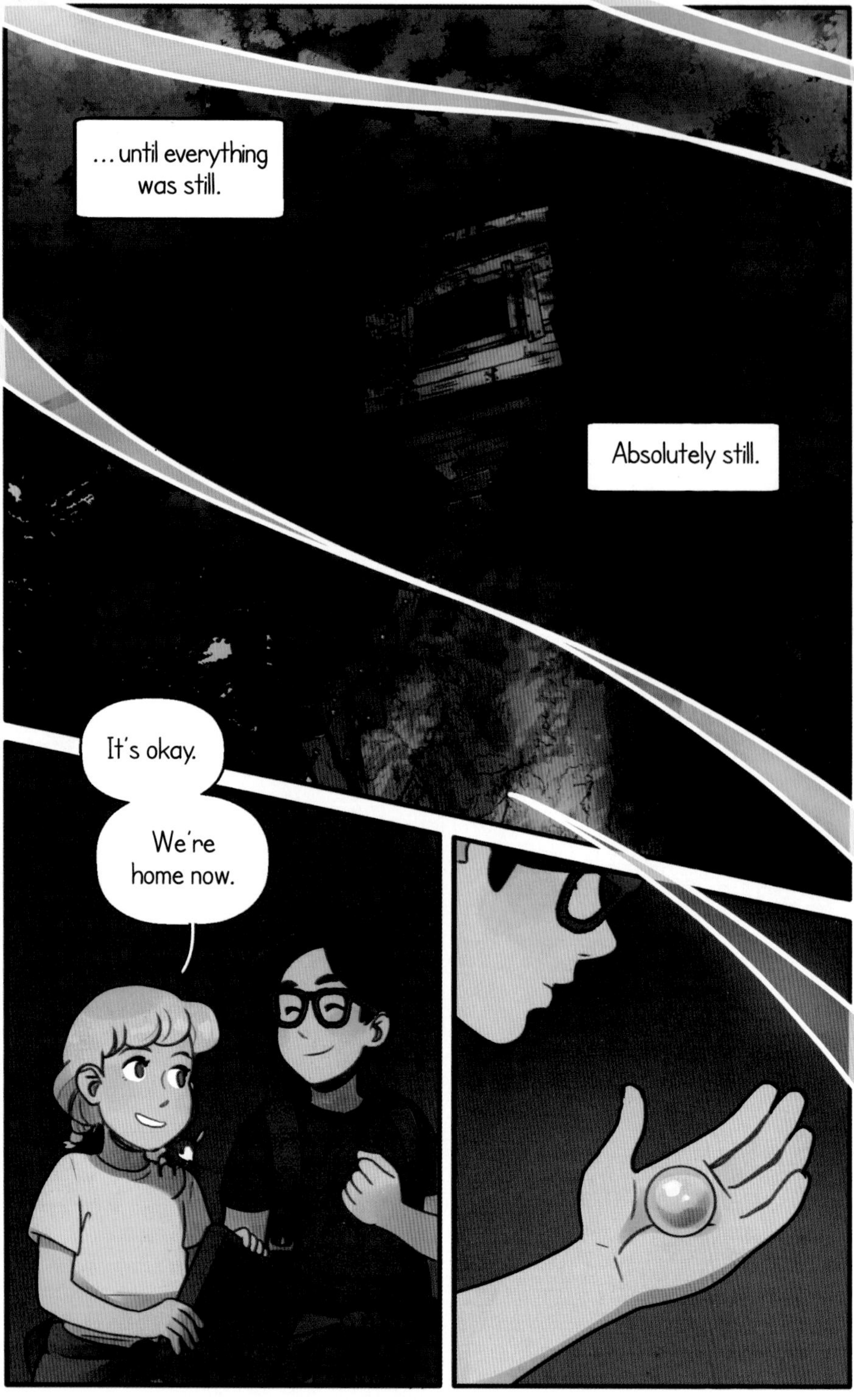
...until everything was still.
Absolutely still.
It's okay.
We're home now.

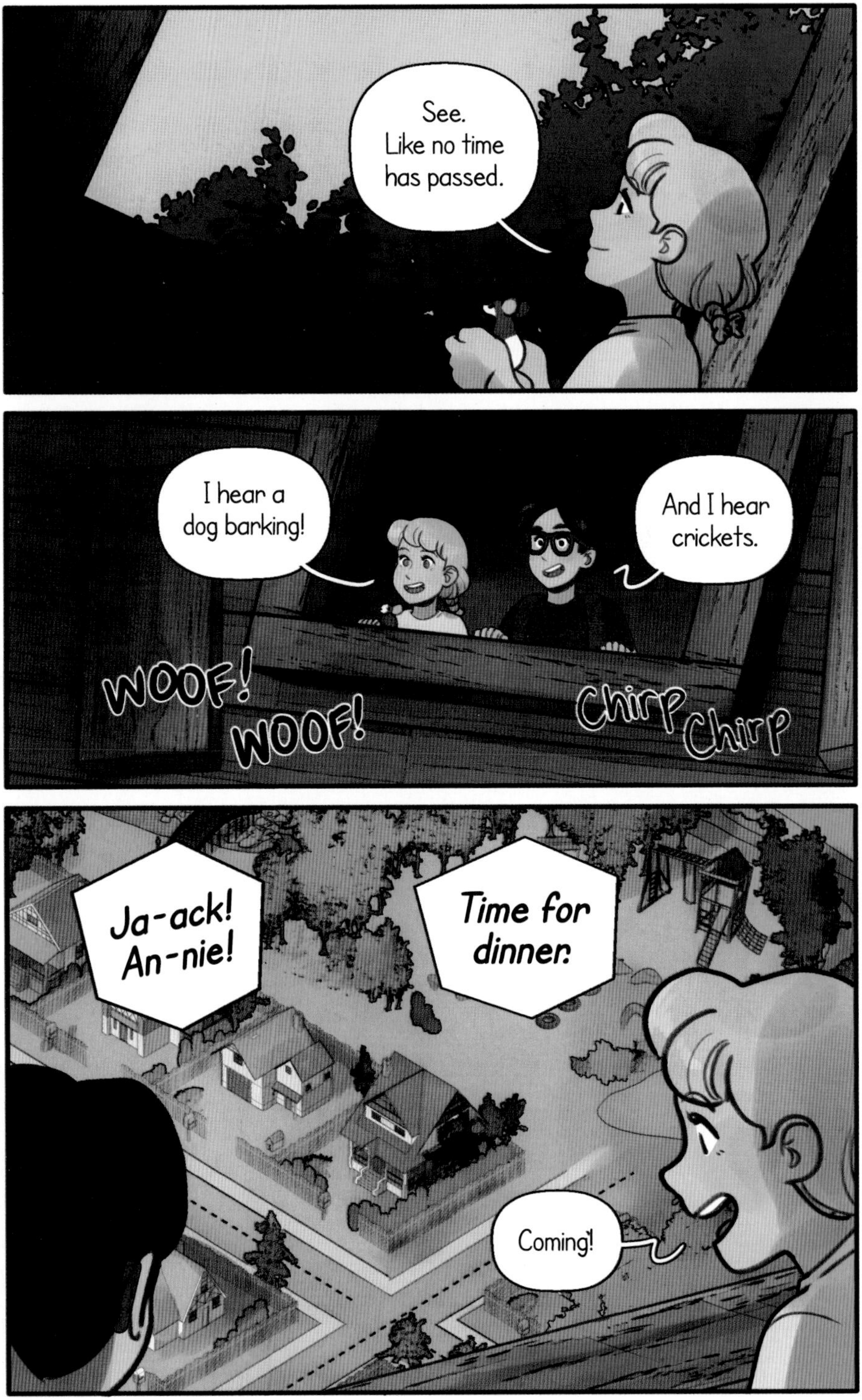
See.
Like no time
has passed.
I hear a
dog barking!
And I hear
crickets.
WOOF!
WOOF!
Chirp
Chirp
Ja-ack!
An-nie!
Time for
dinner.
Coming!

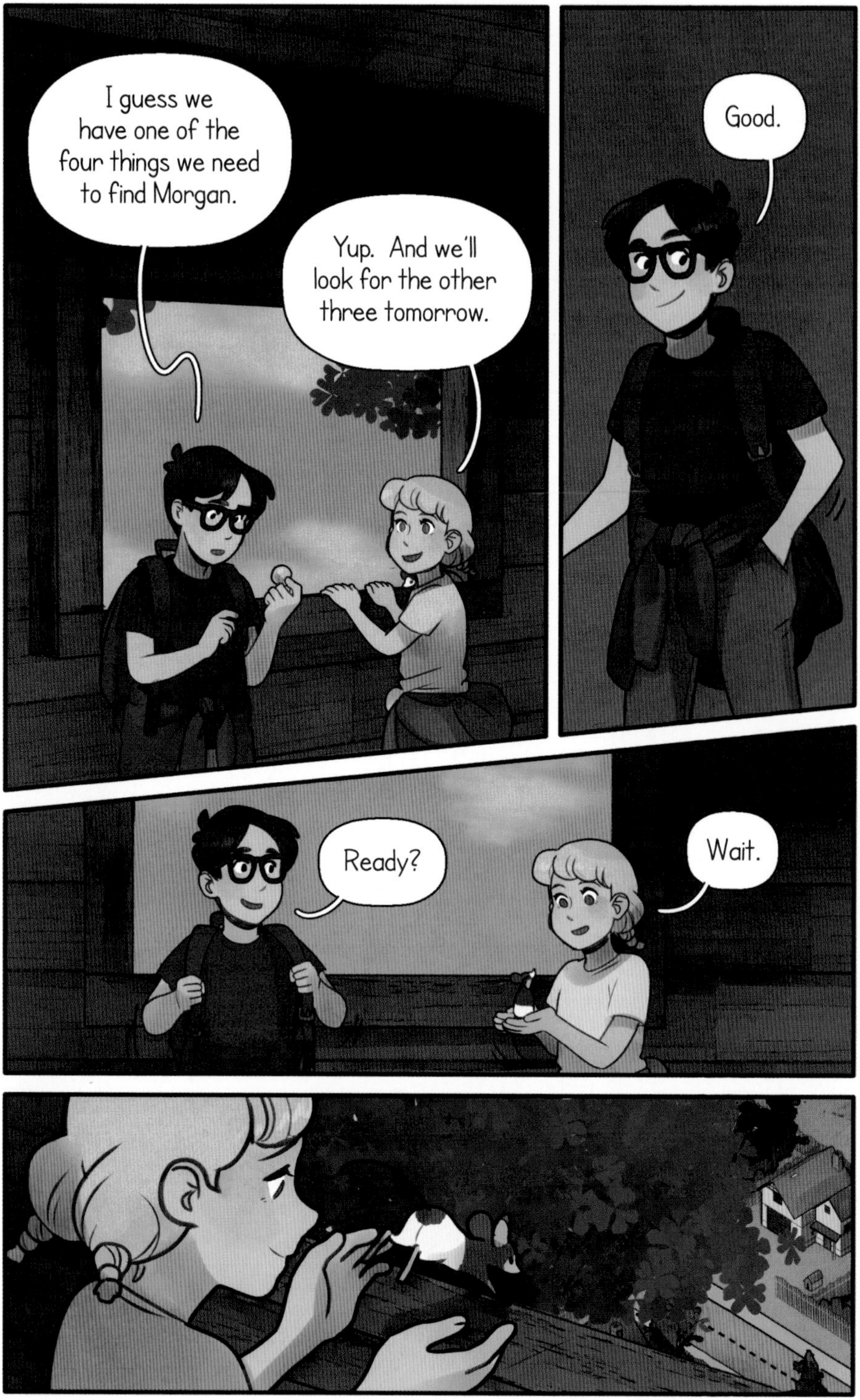
I guess we have one of the four things we need to find Morgan.
Yup. And we'll look for the other three tomorrow.
Good.
Ready?
Wait.

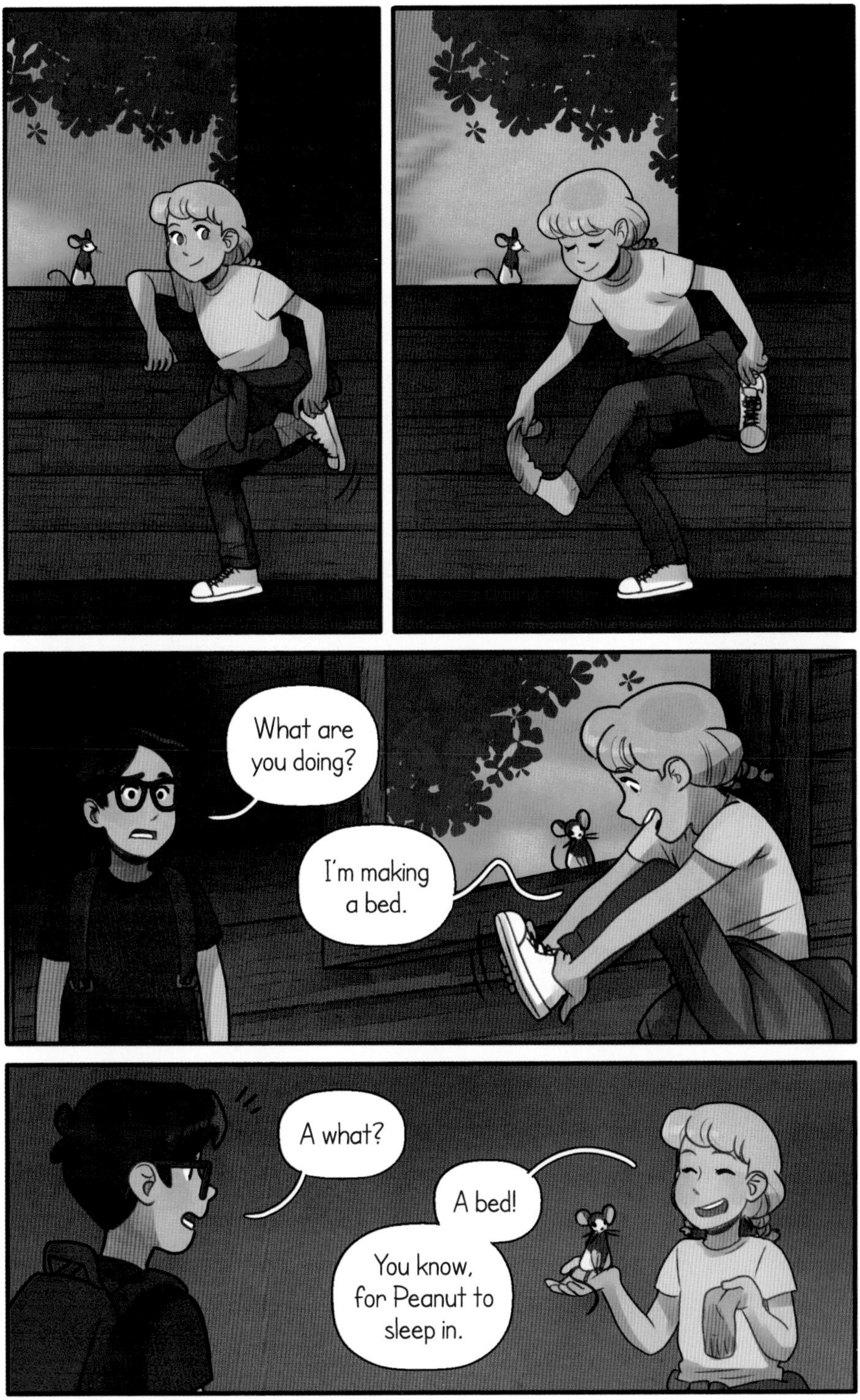
What are you doing?
I'm making a bed.
A what?
A bed!
You know, for Peanut to sleep in.

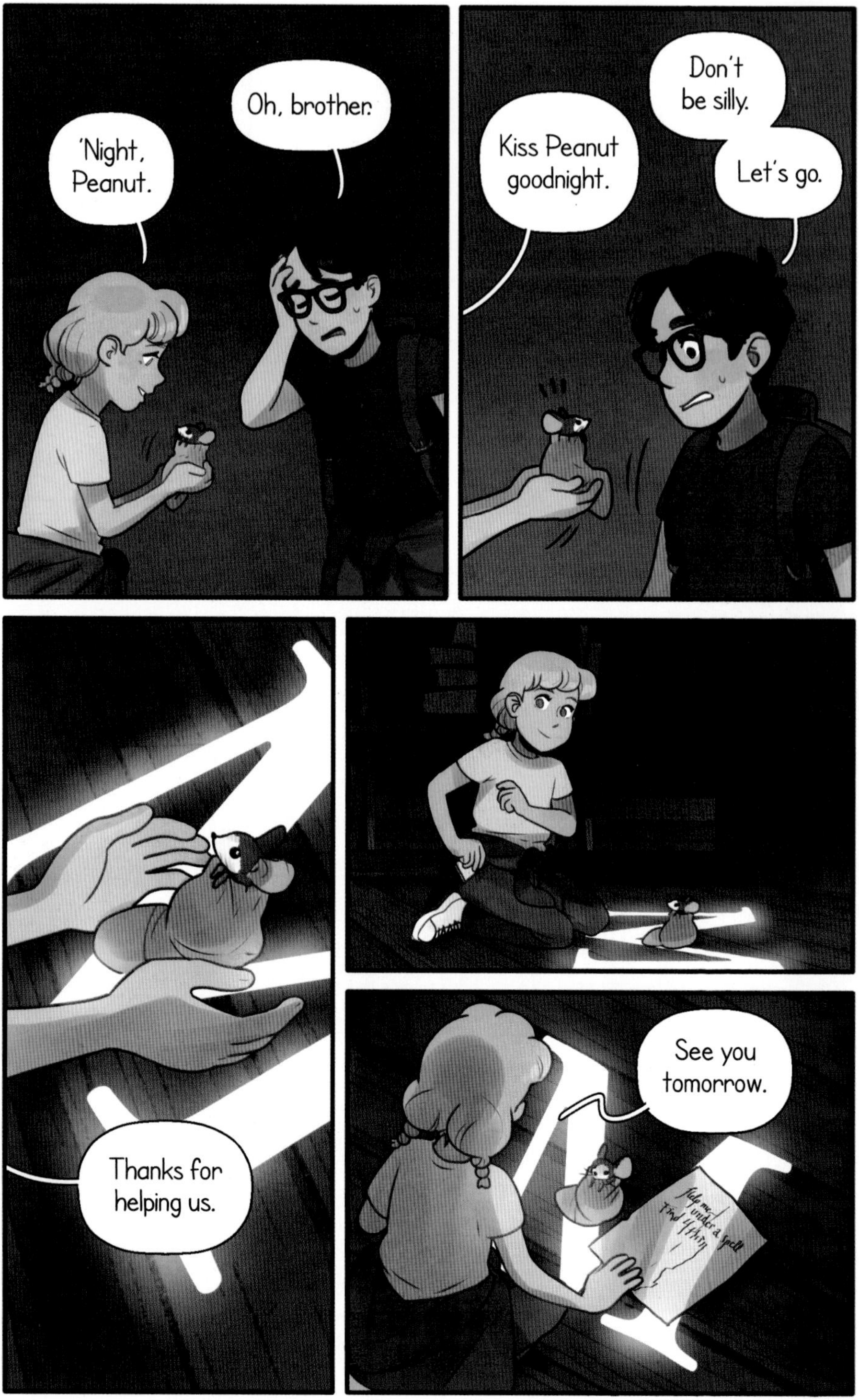
'Night, Peanut.
Oh, brother.
Kiss Peanut goodnight.
Don't be silly.
Let's go.
Thanks for helping us.
See you tomorrow.
Help me
under a spell

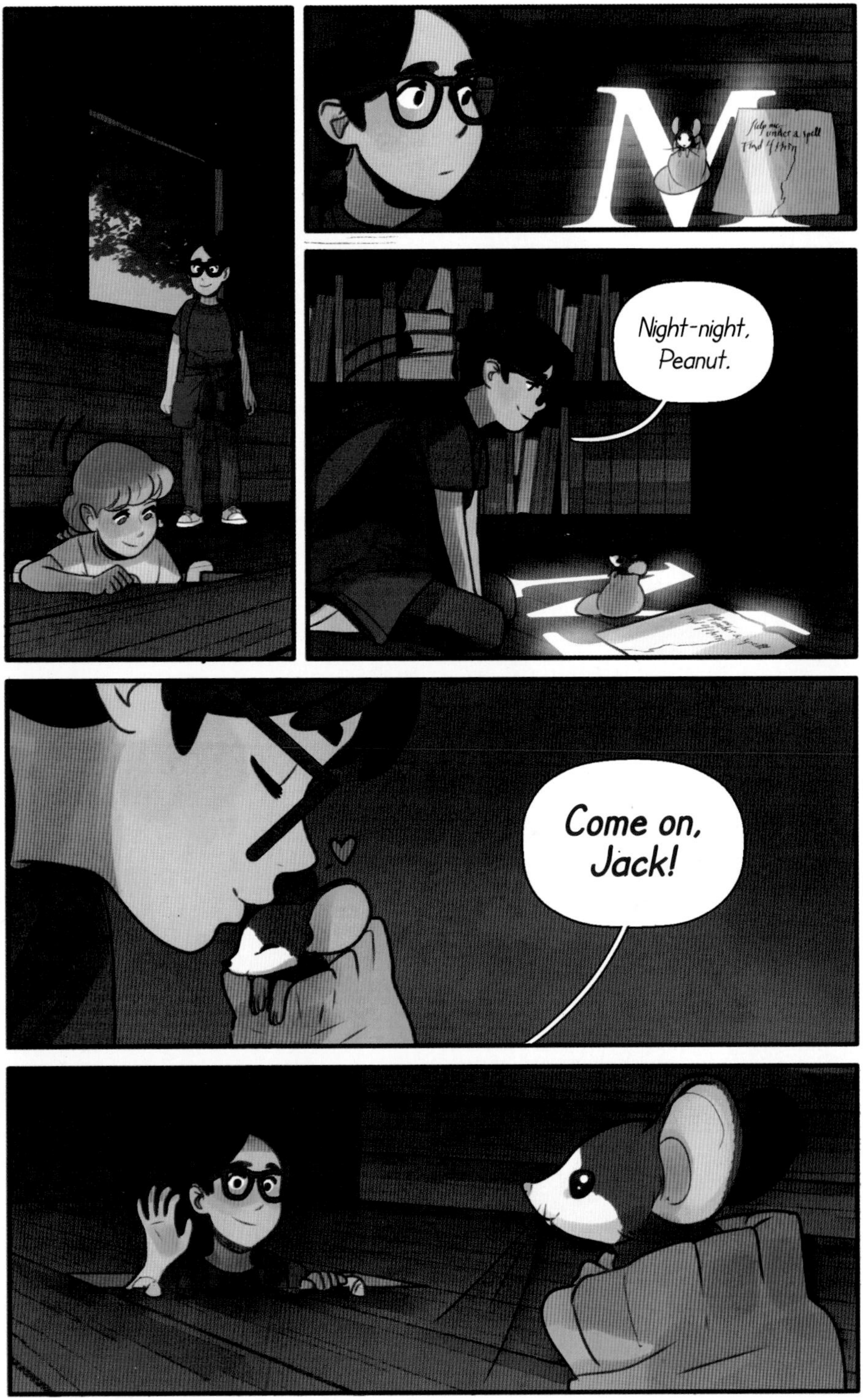
Night-night, Peanut.
Come on, Jack!

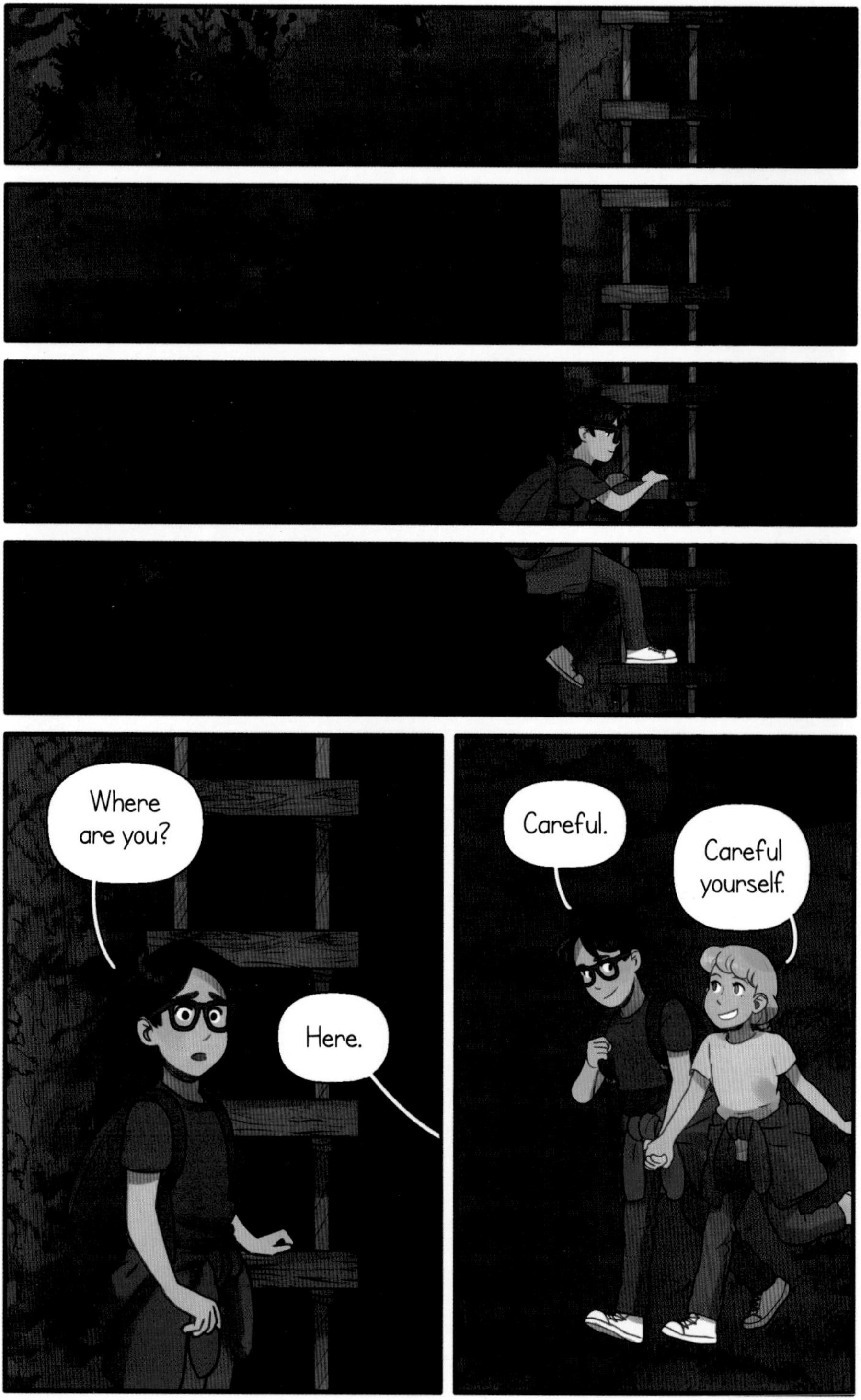
Where are you?
Here.
Careful.
Careful yourself.

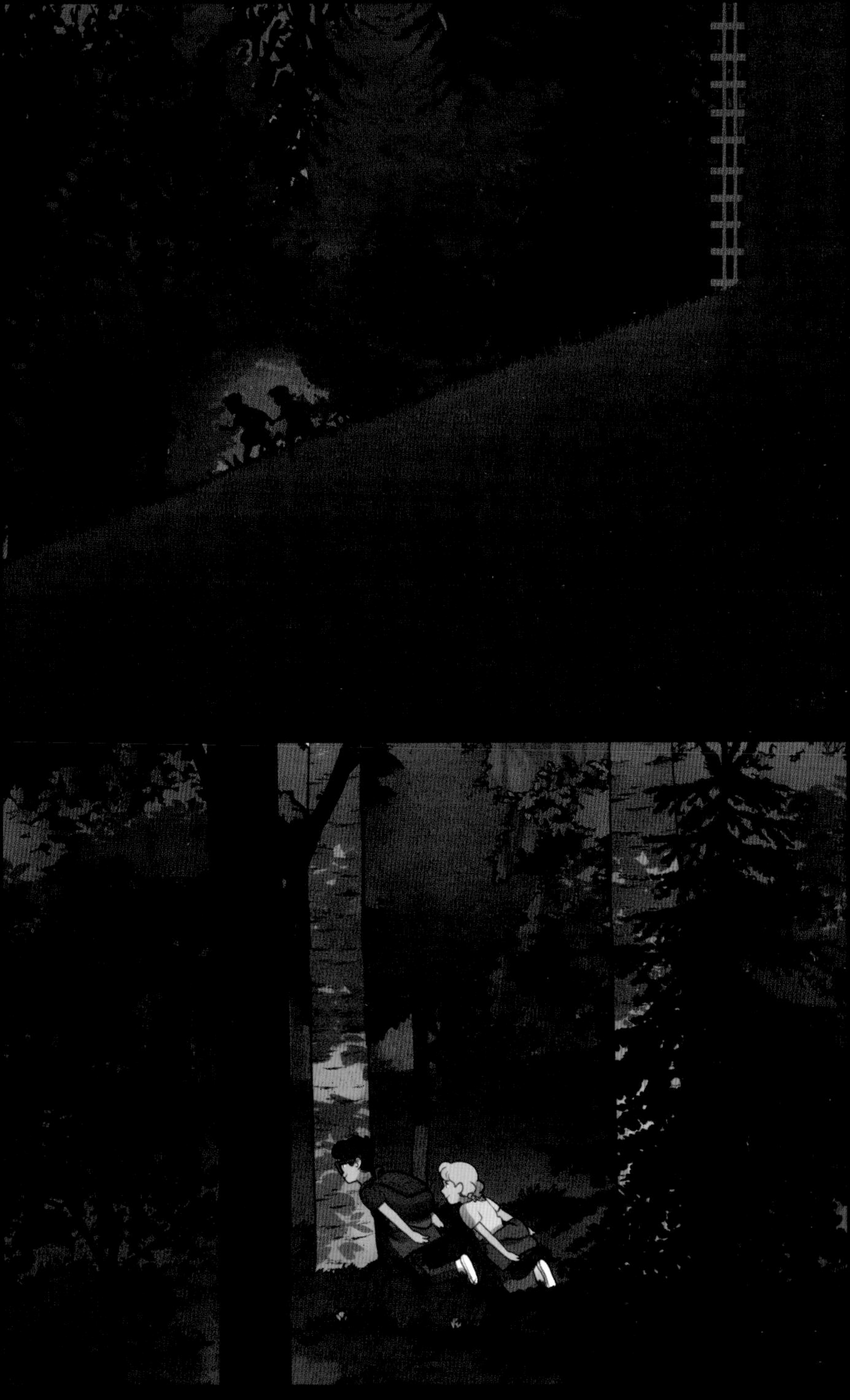

Don't miss another adventure in the
Magic Tree House where Jack and Annie get
whisked away to the time of pirates!

Pirates Past Noon Graphic Novel excerpt text copyright © 2022 by Mary Pope Osborne.
Adapted by Jenny Laird. Cover art and interior illustrations copyright © 2022 by
Kelly & Nichole Matthews. Published by Random House Children's Books,
a division of Penguin Random House LLC, New York.

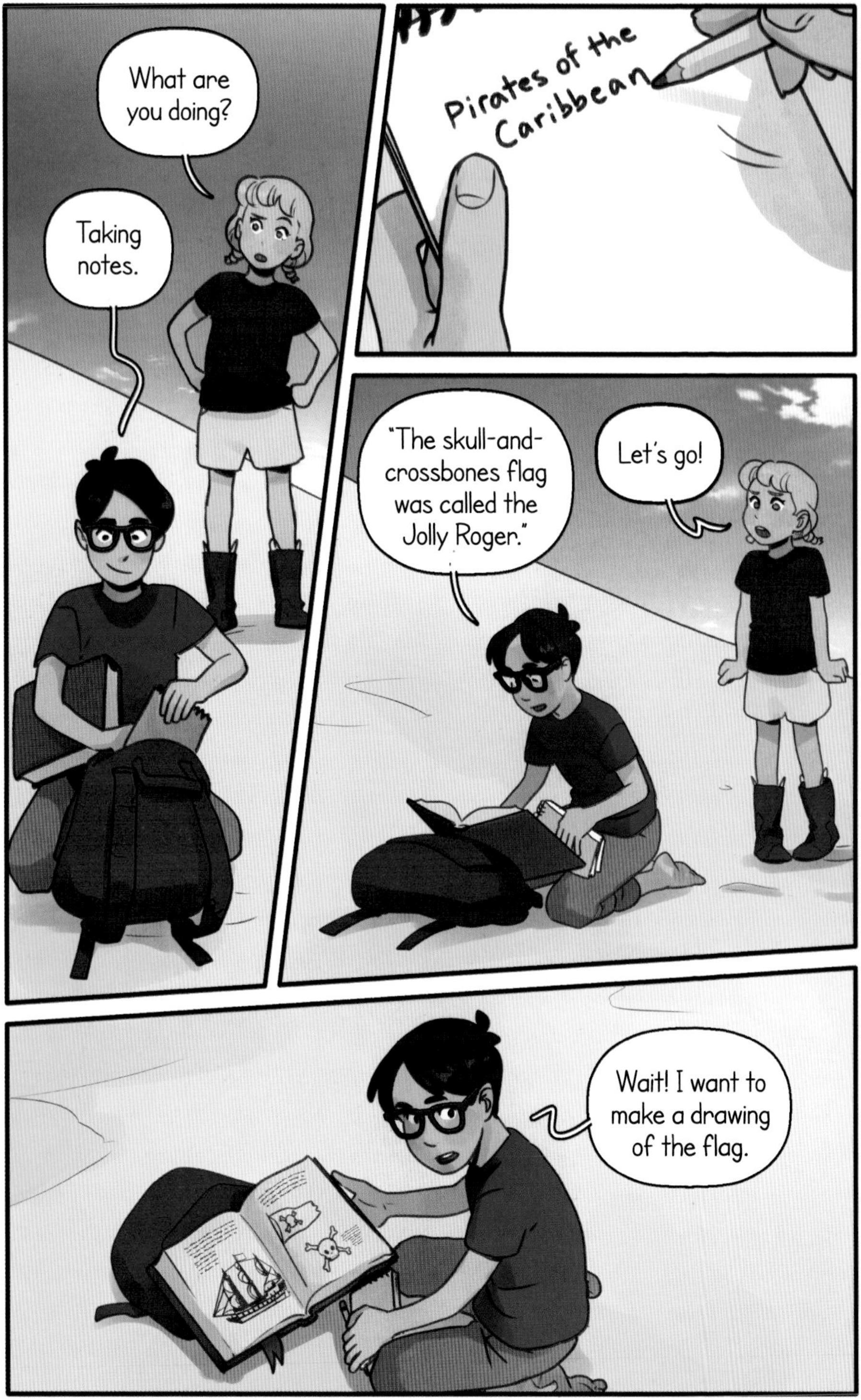
What are you doing?
Taking notes.
Pirates of the Caribbean
"The skull-and-crossbones flag was called the Jolly Roger."
Let's go!
Wait! I want to make a drawing of the flag.

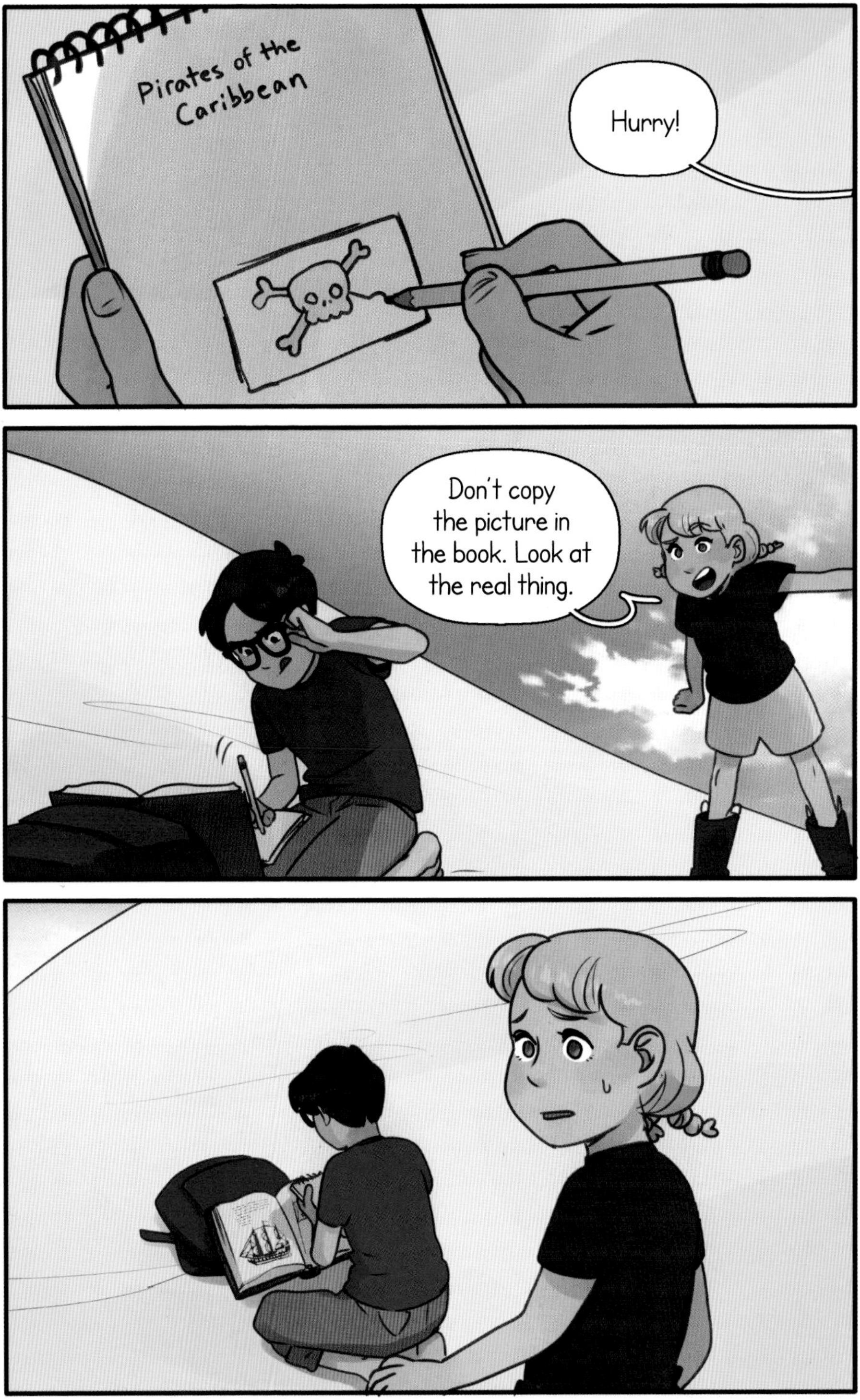
Pirates of the Caribbean
Hurry!
Don't copy the picture in the book. Look at the real thing.

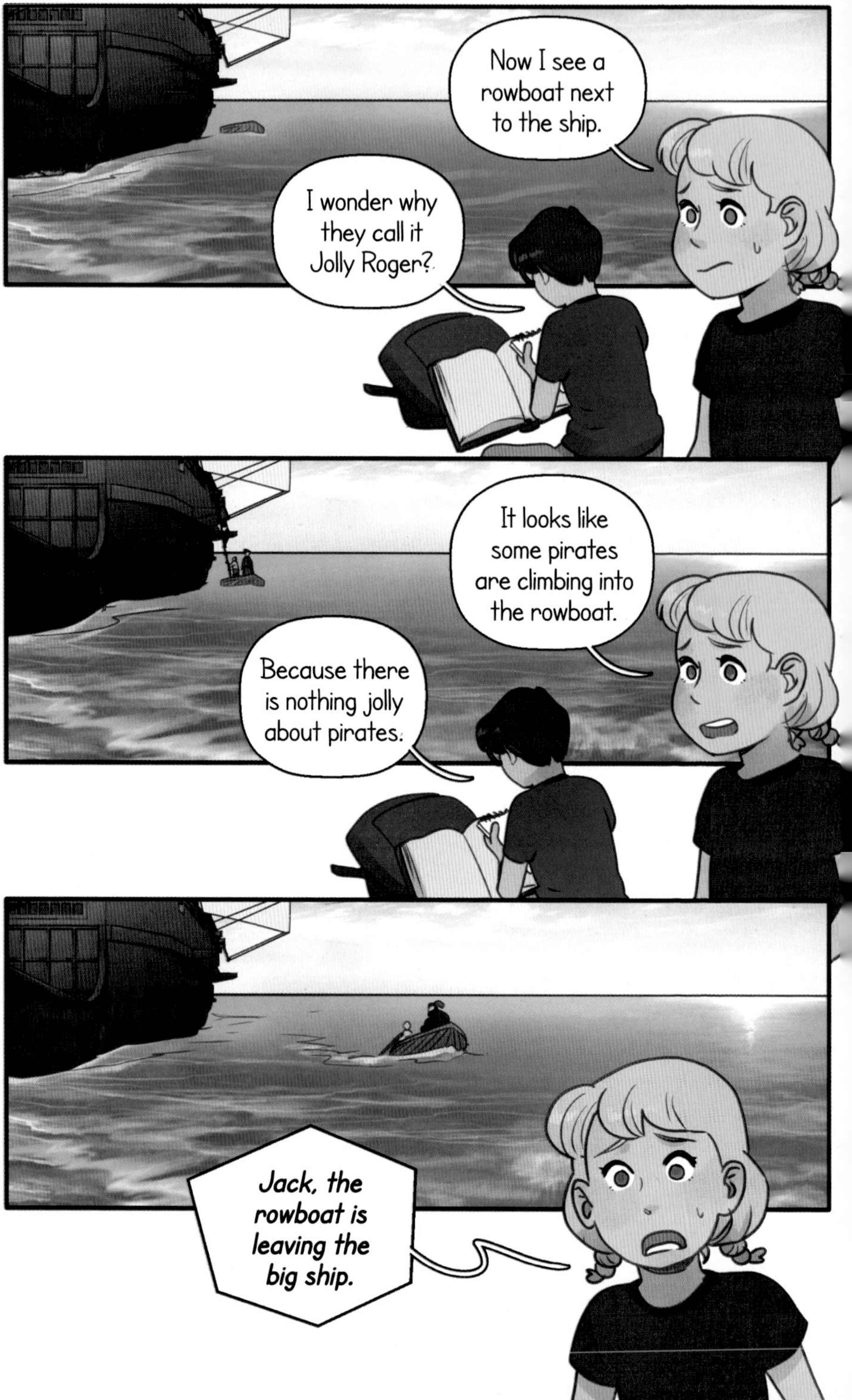
Now I see a rowboat next to the ship.
I wonder why they call it Jolly Roger?
It looks like some pirates are climbing into the rowboat.
Because there is nothing jolly about pirates.
Jack, the rowboat is leaving the big ship.

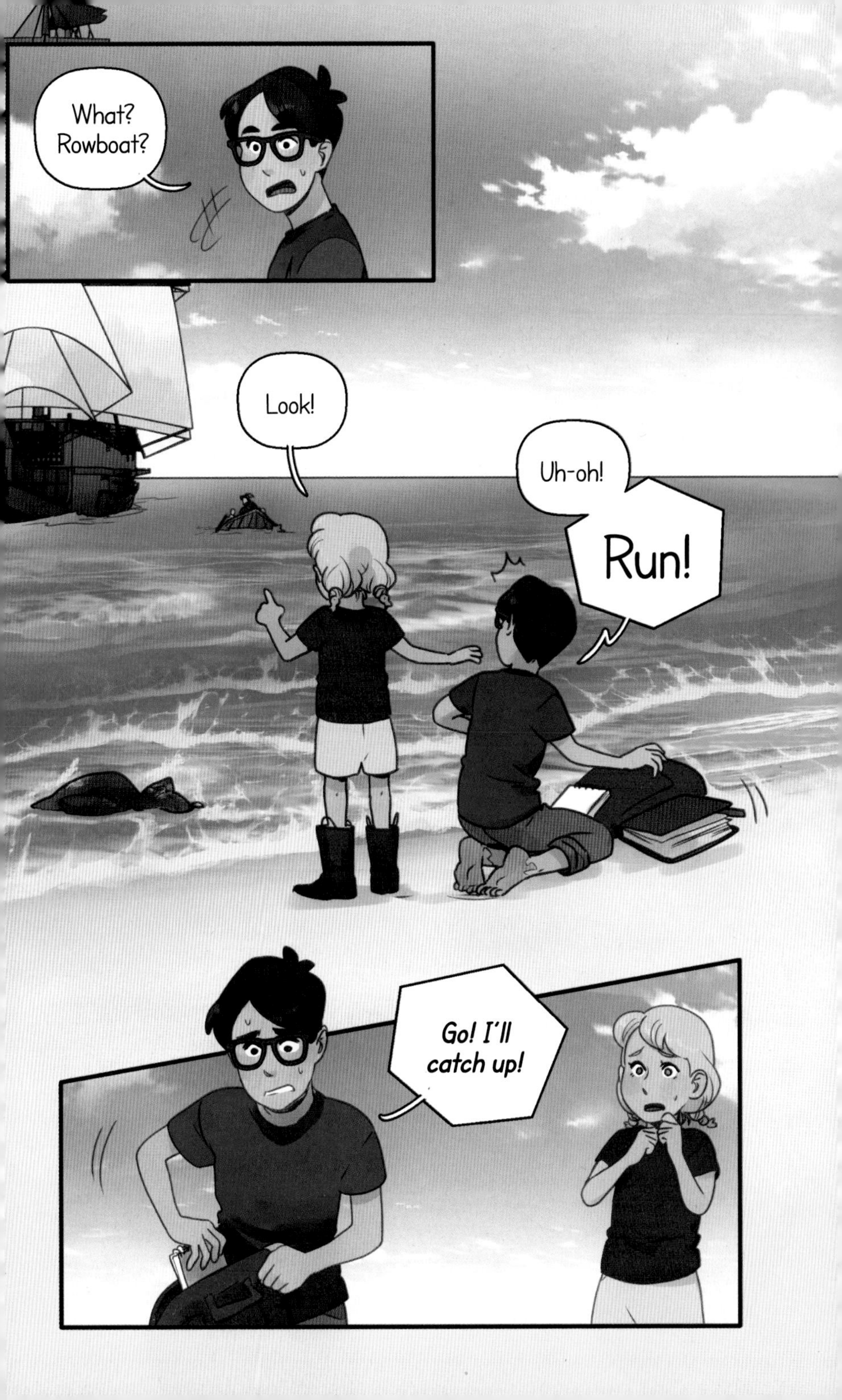
What? Rowboat?
Look!
Uh-oh!
Run!
Go! I'll catch up!

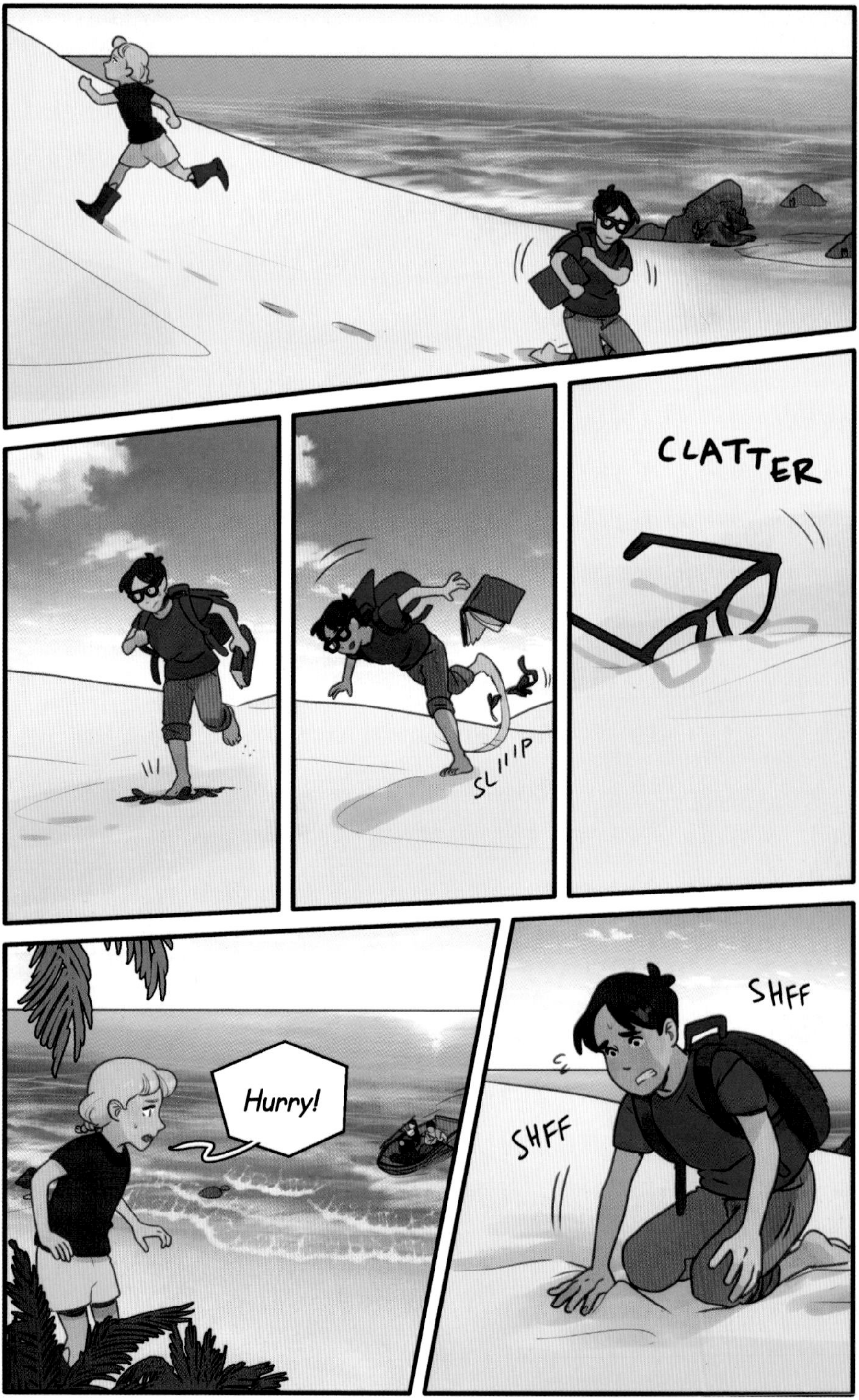
CLATTER
SLIIIP
Hurry!
SHFF
SHFF

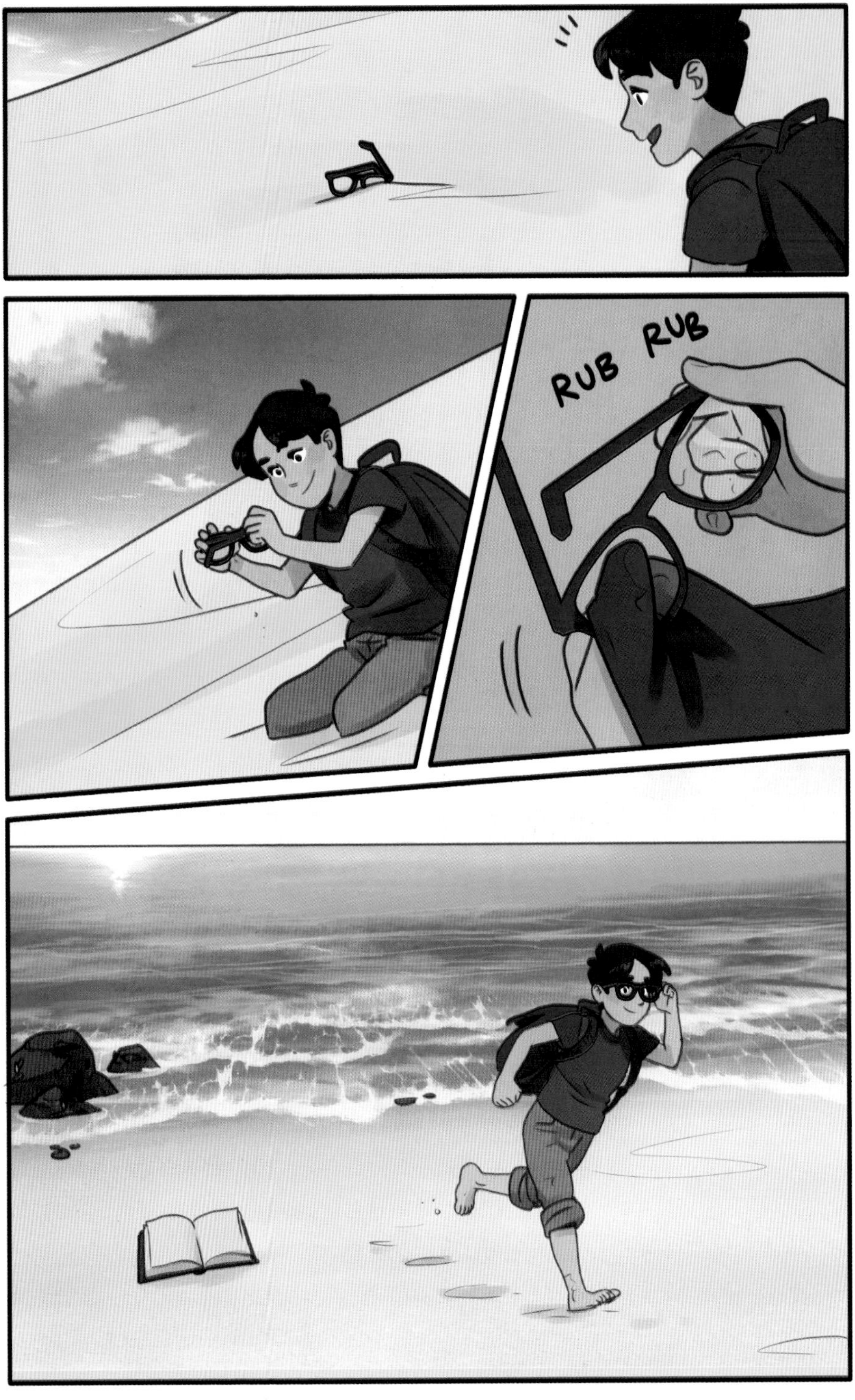
RUB RUB

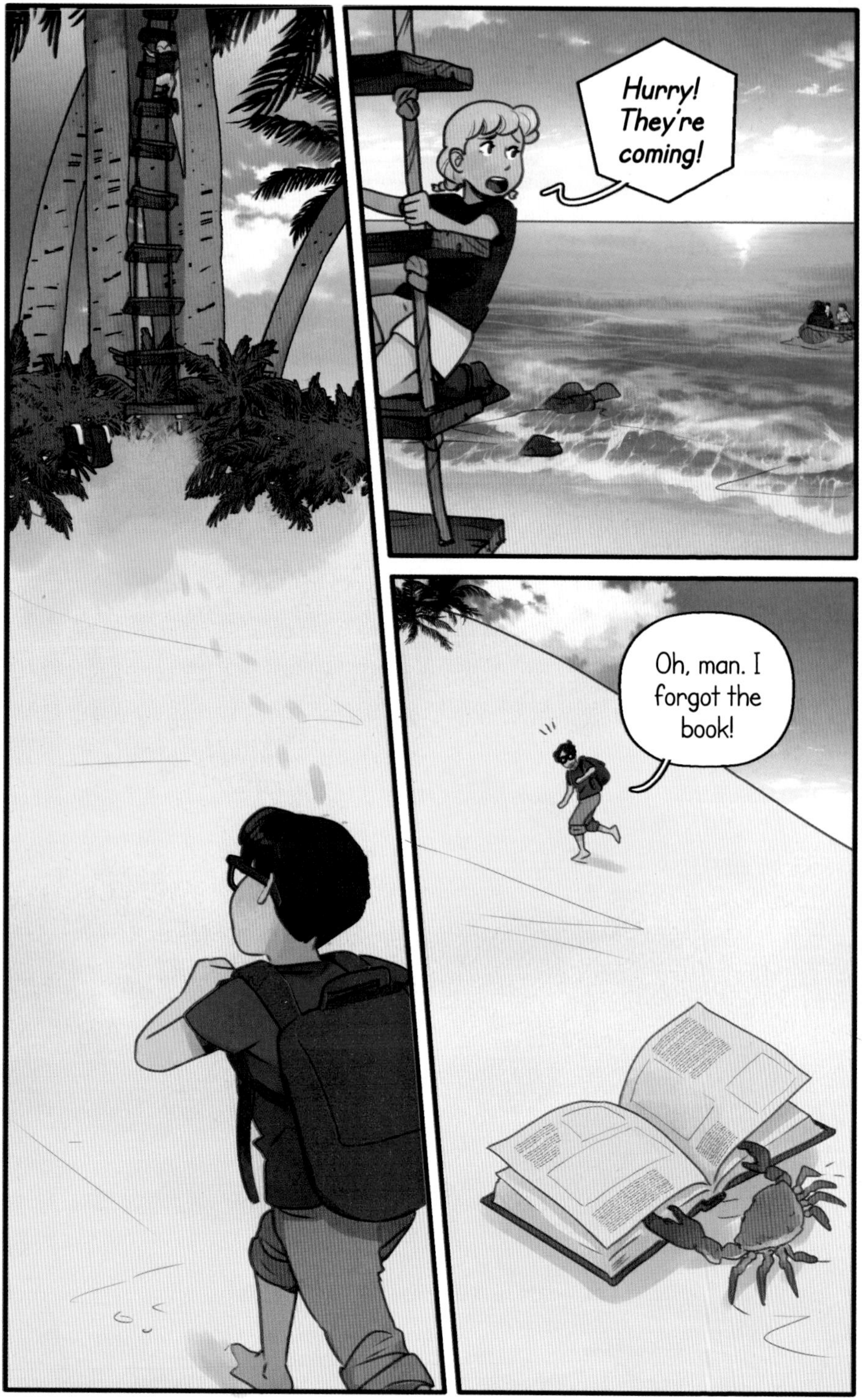
Hurry! They're coming!
Oh, man. I forgot the book!

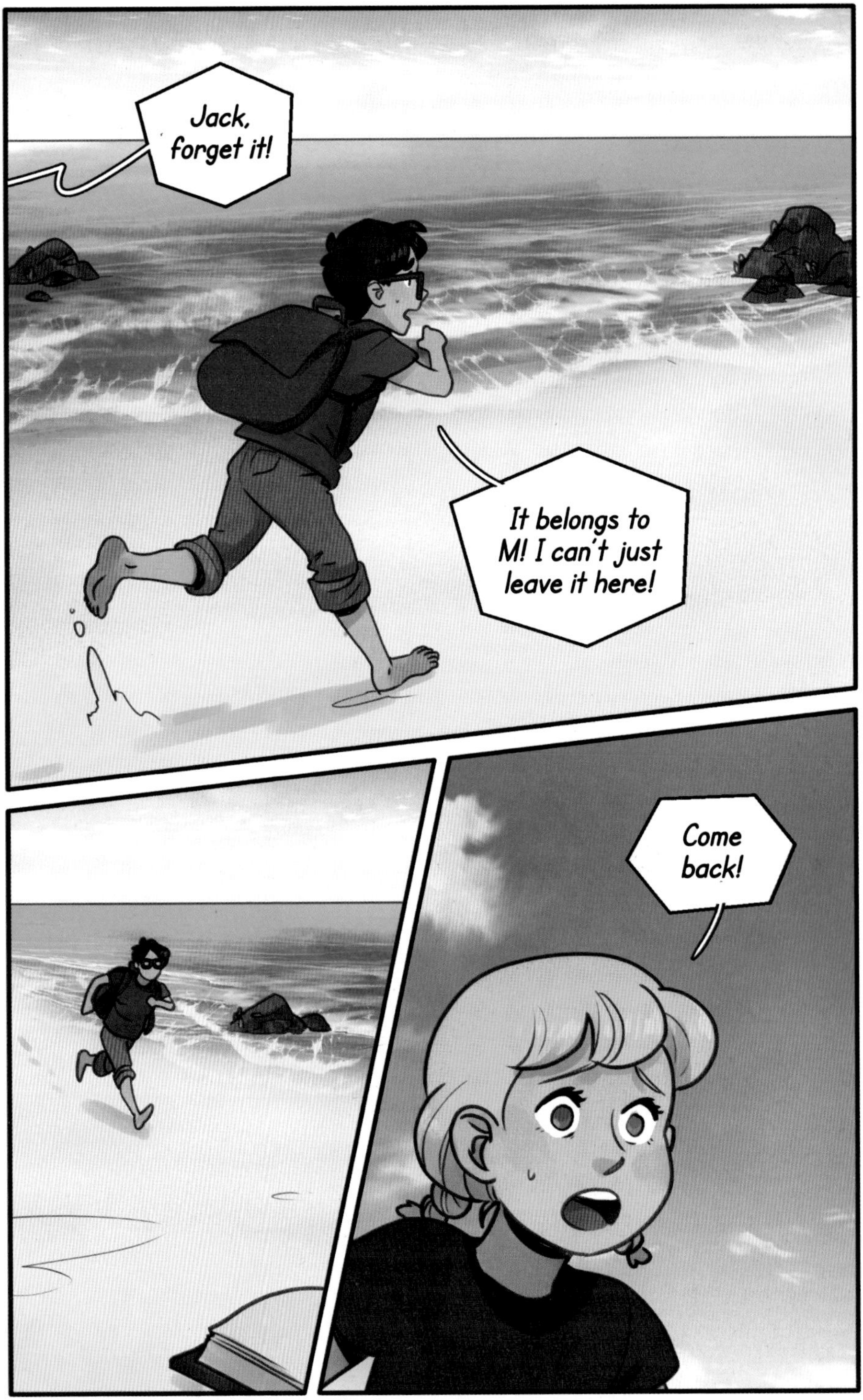
Jack, forget it!
It belongs to M! I can't just leave it here!
Come back!

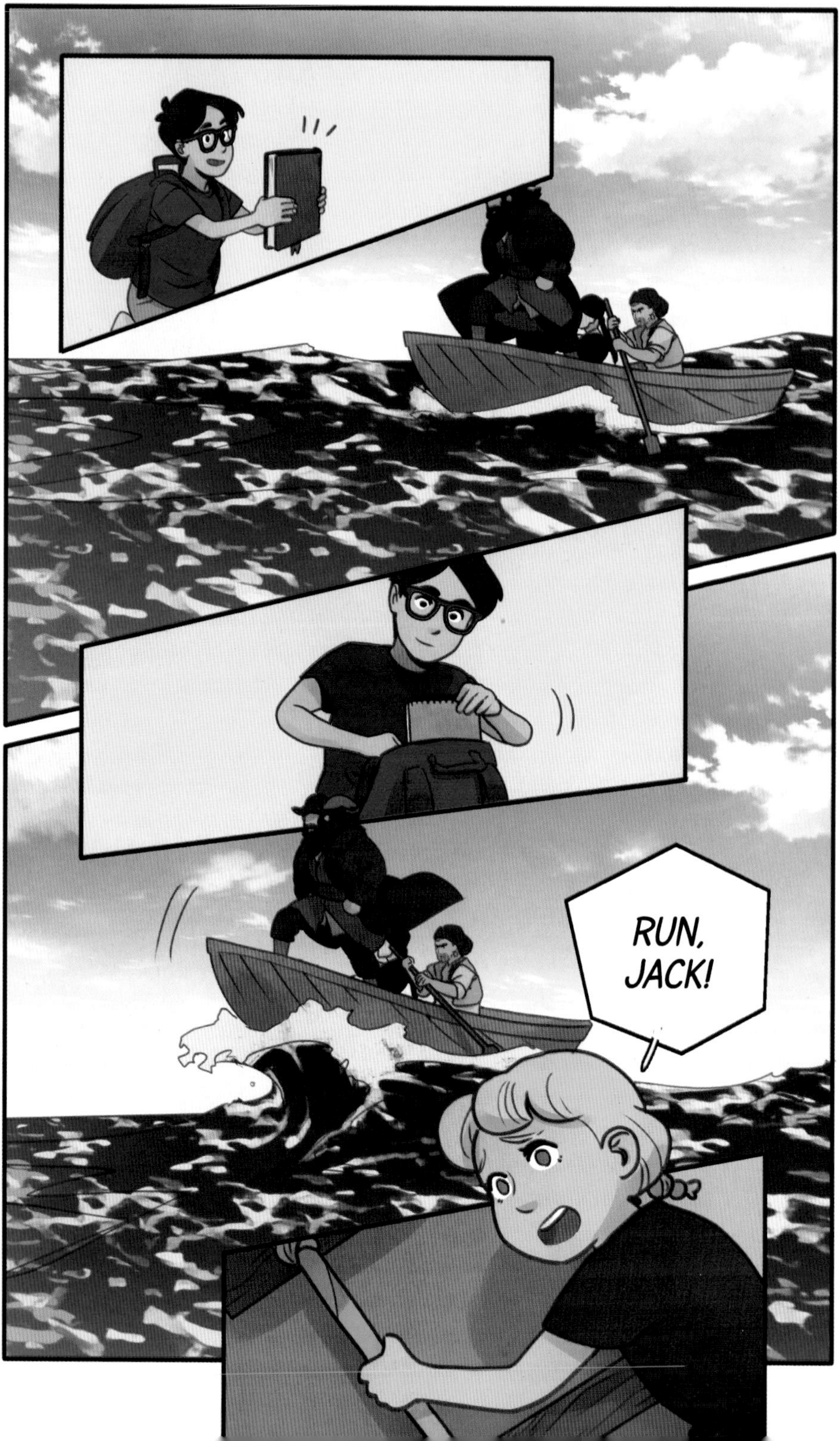
RUN, JACK!

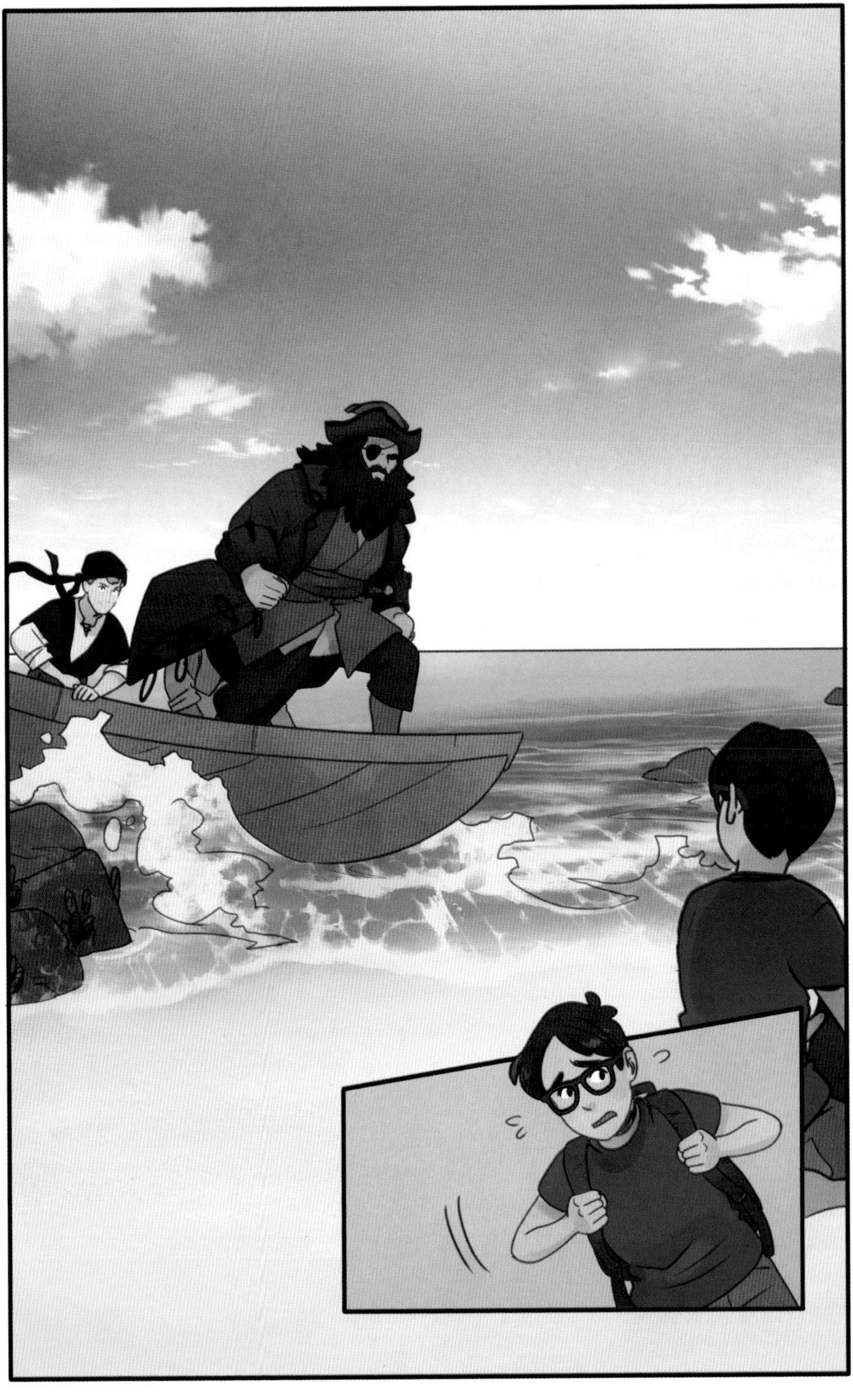

LET THE MAGIC TREE HOUSE® WHISK YOU AWAY!

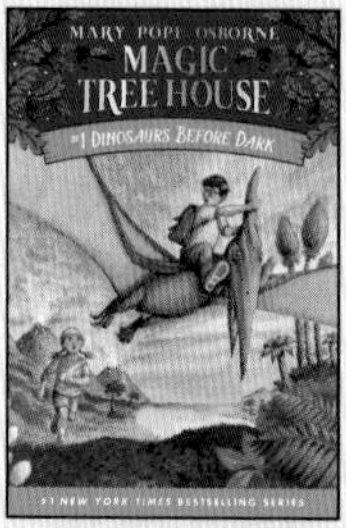
MARY POPE OSBORNE
MAGIC TREE HOUSE
#1 Dinosaurs Before Dark
#1 NEW YORK TIMES BESTSELLING SERIES

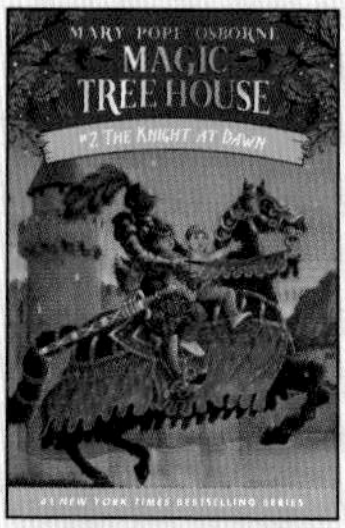
MARY POPE OSBORNE
MAGIC TREE HOUSE
#2 The Knight at Dawn
#1 NEW YORK TIMES BESTSELLING SERIES

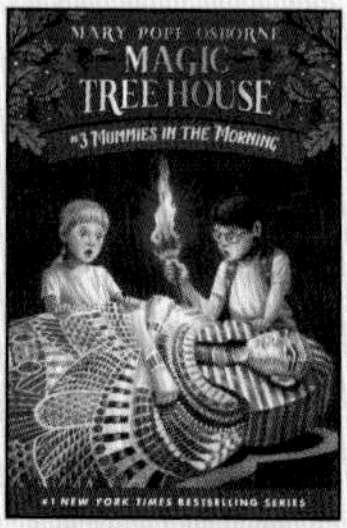
MARY POPE OSBORNE
MAGIC TREE HOUSE
#3 Mummies in the Morning
#1 NEW YORK TIMES BESTSELLING SERIES

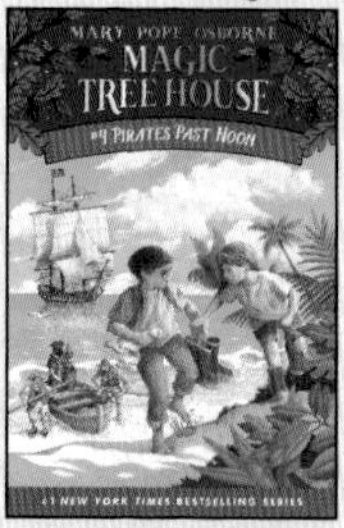
MARY POPE OSBORNE
MAGIC TREE HOUSE
#4 Pirates Past Noon
#1 NEW YORK TIMES BESTSELLING SERIES

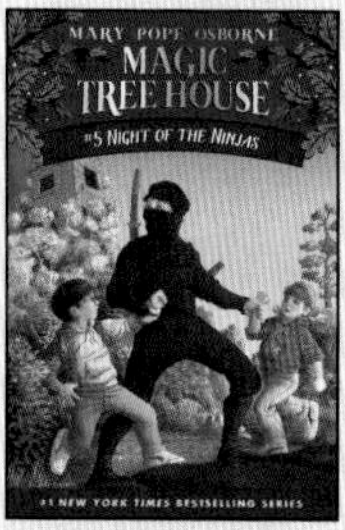
MARY POPE OSBORNE
MAGIC TREE HOUSE
#5 Night of the Ninjas
#1 NEW YORK TIMES BESTSELLING SERIES

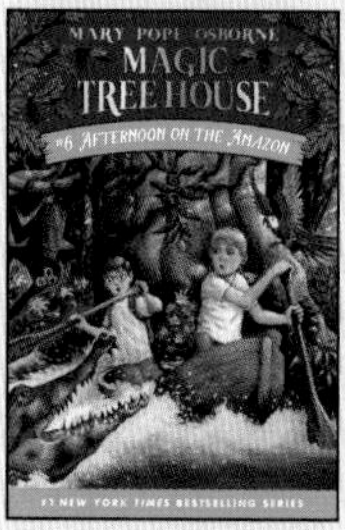
MARY POPE OSBORNE
MAGIC TREE HOUSE
#6 Afternoon on the Amazon
#1 NEW YORK TIMES BESTSELLING SERIES

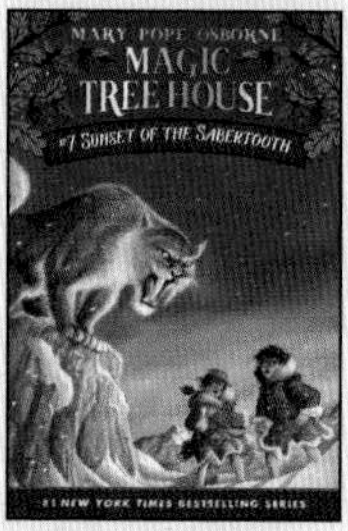
MARY POPE OSBORNE
MAGIC TREE HOUSE
#7 Sunset of the Sabertooth
#1 NEW YORK TIMES BESTSELLING SERIES

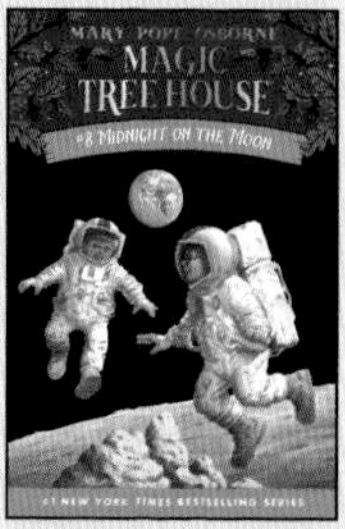
MARY POPE OSBORNE
MAGIC TREE HOUSE
#8 Midnight on the Moon
#1 NEW YORK TIMES BESTSELLING SERIES

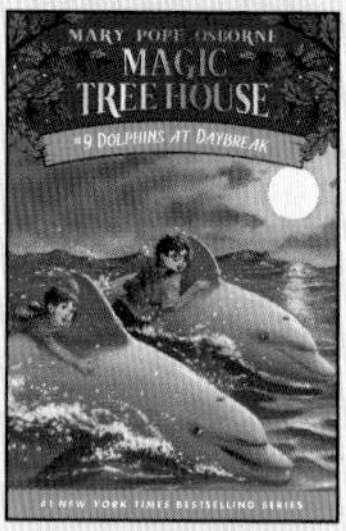
MARY POPE OSBORNE
MAGIC TREE HOUSE
#9 Dolphins at Daybreak
#1 NEW YORK TIMES BESTSELLING SERIES

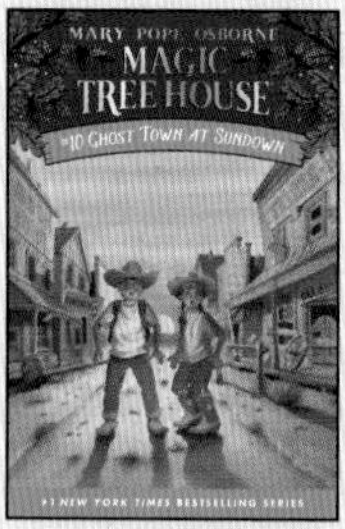
MARY POPE OSBORNE
MAGIC TREE HOUSE
#10 Ghost Town at Sundown
#1 NEW YORK TIMES BESTSELLING SERIES

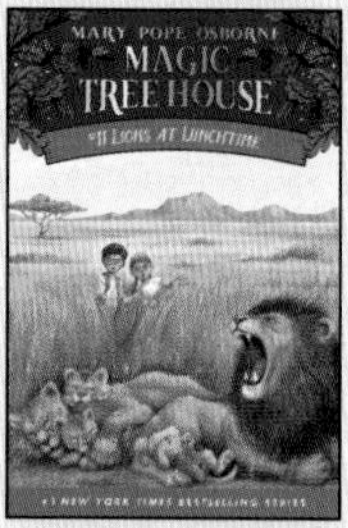
MARY POPE OSBORNE
MAGIC TREE HOUSE
#11 Lions at Lunchtime
#1 NEW YORK TIMES BESTSELLING SERIES

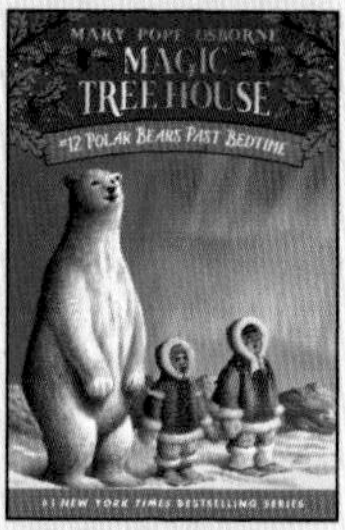
MARY POPE OSBORNE
MAGIC TREE HOUSE
#12 Polar Bears Past Bedtime
#1 NEW YORK TIMES BESTSELLING SERIES

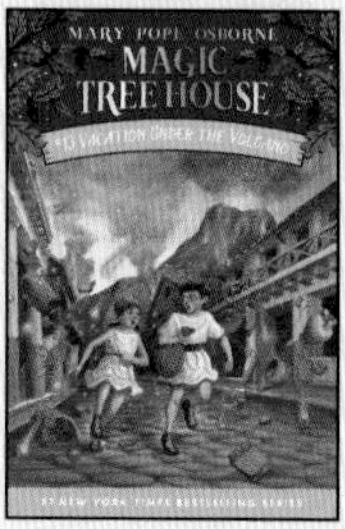
MARY POPE OSBORNE
MAGIC TREE HOUSE
#13 Vacation Under the Volcano
#1 NEW YORK TIMES BESTSELLING SERIES

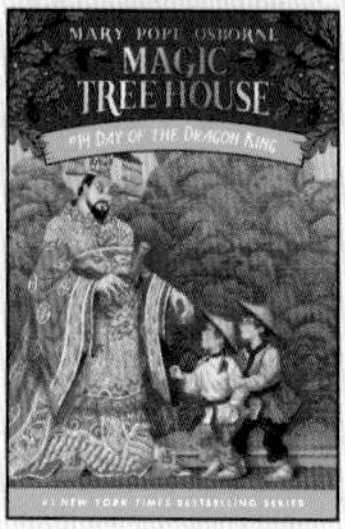
MARY POPE OSBORNE
MAGIC TREE HOUSE
#14 Day of the Dragon King
#1 NEW YORK TIMES BESTSELLING SERIES

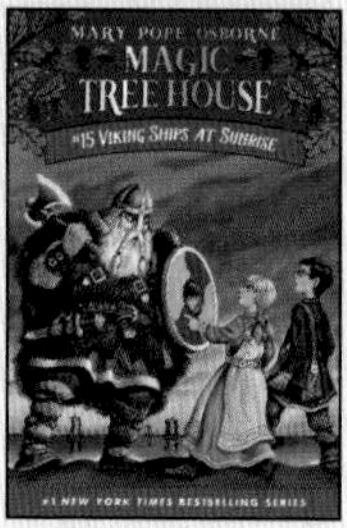
MARY POPE OSBORNE
MAGIC TREE HOUSE
#15 Viking Ships at Sunrise
#1 NEW YORK TIMES BESTSELLING SERIES

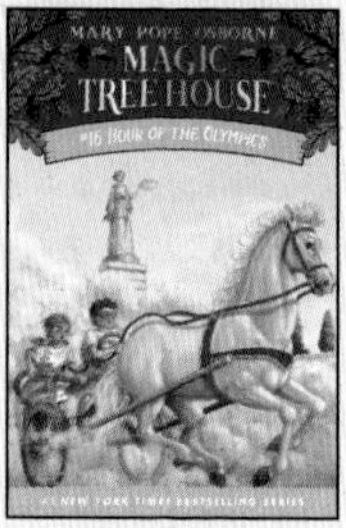
MARY POPE OSBORNE
MAGIC TREE HOUSE
#16 Hour of the Olympics
#1 NEW YORK TIMES BESTSELLING SERIES

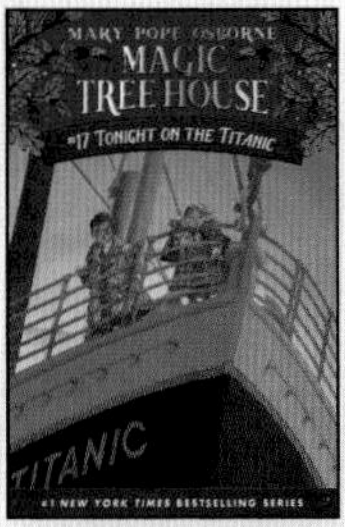
MARY POPE OSBORNE
MAGIC TREE HOUSE
#17 Tonight on the Titanic
TITANIC

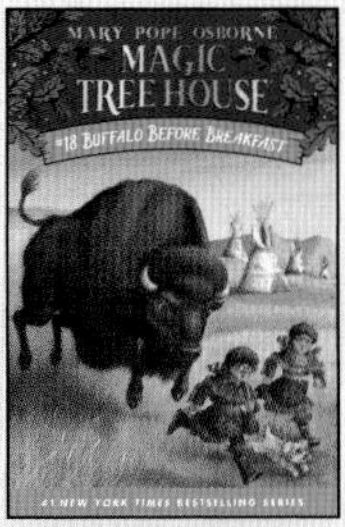
MARY POPE OSBORNE
MAGIC TREE HOUSE
#18 Buffalo Before Breakfast

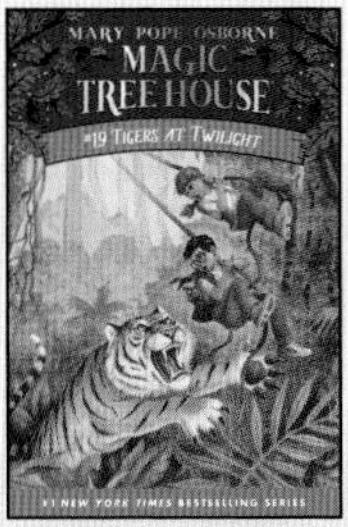
MARY POPE OSBORNE
MAGIC TREE HOUSE
#19 Tigers at Twilight

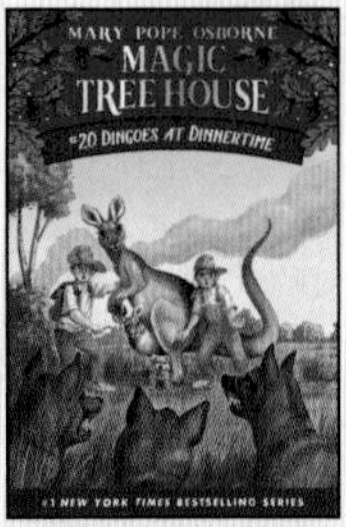
MARY POPE OSBORNE
MAGIC TREE HOUSE
#20 Dingoes at Dinnertime

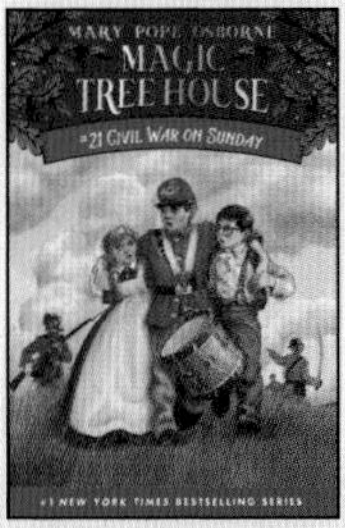
MARY POPE OSBORNE
MAGIC TREE HOUSE
#21 Civil War on Sunday

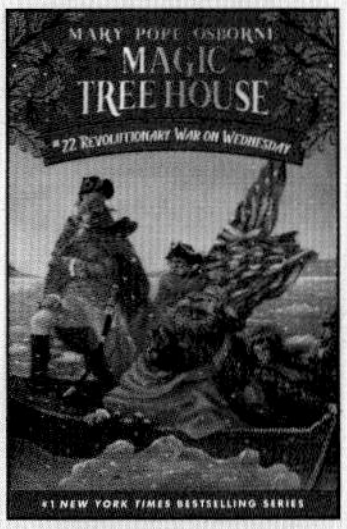
MARY POPE OSBORNE
MAGIC TREE HOUSE
#22 Revolutionary War on Wednesday

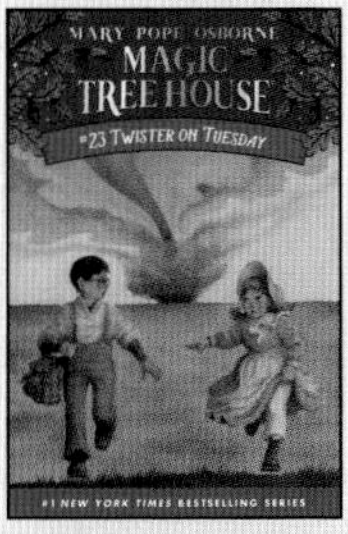
MARY POPE OSBORNE
MAGIC TREE HOUSE
#23 Twister on Tuesday

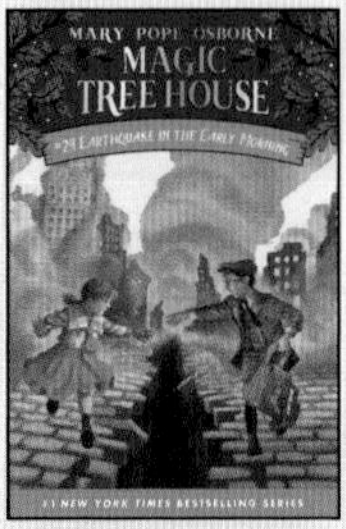
MARY POPE OSBORNE
MAGIC TREE HOUSE
#24 Earthquake in the Early Morning

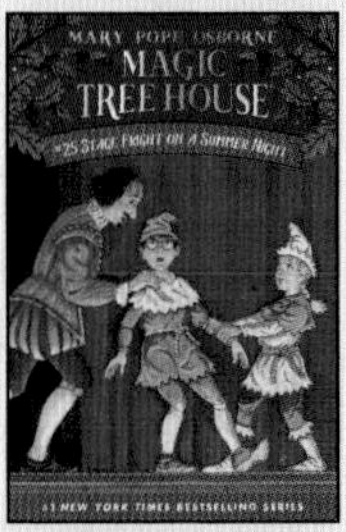
MARY POPE OSBORNE
MAGIC TREE HOUSE
#25 Stage Fright on a Summer Night

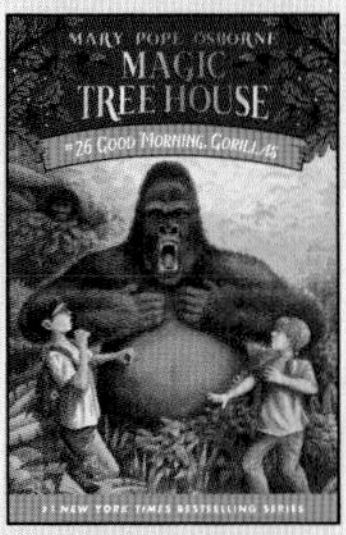
MARY POPE OSBORNE
MAGIC TREE HOUSE
#26 Good Morning, Gorillas

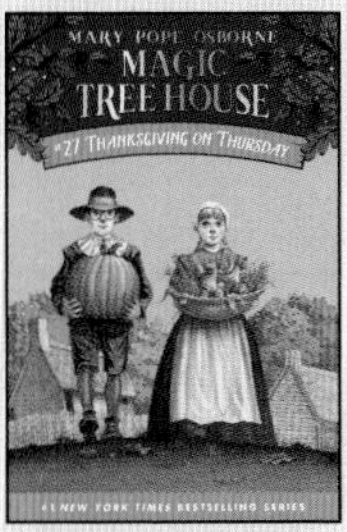
MARY POPE OSBORNE
MAGIC TREE HOUSE
#27 Thanksgiving on Thursday

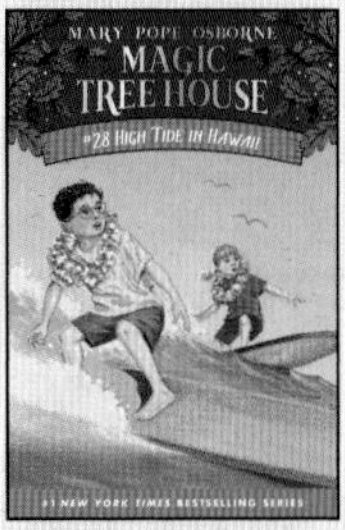
MARY POPE OSBORNE
MAGIC TREE HOUSE
#28 High Tide in Hawaii

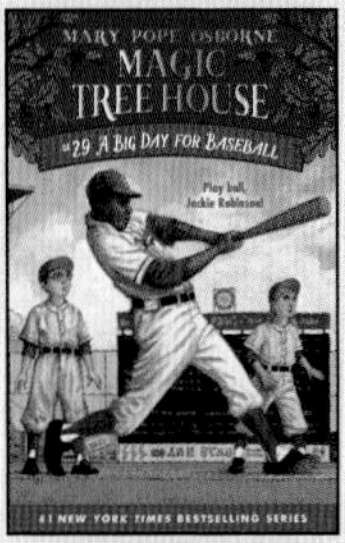
MARY POPE OSBORNE
MAGIC TREE HOUSE
#29 A Big Day for Baseball
Play ball, Jackie Robinson!

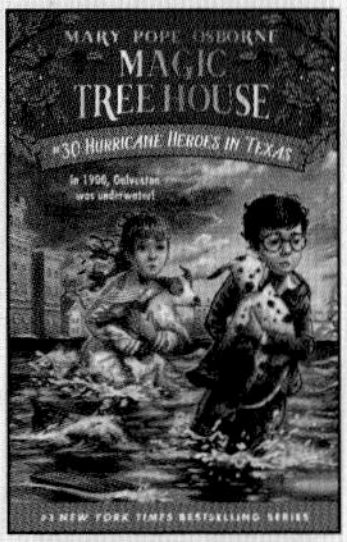
MARY POPE OSBORNE
MAGIC TREE HOUSE
#30 Hurricane Heroes in Texas
In 1900, Galveston was underwater!

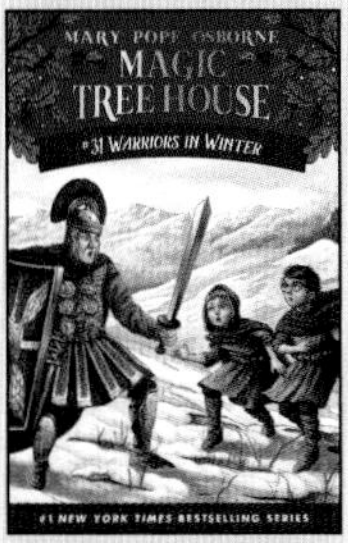
MARY POPE OSBORNE
MAGIC TREE HOUSE
#31 Warriors in Winter

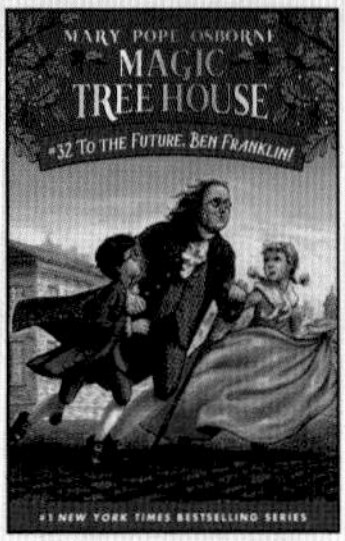
MARY POPE OSBORNE
MAGIC TREE HOUSE
#32 To the Future, Ben Franklin!

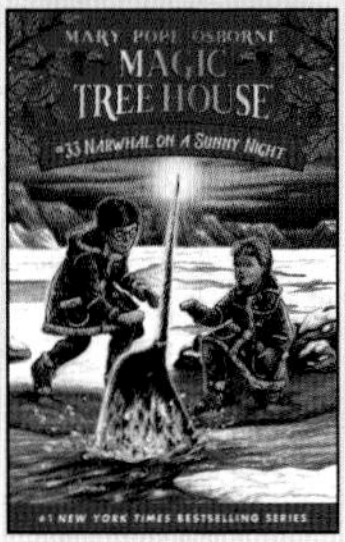
MARY POPE OSBORNE
MAGIC TREE HOUSE
#33 Narwhal on a Sunny Night

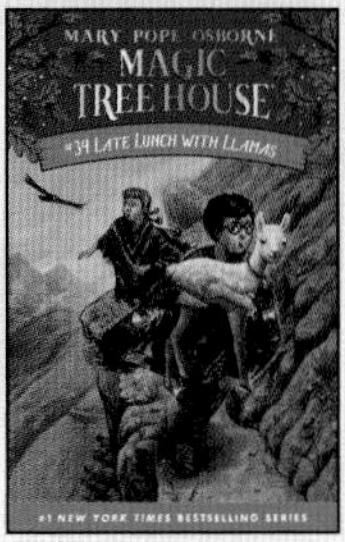
MARY POPE OSBORNE
MAGIC TREE HOUSE
#34 Late Lunch with Llamas

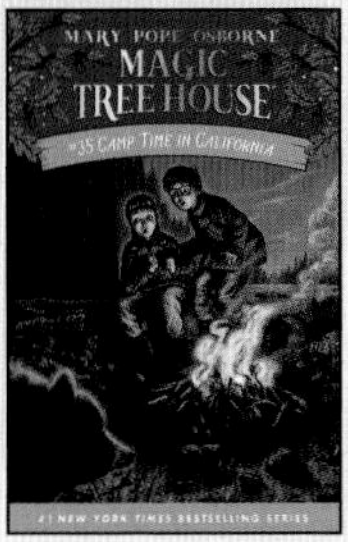
MARY POPE OSBORNE
MAGIC TREE HOUSE
#35 Camp Time in California

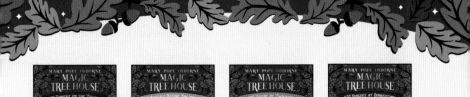

Read all the novels in the #1 bestselling chapter book series of all time!

TRACK THE FACTS WITH JACK & ANNIE!

MAGIC TREE HOUSE FACT TRACKER
Dinosaurs
Will Osborne and Mary Pope Osborne

MAGIC TREE HOUSE FACT TRACKER
Knights and Castles
Will Osborne and Mary Pope Osborne

MAGIC TREE HOUSE FACT TRACKER
Mummies and Pyramids
Will Osborne and Mary Pope Osborne

MAGIC TREE HOUSE FACT TRACKER
Pirates
Will Osborne and Mary Pope Osborne

MAGIC TREE HOUSE FACT TRACKER
Rain Forests
Will Osborne and Mary Pope Osborne

MAGIC TREE HOUSE FACT TRACKER
Space
Will Osborne and Mary Pope Osborne

MAGIC TREE HOUSE FACT TRACKER
Titanic
Will Osborne and Mary Pope Osborne

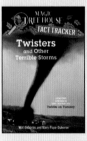
MAGIC TREE HOUSE FACT TRACKER
Twisters and Other Terrible Storms
Will Osborne and Mary Pope Osborne

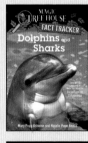
MAGIC TREE HOUSE FACT TRACKER
Dolphins and Sharks
Mary Pope Osborne and Natalie Pope Boyce

MAGIC TREE HOUSE FACT TRACKER
Ancient Greece and the Olympics
Mary Pope Osborne and Natalie Pope Boyce

MAGIC TREE HOUSE FACT TRACKER
American Revolution
Mary Pope Osborne and Natalie Pope Boyce

MAGIC TREE HOUSE FACT TRACKER
Sabertooths and the Ice Age
Mary Pope Osborne and Natalie Pope Boyce

MAGIC TREE HOUSE FACT TRACKER
Pilgrims
Mary Pope Osborne and Natalie Pope Boyce

MAGIC TREE HOUSE FACT TRACKER
Ancient Rome and Pompeii
Mary Pope Osborne and Natalie Pope Boyce

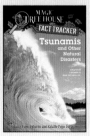
MAGIC TREE HOUSE FACT TRACKER
Tsunamis and Other Natural Disasters
Mary Pope Osborne and Natalie Pope Boyce

MAGIC TREE HOUSE FACT TRACKER
Polar Bears and the Arctic
Mary Pope Osborne and Natalie Pope Boyce

MAGIC TREE HOUSE FACT TRACKER
Sea Monsters
Mary Pope Osborne and Natalie Pope Boyce